THE
NIGHT-HAWKS OF LONDON;

OR,

THE NOBLE HIGHWAYMAN AND THE MISER'S DAUGHTER.

A THRILLING ROMANCE OF LONDON LIFE ONE HUNDRED YEARS AGO.

THE MURDER IN THE LONE HOUSE IN BATTERSEA FIELDS.

CHAPTER I.

THE LONE HOUSE IN BATTERSEA-FIELDS.—A DARK NIGHT AND A DARK DEED.—THE CONSULTATION OF THE COMPANIONS IN CRIME.—THE STRANGER DOOMED. —THE SECRET CHAMBER.—THE VICTIM OF THE LONE HOUSE.—THE STRUGGLE FOR LIFE.—THE JEW AND THE RESURRECTION MAN.—THE HORRIBLE BLACK STREAM BENEATH THE LONE HOUSE.—TRIUMPH OF THE MUR-DERERS—THEIR VICTIM HURLED INTO THE NOISOME WATERS BELOW.—THE FACE AT THE SECRET PANEL.

A BLEAK, drear, and open waste were the fields of Battersea in the last century.

Large tracts of common, covered with marshes and waters from the river, which at times laid near the whole of the fields under its flowing tides, were here and there interspersed with stunted willows.

Open spaces, beside the beaten tract of roadway, were covered with the tall bullrush, rank grass, and dwarf willow, showing the marshy soil around.

It was a wild, dreary spot; the fenny soil in the heat of a summer's sun steamed and bubbled, wafting in the air around a deadly malaria.

In the winter, thick, heavy fogs hung over the open grounds, whilst the blast screamed shrilly across the wide expanse of marsh and common.

On the spot where once stood the old Red House, so well known by all in the year 1786, stood a large old-fashioned residence, built of red brick, with various out-houses, called Battersea Grange, but invariably spoken of as the house by the river, or the lone house in Battersea-fields.

It was a large, rambling building; in the front meandered the silvery Thames; at the back was nought but open common, with here and there a small willow copse. The ghastly aspect of the place was added to by a few grim-looking wych elms, that, with their foliaged trunks and leafy summits, looked like spectral black sentinels standing in the wild waste.

The wintry winds soughed and murmured across the bleak, marshy fields, rustling the pendant branches of the willow, and moaning over the water with a hollow, ghostly sound.

One dark night in the month of October, in the year 1786, two men, seated in an open cart, made their way along the beaten roadway which ran through Battersea-fields.

It was a dark wintry night. The wind blew shrilly over the open common, cold and raw; a thick mist was also falling, threatening to end in a heavy fog. Slowly the drivers in the vehicle made their way along the but half-formed road. Ever and again, with a curse, the man with the reins would pull up the horse, as, diverging from the road, the beast plunged into the marshy soil that edged the tract.

The wind, that had been in stormy gusts careering across the fields, at length subsided into hollow murmurs, while the mist changed to a thick fog.

A fog so dense that nought was discernible in the white cloud.

Curses, loud and deep, fell from the lips of the driver of the cart, whilst, jumping down, he prepared to lead the horse along the dangerous roadway. Scarce, however, had the cart advanced fifty yards after the falling of the fog, ere it stood before a dark mass of building looming, spectre-like, in the darkness of the night and the heavy, thick fog.

An exclamation of surprise, and a curse of satisfaction, fell from the mouth of the man leading the horse, as his eyes discerned the house before which the intelligent animal had halted, aware that it had reached its destination.

"Jump out, Ben. By the devils, we are at the Grange. Curse me, I should have passed it in the infernal fog," said the man, who now led the horse and cart into a large forecourt in front of the lone house, parted off from the fields by some rude black palings.

The wind blew strong and keen from the river, distant not more than a hundred yards from the front of the house.

"Now then, Ben, are yer coming," shouted the leader of the horse, as he proceeded to unloose the reins and let the animal free; "here, take Gray Jane to her stable, and, curse yer, don't stand up there in the cart, looking like a ghost in the darkness of the night. See to the horse, and, d—n yer, I'll manage the rest," muttered the man, as, with a volley of oaths, he drew to the back of the cart, and, pushing aside the form of his companion, dragged forth a muffled figure that lay, without sense or motion, at the bottom of the vehicle.

"Vell, you ish in von cursed hurry, and you knowsh I ish half dead with fatigue; but come, ve vill take our friend into de house, and den I will see about de horse." The speaker, an old Jew, now aided his companion to carry the inert mass, bearing a human form, that they had drawn out of the cart.

Thundering loudly at the door of the lone house for admission, the two men had not waited many minutes ere it was opened by an old shrivelled hag, who, with a small lamp in her hand, stood peering out into the darkness, whilst thick clouds of fog rolled like volumes of smoke into the house.

"Now, then, Mother Ellis, stand aside, and show us into the blue room, and, damme, look alive, or, by the devils, I'll quicken yer with a yard of rope," muttered the man with fierce oaths, pushing past the aged, wrinkled crone, who, with a smothered curse, hurried along the passage, mumbling as she went.

"A rope! Ah! ah! a yard of rope, said he; 'twill be that will grace his neck ere long, I know, I know."

Slamming to the door, the Jew and his companion, with their strange burthen, made their way, led by the old woman, into a large room at the back part of the house, the walls of which, together with the wainscoting, being of a dull dark blue, gave rise to its appellation of the Blue Room.

Depositing their load upon the ground in the corner of the vast apartment, the two men, dismissing the old hag, sat down in front of a fire that blazed and sparkled in a huge grate, and pouring from a decanter some pure brandy, quaffed it off like water, the fiery spirit having no effect upon their hardened frames.

"Ben Abrahams, just search the body of the stiff 'un, and see if we have overlooked anything, whilst I overhaul this pocket-book."

The ruffian now drew nearer to the bright glow of the fire, and opening a book he pulled from his vest, proceeded to inspect its contents, while the villainous old Jew shuffled over to the still, quiet form that lay huddled up in the corner, where it had been thrown upon entering the room.

A hideous-looking villain was the Jew, Ben Abrahams. A cool, horrible smile wreathed his wrinkled, cadaverous, jaundiced face, as he, with a small hand-lamp held in his hand, bent over the form of a young man, from whose features he had now drawn the covering. Deadly pale was the countenance of the senseless form. Placing a shrivelled hand upon the breast of the inanimate corpse-like figure of the young man, the Jew, with a cry, started to his feet, and, uttering an oath, staggered across the room to the spot where his companion was seated, who, startled by the old man's actions, with a curse demanded to know the cause of his alarm.

"He—he—is not dead! not dead!" stuttered the Jew; who, with shaking limbs, stood beside his companion in crime, glaring uneasily into the corner of the room in which laid the form of their victim.

"Not dead, Abrahams! Then, by heavens, we must finish what we have begun. And, as by papers in this pocket-book, I find our man was about to pay a visit to that accursed Guy Essington, I'll not risk selling him to the sawbones. We will convey him to the secret chamber, and hurl his body into the old stream; carried out into the river, and then, perchance, by the tide out to sea, we can defy detection."

A fierce, determined look settled upon the face of the murderer as he gazed upon the form that, still and quiet, rested in the corner of the chamber.

Of huge, herculean proportions, the assassin stood some five feet ten or six feet in height; large square shoulders, and immense brawny arms, told a man of great strength; with low forehead, jet black beetling brows, high features, and a terrific scar down the right cheek, extending from the eye to the jawbone, gave a fearful expression to the face of the villain, who, with coal black hair, hanging in snaky curls over the scanty forehead and about the thick bull-neck, looked a wretch capable of any crime. A fierce glitter shone in the keen gray eye of the villain as he gazed upon the still senseless form before him, and drawing a long dirk or knife from his coat-pocket, he exclaimed,—

"Look you, Ben, we will at once convey that bundle to the secret chamber. A stab or two from double-edged Dick—as I calls my pet knife—will soon settle our friend, who, to have escaped the stunner I gave him at Vauxhall, must have a head as thick as a milestone: but if I arn't been able to crack his skull, curse me if I don't pretty soon make a stiff 'un of him with double-edged Dick!"

The villain coolly drained the decanter of brandy, and made at once for the form of his victim, but even as he was about to seize and raise it up to remove it from the room, three loud knocks were heard, and a voice, sounding strange and hollow in the silence of the night, called loudly from without—

"Open—open! Hawks are out, and on the watch!"

"'Tis Coffin. Open the door, Abrahams; or, stay, we will go together. No one must enter here."

Followed by the villain Jew, the ruffian then left the chamber, locking the door after him. Scarce had they crossed the threshold ere a large, old-fashioned clock in the room, which had been giving a monotonous tick, struck the hour of ten with a sharp, tinkling sound. The ringing noise of the bell was still sounding in the air when the before-quiet figure in the corner of the room began to give signs of life. Wildly the arms of the murderer's victim tossed about in the air; then, rising half up, the young man gazed round the chamber.

"Where am I? The Vauxhall-road; the footsteps in the dark; the blow,—I remember all. But then what follows? A blank—all a blank. Curses on the villains! My first entrance into the metropolis, about which I have heard so much, has cost me dear. But once again my limbs regain their wonted vigour."

The young man now staggered to his feet and tottered to the table by the fire, upon which stood a tumbler half-full of brandy, left by the villain Jew.

Seizing the glass in his hand, the young man raised it up to the bright flames of the fire.

"Hum! brandy good. Come! I shall get on by degrees," he ejaculated. His pale features were lighted up by a smile as he raised the glass to his lips and drank off the ardent spirit.

A glow spread over the face of the stranger as he sank back in a seat, whilst he, apparently forgetful of his perilous position, coolly took a survey of the chamber.

"Well, I'm in snug quarters at present, though how long they intend me to retain them is another matter. Well, I'm certainly in bad hands. Confound them! they have fleeced me of everything—near skinned me! Frank, Frank Hartland, my boy, you are among the breakers on a rocky shore, and deuced unlikely to weather the storm. But no matter; while life remains, there is hope. Ah! by heavens, my accursed murderous foes return; with no weapons to protect me, I am at their mercy. Cunning alone can save me."

The sound of voices in the hall of the lone house could now be plainly heard. Approaching the door of the chamber, darting forwards as he heard the heavy footsteps halt without and the key turned in the lock, the young man, who showed himself possessed of a bold, daring spirit, drew himself upright against the wall of the room just by the door, which now presently thrown open by the Jew and his companion in crime, hung wide upon its hinges. Waiting till the two villains had entered the chamber, the young man bounded through, followed immediately by the villainous assassins, who, with loud yells, execrations, and hideous oaths, dashed in pursuit of their victim, whom they had doomed to a terrible death.

When, bursting out of the room, the young stranger, perceiving the figure of a tall, ungainly-looking man at the hall-door, darted up a broad flight of stairs, followed in his flight by his would-be murderers.

"Stay you below, Tom," shouted the ruffian, who with the old Jew bounded up the wide oaken staircase after the fleeing form of their victim.

Reaching the summit of the stairs, the young man, bewildered, stood for a moment irresolute, then recalled to his dangerous position by the loud report of a pistol, the bullet from which with a whiz went within an inch of his head, the young stranger, with a curse of rage, darted down the long corridor that opened before him.

This passage at the top of the oaken staircase seemed to run the length of the house. Seeing all the doors on either side close shut, and no passage or staircase opening from the corridor, the young man, with fear of death tugging at his heart, rushed on.

His pursuer only a few yards behind him.

"Knife him, Bill! Shoot him down! Ha! ah! ah! Now we have got him," yelled the miscreant Jew, as their victim darted into a room at the end of the passage, the door of which was open.

Quickly following his companion, the Jew darted into the chamber in which their victim had dashed, finding no other means of escape.

Like a caged lion the bold young man stood awaiting his assassins.

The room, a large and lofty one, destitute of any article of furniture save a stool and two old chairs, contained no other means of egress than by the door in the corridor.

Like a sheep at the shambles, the doomed victim stood in the centre of the vast apartment awaiting the attack of his foes.

Of fine form, tall and handsome, was the young stranger, who with blanched cheeks and eyes blazing with fury, stood facing his murderers.

"Villains! cowards! I am unarmed. But by your master, the fiend below, I'll not be tamely butchered." Cool and daring the young man stood before his murderous foes, whilst tearing off a tight-fitting coat that impeded his actions, he awaited an attack.

"Curses on him, he takes it bravely, Abrahams; pity such valour should go unrewarded; but I've sworn to destroy him, and Resurrection Bill never yet broke an oath, nor will he now. Ben, go fetch me a loaded pistol, and by the fiends, I'll scatter his brains upon the walls, and soon end the matter."

The ruffian, whilst giving the order to the Jew, placed his burly frame within the doorway to bar the stranger from an attempt at escape. There was a something in the cool, steady glare of the young man's eye that prevented the ruffian from dashing upon him, unarmed though he was. When the villain Jew, however, had left the chamber, the villain drew forth his formidable-looking knife, and feeling its keen edge, advanced with a murderous smile towards the stranger. The young man, bold, daring, with a fearless heart and scorn of danger, yet felt his frame tremble with a cold shudder, as the villain, Resurrection Bill as he was called, advanced knife in hand before him.

There was no means of escape now!

Now, too, he heard the returning footsteps of the villain Jew!

Was there no hope?

No escape?

Was he so young doomed to perish thus?

How the wintry wind raged round the lone house!

A strange, rushing noise, too, now fell upon the young man's ears.

Like the rush and roar of water.

With a cry of rage, and a yell of fury, the young stranger, nerved to madness by his fearful position, rushed upon the villain Resurrection Bill, and, ere he could raise his hideous knife to stab, seized, with a death grip, his large, bony wrist.

Uttering a volley of horrible oaths, the murdering ruffian struggled with his victim, anticipating an easy victory over the slender form of the young stranger; here, however, the villain was deceived; though young—being only nineteen or twenty years of age—the young man now struggling for his life was possessed of immense strength, which, to look upon his slight frame, was marvellous. Twisting the wrist of the ruffian round in his powerful grasp, he caused the villain to drop his knife, at the same time he gave utterance to a yell of rage and pain.

Wildly, then, the two struggled round the vast apartment.

Like two gladiators they writhed in each other's deadly embrace.

The strong, powerfully-built, herculean frame of the ruffian, Resurrection Bill, shaking in the tenacious grip of his antagonist.

The companion of the murderer now entered the room.

With eyes flashing with rage and malice, the Jew watched the combatants, seeking a favourite moment to fire the pistol that, ready cocked, he held in his hand.

Finding even his prodigious strength giving way to that of the lithe and supple form of the young man, the villain yelled out to the Jew to fire.

"Fire! curses on you; fire, you quaking cur! The whelp has got the sinews of a giant. Curses upon you, Abrahams, fire; and open the trap, I say! The trap—the trap!"

His words were half stifled by the deadly clutch of the young man's hand around his throat. There was a loud report in the chamber as the villain Jew fired but fruitlessly at the figure of the stranger. Then there was the sound of footsteps hurrying along the corridor without, and the crash as the door of a large trap was flung upon the ground; the loud rush of gurgling waters now, too, fell plainly on the ear.

A horrible scene then ensued.

"Help! help! help!" yelled the young man, forgetful that in that lone house no help was nigh.

The two ruffian assassins, now joined by a third, drew the

struggling form of their frenzied victim to the large open trap that yawned in the floor beneath.

The horrible, gurgling rush of the waters could be plainly heard.

Whilst an occasional loud splash in the surgid mass fell upon the ears.

It was the huge water rats in the running stream, that, taking its course beneath the old house, found its way out into the river.

Into the dark, horrible waters the assassins intended to hurl their victim.

How manfully — desperately — the doomed stranger struggled in the arms of his murderers!

They have dragged him now half over the loathsome trap.

The horror of the scene is added to by a loud knocking at the outer door.

With a curse, one of the ruffians darted from the room.

Wild screams of agony now peal through the lone house.

The wretched young man, the victim of the murderous attack, is hurled down the horrible trap. In his fall he clutches despairingly at the edge of the abyss.

With a grasp of dying agony, he seizes the ruffian, Resurrection Bill, by the neckerchief, threatening to drag him, too, into the yawning trap.

"Curses on ye, let go your hold!" The murderer now pulled out a pistol, and fired at his victim. The weapon flashed in the pan.

The villain Jew now, with a howl of triumph, darted away from the trap, and catching up one of the heavy chairs in the room, rushed forwards, and raising it high in the air, brought it down with all his force on the head of the struggling victim. As, however, the chair descended, with a scream of horror the young man, his dark eyes glaring wildly at his murderers, and his death-pale face, like a vision from the grave, disappeared in the grim, horrible darkness. There was a loud plash, followed by a piercing, heartrending shriek. The murderers, startled by the shrill scream, turned from the yawning trap, and gazed round the room.

At a secret panel in the wall of that mysterious chamber of death, they beheld a pale, livid face, a female form bent half through the opening; whilst the jet black, sparkling eyes of the young girl, whose livid face looked wan and corpse-like, glared with a wild, maddened look upon the murderers, as they stood by the side of the open trap.

CHAPTER II.

THE MONEY-LENDER'S IN THE POULTRY.—RALPH FAIRLEY AND HIS CLERKS.—THE MYSTERIOUS STRANGER AND THE DIAMOND NECKLACE.

How cold and drear looks the October sun as it rides high in the heavens.

A piercing north-east wind careers along the streets of London, chilling the wayfarers exposed to its biting blasts.

The orb of day, like a ball of copper, shines brightly in the clear blue sky; but its rays throw out no particle of heat—a dull, cold glare is thrown upon all around.

A change has taken place in the fickle elements. The night before all was wet and stormy; inky clouds had discharged a thick rain or drizzle, whilst a heavy fog had hung upon London and its environs. Now all was bitter frost. The wind, in icy blasts, chills the muffled passengers in the streets, causing them to bend their heads, and hurry along, by rapid progress seeking to warm their numbed limbs.

Now the windows in the houses of public entertainment are encrusted with the thick hoar frost.

The passengers in London's crowded thoroughfares, heedless of each other, jostle along the narrow paths, the wintry wind blowing shrill and keen around them.

The clock of St. Paul's had just boomed out the hour of nine, as a smart, well-built youth made his way alone Cheapside in the direction of the Bank.

Well muffled up against the inclemency of the weather, he bustles along, the frosty air tinging his cheeks with a red glow.

Some three or four-and-twenty years of age; of dark, florid complexion; round, jovial features; a merry twinkle in the bright, dark eyes; and a happy, careless demeanour,—a thorough specimen of a true son of the British isle was the young man who, that keen, frosty morning, made his way hurriedly along the crowded streets of Cheapside, thronged, even at that early hour, with labourers on their way to the docks, artizans, work girls, clerks, and shopmen, all alike hurrying to their several employments in the hive of London.

The clock of Bow church was just ten minutes past nine as the young man halted at the door of a dark, dingy, sombre-looking house in the Poultry.

All city houses look drear and dusty, but this particular house in the Poultry before which the young pedestrian halted that cold, bleak October morning, looked especially dark and dirty.

On the ground-floor—fitted up as offices—a large, yellow blind, yellow with age and dirt, hung from the window, concealing all view of the office from without; a strip of wire blind was covered with some dirty white letters; the paint, yellowish white from age, was dotted over, as was the blind above, with various dots made by the industrious flies of summer, making the texture resemble a dirty pudding-cloth; the glass of the windows was thick with dust, which hid from a passing glance various little bowls of old coins and foreign notes, together with old-fashioned watches and articles of jewellery that were jumbled together in the most admired disorder.

Though so dirty and dingy his abode, the owner of that house was the richest man of business in the Poultry.

A thriving trade had been carried on for years by old Ralph Fairley, goldsmith and money-lender.

The roué, the spendthrift, the embarrassed merchant, the needy tradesman, all alike contributed to increase the wealth of Ralph Fairley, who, lending money at exorbitant interest, revelled in the follies and distresses of others.

Passing through the dingy doorway on arriving at the end of a narrow hall or passage, the young man pushed open a pair of small folding doors, covered with a dark green baize, which, like the blinds of the office windows, had grown dusty, dirty, and yellow in the service.

Entering the large room on the ground floor, he made his way to a desk at the further end of the chamber, and, removing the mufflers and overcoat that had served to protect him from the cold, sat down at the large desk before him, and, taking up some papers, prepared to write.

Scarce had the young clerk seated himself at his desk, before a strange mysterious figure stole forth from an inner office, a kind of closet-like chamber parted off from the large room.

"Are you aware, Mr. Nat Stevens, that you are ten minutes over your time this morning? Eh! eh! eh!" A strange giggle or chuckle here escaped the lips of the questioner, as he halted before the desk of the young clerk.

"I was delayed by an accident on Ludgate-hill; a poor young girl was run over and near lost her life."

"And you saved her? Eh! eh! eh!"

"No, I did not, Mr. Ephraim Rasselton; but if I had, and the so doing had caused me to be an hour late instead of ten minutes, I should not have hesitated in my course!"

"Oh! no, of course not—decidedly not. Eh! eh! eh! How very romantic you are, Nat Stevens. I am afraid, if you think so much of others, you will never do much for yourself."

"Well, you'll lose nothing on that ground, Ephraim Rasselton; for I believe there is only one creature in the universe you care at all for, and that is" ——

"Myself! Eh! eh! eh! Yes, I know it," said the other, while a giggle and low gurgling chuckle escaped him. A strange, hideous looking creature was Ephraim Rasselton, the head clerk of Ralph Fairley. Standing about four feet four, the dwarfish appearance of the man was increased by a huge hump-back; long snakey locks of light hair fell down over his coat collar; with a thin, spare form, he possessed inordinately long arms, which dangled from his body as though strung upon it by wires. Large bony hands and great splay feet increased the grotesque appearance of the man, whose face, however, was even worse than his stunted form to gaze upon. A devilish look of malignity and cunning hung about the features of Ephraim Rasselton. With a receding forehead, he possessed a large hooked nose. This, with a thin, pinched face, ferret eyes, that twinkled and sparkled with malice, and large full lips, with discoloured and projecting teeth, made up the not prepossessing appearance of Ephraim Rasselton, the money-lender's head clerk, who had gained his position in the office by a sneaking, servile demeanour, and his miserly, money-grubbing disposition according well with that of his employer.

Far different in character, appearance, and disposition to Ephraim Rasselton was his fellow-clerk, Nathaniel Stevens. At least twenty years the junior of Ephraim, who was about forty years of age, the young clerk, Nat Stevens, was well-built, good-looking, and of a jovial temperament; one who laughed away dull care, who in the severest distress bore a merry smile upon his face. Left an orphan at an early age, Nat had never known a father's or a mother's care; and when leaving the free school at which he had been brought up, was placed in the office of Ralph Fairley, who for board, lodging, and clothing, received the services of the boy, who, sharp, active, and willing, and with learning above the rank in which he had been thrust by fate, soon was able to act as clerk, in addition to errand-boy and odd hand in the establishment of Ralph Fairley.

For ten years had Nat Stevens been in the house of the money-lender, who, during that time, had presented, as a mark of his esteem, the munificent yearly gift of a crown piece. At no other season save Christmas had Nat Stevens ever received anything in the shape of money from his employer, Ralph Fairley.

It had been suggested to Nat that now it was time he spoke seriously to the money-lender respecting his future position, salary, etc., as other situations might be procured, where he would be far better remunerated than in the office of old Ralph Fairley, the miserly money-lender.

But habit and long servitude, together with the charming friendship of the lovely daughter of the money-lender, kept Nat Stevens in his present situation. Looked upon by Sybil Fairley as almost a member of the family, Nat Stevens could not bear the idea of leaving the situation he had been in since his boyhood; and so, despite all the niggardly conduct of his employer, he still remained, and every morning saw Nat wending his way to the house in the Poultry to his daily toil.

The only thing, however, likely to eventually drive him from the service of Ralph Fairley was the being treated as an inferior by the head clerk, Ephraim Rasselton. This man had only been in the employ of the money-lender for three years, and during that time had made himself thoroughly obnoxious to the young man, Nat Stevens, who hated him with all the bitterness his good-natured disposition could entertain towards anyone with whom he was obliged to be in daily contact.

Hobbling back to his inner office, Ephraim Rasselton left Nat Stevens to himself, having first threatened to complain as to the ten minutes overtime that had occurred twice within the last week.

Muttering a something not a blessing on the head of the deformed clerk, the young man was soon busily employed over the papers he had taken from his desk.

The hour of ten was striking from a clock in the office, which, like all around, was covered with thick dust, when Nat was startled from his work upon the papers by a voice close beside him asking in rough, hoarse tones if Mr. Ralph Fairley was within. Looking up, the young clerk beheld a tall, powerfully-built man, who was muffled up with a large scarf that concealed more than half his visage. A piercing pair of jet-black eyes were fastened upon Nat whilst he was engaged answering the queries of the stranger.

"Mr. Ralph Fairley at home?"

"Yes, sir," replied Nat Stevens, surveying the visitor with a scrutinizing glance.

There were some strange people called sometimes at the money-lender's, and Nat Stevens invariably studied the countenance of every fresh comer.

"Can I see him?"

"You can, sir. I will go and inform Mr. Rasselton, the head clerk, that you wish to see Mr. Fairley."

"Stay," said the stranger, laying his hand upon the arm of the young man as he was about to call Ephraim out of the inner office. "Stay; you can perhaps tell me if you think Mr. Fairley can do anything with this."

The stranger now pulled from his vest a small brown paper packet, and, unfastening it, disclosed a magnificent diamond necklace, the jewels large and of the purest water. The gems glittered and coruscated in the thin rays of the winter sun that stole through the fanlight over the folding doors like stars; the rich gems glittered and sparkled in the hands of the stranger. A cry of astonishment and delight escaped the lips of Nat as he gazed upon the priceless gems. Some of the diamonds, as large as good-sized peas, cast a thousand prismatic rays in the air as the man held the necklace up, the better to show the size and beauty of the jewels.

"There, young man! Do you think, without asking questions as to who I came from, your master, Ralph Fairley, the money-lender, will advance a sum upon the necklace, the diamonds of which are not to be equalled in England or out of it?"

"Well, sir," rejoined the young clerk, still gazing with admiration at the glittering gems; "well, sir, I do not doubt Mr. Fairley will deal with you. He does a great deal of business in this way, has large means, and can advance, when required, heavy sums."

"You think, then, that Mr. Fairley will lend some money on this necklace?"

"I am sure of it," replied Ned; "but here comes Mr. Rasselton; he will see you on the subject and speak to Mr. Fairley." The head clerk now bustled forwards from the other end of the room. Hearing the young man, Stevens, in converse with a stranger, he had hastened out of the little office. The man with the valuable gems gazed upon the person of Rasselton apparently in surprise, a grim smile crossing his features, as he noted the grotesque figure of the strange being that now stood before him.

"What can we do for you, Mr.—Mr."——

"Sharp. Sharp is my name, sir," said the stranger; who, burying his face yet deeper in the thick scarf that he wore round his neck, endeavoured to avoid letting Mr. Rasselton obtain too close a scrutiny of his features: the only thing to be seen by the money-lender's clerk was a pair of dark, piercing eyes, that seemed to search warily round the apartment.

Ephraim Rasselton did not know why, but he did not like the stranger. Nor was the owner of the valuable necklace evidently fascinated with the evil-looking person of Mr. Rasselton; for turning from him to Ned Stevens, he exclaimed—

"Will you let Mr. Fairley know I wish to see him?"

"Certainly, sir," said Ephraim Rasselton, in reply. "Ned, go up to Mr. Fairley. Tell him—eh! eh!—a Mr. Sharp wants to see him. Eh! eh! eh! Cold, sharp morning this. Isn't it, Mr. Sharp?"

"Yes, it is," said the stranger, letting something very much like a curse escape him, as Rasselton followed him up and down the office during the absence of Ned Stevens who had gone for the money-lender.

"Want to change some notes, sir?"

"No."

"Wish to borrow of Mr. Fairley?"

"No."

"Eh! eh! eh!" said Rasselton, annoyed at the stranger's evident determination not to let him know the purport of his visit. "If you don't want to change notes, or borrow some money—eh! eh! eh!—I rather think Mr. Fairley will be vexed; he only cares to be disturbed in the way of business, you see; and"——

"Look you, Mr."——

"Ephraim Rasselton, Mr. Sharp."

"Well, then Mr. Ephraim Rasselton, what I wish to see your employer about is best known to myself. You trouble me, Mr. Ephraim Rasselton, and I'm apt, when annoyed, to settle matters in a rather summary manner. You understand." The eyes of the muffled-up stranger here shone with a savage glare upon the shrinking form of Ephraim; who, starting back, as though fearing an assault from the mysterious visitor, exclaimed—

"Really, Mr. Sharp. Eh! eh! eh! Pardon me, you are very sharp. But here comes Mr. Fairley. I don't like the fellow," muttered Ephraim, hurrying forward to meet his employer. "I don't like him, and, by the fiends, if I can do him an ill turn, why I will. How he glared upon me with his eagle's glance, as though he would read my inmost thoughts. Eh! eh! eh! How carefully, too, he conceals his features. I suspect there is a strong reason for his so doing. I will warn old Fairley ere they have converse." With the privilege of his office, he now, meeting the money-lender, drew him aside, and whispered his suspicions; receiving a nod from his employer, Ephraim then hobbled back to where the stranger was still standing, who cast a quick, searching glance upon the person of the money-lender, who came forward with his clerk.

Nearly seventy years of age, yet Ralph Fairley possessed a firm, upright figure, not bowed by age, with hair white as silver, and a broad, high forehead, with rather prominent features; yet, notwithstanding, he must in his youth have had a fair personal appearance.

The dark gray eyes of the money-lender shifted from the stranger to the outré form of Ephraim. He concurred in the opinion of his clerk. The studious care the visitor took to keep his features concealed assured Ralph Fairley that the stranger did not wish at a future time to be recognised.

"Will you step this way, sir?" The money-lender led his visitor to the inner office, followed by Ephraim Rasselton.

"I wish to see you alone, Mr. Fairley."

"Very good, sir." Motioning his clerk to remain in the outer office, the money-lender ushered the stranger into the little closet-like compartment at the end of the chamber.

"Now, sir," said Ralph Fairley, closing the door; "what is your pleasure? What can I do for you?"

"You advance money upon good security, do you not?"

"Yes, sir; to any amount."

"I require five thousand pounds. Can you advance such a sum?"

"Oh! yes, sir; or treble the amount upon undoubted security."

"What do you think of that for a security?"

The mysterious stranger here handed to Ralph Fairley, the money-lender, the beautiful diamond necklace that had so struck the young man, Nat Stevens.

The eyes of the money-lender fairly danced with joy as he gazed upon the rich gems.

Clutching the necklace in his hands, he gazed, first upon the sparkling diamonds, and then upon the stranger.

"Beautiful, beautiful—lovely," murmured the old man, as he passed the necklace slowly through his fingers. "Oh! how lovely! of the purest water, and the largest I have ever beheld: This jewelled necklace is worth a princely fortune." Lost in admiration, Ralph Fairley uttered aloud his encomiums upon the beautiful diamonds he held in his hands. At length, recovering himself, he exclaimed—

"But whence got you this rare piece of jewellery—this necklace of diamonds, worthy the dower of a princess? It is worth a vast sum!"

"I know it," said the stranger; "yet may you have it for a time for the advance of five thousand pounds; and, if not redeemed within a twelvemonth, it shall be yours."

"But your name, sir?"

"Mr. Sharp."

"And from whom do you come? to whom does the necklace belong?" said Fairley, keenly eyeing the stranger who had brought him such a valuable article.

"That must remain secret. You must deal with me as though I was the actual owner of the diamonds."

"I cannot do that," said the money-lender, still clutching, however, the rich gems in his grasp, as, on receiving this reply, the stranger held out his hand for the necklace.

"If such be the case, I must go elsewhere." The stranger again offered to retake the jewels.

"Stay. You will scarce find anyone to advance money to a stranger upon such an article of value as this diamond necklace without further particulars, unless, indeed, you went to a fence or receiver of stolen property, who would offer you five hundred pound instead of five thousand." The money-lender darted a keen glance of his dark gray eyes upon the muffled features of his companion, as he uttered this speech, who returned his searching look of scrutiny with a gaze as bright and suspicious as his own.

"Look you, Ralph Fairley; let us understand each other. I want money. I bring you a valuable diamond necklace upon which I desire an advance of five thousand pounds. I am not prepared to give you any particulars as to who I came from, whence I come, or where I go. The necklace is worth treble the sum I have named, and to have a chance of securing such a gem deserves some risk."

Whilst the stranger had been speaking, Ralph Fairley had been attentively examining the necklace. On the richly-chased golden clasp he observed a mark that caused him to clutch the rich jewels more firmly in his grasp. The blood of the money-lender and miser bounded like lightning to his heart; his avaricious soul yearned to possess the priceless gems; at any cost they must be his; and now his scrutiny had shown him what would, he thought, help him in his purpose.

"The possession of this diamond necklace you refuse to give any particulars of. You say that to secure them deserves some risk. Are they worth the risk of the gallows?"

A grim smile darted athwart the features of Ralph Fairley as he whispered in the stranger's ears the latter part of his speech. A dark cloud gathered on the other's face, who first uttered a deep curse, then, with a laugh, exclaimed—

"Ha! ha! So you think you are dealing with a robber. Come, old man, give me the necklace; I will go where they will be more civil and less particular. Zounds! to be taken for a thief."

"Ay, or assassin." The keen gray eyes of the money-lender darted a searching glance at the stranger, who, seizing the old man by the arm, with a fierce oath, exclaimed—

"Ralph Fairley, what the fiends mean you by such words as these? By the devils, old man, were it not your gray hairs protect you, I would dash you to the ground at my feet. Give me the necklace, old man."

"Stay!" cried the money-lender, flinching not from the fierce look of his companion. "Can you explain to me the meaning of this dark crimson stain upon the clasp? See! behold! one of the bright crystals are smeared with the same dark stain. Shall I tell you what it is? Nay, your looks fright me not. The crimson smear upon the jewelled necklace is the stain of blood; and you know it!"

The words had scarce left the lips of the money-lender before he was struck to the ground by a violent blow from the stranger's fist; then, kicking open the door, he entered, hastily, the outer office, and, ere the astounded Nat Stevens, who had hurried forward, discovered his master senseless and bleeding on the ground, the mysterious visitor had vanished, but he noted not, when dashing through the outer door, that he was stealthily followed by a shuffling, stunted figure, that darted after his retreating form from the door of the money-lender's house, no other than Ephraim Rasselton.

CHAPTER III.

WANT AND MISERY.—LIZZIE HEYWARD, THE POOR SEAMSTRESS OF THE LAST CENTURY.—THE DYING PARENT.—THE LAST RESOURCE.—NOBLE HEART OF SYBIL FAIRLEY, THE MISER'S DAUGHTER.—THE CHAMBER OF DEATH.

IN one of the darkest and dingiest courts in Leather-Sellers'-buildings, London-wall, which in the last century was even worse than now, with our improvements of gas, drainage, and supply of water, there was an old tumble-down row of houses known as Fuller's-rents.

With doors off the hinges, broken casements, the shattered glass here and there stuffed with old rags, and the broken drain-pipes at the top allowing the rain to pour in floods from the roof to the uneven pathway below, made up a scene of ruin, wretchedness, squalor, and decay. The few panes of glass left whole in the houses of Fuller's-rents were black with a coating of dust and filth, the heavy rains that fell in the winter season but serving to add to the dirt and wretchedness of the place, as it collected together all the refuse of the court, consisting of decayed, rotting vegetables, mud, putrifying fish, and other animal matter, cast from the barrows of the itinerant vendors of these various articles, that lodged in the tumble-down habitations of Fuller's-rents. Strange-looking creatures were the inhabitants of our court, as it was invariably called by those who resided in the place.

The men, composed of the lowest class of costermongers and day-labourers, were seldom seen about our court, and, when visible, seemed to have a total disregard as to matters of apparel, especially coats, as they were seldom to be seen but in dilapidated cotton garments and shirts of mysterious texture that may once have been white, but, from the colour, looking as though half-boiled in pea-soup. These men, who inhabited our court, were always to be seen, at all hours of the day, when at home, with dirty clay pipes, from which they puffed volumes of rank tobacco smoke.

Of the gentler sex, amiability was not a distinctive mark in the character of the ladies of Fuller's-rents. Some there were even of a combative turn of mind, who, at an affront, real or imaginary, it mattered not which, would roll up their sleeves, when their garments boasted such articles, and, with true Amazonian valour, would, to use a common phrase in our court, "fight it out." And, after the belligerents had avenged themselves by a due amount of tearing, scratching, and cursing, would console themselves, with their partizans, in sundry glasses of blue ruin, a favourite beverage, summer or winter, in our court.

Some six months before the incidents we have already detailed, there came to reside at Fuller's-rents a family consisting of a widow and three children, the eldest a lovely young girl of some eighteen summers, the younger ones—a little boy and girl—aged, respectively, nine and eleven years. Far different were these new-comers to the other inhabitants of Fuller's-rents. The widow had evidently seen happy days, though now reduced to abject poverty. An air of the utmost gentility hung about the unfortunate widow and her children, who, by their quiet, reserved manners, won the rude respect of the rough denizens of our court. Lodging in one top room in the meanest and poorest house of Fuller's-rents, the wretched family were wholly supported by the young girl; for within a week after entering their abode of poverty the poor Widow Heyward fell sick and was confined to her bed. Working—toiling like a slave at her needle, the lovely daughter of the widow, beset with temptations by her matchless beauty, sat, night and day, without a murmur, working for the support of her helpless, sick, and dying parent, and little brother and sister. With eyes red and smarting would the poor girl for hours toil in the garret-like dungeon of that old house in Fuller's-rents.

Oh! who shall talk of the sufferings of the wretched negroes, who, we doubt not, lead a terrible life of slavery. Let us look at home; look at our poor, pale daughters of England; poor girls, who, at all hours of the night, toil—toil—till the eyes grow weak, and the heart sick, who, by the accursed slavery of the needle, are born victims to an early grave. Talk not to us of the untutored black—the strong and healthy African—when we look into the pale, ghastly, pinched faces of our poor London work girls, who, in the last century—the time of which we are writing—suffered as now from hard toil and starving pay. Years have passed, still death claims its victims of the needle, which we believe is the worst paid class in England. A manufactured machine is now taking the place of the human one; let us hope still further changes may take place. But to resume.

It was towards the close of the day that the miser and money-lender, Ralph Fairley, had been visited by the mysterious stranger with the diamond necklace, that a pale, shivering, but beautiful girl, timidly knocked at the door of the house in the Poultry, at about eight o'clock at night: the office was closed. In the biting chill of that winter Cheapside was near deserted; the few pedestrians yet walking the streets hurried home to their firesides; whilst the shopkeepers, one after the other, were closing their shops.

A lovely young girl was the summoner for admission at the money-lender's house that dark, bleak, October night. About eighteen years of age, of the medium height, the young girl was possessed of bright, golden hair, that fell in showers of ringlets over her fair brow and plump white shoulders; her features, round and dimpled, were of faultless shape; while her heaving bust and lithe figure were alike formed in admirable contours. A beautiful girl was the young seamstress, Lizzie Heyward, for she it was who stood half-clad, shivering in the wintry wind. Beautiful, very beautiful she was—but oh! so pale, so ghastly pale. Receiving no reply to her first timid knock, the shivering, trembling girl repeated the summons, and this time was answered by a female voice from within, who exclaimed—

"Who's there?"

"It's only me, Miss Watson," replied the poor girl, whose teeth, chattering with the intense cold, and convulsed with grief, could hardly command her voice to utterance.

The rattling of a chain followed the reply of the young girl, who, in a few moments, stood in the hall of Ralph Fairley's residence.

"Why, poor girl, what on earth has brought you out, thus ill-clad, this bitter night?" exclaimed the young woman who had opened the door; at the same time that she cast her eyes with pain and dismay upon the shivering form of the girl before her, who, without a shawl, merely a thin summer scarf, partly covering her shoulders from the shrill blast, had braved the piercing bitterness of that winter's night.

"If you please, can I see Miss Fairley?" said the seamstress with difficulty keeping back the tears that rose to her eyes, called there by the unmistakable looks of commiseration cast upon her by the young girl, Nancy Watson, handmaid to the daughter of the money-lender and miser, Ralph Fairley.

"Well, as it happens, you can see my lady, Miss Heyward, for Mr. Fairley has gone to the officers of justice at Bow-street, for he was violently assaulted this morning in his own office. So, as he is out, I'll show you up to my lady." Followed by the young girl, Nancy Watson, a bright-eyed, merry, roguish little waiting-maid, full of love and kindness, took her way up a flight of stairs, halting at a door, through which fell upon the ear the sounds of a piano, accompanied by the exquisite singing of a young girl, the notes of whose voice sounded sweet and clear. Entering the room, Nancy Watson announced the name of the visitor, whilst, pale and trembling, Lizzie Heyward, the poor seamstress, stood without the door.

Receiving an invitation to enter, she passed through the open door into the large, light room, which, warmed by the fire of a huge grate, looked cheerful and bright after the darkness and cold of the streets without.

Sitting at a piano she beheld Sybil Fairley, the miser's daughter.

A fine contrast were the two beautiful young girls, for Sybil was scarce yet eighteen. If the palm for beauty must have been awarded the lovely maidens, certainly the money-lender and miser's daughter would have carried off the prize. Fair, dazzling fair, was the young girl's skin; her eyes a deep azure, floated in a soft, delicious languor; her features, the direct opposite of Lizzie Heyward's, were of the Grecian type; her beautifully formed head was covered with a mass of dark brown hair, braided after the Madonna, upon the smooth, white, and polished brow. Though so young, the lovely girl possessed a firm, full, and beautifully rounded bust; her plump, soft arms, which, bare to the shoulder, were smooth and white as alabaster, were also beautifully rounded; her hands, soft, white, and dimpled, were like a fairy's, so small were they. Something below the medium height, her figure was cast in the fairest mould; her supple limbs, admirably proportioned, were set off to advantage by a light dress, the folds of which served to show off the graceful figure of the young girl. A lovely creature indeed was Sybil Fairley, the miser's daughter, and many were the suitors she had secured, but none had yet appeared to charm the young girl's heart; nor had any that had offered been sufficiently wealthy to gain the good-will of Ralph Fairley, who was prepared, in his sordid avarice and love of gold, to dispose of his daughter's hand to the highest bidder.

Rising from her seat, the fair girl bade the pale and trembling seamstress to take a chair by the fire. "And tell me," said Sybil, while a look of pity flashed across her face, as she observed the ill-clad figure of the poor girl; "tell me what I can do for you. You have not surely finished the dress I gave you to make yesternight?"

"No, madam; but I have ventured here to-night under the pressure of a severe distress, to—to—ask if you would kindly advance the money you promised me for the work—treble that I have ever before received—and which I feel I am taking an unwarrantable liberty in asking for; but, indeed, I am in great and immediate distress." Unable longer to repress her tears, the young girl sank into a chair, and gave way to a passionate fit of weeping.

"Alas! my good girl, weep not thus. Happy am I to be enabled, through my father's absence, to have seen you; nor do I wish you to suppose I want the heart to assist you. When seeing you yesterday, it never struck me until you were gone that the money for the work might have assisted you; though I remembered after you had left me, that the person who informed me of your expertness at the needle and embroidery, also told me of your distress."

"And you are not angered at the liberty I have taken in intruding upon you to-night?" said the poor seamstress, while the crystal tears poured down her pallid cheeks.

"Angered, my poor girl; no. Here, take this. You can make up the difference some other time." With tears in her own eyes at beholding the deep distress of the young girl, Sybil Fairley pressed a guinea into her hand. Staggering back with a wild look, gazing at the bright coin, she gasped out her thanks; and, without waiting to be shown from the room, tottered out into the passage, down the wide staircase into the hall, and out into the darkness of the night, followed immediately afterwards by the miser's daughter, who, urged by the heartrending distress of poor Lizzie Heyward, had determined to see her to her home, taking from her drawer, ere she left her father's house, a well-filled purse to alleviate, should there be truth in the distress of the unhappy seamstress, the poverty of her home.

Wildly blew the stormy, wintry winds, laden with a frosty keenness from the north; the stars in the bright, frosty sky shone sparkling and beautiful in the keen night air.

The horses' hoofs clattered noisily on the hard roads, while the measured tramp of the watchmen, proceeding to their several rounds, sounded clear and with hollow echoes down the streets and courts of the city.

Heeding not the biting blast, when leaving the kind-hearted daughter of Ralph Fairley, Lizzie Heyward hurried along to the neighbourhood of London-wall, which she reached in a few minutes. With beating heart the young girl hastened through Leather Sellers'-buildings, till reaching Fuller's-rents, she made her way through a mob of the principal inhabitants, who were collected together, shouting and yelling in a drunken brawl.

The poor girl had near approached her own door, when her arm was seized from behind, and a voice exclaimed—

"Lizzie Heyward, I've watched you one hour to-night, daring the chances of insults from the wretched beings who infest this court. I have learned, girl, that your mother is on her death-bed, that want and privation have hastened her end. Can you doom the parent, your only one, your widowed mother, to an untimely grave, whilst it is in your power, mad girl, to save her? Say but the word, and this night your unhappy mother shall be removed from this den of horror, and to-morrow, Lizzie, I will give you riches—all you ask!"

Vainly, during this speech, had the trembling girl endeavoured to withdraw her hand from the grasp of a young man, who, habited in the costume of a civilian, yet bore about him the manner and carriage of an officer in the army.

"Captain Leslie, let go your hold! My mother would sooner perish in this abode of poverty, would sooner be laid in a pauper's grave, than owe her preservation to her daughter's shame, and that, too, wrought by her unfeeling cousin, Captain Leslie. Oh! shame, shame! There is not a poor wretch in this court but who is more manly than thou art. Wretch, quit my sight! and for your discomfort know that I have found a friend who will release me from the distress I have lately endured. With honest industry, Captain Leslie, I shall yet save my mother and myself." Tearing her hand from his grasp, the young girl flew, rather than ran, down the dim, dark court, which, lighted with but one oil lamp which hung in the centre, was cast in gloom and thick darkness, away from the immediate reflection of the pale, yellow, flickering flame.

With a curse, the young man turned on his heel and groped his way out of the court, muttering as he went—

"She shall yet be mine. I will pursue her, though I spend a fortune in securing her to my arms! Her loved Mark will not now return, and she must become my prey. I need but bide my time." Hurrying through the buildings, the stranger who had assaulted the wretched seamstress disappeared in the darkness of the night.

Blindly groping her way up the dark, broken staircase of the house she had entered, Lizzie Heyward was startled by hearing loud voices in the room occupied by her mother, herself, and the two children.

What could it mean? They were always careful never to admit anyone in their only apartment, and now she heard the sound of women's voices, and distinguished the sobbing of her little brother and sister, and her own name pronounced, accompanied with exclamations of pity.

The poor girl halted at the door of the room with a beating heart, trembling to open it; but she must enter it, and, hearing a footstep on the stairs below, and observing a watchman leading a muffled figure up the broken, ladder-like staircase, Lizzie Heyward placed her hand upon the lock and darted into the room.

The sight, however, that met her gaze seemed to change her into stone.

Seated on the floor in the centre of the room was her little sister, with her little brother's arms around her neck.

Upon the bed in the corner of the dark chamber, lit with one small candle, was a quiet, rigid form, which, laid at length upon the mattrass, look ghastly hideous in the dull glimmer of the solitary light. By the couch stood two common-looking women, who, on the girl's entry, had ceased their conversation. They had been attending to the lifeless, rigid form upon the bed, which, without motion or sign of life, laid so still and calm.

Like a statue, Lizzie Heyward stood transfixed in the corner of the room, gazing spell-bound upon the bed.

The words, "Too late! too late!" fell in mournful accents from her lips; and still she stood statue-like in the centre of the room, gazing with distended eyes on the sight before her.

She was gazing on the corpse of her mother!

In the corner of the dim, dark chamber near the broken casement, was seated on the floor the two shivering figures of the little brother and sister of the now orphan seamstress.

Convulsive sobs burst from the bosoms of the poor children, who, alas! were well aware of their position. They knew they had lost their only parent: their fond mother was torn from them for ever.

The two women, who, lodging in the house, had come up in the absence of the wretched Lizzie Heyward, stood by the couch of death with folded arms, gazing with pity upon the poor children, and the speechless, broken-hearted girl.

Still and calm, Lizzie stood erect in the chamber of death.

Like a figure cut from Parian marble she looked as she remained with steadfast gaze glaring on her mother's corpse.

At length, with faltering steps, she made for the couch or rude bedstead, on which reposed, in a last sleep, the parent whom she had so fondly loved. Stopping their sobs, the children gazed in terror and wonder upon the form of their bereaved sister, the women drawing back as she approached the couch upon which reposed her mother's corpse.

The grief of the young girl was speechless, as, drawing down the coverlid that had partly concealed the wax-like features of the dead, she looked on the rigid figure.

How pale, livid, and ghastly was the face of the corpse!

But yet a sweet smile seemed to hover around the handsome features of the dead.

Mrs. Heyward had in her youth been a lovely creature; the traces of extreme beauty still hung upon her pale, livid face.

So haggard, pinched, were the features of the dead, however, that plain and palpable was the cause of death.

It was apparent to all.

The eyes sunk deep in the head, the hollow cheeks, the thin, spectral skeleton hands of the dead one, spoke out the fearful truth.

The unhappy mother of the poor seamstress had died of want.

Wild thoughts darted through the brain of Lizzie Heyward, as she gazed spell-bound upon her mother's corpse.

Her father, upright, honest, of spotless character, had been made the dupe of a villain; losing all his fortune, her parent had perished with despair and want; but, as he lived he died—honest to the last.

The mother, too, now had followed the husband to the grave. Both might have been living if she, Lizzie, had swerved from the rigid paths of virtue she had been taught never to depart from. Gold, gold, would have

THE FLASH KEN IN THE OLD MINT—ARRIVAL OF RESURRECTION BILL AND THE JEW.

saved both of those now dead. And gold she might have obtained.

Horrible thoughts darted through the brain of Lizzie Heyward as she stood by the dead form of her mother.

No tears fell from her glaring eyes; a crimson, hectic flush at times took the place of the deadly pallor, which, when leaving her face, made it resemble that of the corpse beside which she stood.

The two women left her by the couch of the dead, awed and terrified by her speechless despair. A tap sounded at the door as they were about to leave the room; but Lizzie Heyward heard not the inquiry for herself. Speechless she remained by the bed in which rested the corpse of her mother.

"Sissy, sissy; won't you speak to Tarley?" murmured the little brother of the young girl, as, conquering his fear at the scene before him, he ran to his sister's side. Heeding not the poor little fellow, whose eyes were suffused with tears and red with weeping, Lizzie Heyward stood motionless by the bedside. At length her lips parted; a low murmur fell from her mouth; and, perceiving not that the woman of the house had admitted two strangers —a muffled female, and a tall, gentlemanly-looking man— she gave utterance to her thoughts, and her terrible grief.

"And so, then, my mother—father—both are gone, torn from me—dead—dead! Death hath claimed them for his own. Within the year my dear mother has followed my father to the grave; and I might have saved them. But how?" A shudder here shook the young girl's frame; then, turning her eyes from her mother's corpse, she started, a deadly pallor darting across her face, as she beheld the form of the man who stood near the door, in front of the muffled female figure, that was holding a murmured converse with the woman of the house.

"Ha! ha!" screamed the wretched girl, as she beheld the stranger. Laughing wildly and hysterically, and catching his arm, she drew him to the bedside. "See— see you there! She is dead! She—my mother—is a corpse! Death has called her from the world of sin to one of happiness. Thou caus't not harm her there, Captain Leslie. You have returned to behold your accursed work. Ay, yours! You who defrauded my dear father! You who would have had the daughter purchase life for her mother by her shame! Ha! ha! are you not pleased, wretch, with your work? Doubtless, now the parents are removed, you think your prey must fall into your arms. But rather, Captain Leslie, would I take a leap into the dark waters of the river. Rather meet death this moment than become thine. I am now alone, wretch, and defy you; for she—she, for whom I might have given honour itself to save from such a fate as this, is now removed for ever."

"And your brother, sister, would you doom them to a fearful death by want?" said the stranger, the cousin of the wretched girl's mother, who had assailed her but shortly before in the court, for he it was who now stood in the chamber of death. A shudder and gasp of pain escaped the lips of the poor girl, as she cast her eyes upon the cowering figures of the two poor children, whose very tears were choked by the scene before them.

"I had forgot! I had forgot! They must not, too, be torn from me by a cruel death, Captain Leslie. To save them I may at length accede to your wishes; but leave me now. Leave me alone—alone with her." The poor girl here pointed to the still, stark form that laid in a death sleep upon the bed. A smile of joy irradiated the features of the young man, who, throwing a purse of gold upon the table in the centre of the room, turned to go.

"I leave you the wherewithal to defray any little expense of to-night, dear girl, and will return hither on the morrow. For the present, farewell!"

The wretched orphan, catching the young man by the arm, drew him near the death-bed of her mother, and exclaimed—

"See you here! Look upon that attenuated form, those wan, thin features. She, your cousin, has died a terrible death from starvation. Say you will, for the sake of the dead one, provide for her unhappy children without the terrible price of her daughter's shame."

"Lizzie, I have sworn long past to make you mine. Accede to my wishes, and all the world can give shall be yours; refuse, and your innocent brother and sister will meet their wretched parents' doom."

"Wretch! inhuman monster! heaven will aid your cousin to save the children from the fate you have predicted. I, myself, will assist, and enable her to foil you in your villainous purpose."

A cry of joy escaped the lips of the poor seamstress as the veiled form burst forward. Throwing aside the cloak that had concealed her figure, Sybil Fairley—for it was indeed the miser's daughter who had stood thus long silent in the death chamber—appeared with flashing eyes before the villain, who had pursued his victim even to the death-bed of her parent. A dark frown gathered on the face of the young man, as he gazed upon the beautiful girl, who had started forward with offers of aid to her whom he had thought all but in his grasp. Hanging on the arm of the noble-hearted Sybil Fairley, the poor seamstress murmured her thanks, whilst in accents of abhorrence she bade the villain-cousin quit the chamber, and take the gold with which he had thought to purchase her ruin. "Heaven," ejaculated the poor girl, "has sent a friend, and, villain, I defy you! At once leave the room. Your presence is a desecration to the dead." Then, at length giving way to her sorrow, with wild hysterical sobs, Lizzie Heyward threw herself over the corpse of her mother. A curse escaped the lips of Captain Leslie, who, in obedience to the extended finger of the young girl, Sybil Fairley, turned to the door, and quitted the room, muttering as he went—

"By heavens! my cousin's friend is fairer than herself. She has started forward between me and mine. Let her look to it, or she, too, may become my prey! By the fiends! she is a lovely girl, and of her I will soon know more."

The clock of St. Paul's was booming out the hour of ten, when Sybil Fairley rose from her knees in the dark chamber of the old house in Fuller's-rents. With the poor bereaved orphan, the noble, kind-hearted daughter of the money-lender of the Poultry had been praying for the dead, and left the house with proud and beating heart, arranging in her mind how best to assist the poor girl who was the victim of such terrible distress. The good angels hovered round the couch of Sybil Fairley that night, who slept far more calm upon the good deed of the day before than her parent, the miser, who dreamed of the one object of his life—the procuring of the bright yellow gold, for which he would have bartered his immortal soul.

CHAPTER IV.

THE FLASH KEN IN THE OLD MINT AT SOUTHWARK.— BURKING SAM AND THE COFFIN. — ARRIVAL OF RESURRECTION BILL. — THE SIGNAL OF THE NIGHT-HAWKS.—THE MUFFLED STRANGER AND BROWN BET.— THE FRACAS, GUY ESSINGTON, AND THE NIGHT-HAWKS.—THE SECRET CHAMBER IN THE FLASH KEN.— THE INTRODUCTION OF THE MUFFLED STRANGER.— SURPRISE AND DISMAY OF RESURRECTION BILL AND ABRAHAMS, THE JEW.—THE DEAD ALIVE.

THE Mint at Southwark in the last century was far different to that of the present day. The thoroughfare now known as Mint-street has much more improved than its neighbour, the dark, ill-paved turning leading out of the Borough to the Kent-road, and named Kent-street. The old Mint has quite disappeared; some well and newly-built houses now stand in the street, once the haunt of thieves of the vilest class.

A dark, murky, murderous-looking place was the old Mint at Southwark. In the last century, when night had fallen, lighted here and there with a dim, flickering oil lamp, it looked, indeed, a fit abode for crime.

The night following the incidents related in our last chapter, two men proceeded from the neighbourhood of Kennington-common (then a dark, bleak, open spot) towards the Borough. Slowly they plodded on, side by side, holding a converse in an under-tone, thickly interspersed with oaths and imprecations.

"Then, does yer mean to say, Coffin, as how Resurrection Bill and old Abrahams really made a stiff-un of the stranger what he hocussed and floored in the Wauxhall-road the night afore last?"

"Yes, Burker. Not content with the swag as we collared from the young bloke, Resurrectioner must needs walk off the body to the old house in Battersea-fields, making up his mind to sell the stiff-un to the saw-bones."

"Ah! he is very downy, is Bill. Not a bad hidea, don't yer know. 'Cos why? Resurrectioner gained two ends," ejaculated the other ruffian to his companion. "Don't yer see as how the body sold by Bill to the doctors, and cut up, prevented it from turning up agin us coves what made it a stiff-un?"

"Right you is, Burker; but you arn't heard all. You see as how when I went the same night to the old house, who should I find struggling with Resurrectioner and old Abrahams but the identical young swell, who hadn't been done for by the crack we gave him on his cocoa-nut, but came to life agin, out of spite, and fought like a fiend; but," added the ruffian, with a fearful oath, "Resurrectioner soon settled him. Assisted by Ben Abrahams, he toppled him down the trap, over the waters, and by this time his blessed corpse is pretty well pickled, I calculate, out at sea."

"Do yer know, Coffin, what Bill wants to see us for to-night? What's the lay?"

"Doesn't know."

"'Cos why, Resurrectioner is such a down-pin, he always keeps his tater-trap shut till the last moment; however, we shall hear whether it's a crib or a graveyard Bill purposes cracking. Lor, Burker, what a cove he is. He is as good a cracksman as ever danced a hornpipe on nothing at Tyburn Tree, and as quick and expert a snatcher as ever prized open a wooden box of cold meat on a dark night in a graveyard. Ah! if as how he were the leader of the brave Hawks instead of that cove Guy Essington, who turns up his nose at churchyard business, which, arter all, pays as well as cracking a crib, padding, or doing the highway, to which he is so very partial."

"Curses on Guy Essington," ejaculated the man called by his companion Burker; "he is a doing on us all. There is that precious prize what we collared from that young sailor cove as I burked down by the river, and then tumbled over into the stream. What has come of that haul? I, for one, will know; ay, and this very night, or, curse me, I'll blow the gaff-snitch nose upon the gang, and risk a lag myself. Guy Essington don't do the blind on Burking Sam, not if he knows it."

"Well, there is four on us, as is pretty nigh agreed. As to Captain Guy, we all votes for another leader. The captain has owned himself that he arn't as young as he was, and the Night-Hawks want a young, bold, or a known hand, as is up to every move on the board, keen, daring, and as ready to knife a cove as to eat a dinner. The Hawks is a large body now, and, cuss me, if we don't get lots of swag, and defy the runners and the beaks, wot is so werry anxious as to our welfare; but here is Sam, and arter business has been talked over with Resurrectioner, let us sound him as to a new leader for the Night-Hawks of London."

The two members of a daring gang, that at that time haunted London and its environs, had now reached the corner of the old Mint of Southwark, the clock of St. Saviour's was tolling out the hour of nine as they entered the dark, dismal, murky purlieus of the Mint.

A dark night made the old Mint yet look more dreary, murky, and murderous.

The thick black clouds hung like a funereal pall aloft; not a star was visible in the sky; all was black—black as the raven's wing.

The darkness of the night seemed to be increased as the two men entered, from the Borough, the ghastly, narrow entrance of the old Mint.

The dim light from the oil lamps swinging in the streets served but to increase the dreary aspect of the place.

Oaths, shouts of drunken revelry, mingled with the uproar of an occasional brawl, rang upon the air.

Anon the shrill scream of a woman sounded from one of the narrow courts that lined the street, followed by the noise of blows, curses, and even the startling cry of murder, woke up an echo in the den of crime.

Stumbling along, the two companions made their way to a house about halfway up the street, before which was a large lamp, enclosed in a hoop lined with red calico, on which was daubed some large yellow letters, "Josh Jordan, innkeeper," and underneath the sign, "The Fox in the Hole." Entering the house, the two men passed the bar, which was filled even at that early hour of the night with a noisy, fighting crowd, and made their way to a room at the back of the premises on the ground floor. A tall slattern, with loose hair, like dirty tow, hanging down her back, and large red eyes, with a face covered with blotches, caused by a frequent use of intoxicating liquors, followed the men in, and desired to know their orders.

Bidding this disgusting-looking parlour-maid bring in some brandy hot, the two ruffians sat down near a large blazing fire, which crackled and gleamed merrily in the frosty air. It was a bitter night, and with curses on the weather, the two men, placing their feet upon the hob of the huge grate, prepared to make themselves comfortable in their present quarters.

The room, a large one, lighted by an oil lamp and the ruddy glow from the fire, looked cheerful that winter evening.

The brandy at length making its appearance, the companions in crime again fell into conversation, emptying glass after glass of the burning spirit, whilst waiting the arrival of their comrade.

As the two outcasts of society play a prominent part in this romance of life, we must here describe their calling and appearance.

The ruffian Burking Sam was a villain who hesitated at no crime. In the habit of destroying his victims, strangling them Thug fashion with a handkerchief or a pitch-plaster over the mouth, his expertness in his devilish calling had gained for him the appellation of Burking Sam, the real name of the wretch being Barney Samuels. Originally of Irish family, the man possessed the prominent high features and high cheek-bones of the Connaught Irish, with broad, square shoulders; he also possessed an herculean frame, with a forehead low and receding. His ugliness was further enhanced by a deep scar from the temple to the eyebrow, which gave a terrible sinister expression to the strongly-marked features of the man, deeply pitted with the small-pox, and with tawny, reddish hair, which fell over his bull-neck, the villain looked, indeed, the personification of ruffianism.

The companion who sat beside him, puffing thick clouds of stifling smoke from a pipe filled with rank tobacco, was universally known by the somewhat ominous name of the Coffin. Coffin-Faced Jem, or Jem Coffin, was of tall, spare figure, and cadaverous features, with a face long, thin, and pale. He had a large flat chin and immense jaw, while a dark, ferocious expression was given to his pallid features by heavy, beetling eyebrows, whilst a keen gray eye sparkled and shone with a sinister glare from beneath the half-closed eyelids. The length of his face had gained for the ruffian the *soubriquet* of Coffin-Faced Jem, but he was generally called by the short, abbreviated term of Coffin. Originally an undertaker, he had by nefarious practices been imprisoned within the strong portals of Newgate, leaving which he joined with the criminals with whom he had before been engaged, and was now one of a gang called the Night-Hawks of London. Composed of daring ruffians, the gang had its members in almost every county, and had hitherto defied with success the officers of justice. So strong was the league, that when a Night-Hawk was captured, the best of counsel was obtained for the victim in the clutches of the law; and if all failed to free the captive, and he was led to the gibbet or the hulks, no word of betrayal issued from his lips regarding his companions, so strong was the chain that bound the Night-Hawks. Several of its members had perished, but the band still remained united, and gaining strength daily.

It was near the hour of ten that the companions of crime in the large back room of the "Fox in the Hole" were startled by the entrance of a stranger, who, muffled up, seemed anxious to avoid, as much as possible, the observations of the men and women who at that moment crowded into the chamber.

Foremost in the crowd that thronged the room was a tall, dark beauty, with olive complexion, jet black eyes, and finely pencilled eyebrows, that, shaded off and delicately curved, were black as the raven's wing. The young girl possessed fine features, full glowing lips, with pearly white and even teeth. She had also a fully developed, firm, round, and swelling bust; indeed her figure was almost faultless. A lovely brunette or gipsy was this girl, who, on entering the room, assailed the muffled stranger, who, seated in a corner, endeavoured to avoid her importunities. The girl, however, nothing abashed, persevered in her unwelcome attentions.

"How now, Brown Bet; don't disturb the stranger, but come over here, and I'll treat you to a glass of brandy hot," said the man Coffin, banging his fist on the table, and shouting with stentorian lungs for more of the fiery fluid.

"Ha! ha! ha!" shouted the girl, with a burst of laughter. "And do you think, Coffin-Faced Jem, the likes of Brown Bet is going to cast her smiles upon you for your paltry glass of brandy? Now, I'd wager beef-steaks and onions all round, that the swell cove here will treat Gipsy Bet to some of Josh Jordan's best wine; for Josh does sell good wine, stranger, and I'll drink your health this night in some of his old port." Calling the landlord, a rubicund-faced, stout, and ill-looking fellow, she pointed to the muffled figure of the young man before her, and ordered a bottle of the best port. The landlord, on receiving a nod from the stranger, hurried away to procure the necessary drink, whilst, with a ringing laugh, the dark beauty threw herself half into the arms of the young man, whose features, only partly concealed by a slouched cap and collar of a large cloak, it could be seen was good-looking, and in general deportment far above the average visitors of the "Fox in the Hole."

"Curse me, who the devil is it? By the fiends, Gipsy Bet seems to have fallen into the good graces of the strange one. Damn him, why don't he show his mug?" exclaimed Coffin.

"That he'll pretty soon have to do if Resurrection Bill comes in and finds Bet's arms around his neck. Curse me, if I'd change places with the swell cove; for if Bill finds Bet at all on, the swell is as good as corpsed, and by ——" added the ruffian, with a fierce oath, "here is Resurrectioner. Look! See! How quickly he has fastened his peepers on them. Well, I guess Brown Bet will begin to grow nervous on it. Resurrectioner arn't a cove to put up with any nonsense from a blowen. Don't he look savage at them."

On first entering the room, the murderer of the lone house in Battersea-fields had caught sight of Gipsy Bet, as the dark beauty was called, sitting beside the muffled form of a young man, with her arms wound round his neck. A dark, ominous flash, a ferocious look of deadly rage, rested on the features of the man as he cast his eyes upon the young girl, who, staying the merry laugh upon her lips, grew deadly pale, and, slowly drawing her arms from the stranger's neck, made as if she would rise; but she found herself stayed and deterred from her purpose by her companion, who, pulling her gently back, in a voice loud enough to reach everyone in the room, exclaimed—

"Sit down, my beauty; don't be frightened at the looks of that ugly baboon. I'll twist his bull neck, if he says aught to you while you're near me."

A buzz ran round the room at this bold speech of the stranger, while the woman motioned him entreatingly to go; but, firm in his seat, and apparently unmoved by the looks of alarm in the visage of the poor girl, Brown Bet, the stranger remained; whilst the burly ruffian, twice his size, with dark, ferocious looks, threw off his coat and bared a brawny arm, covered from the wrist upwards with tawny-coloured hair. The face of the young girl grew of a livid hue as she gazed at the villain, whilst a grim silence fell on the room; all awaited, in anxious suspense, the issue of the inevitable encounter between the young stranger and the herculean form of the resurrection man.

"Now, then, you black-faced ——," said the ruffian, with a horrible oath, "just come here! Come here, and see how soon I'll spoil your dainty features you think so much of!" The ruffian here strode forwards; and, as the trembling, shrinking figure of the young girl clung to the stranger, he grasped her by the arm, and, ere she or her protector were aware, dragged her away, and flung her with all his force across the room. With a scream the poor girl fell into the arms of Coffin and the Burker, as they rose up from their seats. Scarce, however, had the ruffian turned round, with a demon look of rage upon his hideous features, ere, to his astonishment, and that of everyone in the room, the stranger sprang up, and ejaculating the words—

"Scoundrel—thief—assassin, look to yourself!" Seizing the burly form of the resurrection man in his grasp, he held him with a firm, deadly grip, whilst like two wild animals they writhed in each other's arms round the chamber, overturning with a crash, tables, glasses, and chairs in their mad struggle.

The lawless crew congregated in the parlour of the "Fox in the Hole" stood round the room in a ring, gazing upon the burly form of the resurrection man and his slim, but lithe, antagonist, as they twisted and struggled in a deadly grip of hate.

"Stand back!"

"Give them room."

"Let 'em have it out."

"Twenty to one on the little 'un."

"He's werry game. Resurrection 'as got his match at last, he has."

"Trip him up, Bill!"

"Knife him!"

These and such like cries, accompanied by hideous oaths and imprecations, burst from the lips of those who stood eyeing the stranger, whose lithe and active form seemed to defy the resurrection man.

Suddenly, as the ruffian was about to bear down the young man by his sheer weight, hoping by a heavy fall to deprive his antagonist of sense or motion, the stranger, as if aware of his intention, suddenly shifted his grasp from the arms of the resurrectionist, and, clasping him upon the hips, lifted his gigantic body right off the floor, and threw it with great force upon the ground—the head of the ruffian striking against one of the legs of a heavy table, causing momentary insensibility. Looks of amazement and admiration were cast upon the young stranger, who had thus easily vanquished the giant.

But anon dark looks settled on the faces of the partizans of the discomfited villain as they lifted up his senseless and bleeding form, and as the girl, Brown Bet, the original cause of the disturbance, was about to hurry the stranger from the room, loud yells burst forth, and several ruffians dashed at the unarmed stranger, knife in hand, with murderous looks.

"Cut him up! Mincemeat the whelp!"

"Slit his weazand!"

"Dowse the glim, and at him!"

The light in the room was now kicked over; the embers in the grate giving out a strange, spectral, ruddy glow in the chamber of the old inn.

Then ensued a fearful scene. The sounds of noisy conflict, oaths, cries, and imprecations, mingled with the shrill screams of women. The daring young stranger, who had boldly defied the ruffian frequenters of the flash ken, was now struggling in the grasp of four or five of the villains, that, like wild cats, had dashed upon him at the moment when his strength was giving way to numbers. Three loud knocks were heard at the door of the old inn without, and a voice ejaculated in the passage of the old house—

"Hawks, to your nest for the midnight meeting!"

"The door of the chamber in which the conflict had taken place was then dashed open by a kick from without, and all in the room started back, as a tall, herculean-looking man stood before them. On catching sight of his features, the late antagonist of the resurrectionist started from the grasp of Coffin Jem and the burker, and, throwing off his cap, seized the new comer by the arm, and whispered in his ear—

"Guy Essington, I am here! Though at peril to my life!"

Then, as several of those in the chamber were about to dash at the young man, the tall stranger, who appeared known by all, raised his arm, and bidding them hold their hands, ejaculated—

"Night-Hawks, to the council-chamber! Come, boy, come, and fear not."

Taking the young man by the hand, the mysterious stranger, who seemed to hold some authority over the lawless ruffians in the house, led the way down a dark, narrow passage, which terminated in a door. Giving three knocks, and the warning words, "Hawks are in and want to nest," awaited a reply. In a few moments the sound of bolts and bars fell upon their ears, and the falling of a chain; the door then swinging open, revealed a steep flight of stone stairs, leading down apparently beneath the foundations of the old house. Guy Essington passed through the door, followed by some dozen men from the parlour of the flash ken, who, with looks of amazement, gazed in wonder upon the young stranger, who trod in the steps of their leader, confident and defiant, seeming indifferent to any danger that might beset him. Descending the rude flight of stairs, they now halted in a long, winding passage, lighted here and there by a small oil lamp, that shed a kind of ghostly ray about the darksome, underground passage. As they proceeded on, the murmur of voices could be heard; and, at length reaching a door at the end of the winding, gloomy passage, the leader again gave the three knocks and the pass, "Hawks are in and want to nest." No sooner had he given utterance to these words, than the door before them was swiftly opened, and, seizing the dauntless young stranger by the arm, Guy Essington pushed aside some thick, heavy curtains that hung within, and they entered a handsome, spacious apartment, lighted up by innumerable oil lamps. At a large table in the centre of the room were seated about three dozen men, regaling themselves with hot spirits, punch, cigars, and tobacco, the latter they helped themselves to from a huge bowl on the table.

A strange, wild scene was that in the underground apartment of the flash ken in the old Mint.

The young stranger gazed in wonder at the sight before him.

Every eye was turned upon Guy Essington, whilst loud cheers rung through the apartment, mingled with cries of "Order! order!" During the tumult occasioned by his appearance, the leader made his way to the head of the table, and seating himself in a chair elevated above the rest, bade the young stranger sit beside him. A silence now fell upon the scene, and all awaited the words of their chief; who, first raising a glass high in the air, exclaimed, "Long and prosperous career to the Night-Hawks!" A loud cheer then burst forth, whilst every goblet was drained of its contents. Then, as silence once more took the place of the loud cheering, Essington rose, and prepared to address the assemblage before him, amidst reiterated cheers giving the following speech—

"Knights of the road, hightobymen, cracksmen, and rum culls, 'tis known to all here that I, your leader for the past ten years, am now, by our increased numbers, in want of a lieutenant—a young, quick, and daring fellow, one in whom I can place implicit faith; one who will never disgrace our bold band; one that will not turn pale at sight of Tyburn Tree, or ever noze upon a pal in the hour of danger. You know that I, Guy Essington, have served you long and faithfully, but I am not now so young as formerly; I require a kindred spirit to my own, and that I have found. Yes, pals, my own nephew, one of my own flesh and blood, I will introduce to your notice this night, and by your leave will dub him my lieutenant."

"Hear! hear! hear!"

"What line does your *protegé* propose taking to?" exclaimed a tall, wiry man, known by his companions as Gentleman Jack.

"Your own, Jack."

"What! moonlight rides on a bonny brown mare, with the sententious demand of 'Money, or your life!' Takes he to the road?"

"Ay, Jack; nor would I wish for a better one to join him on his maiden trip than yourself."

"With all my heart, if he is daring, and will not flinch in the hour of danger, then would I gladly have him for a pal to join me on my canters over Hounslow heath."

"As you will, Jack. You will not find Eustace Maltravers, or Dashing Dick, as I call him, disgrace my encomiums. And now, knights of the road, flash and high-tobymen, forgers, and rum culls, allow me, with all the honours, to introduce to your notice my future lieutenant, and your future captain, when Guy Essington has gone his road. Gentlemen all, fill your glasses; no heel-taps—fill, fill to the brim, and drink to the health of Dashing Dick, who, though but a lad, in an encounter within the last hour with a member of the band, Resurrection Bill, threw his man! ay, hurled him to the ground as he would a child. See, the victor of Resurrection Bill stands before you."

The young stranger now, at a whisper from Guy Essington, rose to his feet and bowed to the dark line of figures that stood up at the long table, shouting and drinking off the contents of their glasses to the dregs.

"To the health of Dashing Dick!"

Loud cheers and the rattling of glasses followed this, which were quelled when the young man began to speak. Returning thanks for the honour bestowed upon him, he then detailed how he had met the resurrection man an hour before in the parlour of the house. "He is one of the band, I understand, so I must forget the incidents of the past hour: but there is another matter will ever cause Eustace Maltravers to be a bitter, unceasing foe to the resurrection man; but this enmity shall not, for my uncle's sake, cause me in respect of my enemy to break any rule of our band—but see, by heavens! he is here."

At this moment the hangings which concealed the door were drawn back, and Resurrection Bill, followed by the old Jew, Ben Abrahams, entered the room. The hideous face of the resurrectionist was made even more repulsive than ordinary by a stream of blood trickling from a deep jagged wound in the temple, received in the struggle with Dashing Dick an hour before. Standing erect by the side of Guy Essington, Eustace Maltravers was first noted by the resurrectionst and the Jew. The features of the young man in their encounter in the room of the inn had been unperceived by the ruffian, but now the full glare of the many lamps fell fully upon his handsome face. On casting their eyes upon him, a deadly pallor spread itself across the features of the resurrectionist and the old Jew; wildly and with distended eyes they gazed upon the figure before them. Low ejaculations of terror burst from the mouth of the Jew, whilst the resurrection man advanced nearer to the table, eyeing Dashing Dick in a strange wild manner. With a curse he drew his hands over his eyes, and then, noting that he was observed curiously by all present, endeavoured to shake off the horror that oppressed him.

At length, unable to bear up longer, he quitted the chamber, followed by the old Jew, and as he hurried forth, strange words fell from his lips.

"The dead returned to life? No, no! The living, the prey escaped, and once again before me. 'Tis well, he is my fate! I am his, and he or I must perish—by all the devils, I swear it! With a strange, wild demeanour, Resurrection Bill rushed from the "Fox in the Hole." But what caused the consternation and surprise of the ruffian Jew and the resurrectionist?

They had gazed upon their victim of the lone house at Battersea.

The figure thrown struggling down the loathsome trap in the murder done in Battersea-fields stood again in life before them. The villains were confounded—time alone could solve the mystery, to them inexplicable.

CHAPTER V.

EPHRAIM RASSELTON AND THE OWNER OF THE DIAMOND NECKLACE.—THE HARE AND THE HOUND.—CAUGHT IN A TRAP.—PERIL OF EPHRAIM.—THE LONE HOUSE AT BANK-SIDE.—MYSTERY AND MURDER.—TERROR OF EPHRAIM.—LUCY MASTERTON AND THE MONEY-LENDER'S CLERK.—ESCAPE OF EPHRAIM AND ARRIVAL OF THE UNKNOWN.

ON leaving the office in the Poultry, Ephraim Rasselton followed stealthily in the footsteps of the mysterious stranger, who carried with him a valuable diamond necklace worth some thousands of pounds. Aware of all that had passed in the inner office between the strange visitor and his employer, he determined to find out who the owner of the diamonds really was; and in his own mind judging them to be the proceeds of some robbery, with low cunning followed up the present owner with the idea of in some way securing the diamonds for himself.

"He is very sharp, is this Mr. Sharp; but—eh! eh! eh! —if Ephraim Rasselton don't out-wit him, I'm grievously mistaken," and so muttering to himself as he pursued his path through the crowded streets, the money-lender's clerk, with wary eye kept the stranger in sight down Cheapside, Ludgate-hill, and the neighbourhood of Whitefriars; here for a few moments Mr. Fairley's clerk was off the scent, his prey had disappeared. A deep curse passed the lips of Ephraim, which was followed by his usual giggle or chuckle which invariably escaped him when pleased. His mark, the mysterious stranger, again appeared, from the entrance of a dark, dirty-looking beer-house near the water-side. Ephraim, now again upon the track, hobbled along in pursuit, till at length the stranger, making his way to the Temple stairs, called for a boat.

This was awkward.

In the crowded streets 'twas easy to follow a man without notice, but upon the open river in a wherry was another matter; he would be soon discovered. His man would elude him.

What was to be done?

"Eh! eh! eh! I'll chance it. I'll follow him up to his lair; he is a thief, an assassin, and I have sworn to foil him in his plans. We only met this morning, but, damn him, I hate him! He jeered, scoffed me, treated me with scorn, and—eh! eh! eh!—he shall live to rue it—he shall live to rue it!"

With his spiteful cat-like eyes gleaming with malice, and his thin lips compressed, whilst a hectic flush of rage rested on either cheek, the stunted, dwarfish form of Ephraim Rasselton hurried down to the water-side, and as he muttered his soliloquy, he beckoned one of the watermen near for a boat.

A rough, jolly-looking, red-faced fellow answered the summons.

"Do you see that wherry half out in the river?" said Rasselton, pointing to the boat containing the man he was spying to his residence, and the waterman of which was pulling towards Lambeth.

"Yes, I sees it, governor; it's a pal of mine in that there wherry. The cove what is in it has engaged him to carry him to the old Bankside."

"Eh! eh! eh! 'tis well; I'm running down the hare!" muttered Ephraim. Then looking up at the man, who had now unfastened his boat, which tossed like a cork upon the mimic waves caused by a slight wind and a high tide, he exclaimed, "Well, you see that boat, and know, you say, its destination; pull at once for the same place, but do not let them see they are being followed. You understand?"

"Perfectly, sir," replied the boatman; who, Ephraim having seated himself, pulled his wherry out into the river. "You is a follerin' that muffled-up cove, and don't want to be twigged. I'm fly."

Returning no answer to the boatman—a rather talkative fellow—Ephraim, with folded arms, brooded upon the likely result of his present errand. That the rich and valuable diamond necklace, in the possession of the man whom he was thus tracking in broad day, was the proceeds of a daring robbery he doubted not, and Ephraim inwardly vowed to gain the precious gems himself, though life itself was risked in the attempt.

The wind blew piercing cold that winter morning over the broad and ruffled bosom of the noble Thames.

Large pieces of ice floated with the tide, surging and rattling in the water, and dashing with a crash like broken glass against the sides of the boat.

The sun, now high up in the heavens, shone like a ball of copper in the blue vault above, its dull, red glare but adding to the intense cold.

Finding his fare wrapped in a moody silence, with a muttered curse on his stolid manners, the waterman began to blow a cloud from a dirty clay pipe he pulled from his pocket, at the same time ruminating as to who and what his fare was who had desired him to follow the man who had only a few minutes before asked for a boat to convey him to Bankside.

"He is a rum 'un, darn him," muttered the waterman, dissatisfied with the silence of Ephraim Rasselton; "and, cuss me, if I don't look arter my coin."

Proceeding at a quick rate with the tide, the vessel which Ephraim was following soon reached Bankside, its destination, and pulling close in shore by the boatman, landed the mysterious stranger, the object of Rasselton's pursuit, near a large, old-fashioned, tumble-down inn, the back windows of which overlooked the waters of the river.

Jumping out of the wherry on to a rough landing of logs, surrounded by boats belonging to a boat-builder near at hand, the stranger disappeared. Scarce had the boat which conveyed him to his destination again dashed into the surging tide, urged by the sturdy rower, when that of Ephraim's, with a sharp jerk, grated against the logs, and in his hurry forgetting his fare, the old clerk was pursued across the rough landing-place by the waterman, who, with a volley of oaths, swore "he warn't a going to be done out of his fare."

Throwing him some money, with a curse, Ephraim darted on, fearful of losing his man; but about to pass the tavern, he started as he perceived the stranger conversing with the landlord of the house at the bar. Diving into the shadow of the wall, out of sight to those within, the shrewd clerk stayed his steps, and began to arrange his future course. Should he dare all, boldly call for aid, and give over to the officers of justice the man who, that morning, a short hour before, had assailed Ralph Fairley, the money-lender, in his own house? But should he do this, what would be the gain to him, Ephraim Rasselton?

Nothing! All his cunning pursuit, at present so successful in its results, would be vain.

No; he must drive a bargain with Mr. Sharp; frighten him; prove how he (Ephraim) held him in his power, and by that means extort from him a handsome sum, the proceeds of the rich necklace, which might even yet become his.

Boldly entering the house, Ephraim Rasselton, calling for refreshment, looked round for the owner of the diamonds.

He was not now at the bar.

He was well known, then, at the house, for he had not left it, and must have gone into the coffee-room or parlour.

Ephraim looked into a large, dirty chamber with a sawdust-covered floor, luxuriating in the appellation of parlour, but there was no one there.

He hastened back to the bar.

Had the stranger really after all escaped him, by leaving the house another way?

No, he was there. At the moment Ephraim was about to raise the glass to his lips, the tall stranger emerged from a door at the end of the passage which ran from the bar.

The man gave a start on perceiving Ephraim, who, with a knowing smile, beckoned him forwards.

"Eh! eh! eh! Met again, Mr. Sharp. You left us so hurriedly, really there was no time to say good-bye. The governor, too—serious matter—you have knocked his brains out!"

The keen dark eyes of Ephraim Rasselton searched into those of the man before him as he gave utterance to the lie. The stranger again started. With an oath, he stepped forward, and, seizing Ephraim by the arm, exclaimed—

"Mr. Ephraim Rasselton, you are a fool, a villain, and a liar! A fool to have tracked me thus; a villain and a liar to accuse me of having destroyed your master—the man who, refusing to purchase what I offered, dared to accuse me of that he nor you could prove."

"Eh! eh! eh! Indeed! How about the stains upon the clasp of that pretty necklace of yours? Eh! eh! eh! Blood, blood—you know; blood! Eh! eh! eh!"

The brow and forehead of the stranger flushed with rage and fury as he gazed upon the hideous features of the man Rasselton, who, with his chuckling giggle of malice, seemed to enjoy the other's rage.

"Eh! eh! eh! Hadn't we better come to terms?"

"What do you want?"

"Eh! eh! eh! Money, of course."

"What for?"

"My silence upon the little affair at the office of Ralph Fairley, the money-lender's, in the Poultry."

"Well, you step in here. The stranger opened the door of the by no means elegant coffee-room or parlour.

"Step in, did you say? Eh! eh! eh! with pleasure. Glad to see you understand me, Mr. Sharp."

Following in the stranger with a chuckle, Ephraim seated himself by a window overlooking the river, and coolly rapping with his knuckles on the table, awaited what the other should say.

"Now, Mr. Ephraim Rasselton, tell me how much of my converse did you overhear with your employer, Mr. Ralph Fairley?

"All! Eh! eh! eh! I heard the accusation of Ralph Fairley, about the blood stain on the clasp, and then the scuffle, the blow, the crash upon the floor, as the old man's brains were dashed out by the fearful fall against the iron stove. I said to myself this is a hanging matter, and must be seen to. Whilst others were busy with the body, I made after you, and—eh! eh! eh!—I am here."

"And you mean to tell me that Ralph Fairley is dead?"

"Dead as a man can be, with his brains out!"

"Liar!"

Ephraim Rasselton's blood grew cold in his veins as he gazed into the dark, gleaming eyes of the man before him; they bore in them a look of such vindictive rage that he trembled for himself, alone with a man whom he doubted not would scarce hesitate to imbrue his hands in his blood.

Ephraim Rasselton was a cunning, cautious man, well weighing his actions ere committed; and as he sat in the large, gloomy-looking apartment of that old house by the water-side, he shuddered as he thought what might be his fate should he have gone too far with the man before him.

He got up to go, muttering that he would call again to resume their conversation; but, seizing him by the wrist, the stranger thrust him down again in his chair, whilst hissing out words from between his clenched teeth, that caused the blood in the veins of Ephraim Rasselton to run like ice.

"Look, you fool! Idiot! You have, 'tis true, followed me to my lair. You have run the fox to earth that will now turn and double on you. Ephraim Rasselton, you have blindly entered the tiger's den, from which hope not again to leave with life. This old house is tenanted by those in my pay. One word of mine and your lifeless body would ere an hour be rushing down with the tide in the open river."

"But that would be murder."

"And why should I, that have slain your master, spare you, his tool?"

"Why, you see, he may not after all be dead. I am not quite sure as to whether he really perished. Release me, and I swear I will keep silent upon all that has passed."

"Dog, I'll trust you not. You have barked and shown your teeth, but, by ——, I swear you shall have no chance to bite." He now dragged him off the chair, and drawing him towards a large door, opposite to that which led to the passage in front, threw it open, disclosing not a closet but a flight of stone steps, some twenty or thirty in number. Despite the yells of the horrified Ephraim, the stranger, with a curse, hurled him down the dark staircase to the gloomy cellarage or vault below, his head in the fall striking upon the edge of the stone at the bottom of the stairs, rendering him for a few moments insensible. On returning to consciousness, the horrified clerk of Ralph Fairley found himself in a large, dark cellar or vault, the walls of which were dripping with moisture, proving its close vicinity to the river. At first about to utter a loud scream for help, the horrified clerk checked himself. Had not his aggressor informed him that all in the house were in his pay? Of what avail a cry for aid, that might but hasten his doom, bring upon him his assassins? How he cursed the folly that had led him to enter the house, and yet more the false step he had taken in defying the stranger, who, driven to desperation by his threats, had pursued his present course.

Staggering to his feet, he peered into the darkness of the underground chamber to ascertain if there were no means of egress. Groping his way round the vault-like chamber, he found that there was no outlet save the one by the steps, down which he had been hurled a few moments before.

Cold drops of fear started out upon the brow of Ephraim Rasselton as he reflected upon what might possibly be his fate.

A villain unscrupulous, and capable of any crime to answer his ends, yet was the man, Ephraim Rasselton, a very coward at heart; and, as he stood in the dark, gloomy vault, a terrible fear took possession of the craven wretch, who, by his own act, had placed himself in his dangerous position.

Groping once more round the vault, a half-smothered shriek escaped his lips, as his foot trod upon a soft mass, occasioning a shrill, squeaking noise to echo through the darksome chamber.

The noise was taken up by others of like description, accompanied with a loud, pattering, scampering rush on the floor of the cellar.

The dark chamber suddenly seemed studded all round with glittering, fiery sparks.

Like beads of fire scattered about the earthern flooring of the cellar, these strange sparks kept darting hither and thither.

Whilst the horrible shrill squeaking increased in violence.

With a howl of horror, Ephraim Rasselton rushed up the stone steps, and, reaching the top, he turned with horrid fascination gazing into the cellar below, which was now covered with the fiery sparks.

The vault-like chamber in that old house by the river was swarming alive with rats.

Rats, large, fierce, and daring, that, gathering in numbers, literally covered the floor of the cellar below.

Ephraim Rasselton tried to murmur a prayer, but the words faltered on his lips—he remembered nought.

A strange, rushing noise now sounded in the vault below.

A gurgling, surging, rushing sound, as though of a body of water near at hand.

Meanwhile, the screeching of the huge vermin below increased; whilst some, more daring than others, appeared upon the lower steps.

Ephraim fairly shook with terror as he gazed upon the scene below.

Drops of cold perspiration, in beads like ice, trickled down his brow.

Was it in broad day, without did the sun shine bright and fair, while he was doomed to die a fearful death.

A death, the thought of which chilled the very marrow in his bones.

How the gurgling rush of water, too, continued!

Ephraim, with a horrible shudder, well knew what its sound meant, and whence it came.

It was the water of the river rising; all the underground places at Bankside were flooded at high tide.

And he had been thrown into the horrible cellar to perish by a fearful, hideous death.

His eyes accustomed to the darkness, Ephraim now discovered the dark mass of waters which covered the whole of the flooring below.

He beheld, too, the huge rats swimming and paddling about in the inky stream.

Some ascended the stairs as the water rose, approaching his very feet.

Wild screams of terror escaped the lips of the despairing man, awaking up the echoes in that dark, horrible vault, and scaring for a moment the loathsome reptiles, but no answering voice replied from without.

They had left him to his doom.

Tears—scalding tears—coursed each other down the cheeks of the poor wretch. He who had never felt for others could now feel for himself.

The waters now rose higher and higher. They would presently reach his feet.

Wildly, frantically, he hammered at the door.

But no note was paid to his maddened cries for aid.

He was lost—doomed.

Doomed to perish—to die.

And what a death!

How the water gurgled and dashed about in the cellar of the old house!

While the plash and shrill, piercing notes of the vermin made a hideous echo in the place.

Ephraim Rasselton foamed and raved with rage and terror as the horrible water-rats at length dashed upon him, snapping viciously at his feet and hands, as he, in frantic terror, tore them off his clothing and hurled them back into the water.

Was there no escape?

Was he to perish thus, his fate unknown—unavenged?

How he cursed the blind folly that had placed him in the power of a villain who had left him to such a fearful, hideous death!

The gurgling rush of water ceased.

The tide had risen to its height.

It reached within three steps of the top of the stone staircase.

He could not drown, then.

But the rats?

Would they cease their bold attacks?

Or, persevering in their purpose, at length deprive him of strength to resist?

Already he felt a numbed feeling as of approaching faintness creeping over him.

The eyes of the rats shone like glittering sparks of fire on the stairs, and in the dark mass of water that, four or five feet deep, flowed in the cellar below.

A humming, buzzing noise rang in the ears of Ephraim Rasselton.

Oh! how he wished in that moment that he could murmur but one prayer, only one, ere he perished so awfully in the horrible vault.

Powerless to resist the ravenous vermin that now fastened on his flesh, he sank upon the topmost stair.

Incapable of uttering a cry, he was near losing all consciousness.

His tongue, dry and parched, clung to the roof of his mouth.

The sound as of ringing of bells surged in his ears.

He was relapsing into total insensibility.

When, with a last despairing effort, he gave utterance to a wild, thrilling, piercing scream for help.

Scarce had his agonized shriek died upon the air, when the door behind him was thrown open, letting in a flood of light to the darkened cellar, which caused the hideous rats to run screeching and scampering down the stairs, disappearing with a loud plash into the inky waters below.

Ephraim Rasselton scarce noticed the face of a lovely young girl that appeared at the open door convulsed with terror, nor felt he the feeble hand that dragged him from the horrible staircase into the apartment of the old house, as the door of the terrible cellar that had so near been his tomb closed again, hiding the loathsome vault, he once more relapsed into insensibility.

When he recovered he found himself seated near the window of the apartment overlooking the river, whilst near him stood the young girl who had saved him from a loathsome death.

Wildly Ephraim looked round the room, and then with a shudder at the door leading to the cellar where he so near had perished.

A low muttered curse escaped his lips.

While a dark shadow overhung his brow.

He registered a vow of vengeance on the man to whom he owed the sufferings of the past hour.

Instead of thanking his deliverer who had rescued him from his deadly peril, he thought but of revenge! revenge! upon the man who had so cleverly outwitted him, and who had doomed him to such a fearful death!

"I'll have his life! I'll have his life!" hissed Ephraim between his clenched teeth.

"Of whom do you speak?" said the young girl, who had caught the words that fell from the lips of Rasselton.

"Of whom should I speak but of the murderer who thrust me into that dark hole of death! but—eh! eh! eh!— he shall see. The game was his this morning; perhaps when next we meet the cards may change hands. I may hold the winning one, and dearly shall my worthy Mr. Sharp, as he styles himself, rue the hour he entered the lists with Ephraim Rasselton. I'll follow him up till I bring him to the gallows! Eh! eh! eh! Yes, I'll bring him to the gibbet!"

"No, you will not!" The words were said with such sternness and decision that Ephraim fairly started up from his recumbent posture, and gazed with savage fury upon the young girl who, a short time before, had saved him from death!

"No, you will not!" reiterated the young girl, returning the vengeful glance of Ephraim with one of scorn and loathing. It was evident that she was disgusted at the ingratitude of the wretch who returned no thanks for the saving of his life.

"Wont I! Eh! eh! eh! We shall see! I say again, I'll bring Mr. Sharp, clever, wily, murdering, thieving Mr. Sharp, to the gallows," snarled Rasselton, his before hideously palled features changing to a purple tint with suppressed passion. "Do you hear me, girl? I'll gibbet him though he was your own father. Eh! eh! eh! What's to prevent me?"

"The saving of your own life!"

"What mean you?"

"You are yet in the power of your enemies."

The face of Ephraim turned again a ghastly, grave-like hue.

"What is to prevent me calling in those who, without the least hesitation, will thrust you back to the dark cellar of death from which I snatched you?" said the young girl.

"But—but—this would be murder!" ejaculated Ephraim in a gasping voice.

"Granted; but you must be aware that the man whose anger you aroused hesitates not when driven to extremities, else would he have hurled you into the dark den where he knew the tide would destroy you, if, indeed, the hideous rats spared you; believe me, you have escaped a terrible end!"

"I know it; therefore I swear to have a terrible revenge, tooth for tooth, nail for nail. Eh! eh! eh! I'll have his life—he shall swing, swing upon the gallows."

"No, he will not! You will leave this house, nor ever drop a word as to what has passed within its walls; you will give up your vengeance to save your life; you will, ere you depart, take an oath, by your dead parent's grave, to keep locked within your bosom all the secrets of this old house; you will do this. Refuse to take the oath, and, despite my will, your body will be thrown into the darksome cellar from which you so narrowly escaped but now.

A livid pallor had gathered on the features of Ephraim Rasselton when the young girl before him pointed to the cellar, and told him that again he might expect to be thrown into its dark recesses, should he refuse to take the oath binding himself to keep unrevealed the secrets of that old house by the bank side.

Recovering from his panic, a grim smile crossed the features of Ephraim, who made up his mind to take the oath required, and when well clear of the murder-den—for such he set it down—to break the oath and reveal all, following like a bloodhound the man who had hurled him into the loathsome cellar of death.

As if divining his thoughts, the young girl seized him by the arm, and ejaculated—

"Wretch! I can read as in a book the dark purpose of your soul. But know, ere you depart, measures will be adopted to convince you that any treachery will immediately be the signal of your death-warrant!"

At this moment the sound of a loud voice without caused the young girl to start, and dart forwards to the door of the room. Seizing the opportunity for escape, Ephraim Rasselton bounded to the casement looking out upon the river. He discovered a large shed, the roof of which reached within a couple of feet of the casement. Throwing up the window, Ephraim was about to dash through, when he was dragged back by a powerful hand; not that, however, of his foe, as he expected, but of a tall, handsome young man, who had stepped into the chamber as Ephraim was about to quit it by the window.

The young girl, with pallid cheeks, clutched the stranger by the arm, scarce noting the trembling form of Ephraim, who twisted and writhed like an unwieldy snake in the tenacious grasp of his captor.

"In heaven's name, oh! Eustace, what prompted you to enter this house?"

"The sound of your pretty voice, my love, which I heard as I stood in the bar a moment ago. A something, I know not what, led me to look into the old house in which you informed me you sometimes resided; and though so strongly cautioned against entering here in quest of you, all powerful love, my Lucy, gained the victory over my scruples, and I boldly walked into the bar, ordered refreshments, caught the tones of your silvery voice, made my way into this room in time to prevent this interesting specimen of humanity making an exit by the window there. And now, tell me, Lucy, what shall I do with the fellow—pitch him through the casement, or kick him from the house?"

"Leave him here, dear Eustace, and fly the house this moment. Should you be discovered here with me, I know not what might hap. Away, then, at once. I will meet you to-night at the lane by Vauxhall-gardens, and till then, dearest, farewell. Oh! hasten hence, as you love me."

"Well, confound it, this is strange. Lucy, what is there to fear, unless, indeed, there be some second claimant with me for your love? If so, then I will dare all the danger, the thought of which I perceive has sent the damask rose from your lovely cheeks, placing in its stead the white of the lily, and stay with you, dearest, spite of all; and for this ugly ape here, I guess we can very well dispense with his company, so here goes to find him other lodgings."

With a loud laugh, the young man drew the shivering, craven Ephraim to the door of the room, and was about to hurl it open, when it was thrown wide upon its hinges, and three dark figuures stood before him. The young girl had flown to her lover's side, and with her hands upon his arm was about to draw him back.

For a few moments the group stood silently watching each other; then the three men entered the room, and banged-to the door, whilst the young girl, pale and trembling, stood beside her lover. The cowering Ephraim Rasselton, with horrified gaze, glared wildly at the figures before him, watching the opportunity of an escape from the mysterious house with torturing suspense.

One of the new comers, a dark, forbidding-looking man, clad in half-sailor costume, stepped forward, and speaking to the pale and shivering girl, pointed to the terrified figure of Rasselton, exclaiming—

"Who is that devil's whelp? What does he here?"

"He was thrown into the cellar by a Night-Hawk, who had been watched hither. I, fearing the tide would destroy him, released him from his perilous position. He will take oath to keep secret all he has seen," faltered the young girl, as she glanced with terrified eyes upon her lover, who, in mute amaze, listened to the strange discourse, looking first upon the three stalwart ruffians before him, and then at the girl, who seemed to fear some terrible ending to the strange scene.

"A spy, eh?" said the man who had first addressed the girl; "well, if the party who threw him into the cell meant him to escape with life, he wouldn't have left the house without releasing his man. He must have known well the tide would rise within the hour; but we will keep him secured till he who placed him in the cellar returns. And now, girl, for that young spark, there. Who the fiends is he?" A dark frown gathered on the brow of the man as he here pointed to the figure of the young stranger, who gazed with a scornful smile upon the dark, lowering brows that were bent upon him. Stepping forwards, the young stranger took upon himself to reply to this last question of the seaman-looking ruffian before him.

"Look you," he exclaimed as he stepped forwards, "I am one rough and ready, easy to take an affront, and give a blow. Your question, as to who and what I am, will not be answered; suffice it, I love the girl there, and will see her here or anywhere at my pleasure. And now, if you don't like what I have said, why, my handsome friends, you had better set about taking the measure of your wrath out of my body—that's if you can."

The young stranger here darted forwards, and, ere the man was aware, had wrenched from his grasp a heavy bludgeon that he had held nervously clutched in his hand, as though only waiting a word from his leader to attack the unarmed stranger.

THE MURDER DEN AT THE OLD BANKSIDE—THE CONFLICT.

A yell of rage broke from the lips of the ruffians, as with glowing looks of scorn and defiance, the stranger stood, bludgeon in hand, before them.

"Upon him, lads, and convey them both to the red chamber!"

A shrill scream burst from the lips of the young girl, followed by the sounds of a fierce struggle, in the midst of which there was a loud crash of glass and a yell of pain.

With a bound of terror Ephraim Rasselton had burst right through the window, rolling like a ball over the roof of the shed without into the yard at the back; with frantic haste he scrambled over a low wall, and in a few minutes was speeding for his life along the muddy banks of the river.

The young stranger, scorning to fly, remained in the chamber of the old house, boldly contending with his murderous assailants.

Oaths, curses, and wild screams rang in the air.

"Knife him, Randle!"

"Hurl him into the cellar—the tide's in."

"Let him have the contents of your barking irons, Snatchem."

"Trip him up!"

"Run in at him, dash out the brains of the ——!"

These cries from the ruffians were mingled with wild screams from the young girl, and the clashing of steel against the heavy bludgeon that was wielded by the young man to protect him from his assailants, whilst he stood with his back to the casement that overlooked the river.

With a heavy groan, one of the ruffians fell on the floor, a fearful blow from the bludgeon wielded by the young stranger's powerful arm stretching him senseless at the feet of his comrades. The report of a pistol now rang, with a sharp, clear report, through the house. Lowering his head, the young man avoided the shot, and it was now when he was likely to be overpowered by the two remaining ruffians, that a dark, hairy face was thrust through the door, which was opened just wide enough to admit the head of the speaker, who exclaimed—

"Stow the game, lads! The wheese is cracked! The runner is up. You have alarmed the neighbourhood, and I suspect the young buck at bay is guarded by the cursed Night-Hawks. Where away, and take to the river. Hillo! the hounds are here!"

The mysterious, hairy-looking face disappeared; the two ruffians left off their sssault of the young stranger, and, lifting up the body of their wounded companion, hurried from the chamber. The young girl, with a shriek of joy, sunk upon her knees, whilst the young man coolly wiped his brow with a snow white kerchief, whistling the while a popular melody of the day.

He was a strange mixture of bravery and audacity, was the young man who stood so quietly in that room, which a few moments before had resounded with the noise of a conflict—a conflict which imperilled his very life. It was not his first peril, however, for the stranger was none other than—

Eustace Maltravers! He who had escaped by a miracle from the murder-house in Battersea-fields, and who had discomfited Resurrection Bill, at the ken in the old Mint.

Eustace Maltravers was a thorough believer in fate, and rushed dauntless into danger, without fear of meeting that death which it was decreed would seize upon him sooner or later, as upon all else in life.

On the entrance of several officers, Eustace Maltravers had no information to give them. He had been attacked, he said, by some drunken ruffians who had fled. He feared by describing too minutely his foes, criminating the young girl who, with blanched cheeks, stood trembling beside him. A mystery he could not fathom linked her fate with the ruffian gang, who evidently made the old house by the river-side their rendezvous. Determined to unravel the secret skein of guilt that connected one so fair and lovely with the villain crew that haunted the old house, Eustace Maltravers, the bold and dashing hero of this romance of real life, waited, with lynx eyes, watching for any incident that might help to discover his foes.

Left alone with the fair, terror-stricken girl, he endeavoured to cheer her drooping spirits; and at her earnest wish bid her adieu, with the understanding that they were to meet that night near Vauxhall Gardens.

With a sigh of relief the young girl beheld her lover quit the old house. A quiet smile wreathed the face of Eustace Maltravers as he left the old inn. A dark figure stole cautiously after him, evidently tracking his footsteps. With a chuckle and a smile he passed on his way, acting as though quite unaware that a man was dogging his every footstep.

CHAPTER VI.

LIZZIE HEYWOOD AND THE MONEY-LENDER'S DAUGHTER.
—LOVE AND CONSTANCY.—NAT STEVENS AND EPHRAIM RASSELTON.—THE MYSTERIOUS WARNING.—CAPTAIN LESLIE'S VISIT TO THE "FOX IN THE HOLE."—PLOT AND PASSION.—THE BURGLARY AND THE ABDUCTION. —THE FIRE IN SOHO SQUARE.

"Is Miss Sybil within?"

The voice is that of Lizzie Heywood, the seamstress, who, clad in humble but neat mourning, stands at the door of Ralph Fairley, the money-lender's, in the Poultry. The reply of the smart little handmaiden, Nancy Watson, is in the negative. Her young mistress has just stepped out, but had left orders, should her young *protegée* arrive during her absence, she was to await her return, and Lizzie Heywood was accordingly shown into the dressing-room of Sybil Fairley, to await her coming. The poor seamstress was much changed since her mother's decease. Still beautiful, there was a pallor as of death on her lovely face. Yet was there a happy smile at times upon her features. Thanks to the kind-hearted Sybil Fairley, she was now removed from the chance of abject want, enabled by honest industry to support herself and orphan brother and sister. Introduced to some ladies of Sybil's acquaintance, she received as much work as her hands could accomplish, and was paid, too, a remunerative and fair price for her toil. She had called upon Sybil, her benefactress, respecting some embroidery work to be executed ere she left London in a few days for her father's country residence at Harrow.

Lizzie Heywood had not long been seated in the chamber of the miser's house ere the light footsteps of Sybil could be heard ascending the stairs, and in a few moments the two young girls were seated alone.

Both young and beautiful, there was a delightful contrast in the looks of the rival beauties.

Like the lily and the rose they looked as they sat side by side.

Nor did the exquisite beauty of Lizzie Heywood lessen the feeling of friendship entertained for her by Sybil Fairley, who was, in her sweet disposition, above the petty feeling of jealousy of beauty akin to her own, so common among her sex.

"And so you are pleased, my dear Miss Heywood, with the little I have been able to do for you in the way of introduction to ladies of my acquaintance?"

"Indeed, dear Mistress Fairley, I owe you a life-long debt of gratitude; but for you, my mother must have been consigned to a beggar's grave; but for you, my dear little brother and sister forced to wear a workhouse garb unless I had done that I shudder but to think upon. I cannot find words, dear lady, to express the gratitude I feel to one who has done so much to save me and mine from ruin and death." The young girl here hid her beautiful face in her little hands to conceal the crystal drops that started from her eyes as she thought of the past, and how different matters might have been had she met with Sybil Fairley ere her mother's death.

"Nay, my dear girl, do not weep. I can guess the source of your grief; but doubt not that your dear mother is happy in another world—a happier one far than this. And now, here is a letter I have got for you, that will gain an entrance into a charitable home for orphan children. In that abode your little relatives will be removed from harm, and you, poor girl, not have the care of guarding them in addition to your daily toil. Nay, give me no thanks, unless you wish to pain me, for what, after all, is but a trifling act of kindness. And now, Lizzie," added the lovely girl, with a merry smile, "tell me about that affair of which you were speaking when I saw you last, respecting the mysterious non-appearance of your cousin, Will Stacy, whose ship, you told me, you ascertained had arrived in London ten days ago. Have you heard anything to clear up the mystery?"

"Nothing, dear madam," replied the young seamstress, "save that my dear cousin left the vessel alive and well—left, too, telling a messmate that he was going to visit his cousin, who lived, he believed, not very far from the docks into which their ship had been anchored. This much I have ascertained, but nought else; all is a mystery, that time alone can solve; he has been seen by no one since the day that he left his vessel. A terrible fear weighs upon my spirits at times as to whether he has met with some dreadful accident—or, worse, foul play at the hands of the wretches who haunt the neighbourhood of the docks in search of prey."

The young girl shuddered, and her face grew yet more ashy pale as she thought of what might have befallen her cousin the young sailor, Will Stacy, between whom and herself there was a bond of affection and vows of love, which each had sworn should never be broken.

A few days before, Lizzie Heyward had mentioned the mystery of her cousin's disappearance to Sybil Fairley, asking the young girl's opinion of the matter; and Sybil, though fearing some terrible incident had taken place in reference to the non-arrival of the young sailor at his cousin's residence, yet had endeavoured to cheer the young girl's spirits, bidding her hope for the best; but when, on again inquiring, she learned the particulars just given her by her humble friend, she trembled to think what might have happened, and in her own mind felt convinced that the young man had met with foul play on leaving his ship. Hearing her name pronounced by her parent, Sybil Fairley rose, and bidding the poor girl, Lizzie, in whom she felt deeply interested, call upon her again, rose to leave the room.

With heartfelt thanks, Lizzie Heyward prepared to depart, promising to return on the morrow; and, in a few moments, the young girl had left the house.

Strange, terrible incidents occurred ere those two young girls met again.

Descend we now into the office of the money-lender, 'Tis four o'clock; darkness has fallen on the city; and the light of day is but partially supplied by numerous oil lamps.

The dusty, grim-looking office of Ralph Fairley was dimly lighted up by two large oil lamps, the dull yellow flicker from which gave but a faint, subdued light through the office.

Seated at his desk at the end of the large apartment that comprised the old money-lender's office, was our young friend, Nat Stevens, looking rosy and jolly as usual; the merry face of the young clerk seeming a kind of reproach upon the musty, sombre-looking office, which was redolent of stale, dusty parchments and time-worn ledgers.

Throwing down his pen as the clock struck four, Nat jumped off his stool, and, tripping to the little inner office, opened the door, and, thrusting in his head, exclaimed—

"Time's up, Ephraim; sink the quills and ink, and come with me to the 'Magpie and Stump,' in Bell-yard, and have a stiff glass of hot grog to cheer you up."

Ephraim Rasselton, who was standing by a desk, his head leaning on his hand, looked up as he heard the merry voice of his young fellow-clerk. Ephraim Rasselton looked ghastly pale; he had not yet recovered from the effects of the terrible adventure the day before, and had found it quite impossible to hide his distress from his fellow-clerk, Nat, who, despite his natural dislike of Ephraim, pitied his worn, dejected appearance, and endeavoured to revive the drooping spirits of the man who, at another time, he would have gloried in doing an ill turn. But Nat Stevens was a good-hearted young fellow, and could not bear to see his worst enemy suffer without attempting to alleviate his distress.

"Thank you, Nat, for your invitation," said Ephraim, "but I shall not go out to-night."

"Oh! bosh. Come along, old fellow; a glass of hot brandy-and-water will drive away those blue devils you have had hanging upon you since your return to the office yesterday. Hang it! old boy, care killed a cat; come, put on your tile; eschew business for to-night, and come and hear a song at the 'Magpie and Stump;' there are some jolly birds there, I can tell you—some of the right sort. Now, I won't hear of a denial. Come on!"

"Indeed, I thank you, Nat; not to-night. Heavens! what's that?"

The face of Ephraim Rasselton grew a livid paleness at the sound of a single loud knock at the door.

Nat Stevens, despite his merry disposition, began to grow nervous in the company of his fellow-clerk. There was nothing to be alarmed at certainly in a loud dab at the house door, and yet Nat shared his companion's alarm upon hearing that one loud, imperative summons for admission. The scene of the diamond necklace had caused a nervous feeling to fill the bosoms of the two men, left alone in that office, in which there was a goodly sum in gold, silver, and trinkets.

"I'll go," said Nat Stevens; "and if it is anybody having a game with the knocker, why, damme, I'll warm 'em."

Another loud, startling knock caused Nat to give a jump as he left the inner office. Leaving Ephraim Rasselton standing pale and ghastly with terror at his desk, the young man hastened to the door and threw it open.

There was no one there.

"As I thought, cuss 'em," said Nat; "a runaway knock. Halloa!" he added, "what the devil's this?" Closing the door, he came back holding in his hand a letter he had picked up on the threshold of the door. On reaching the inner office, and holding up the mysterious epistle, Nat found it was directed to his fellow-clerk, Ephraim Rasselton.

"Why, it's a letter for you, Ephraim. What a mysterious-looking affair!"

Snatching it from him, Ephraim Rasselton glanced at the superscription and then at the seal, but could make nothing of it.

Not wishing to pry into his companion's secrets, Nat Stevens walked away. For a few moments Rasselton stood holding the strangely-delivered document in his hand, undecided as to whether he should open it; at length, breaking the seal, he tore it open, and held it up to the rays of the lamp.

Biting his nether lip till the blood came, Ephraim read the letter, which was written in red ink:—

"Ephraim Rasselton, you are watched and warned that your every action is noted down. Breathe but one word of the matter in connexion with your adventure at the old Bankside yesterday morning, and two hours after your body will be floating down with the tide. Beware, then! —Signed."

There was no signature to the above note of warning; but a large cross in blood red was printed at the foot of the letter; and, underneath, a hideous figure of death.

For some minutes Ephraim Rasselton gazed upon the strange letter which he held up to the light, reading it over and over again; with a shudder, he held it to the flame of the lamp, nor dropped the paper till it was reduced to ashes. Then, taking from his desk a note, he held that up to the lamp; as the flame devoured it, the superscription met the eyes of Nat Stevens, who entered at that moment. Some surprise was felt by the young man as he caught sight of the note; it was addressed to James Hanway, Detective, Bow-street, and written in the hand of Ephraim Rasselton.

The warning note from the mystic hand had done its work. Recalling the dread scene in the cellar of the old house by the river, the coward soul of Rasselton trembled at the risk he felt he might run in placing the officers on the track of his foes. He would await the course of events; he yet might have revenge upon the man who had so near destroyed him; and Ephraim Rasselton had registered an oath to bring his enemy to the gallows.

"Slow and steady yet may win. Eh! eh! eh! Like the deadly snake, I'll turn and sting him yet! By all the fiends below, he yet shall be in my power! By Satan himself, I swear it!"

On the same night that the above incident took place at the office of Ralph Fairley, a tall, handsome, military man made his way through the Borough over London-bridge, and pursued his course till he reached the old Mint; here, leaving the high road, he dived, without hesitation, into the dark, half-lighted turning known as Mint-street. All was squalor and wretchedness in the stranger's path. Drawing the folds of his cloak yet closer round him, he stumbled on up the ill-lighted street, till he reached the "Fox in the Hole" public-house. The stranger hesitated a moment or two in front of the door of the house, and then, with a curse of impatience at his own folly, walked boldly in. There was a rough assemblage at the bar, all of whom made way for the fashionably-dressed stranger. Making his way to the bar, he asked the landlord if Guy Essington was within. Receiving a reply in the affirmative, and saying that he wished to see him, the stranger was ushered into the little parlour at the back of the bar, where, in a few minutes, he was joined by the man whom he wished to see.

"Your servant, sir," said Guy Essington, the leader of the Night-Hawks. "Your servant, sir. To what may I attribute the pleasure of this visit; and who, may I ask, have I the honour of addressing?"

Guy Essington keenly eyed his visitor, but acknowledged to himself that they had never met before.

"Your name is Essington?"

"It is, sir."

"You undertake almost anything, do you not?"

"I do at a price."

"Of course. Now I suppose you have some rough hands at command, to carry out any project that may be attended with danger?"

"Oh! yes; but, of course, the greater the danger and risk, the larger the sum required for the job."

"Exactly. Now look you," said the stranger, "you don't know me, though you executed for me some business a year or two ago; but, as we never met, why, of course, you know me not. My name is Leslie."

"What, Captain Leslie, for whom I got up the forged —— ?" Then, correcting himself as he observed the stranger give an angry start, he exclaimed, "Pardon me, Captain Leslie, I seldom revive past business. I transact my customers' affairs, and, when paid, dismiss the matter ever from my mind. And now, to the point. What is the lay?"

"I require you to carry off for me a young girl, now residing with a family in Soho-square."

"Hum! a nasty job. How many are there in the family?"

"That I don't know."

"Where do you wish the girl conveyed?"

"To an old mansion in Hampshire, some fifty miles from London."

"You wish her taken straight there?"

"I do."

"And the terms."

"Name your charge. We have dealt before. You executed the business to my satisfaction. Secure the girl, lodge her safely in the manor, and make your own charge."

"Enough; consider the job as done. When do you wish the affair to come off?"

"At once. This very night if it can be managed."

"It is short time, but I think I can do it. Of course you have come prepared with money?"

"Ay; you can have aught you desire."

"Say you so? Then, Captain Leslie, the abduction shall take place to-night, if I undertake the hazard myself. Ringing the bell, at the appearance of the waitress, Guy Essington desired her to send in the landlord. On his appearance he drew him aside, calling over the names of two or three of his band, asked if they were in the house. Receiving a reply in the affirmative, he turned to Captain Leslie, and informed him that the job could come off that very night.

"'Tis well," said the captain. "Here is a purse containing one hundred guineas. Do the job effectually, bear off the girl without fear of discovery, and I'll not hesitate to double the amount." Then, giving directions as to the exact locality of the place where he wished his prey conveyed, the villain *roue* left the "Fox in the Hole" well satisfied with the success of his visit.

"All goes well and bravely on," he muttered, "and ere another week I'm safe, secure from any accident that may occur at a future date."

CHAPTER VII.

THE HOUSEBREAKERS.—SOHO-SQUARE BY MIDNIGHT.—THE BURGLARY.—THE MEETING ON THE STAIRS.—THE SHRIEK FOR AID.—THE STRUGGLE.—THE VICTIM CARRIED OFF.—FURY OF THE COFFIN AND THE PIPING BULLFINCH.—THE TIGERS CAGED.—FIRING OF THE OLD HOUSE BY THE BURGLARS AND ESCAPE OVER THE LEADS.—TRIUMPH OF THE NIGHT-HAWKS.

THE hour of twelve was booming from the old tower of Westminster Abbey as three figures made their way across Soho-square to a house in the corner nearest to Dean-street.

Keeping cautiously in the shade of the houses, the moon riding high and bright in the heavens, making all as light as day, the three figures at length halted and stood before a house that stood right in the corner of the square, the top back casements of which looked out into Dean-street.

All was quiet in the square that midnight hour. Not even a solitary watchman was to be seen. The burglars, for such they were, had well timed their visit. Not a human being was in sight to interrupt their movements.

How still, calm, and quiet was the scene, soon to be awakened by shouts of terror and alarm.

Like demons of darkness, the midnight marauders proceeded in their fell work.

The master fiend—he who had planned, plotted the deed—appeared at that moment at the other end of the square. The burglars saw, but took no note of the appearance of the muffled figure that keenly watched their actions.

He it was who paid liberally for the task in hand.

And who watched with feverish impatience the result of his scheme of villainy.

"Now the Coffin," said the leader of the men, Guy Essington, who himself headed the burglars that night, "prize open the door with as little noise as may be, or ascertain the best means of entrance."

"The door arn't no use, captain; it's sheeted with iron."

"How about the window?"

"That's our only chance. Here, Bullfinch," addressing a tall, gaunt, savage-looking man by his side, "hold the glim, while I look to the glass."

Making their way over the railings that guarded the area, the two burglars now stood upon a ledge of bricks that ran the length of the house, just beneath the window sills.

Drawing some brown paper from his pocket, which was thickly covered with pitch, the burglar, Coffin, fastened it down firmly on one of the panes of glass, and then, dashing his hand through, it broke and fell to the ground without the usual noise. There was now a shutter to resist an attempt at entering the house. Prepared for this obstacle, the Coffin took from his pocket a gimlet and peculiarly-shaped saw. These, with one or two other housebreaking implements, soon enabled the burglar to make an opening in the shutters large enough to admit of his thrusting through his hand. With some trouble, he then lifted up a bar that ran across the shutters inside. Dislodging this from its staple—with due care preventing it falling with a clang to the ground—the housebreaker presently forced open the window, and scrambling through, closed to the shutter, and admitted his companions by the house door.

All was quiet within the house, the inmates sleeping unconscious of the entrance of the midnight marauders.

Slowly, cautiously, the burglars now ascended the stairs.

Like grim, black spectres, they moved up the wide, old-fashioned staircase.

The moon cast her bright blue rays in a silvery flood through a window on a landing of the staircase, which, alighting on the three figures, as noiselessly they ascended, made them look like dark shadows of the night.

On reaching the top, a whispered consultation took place between the burglars and their chief.

They knew not the situation of the chamber in which reposed the young girl, to carry off whom they burglariously forced their way into the house.

Suddenly they all three bend down in the shadow of the wall, as a white, spectral-looking form approaches from a chamber at the further end of a corridor.

Breathless, the three men wait the moment that must inevitably discover them.

The figure that makes its way down the corridor is that of a young girl.

Halting a few yards from the staircase, she strikes a light; the sound of the flint and steel sounding strangely in the silence of the midnight hour.

"I may have been mistaken," murmured the young girl, "but I could stake my life I heard an unwonted noise in the chamber below."

A ruddy glow of light now darted out upon the scene.

And the young girl, lamp in hand, approached the staircase.

Not observing the dark figures by the wall, the young girl cast her eyes over the balusters.

All was still and quiet in the house.

Nought breaking upon the silence of the night, save the tick, tick, of a large old eight-day clock in the hall below.

"I must have been dreaming," muttered the young girl. "All is safe; 'tis well I alarmed not the house."

Turning round to proceed down the corridor, she finds her path obstructed by three dark figures.

Men with their faces concealed by half-masks.

Looking grim and horrible by the flickering rays of the lamp.

A shriek echoed through the house—a wild, despairing, heartrending shriek of horror and alarm.

A shriek that woke up echoes through the old house.

A shriek that startled the passing wayfarer without.

That, prolonged with loud, clear shrillness, told of horror and fright.

The wild scream of the young girl was followed by the sound of footsteps.

A door was thrown open at the end of the corridor, and a young man darted forwards without clothing, appearing upon the scene just as he had been startled from his sleep by the wild, despairing shriek of the young girl.

A moment afterwards there was the sound of a terrific struggle in the old house, accompanied with fierce oaths and yells of rage, mingled with loud cries for help.

A loud knocking at the hall-door gives notice to the burglars that they are discovered.

The neighbourhood is alarmed.

The rattles of the watchmen sound loudly on the air.

Whilst cries of "Thieves! thieves! Murder!" are caught up from mouth to mouth.

The burglars struggle desperately with the young man who darted out upon them when first hearing the shriek of the poor girl, who was borne off in the arms of Guy Essington.

Passing hastily down the stairs with his now insensible

burden, Guy Essington, with unparalleled audacity and daring, threw the door wide open on its hinges, first having torn off the mask that he had before worn to disguise his features.

There was a crowd of watchmen poured into the hall. Struggling his way out, Guy exclaimed—

" Haste you to those above, whilst I carry this poor girl to a surgeon near at hand !"

The guardians of the night bounded up the stairs ; and, with his insensible victim in his arms, Guy Essington, with a chuckle, darted across the square, met on his road by the dark figure that had paced anxiously to and fro during the committal of the burglary.

In a few moments the senseless girl was placed in a carriage near at hand, first wrapped up in a heavy cloak that laid upon the seat ; for, startled up from her sleep, the poor girl had only on her a loose morning gown, thrown on ere she quitted her bed chamber. With a warning to the coachman that some figures were rushing towards the carriage from the direction of the house that had been so buglariously broken into, the horses were lashed into full speed, and in a few moments they were far from the spot. A strange, red glare lighted up the sky from the roof of the old house in Soho-square, to account for which we must return to the buglars, Jem Coffin and the Piping Bullfinch, left by their leader to make their escape as best they could.

Struggling violently with the young man belonging to the house, they had been unable to release themselves before the hall door opened, and the watchmen, in force, darted up the stairs.

With loud curses at length the burglars hurled their tenacious foe off, and dashed into a room behind them. With a shout the young man who had so courageously struggled with the ruffians dashed after them, and pulling to the door when they had entered the chamber, turned the key which was outside, and thus locked the villains in.

" Safely caged ! What ho ! Help, help ! I have them ! They cannot escape !" yelled the young man triumphantly, as he stood beside the door.

Some few minutes afterwards, on attempting to open the door, it was found to be barricaded inside.

" It's no use, you know," exclaimed a purple-nosed keeper of the peace. " Its no use trying to dodge from us, so come out quietly and let me slip on the darbies."

No reply was received to this very polite invitation, but the officers were soon startled by a strange crackling inside in the chamber, accompanied by a red glare from under the door, and a strong smell of burning wood.

At length the door was burst open with a loud crash. The furniture that had been piled against it fell to the ground, and all started back with loud cries of alarm ; the whole chamber was a mass of flame ; every article contained in the room was fast becoming a prey to the devouring element.

The burglars, before making their escape through the window, from whence they had made their way on to the leads or roof of the house, had, with infernal malice, set light to the various articles of imflammable material in the chamber, such as window curtains, etc. ; these in turn set light to the furniture, and ere the door was burst from its hinges the room was one blaze of fire.

How the forked tongues of flame, in hot and hungry glow, licked up the walls, and curled and darted out of the window, with a hissing sound that soon increased to the roar of a furnace, and spread alarm both far and near.

" Fire ! fire !" How the cry echoes from mouth to mouth !

The sky is now lighted up with the red glow.

The house is doomed.

Engines arrive, but fail, with their limited supply of water, to stay the flames.

In the morning, when the sun tipped the eastern skies with its golden rays, the house in Soho-square, that had been broken into by the burglars the night before, was a smouldering ruin, a charred and blackened mass.

And an old lady who had resided in the house was missing, fears being entertained that she had perished in the flames ; much anxiety was also felt respecting a young girl who had been carried off during the confusion ; she had disappeared, and could not be found.

———

CHAPTER VIII.

THE OLD RED GRANGE.—THE PRISONER.—THE MAN OF CRIME AND HIS VICTIM.—THE STRUGGLE.—THE LOST ONE.—THE PERPETRATION OF VILLAINY AND CURSE OF THE BLIGHTED ONE.

FAR out from the busy haunt of London, standing alone near a green, dark copse, was the old Red Grange.

Built of red brick, in the gothic style of architecture, with a little turreted clock tower, a gloomy, sad, and spectral-looking house was the old Red Grange.

The ivy grew in wild luxuriance about the old building, whilst a row of tall, dark pines in front of the Grange increased the sombre aspect of the building.

The caw, caw, caw of the rooks as they hovered above the Grange, or circled round the grim, dark pines, alone woke up the stillness of the scene.

The inhabitants of the little village of ——, distant some three miles from the Grange, held firm to the belief that the old building was haunted.

For some years it had stood alone and deserted, falling into ruin and decay, whilst, at length, an heir of the estate took possession of the Red Grange, and coming down with the retinue of servants had tenanted the old dwelling.

There were some strange reports in connexion with the resident and proprietor of the old Red Grange.

He bore, among the simple villagers around, not the best of characters.

But, being rich and powerful, he extorted respect and deference from all.

No one dared offend Captain Leslie, the owner of the estates appertaining to the old Red Grange.

Though, from incidents that had become blazoned abroad, he was universally detested.

The deaths of a worthy young couple, who had resided in the village near the Grange, was laid to his charge.

A lovely young girl, the daughter of a small farmer living on the Grange estates, was known to have been somewhat intimate with the libertine, Captain Leslie, but none knew the whole of the fatal truth.

Until one morning the lifeless body of the poor girl was discovered in a dark, dank pool in the woods surrounding the Grange.

A letter found upon her explained all.

The dread of exposure of her frailty had caused her to end her miseries, her shame, by death.

Driven to frenzy by her loss, and the hearing of her dishonour, her lover, an honest, hard-working young farmer, hung himself in a fit of temporary insanity from the branches of a tree that stood near the lone pool where the poor girl had destroyed herself.

Captain Leslie it was who had villainously seduced the poor girl, and was thus the means of driving these two young people, by suicide, to an early grave.

Execrated by all, yet none dared openly attack the rich Captain Leslie.

The night following the one that beheld the destruction of the house in Soho-square by fire, a scene of horror took place at the old Red Grange.

The evening, a dark and stormy one, had closed in black and drear.

A wild tempest roared through the copse that stood near the old Red Grange.

The wintry blast moaned and whistled shrilly through the dark branches of the tall pine and stately beech.

The decayed leaves were whirled in fantastic eddies through the air.

Whilst the occasional caw of a restless rook harmonized in dismal concert with the blast.

How the rain pattered upon the fallen leaves that lay thickly all around !

It was, indeed, a wild, dismal night.

A night that made one shiver to look abroad.

A night of mist, rain, wind, and desolation.

A night that caused the sick to shudder as they lie listening to the wintry winds.

On this wild, dark night a dark deed was enacted in the old Red Grange.

A deed of villainy and crime.

In a large apartment, in the east wing of the old house, was seated a young and beautiful girl.

So young, so lovely.

Like a beautiful lily, or being of the other world, looked the pale, drooping girl, that sat despairingly, with hands clasped over her bosom, in that large silent apartment of that old house.

The pearly drops fell from her light blue eyes in showers, as she gazed distractedly around her.

Her soul sickened at her desolate position.

That young and beautiful girl, like the image of death, in her despair, sat a prisoner in the old Grange, was the same borne off from London the night before.

She that had been torn from her residence in Soho-square.

And this fair, despairing girl was no other than Lizzie Heyward, the young seamstress, the *protigée* of Sybil Fairley, the miser's daughter.

Little did either of the young girls think what suffering was in store ere they would meet again, when parting at the money-lender's house in the Poultry.

Borne off by her cousin, Captain Leslie.

The fate of poor Lizzie seemed sealed.

What could now intervene to snatch her from the power of so base a villain ?

The fair bosom of the lovely girl heaved convulsively as she thought upon her fate.

There was no escape now !

She was doomed !

Doomed, and to what !

To fall a victim to the brutal passion of her evil-minded relative.

The young girl shuddered as she reflected upon what might happen.

Alone with the villain who had daringly borne her from her friends.

What hope had she !

None !

She was lost.

The wind, howling dismally without, added to the horror of the young girl's thoughts, who uttered a piercing shriek as the door of the chamber opened, admitting the form of Captain Leslie, who, with a grim smile, gazed upon the shrinking girl before him.

"Well, Lizzie, have you weighed over in your mind my proposition of the morning ?"

"I have," gasped the young girl, who, feeling a sense of faintness creeping over her, staggered into her seat, from which she had started up as her cousin entered the room.

"Well, and your reply ?" eagerly ejaculated Captain Leslie.

"Is never to consent to be yours, come what will."

A wild glare of savage fury darted from the eyes of Leslie as he heard the words of the pale but lovely figure before him.

He was rejected, scorned by the young girl who, in the morning of that day, he had sued to become his bride.

"And you refuse to give me your hand ?"

"Captain Leslie," gasped the lovely girl, staggering forwards, "were it to save my life I could never consent to be yours. What, forget my early love—he to whom I have pledged my young heart, and who may yet return to claim me for his own ? Consent to forget him, to forswear my vows, my oath registered in heaven never to be other than his ; consent to wed the man who left my sick, suffering mother to die of want, to perish in a garret; give my hand to him who robbed my father of all; fool, villain, you are mad to ask it. I am in your power and may not escape, but to save my life I will never consent to be yours."

"Indeed ! So you defy me ; but by the fiends, you shall live, girl, to sue for that which now you refuse, the title of my wife. I will make you mine, proud beauty. You are in my power, nor the enemy of mankind should tear you from my arms this night."

A livid, death-like pallor stole over the features of the beautiful girl, as she listened to the threats of her base cousin, whose eyes shone with the fierce glitter of passion.

Falling on her knees the poor girl raised her hands supplicatingly to the villain, who, with folded arms, gazed with passion upon the lovely form pleading at his feet.

"In mercy spare me, Leslie ; for she who now rests in the cold grave, for your own honour's sake. Oh ! let me free. I may not be yours, for I have long loved another ; in mercy have pity on me. Say you will spare me ; you mean not to fulfil your threat, you did but jest. You would not, could not, be so cruel as to execute the crime of which you spoke. Oh ! in mercy, for my dead mother's sake, spare her orphan child."

Sobbing convulsively, and clinging despairingly to her consin's knees, the poor girl prayed for mercy, for exemption from her cruel fate.

But as well might the hunter pray for mercy in the deadly embrace of the grizzly bear ; as well sue to the tiger or the panther for release, as have softened the heart of Leslie.

Whilst the fair young girl was kneeling at his feet, the eyes of her cousin had caught sight of the white swelling globes of her bust, revealed as the boddice of her dress partly unfastened as she sunk upon the ground.

The blood of the libertine ran like lava through his veins as he beheld the firm, white, and heaving bust of the beauteous girl.

He would have perilled life itself at that moment to have made her his.

Wildly the young girl shrieked, as, lifting her up, he wound his arms round her in a close embrace.

Madly he glued his lips to hers,

Which, full, luscious, and covered with a dewy moisture, wore the colour of the damask rose.

The deadly pallor of the lovely girl heightened her extreme beauty.

Fiercely she struggled with the villain ; who, mad with passion, held her tightly in his embrace.

How the wild frenzied shrieks of the poor girl rang through the old Red Grange !

But no help was nigh.

Nought answered that cry for succour save the shrill blast without.

That, raging round the old mansion, seemed to exult at the scene within.

"Mercy ! mercy ! Spare, oh ! spare me," sobbed the poor girl.

But her struggles for release had but inflamed the passions of Captain Leslie, who devoured the glowing charms of the young girl's bust, now fully revealed, her dress being torn from her bosom in her struggle to get free.

At length the poor girl's cries ceased, and in a death-like swoon she sank upon the couch to which she had been borne by her villain relative.

How the eyes of the libertine now gloated upon the charms of the lovely girl !

Her round, smooth, polished bust, white as ivory, was revealed in all its exquisite loveliness.

The soft, round arms hung by her side as she lay in her death-like swoon.

Kneeling down, the *roué* pressed his lips to those of the beautiful girl.

The shrieks of the doomed girl again rang wildly upon the night air, which gradually subsided ; then all was silent.

In the morning the sun rose bright and clear, darting its golden rays full into the chamber of the old Red Grange, that had witnessed the ruin of the unhappy Lizzie Heyward the night before.

The poor girl staggered from the couch, and gazed wildly upon the lovely scene without.

The thaw of the preceding night had again given place to a severe and bitter frost.

The trees and bushes sparkling in the rays of the sun, which were covered with hoar-frost and icicles, formed from the rain that had frozen upon the trees, shrubs, and pathway during the early morning.

The eyes of the poor girl ached as she gazed on the beautiful scene. All nature seemed bright and joyous. The robin twittered merrily as he flew from shrub to shrub, and the rooks, with their caw ! caw ! caw ! woke up the silence of the wintry scene.

At this moment the poor girl started, and turned from the window with a nervous start of terror.

Her cousin again stood before her.

A dreadful scene took place between the *roué* and his victim, whose offer to make her his wife was rejected with scorn and passion.

"Look you, Ernest Leslie ; by a foul deed of crime you last night effected my ruin. Know by this act you have changed the meek girl into a vengeful woman. When awakening to my terrible position, thoughts of suicide flashed across my mind, which at length gave way to other feelings. A longing for revenge took possession of me. I registered an oath to execute upon you a deadly revenge, and I will keep my vow, though years elapse in its fulfilment. I will follow you, Ernest Leslie, like your shadow—your fate. I will cross you at every turn. I will pursue you, in my just revenge, like a bloodhound the fugitive slave, and I here breathe upon you my bitterest curse. May you be pursued by every evil of misfortune. Should you ever wed, may your offspring turn upon and sting you to the death. Ernest Leslie, from this time forth Lizzie Heyward, she whom you have destroyed and condemned to a life of misery, will follow you in all your actions, like your shadow. I will be ever your evil genius, thwarting you in all your deeds of good or ill. Ha! ha! ha! Captain Leslie, what, you turn pale at the curse of the blighted one? and you shall live to see its fulfilment!" With a wild, hysterical shriek of laughter, the wretched girl sank upon the floor in a death swoon.

The bright rays of the wintry sun poured in a flood upon the pale, livid features of Captain Leslie, who, with knitted brow, stood gazing upon the still form of his victim, that like a corpse lay stretched at his feet.

CHAPTER IX.

THE RUINED HOUSE IN THE VAUXHALL-ROAD.—THE MEETING.—LUCY MASTERTON AND HER LOVER.—THE HALL OF TERROR.—THE SURPRISE.—THE RIVER PIRATE.—ANTHONY REDRUTH, ALIAS TONY REDHEAD, AND EUSTACE MALTRAVERS.—THE CAPTURE.—STUGGLE IN THE RUINED HOUSE.—THE ESCAPE.—THE BOAT UPON THE RIVER.—THE PURSUIT, THE FIGHT, AND DARING LEAP OF EUSTACE MALTRAVERS INTO THE DARK WATERS OF THE THAMES.

THE hour of nine was striking as the young man who had had the encounter with the ruffians in the old house at Bankside the evening of the same day, made his way to the neighbourhood of old Vauxhall.

It was a lovely night, the moon shining bright and clear in the frosty sky.

Proceeding down the Vauxhall-road, the young man halted at an old ruined house, that, standing for many years untenanted, was falling into decay.

It was in chancery.

And, like everything else, once in chancery was likely to remain so.

Standing alone, quite detached from every other building, the ruined house in the Vauxhall-road was well known.

And it had been arranged between the young man to meet the fair girl, Lucy Masterton, of the inn at Bankside, near the ruined house in the Vauxhall-road, as that was a spot little likely to be frequented at nine in the evening, and, therefore, one where they could converse uninterrupted.

The hour of nine had barely ceased ringing on the air, before the young stranger was joined by a light, sylph-like form, who, tripping forwards in the moonlight, looked some beautiful fay.

"Oh! dear girl, this, indeed, is kind. I feared that, in consequence of the incident this morning at your father's inn, that you would not be able to keep your meeting with me this night. Dear, dear Lucy, this happy moment repays me for all the danger I may have passed in gaining you to my arms."

His eyes beaming with passion, the young man strained the fair young girl to his breast in a close embrace.

The maiden, a lovely young creature, some eighteen or nineteen years of age, looked up, with eyes of love, into her companion's face; and then, partly disengaging herself from his too close embrace, gazed round her in terror, exclaiming—

"Eustace, you must not stay here. I fear I have been watched by a companion of my father's, one Anthony Redruth, a man who, professing attachment for me, would hesitate at nought to gratify his hate and revenge upon you. Should he discover us together, you must then haste away, dear Eustace, and we will meet again. I tremble lest we should be discovered."

The young girl clung in terror to her lover, as she fancied she heard footsteps approaching, but nought was discernible; the broad, white light of the moon cast a glare upon all around; the Vauxhall-road was at that moment deserted, not a single person was in sight.

"Nay, tremble not thus, dear Lucy; believe me, if indeed your suspicions were correct, I am well able to meet any danger that may occur. Witness the scene in your father's inn at the old Bankside this morning. I am one, Lucy Masterton, that laughs danger to scorn, like the hardy mariner in a storm, or the brave soldier when storming the breach. I am oblivious of danger, and know it but by name. I could tell you of an adventure, dear girl, that befell me when first I entered the great city, only a few days back, that would startle you with horror, but, to hear of the recital, the strange incidents, the perils I have encountered, seem to me like some wild dream."

"How strange, dear Lucy," said the young man, now drawing her nearer to his side. "How strange our meeting the day I entered London. Who would have imagined when you left our peaceful little village in Hampshire, where we first met and loved, that we should come across each other in this gay city; and yet, Lucy, when torn from my side so many months back, when told by you that your parent in London insisted on your joining him after your mother's death, yet still, I said to myself, we shall meet again; and, entering London, my Lucy is the first I happen to cross in my path."

"And what, dear Eustace, was the dreadful peril of which you spoke? You never hinted of this before."

"No, dear one, I thought it would but distress and frighten you with its horror; but I will tell you now, dear girl, to prove to you that not only am I well prepared to meet and encounter any danger that may hap, but also that I am protected by an all-wise Providence above, else could I never have lived to tell that which now I relate."

Pacing up and down before the ruined house, the young man gazing fondly upon the beautiful features of the young girl by his side, exclaimed—

"It was a dark, foggy night, dear Lucy, you may remember, which closed the day that first found me in London. Business compelled me to go abroad notwithstanding the inclemency of the night.

"It had been well if I had let the affair in hand stand over, but I was eager to present myself to those who had commanded my presence in London, and, unacquainted with the hour, I made my way blindly through the thoroughfares, which were all thickly enveloped in fog. I had, at length, I found, wandered from my path, getting into the neighbourhood of a dark turning, called, they told me, Kennington-lane, and not far from where we now stand. I was about to make further inquiries, when I was suddenly struck violently to the earth from some one behind, and was stretched senseless and bleeding on the earth.

"I remembered no more, and returned not to consciousness till I found myself lying, partly covered with a sack, in a corner of a large, old-fashioned apartment of some house in the country, as I guessed, the shrill winds raging and roaring without, as though the house were situated by the sea-side.

"I had barely time to stagger to my feet when two ruffians entered the room. I fled, made my way up a wide flight of stairs that opened before me, followed in my flight by the yelling hounds of the lone murder-den. In my mad flight I made my way into a chamber, the door of which stood open before me. I cannot recal the scene now, dear girl, to my memory without a shudder.

"I was hurled, after a desperate struggle for my life, down a hideous, yawning trap, that opened in the floor of that den of murderers, and, with a wild shriek of agony, sank into the depths of a turpid stream that ran beneath the old house.

"For a few moments I lost all consciousness, but a love of life endued me with powers and courage that I never thought to possess. In that dread moment I reflected that the stream, a large one, must have some outlet, possibly it made its way to the river. I was an excellent diver, had been often spoken of as a wonder by my schoolfellows at my feats in the water, and power I had of retaining my breath when beneath the life-destroying fluid. This gift stood me in good stead on that night of horror.

"I sunk beneath the turbid stream, and let my body rush headlong in the current for a few minutes, which seemed an age. I appeared as though forced through a dark, horrible tunnel, a loud, roaring noise ringing like thunder in my ears.

"At length a white light shone on the top of the waters that before had been black—dark like ink.

"I then knew I was in the open air, and near suffocated by my long stay beneath the waters.

"I rose to the surface, and discovered myself rushing with fearful velocity out into the centre of a broad, wide stream.

"The fog lifting, showed me a large, deserted house, standing alone in an open field close to the water, in which I was now swimming vigorously to reach the shore. But, leaving the house behind me, I made for the opposite shore of the stream.

"I had not the courage to return near the vicinity of that lone house in which I had so near met my death.

"As I had conjectured, the stream beneath the lone den of murder made its way out into the river, and by a a miracle—a blessing of Providence—I was saved. I reached the opposite shore in safety, procured assistance, and the next morning could at first only think of the occurrence as of a horrible dream.

"I have since met the villains at whose hands I nearly lost my life. Certain reasons compel my silence of the past, but I will yet be amply avenged for the horrors of that night."

The young girl had listened to her companion with breathless interest, her face assuming a death-like tint as her lover recounted the horrible adventure. About to ask him who and what the villains were who had thus murderously hurled him down the trap in the den of death, she was startled by the shadow of a dark figure that emerged from the vicinity of the ruined house.

Seizing her lover's arm, the young girl, pale and gasping, exclaimed—

"Oh! Eustace, all—all is lost. We are watched, and you are"——

The remainder of the sentence was lost in the loud scuffle of approaching footsteps, and a piercing shriek issued from the young girl's lips as three men darted out of the shadow of the ruined house and sprang upon her lover.

Seized from behind, and partly stunned by a violent blow on the head, with a single cry for help, the young man was struck to the ground.

No answering voice echoed the cry for aid.

It was a deserted, solitary spot—but few wayfarers passing after dark.

"Bring him along; off with the gal to Bankside, Harry; leave me to look after the rum cull."

"What are yer going to do with the swell, Toney?" exclaimed one of the ruffians who had seized upon the young girl, Lucy Masterton, who, on beholding her lover struck senseless to the earth, had fallen into a death swoon.

"Oh! leave him to me, Harry. I shall take him into the slum (house), search his pockets for jack, inguns, or flimsies (watch, seals, or bank notes), give him one on his cocoa-nut, knock out his cussed fine ivories (teeth) for the sawbones (doctor), and topple his carcase into the river at the back of the old house."

"Well, as your dolly begins to show signs of coming to, while you settle accounts with the swell, why, I'll convey the gal to her father's house. But hasten back, Tony, for we've much to do to-night."

"Right you are! I'll be with yer at twelve, never fear."

"Where shall we meet?"

"At the 'Devil's Punch Bowl,' in the highway."

"You'll bring Nosy and Bony with you?"

"Of course! But haste away, for I can hear the tread of the watch."

Whilst the men had been conversing, the two who held the young stranger in their arms had made their way to the door of the ruined house, that, despite the apparent secure fastening, they pushed open.

The leader of the ruffians now approached, and, as the companion to whom he had been speaking hurried off with the still senseless girl, the others made their way into the hall of the ruined house, bearing the young man in their arms.

Closing the door, the leader of the gang—a tall, herculean ruffian, with a dark, forbidding-looking countenance and shock of red hair, and wearing a huge red beard—struck a light. As the faint glimmer of the taper lighted up the dark passage or hall of the house, the young man, reviving from the half-senseless state he had been in, opened his eyes and glared wildly round.

"Hum! So you have recovered that crack on the nut! It's a pity; 'cos why, I'm fixed to make cold meat of yer!"

"And sell his dominoes to the sawbones, Tony!"

"Of course. Just so, Bony; neither more nor less."

"The wery identical!" echoed another of the ruffians.

"Right you is," sententiously muttered a third—a fellow who, possessing a huge Roman nose, luxuriated in the cognomen of Nosy.

"Villains, would you murder me?" exclaimed Eustace Maltravers, who, for the third time, found himself in danger of his life, and who, remembering his former escapes, called in all his wit and cunning to elude the villains into whose hands he had fallen.

"Well, if yer likes to call things by their right names, that is just what we is agoing to do."

"Precisely!" muttered Bony.

"Just the wery ticket!" echoed Nosy.

"But your object, villains? my death will avail you not," exclaimed Eustace, willing to gain time by parleying with the ruffians.

"Why, as to that, yer see, my swell cove, there is one or two reasons which, as we means making a stiff-'un of yer, don't signify yer knowing."

"In course not, Tony; that's jest it."

"Spoken like a parient," said Nosy.

"Now yer see, my dandy cove, in the first place a pal of ourn, one Bill Slasher, or Resurrection Bill as we calls him, owes yer one."

"Just so; owes yer one."

"And we pays yer."

"Like beans."

"No flies; we'll behave like gemmens."

"Exactly," continued the ruffian; "Tony Redhead, my pals, speak like blessed oracles. Well, now, in addition to this, yer see, I have a nasty habit of slitting the weazands of any cove what interferes with me or mine. You have cottoned on to the gal, Lucy Masterton, curse yer, and I'll make yer a stiff-'un, if only to remove you from my path."

"In course, yer got the gal, and now yer'll get summat else."

"And no flies."

"Shall I give him one on his nut, Tony?" ejaculated Bony, who drew from his pocket a small bludgeon or life-preserver, the end of which was loaded with lead—a fearful instrument in the hands of a determined man.

Like a cat watching her prey, Eustace Maltravers kept his eyes fixed intently upon the three ruffians who stood before him.

During the above brief converse he had ascertained that behind him was a wide oaken staircase. At the sides of the hall were various doors, and a large door at the extreme end of the passage evidently opened out upon the gardens at the back, as a stream of moonlight fell into the hall through a broken fanlight over the entrance.

All this Eustace Maltravers gathered in his eye at a glance.

The only chance of escape from his enemies was by the door he had entered, or that at the other end of the passage.

To reach either of these, he must put his foes *hors de combat*.

With a shudder, Maltravers acknowledged to himself that his chances were small.

Unarmed, against three determined ruffians, his escape seemed hopeless.

"Now then, my tulip, say yer prayers if yer knows any, 'cos yer time is but short," ejaculated the villain Bony, grasping the formidable weapon loaded with lead. "In ten minutes from this yer'll turn up your toes, and be a blessed subject, what we shall take to the sawbones, leastways yer ivories, of which yer arn't got a bad set. On to him Bony, let him have it."

The wretch Tony, followed by his companions, rush upon Eustace, but the determined and courageous young man was well prepared for the onslaught.

Seizing the wrist of the man Bony, he wrenched the life-preserver from the villain, making him shriek as he nearly twisted his hand from the socket.

Endowed with amazing strength, the ruffian was as a child in the grasp of Eustace Maltravers. Starting back, our hero now darted for the door at the back, and seizing the handle, ere his foes were aware of his purpose, had

THE STRUGGLE FOR LIFE—THE CAPTAIN IN PERIL.

torn it open, fortunately the rusty lock gave way instantly to the young man's grasp.

"Upon him, Bony. Curses, he'll escape."

"Not he, Tony; not if I knows it. Cut round to the back, through the parlour winder."

"Nosy, we'll soon settle him," shouted the ruffian, who, yelling with the pain of his injured wrist, and mad with fury, rushed upon Eustace, as he was about to dart through the door.

Turning round, Maltravers raised the formidable weapon he had secured in the air, and the man Bony, starting aside to avoid the blow received, fell upon the upper part of his right arm, in the hand of which he held a large knife. With a scream of agony, and fierce curses, the ruffian staggered back, at the same moment a sharp report rang through the old ruined house, as Tony Redhead fired a pistol full at the body of their victim, who, however, seeing the glitter of the pistol-barrel in the bright rays of the moon, that streamed into the passage,

ducked his head, and as the report reverberated through the old house, threw open the door and darted out into the garden at the back.

The bright moon shone with her silvery rays upon all around, making the hoar-frost upon the trees and shrubs glitter like diamonds.

Dashing along the grass-grown walk, Eustace made for a low wall he discerned at the bottom of the garden.

As he darted along, a dark shadow appeared upon the path before him.

There was a deep-breathed curse, and sounds of a fierce struggle.

Eustace in his flight had rushed into the arms of the ruffian, who, executing his comrade's orders, had made his way into the grounds during the struggle in the passage.

"Let go your hold! or, by the heavens above us, I'll beat in your villainous skull with the bludgeon I hold in my hand."

"Come on, Tony.   It's all right; I've nabbed him. I've got him hard and fast."

"Then mind you keep him, lad."

There was the sound of a crushing blow, a yell of pain, and, released from the villain's clutches, Eustace dashed on as the other two ruffians came rushing up the pathway.

"After him, hell-devils!   Don't let the —— escape."

"Let him have one from your barking-irons, Tony."

Then followed a loud report, answered by a shout of laughter and yell of defiance from their victim, as mounting the wall uninjured, he, a moment afterwards, disappeared.

With hideous oaths and curses, the villains, with murder in their souls, bounded on, and, reaching the wall, scrambled over, and just discerned the form of their victim turning the corner of the lane that ran at the back of the house.

No one appeared about that lone spot, and the ruffians, with the daring of fury and longings for revenge upon the man who had, single-handed, evaded them, kept up their pursuit.

Finding he was still pursued, and aware that it was a race for life, Eustace glanced round in hopes of perceiving some solitary watchman, but it was a lone spot and a late hour—not a living creature could be seen.

The neighbourhood of Vauxhall was not then as now; 'twas simply a rural spot, out of town, with but few habitations, and those far apart.

Darting onwards in his course, Eustace now turned off the road he had been pursuing, and rushed down a dark, narrow turning.

A slight tremor shook his frame as he darted on.

The court or alley was dark, with a brick wall high up on each side.

What if there should be no thoroughfare?

His enemies were close behind him.

He could hear the clatter of their iron-shod shoes upon the frozen pathway.

Should there be no escape from the alley, he was lost.

He had lost the fearful weapon he had wrested from his foes when bounding over the wall, and was now unarmed.

Suddenly a thrill of joy darted through his frame.

He could hear far off the rush and murmur of waters.

The lane or alley down which he ran with frantic speed led to the river.

He might yet escape.

Keeping on his mad career, Maltravers darted out of the long, dark lane, and found himself at the top of a flight of stone steps.

At the bottom plashed the waters of the Thames.

Whilst a jarring, creaking sound fell upon the ear, as three or four wherries, fastened together, dashed against each other as they were rocked up and down by the tide.

Rushing down the steps, taking no heed of a waterman who lay coiled up in a thick rug at the bottom of a boat, Eustace unfastened one of the wherries, and, jumping in, seizing a pair of oars, pushed her off as the eager villains who pursued him made their appearance at the top of the steps.

Such a shout of fury escaped them as they beheld our hero making his way out into the river, that, starting up from his doze, the old boatman, with a curse, halloaed upon Eustace to come back.

"Here, you vagabond, come back with that there boat!"

"It ain't no use calling on him, he is an escaped burglar; we are detectives, so we must follow our man; we'll soon return, old cove."

Jumping in, to the astonishment of the old waterman, another boat was unloosed, and soon darting over the waters in pursuit of the one containing our hero now far out in the stream.

"Well, dowse my toplights! may I never chew another quid if this ere arn't a rummy go!   Cuss 'em, they don't do me that way though.   Cuss 'em, I warn't born yesterday;" so saying the red-faced old waterman cast off the painter of the craft in which he had been sleeping, and was soon pulling strenuously for the two wherries that without his leave had been taken away.

The moon shone bright and clear in the frosty sky, tipping the waters of the silent highway with a silvery radiance.

In the centre of the stream Eustace Maltravers urged his boat forward, endeavouring to reach a barge upon which he discovered two men; but the current of the river was against him, the tide was up and running strong, the barge far ahead, and the boat with the villain assassins rapidly approaching.   He could hear the men, with horrible oaths, vowing vengeance against him.

With a shudder Eustace acknowledged to himself that his only chance now was in being able to reach the stairs, by the Houses of Parliament, at Westminster-bridge.

But he was some distance from the spot, and his foes each moment gaining upon him.

"Pull away, Bony; we shall have him now!"

"But how about the waterman, Tony?   He'll blow the gaff on us; he'll twig us, do the job-nose (give evidence) on us, and we'll have a lifer (be transported), or be topped (hanged) at Tyburn!"

"Kious (keep still), I'll see to it, by ——," said the ruffian Tony, with a fierce oath; "the swell cove shan't escape.   Pity Lady Blue shines so bright, but it shan't save our covey; who knows, his gropers (pockets) may be well lined."

"Right yer is, Tony.   Besides," muttered the wounded wretch Nosy, who, groaning from the pain of his fractured arm, sat by the rudder guiding the boat, "besides, didn't Resurrectioner say as how he'd give fifty couters (sovereigns) if as how we succeeded in slitting the weazand of the cove?   And mind as how, afore we throw him to soak in the river, yer knock out his ivories (teeth); his dominoes are worth a goldfinch (guinea) to any front railing maker in the long village (dentist in London)."

"No, no, Nosy, that can't be done; the old bloak in t'other boat must be thought of," said the man Tony.   "If as how we merely as a struggle and knocks our man over, we can say anything; but, by the devils, here we is alongside him.   Now for a scrimmage."

Their boat was now parallel with that of Eustace Maltravers.   Finding further escape useless, the young man started up; seizing one of the skulls, and raising it above his head as the only means of defence at hand, he prepared to encounter his assailants.

"Help! help! help!"

The voice of the young man sounded loud and shrill over the waters.

"End the business, Tony; curse him, we shall be collared by the crabs (officers) for the job if we don't do for him pretty soon."

The boats now dashed against each other with a dull crash.

The one containing the ruffians pulled forwards in such a way as to almost overtopple the other.

"Let him have it."

"Knife him."

"Knock in his brain pan."

"Chive (stab) him."

Such like exclamations, with vollies of oaths and curses, fell from the mouths of the villains, as rising up they endeavoured to hurl their victim into the dark waters of the river.

Rising the skull in his hands, driven to desperation, Eustace brought it down with all his force on the head of the unfortunate ruffian at the bow of the craft, the villain Nosy.   With a groan the wretch sank back senseless at the bottom of the boat.

But the force of the blow had broken the scull in two, and Eustace now stood before his would-be assassins incapable of offering further resistance.   Watching the desperate conflict, and fearing to join in the affray, uncertain as to who was the guilty party, the old waterman held himself aloof, resting on his sculls.

A cry of surprise, however, escaped his lips, echoed by a yell from the mouths of the villains, Tony and his companions, as with a defying shout at his foes, Eustace, whom they had thought all but in their power, leaped from his boat, disappearing in the dark, deep waters of the river.

Three minutes later a long boat, in which was seated some half-dozen of the river police, made their appearance, causing the ruffians who had so daringly pursued their victim, to beat an ignominious retreat.

As they pulled away from the spot, a cry of fury escaped them, as they beheld the body of a man drawn from the river into the boat belonging to the police.

Eustace Maltravers was rescued and perished not, as his enemies had hoped, in the dark, dismal waters of the silent highway.

CHAPTER VIII.

THE HOLLY-TREE FARM.—A TALE OF SORROW.—A SISTER
DISHONOURED, AND A BROTHER'S VENGEANCE.—THE
EARLY GRAVE.—THE FUNERAL.—THE WATCHERS IN
THE CHURCHYARD. — THE MIDNIGHT HOUR. — THE
RESURRECTION MEN. — THE DISINTERRING OF THE
DEAD.—THE FRIGHT OF THE OLD JEW.—THE DEAD
ALIVE.—TERROR OF THE ISRAELITE. — INCREDULITY
AND BRAVADO OF RESURRECTION BILL.—THE WHITE
FACE BEHIND THE TOMBSTONE.—THE ALARM.

STANDING some seven miles from London, on the road to
Finchley, at the time of which we are writing, was a large
farm, known as the Holly-tree Farm.

Holly-tree Farm was situate some quarter of a mile
or more from the high road. Built of red brick, with
innumerable barns and outhouses, a pleasant, thriving-
looking tenement was Holly-tree Farm.

In the front of the house was a row of fine holly trees,
from which the farm derived its name.

Beautiful they looked in the winter time of year, with
their dark green foliage and countless red berries hanging like clusters of coral from the branches.

A pleasant, cosy-looking retreat was Holly-tree Farm.

Its tenant, Mathew Templeton, a bluff, jovial, real old
English yeoman, was well known and respected by all
around.

Much pity was felt for him when a cruel and terrible
misfortune fell upon him.

The whole neighbourhood, for miles round, pitied and
sorrowed for the sad incident in connexion with Mathew
Templeton, of Holly-Tree farm.

A terrible tragedy had taken place.

A tragedy casting one and all in gloom.

'Twas the old story; but one finishing with more than
usual horror and calamity.

Farmer Templeton had for some years been a widower,
left with a lovely daughter and two fine-grown boys, who
all loved and revered their parent. Mathew Templeton,
with a fair allowance of the world's riches, and blessed
with health, thus lived in happiness and joy.

Years passed on. Bessie Templeton, from a beautiful
child, budded into a lovely, fair young girl.

Many sought the hand of the farmer's lovely daughter;
but she was young, loved her father and her home, and
cared not to change it for another.

At length, however, Bessie chanced one day, in the
neighbourhood of the farm, to meet a gay, handsome,
dashing stranger, an officer of the army, who was admired,
and introduced himself to the lovely girl.

Despite her blushes and alarm, the stranger persevered
in following her within a short distance of her father's
farm.

Flattered by the compliments of the handsome officer,
though hastening away alarmed from his presence, Bessie
Templeton throughout that day occupied her thoughts
solely with the incident of the morning; but the approach
of evening dispelled these reflections. A grand ball was
to take place that night at the Manor-house, near the
farm.

The manor belonged to the owner of the estates, who
thus gave an invitation to all his tenantry round. To this
ball the Templetons, of course, were invited; and, accordingly, Bessie, the belle of the village, with her father
and young brothers, proceeded there at the appointed
hour.

A nervous tremor shook the frame of the lovely farmer's
daughter as, in the course of the evening, she was introduced by a friend to the very stranger from whom she had
fled in the morning, and who had occupied her thoughts
all day.

Blushing scarlet, the beautiful girl hung down her head
as the handsome stranger breathed his soft adulations in
her ear.

The whole of the evening the handsome officer retained
the lovely Bessie by his side.

The next day they met again, secretly and alone.

Time passed on. The handsome stranger visited at the
farm, amused the worthy yeoman, eventually proposed,
and was the accepted suitor for the hand of the innocent
and lovely Bessie.

One fine summer morning, the ardent and enthusiastic
lover left his mistress to proceed to his residence in Hampshire.

He returned in five weeks.

Better had he never come back!

Better had he and the lovely girl never met!

Weeks rolled on; months passed away; the betrothed
of the farmer's daughter at various times absented himself from the farm, and returned as before.

Winter now fell with iron hand upon the scene.

Dark, stern, gloomy winter, with its shrill winds and
biting frosts.

It was on a bleak, frosty day in February, that Bessie
and her lover met near the Hollies.

He had just returned from one of his visits to his home,
and was met by the lovely girl as he neared the farm.

Together they wandered from the house, arm in arm.

Bessie had noted a dark, heavy cloud on her lover's
brow; and, in terror and alarm, linked her arm in his,
and followed him from the farm along the open road leading to picturesque Finchley.

What passed at that interview was never known.

Some hours after the meeting of Bessie and her lover,
Miles Templeton, the farmer's eldest son, a young man
about nineteen years of age, staggered wildly along the
road to the farm with fury and horror in his looks.

There was a terrible scene at the Holly-tree Farm that
cold winter's day.

In the afternoon, the farmer, with his sons and some
villagers, searched for his daughter, who, it appeared,
had fled at her brother's approach, when he had burst
upon her with her lover in the morning in a coppice off
the Finchley-road, and had not since returned.

Nought, however, could be discovered.

Bessie Templeton returned not that night to the farm.

Early the next morning she was found cold and lifeless
in the coppice.

A sad party conveyed the poor girl to her home.

The unfortunate yeoman, upon beholding the lifeless
form of his child, with a wild shriek of horror sank in
convulsions upon the ground.

The next hour Mathew Templeton was a raging maniac.

Late the same day Miles, the eldest brother of the
unfortunate girl, met and attacked the lover and seducer
of his sister.

What passed was related by the young farming man,
who was in the company of his master.

Miles Templeton, with a howl of fury, attacked the
villain seducer, upbraiding him with his accursed deed of
treachery. In the struggle the young man was thrown
violently, and, striking his head against the root of a tree,
was stretched senseless at the foot of his adversary.

On his recovery there was a recrimination between the
two men, and a meeting was arranged for the next
morning, wrung unwillingly from the libertine by the
brother of the unfortunate girl.

The two men met, the brother of the ill-fated Bessie
Templeton falling beneath the fire of his adversary.

The libertine hastily left the neighbourhood, making
good his escape, nor could he be traced in his flight.

The unhappy girl and her elder brother, thus, by the
heartless roué and seducer, sent to an early grave, were
mourned by all, and a sorrowful gloom was cast over the
village at the terrible tragedy that had taken place in
the family of Mathew Templeton, the owner of Holly-
tree Farm.

It was towards the close of a dark, wintry afternoon
that the bodies of the unfortunate brother and sister were
conveyed to the village churchyard.

It was a sad procession that which conveyed poor Bessie
Templeton and her brother to their early grave.

The dull clang, clang of the bell, as it tolled the death-
knell, sounded sad and gloomily on the air.

Darkness at length fell upon the scene. All was finished.
In one grave the loving doomed ones were buried. As
their bodies were consigned to the earth, many a deep-
breathed curse was vented upon the villain who had
hurried them from the world.

One young lad, of perhaps eighteen years of age, as the
last sod was beaten down upon the grave, kneeled beside
it, and, raising his hands to heaven, swore never to rest
upon earth until he had consummated a terrible revenge
upon the head of the destroyer.

With white, pallid cheeks, and eyes blazing with a fiery
light of savage determination, the lad then bounded from
the churchyard.

That poor youth was the younger brother of Bessie

Templeton, and one doomed to play no insignificant part in this drama of real life.

As the youth hurriedly dashed away from the church, he noted not two dark figures closely following him from the resting-place of the dead. On his reaching the farm, however, they kept on the road making their way to the village near.

It was a cold, bitter, bleak winter's night that followed the day that beheld the funeral of poor Bessie Templeton and her brother.

Cold, dark, and drear!

Thick, heavy clouds, surcharged with snow, hung in the horizon.

Whilst the wind from the north-east blew in piercing, chilling gusts.

The clock of the church, in the burial-grounds of which now reposed the bodies of the unfortunate farmer's children, was striking the hour of eleven as two dark figures appeared at the gate of the churchyard.

Spectre-like, grim, and shadowy looked the muffled forms as they stood by the gate of the village churchyard.

"It ish very cold, Bill. Curses, how de vind do cut one, as it blows, laden wit de frost of de cussed winter night. By Satan! I vish the job was over."

"Kious (softly), or——! you'll give the office to anyone should they be passing. Tie the horse up to the gate, get the sack out of the rumbler (cart), ready for the stiff-'un, and follow me. ·Curse yer! don't stand shivering there, with yer dominoes clattering like castanets, but follow me."

"Bill, you ish von daring devil, and I believe if yer wash lagged, yer would be as cool as ven sharing the regulars after a good lay."

Having opened the gate, Resurrection Bill and his companion, the Jew, Ben Abrahams, now entered the churchyard, for it was, indeed, these two villains who had made their way to the burial-ground that bitter, dark, wintry night.

"Now then, Ben, old boy, kim on. We must get back to the long village (London) by two, and we've a good hour's work afore us ere we get the stiff-'uns up out of the parson's lodging (grave)."

The two men had cautiously groped their way through the burial-ground, and now halted beside a newly-made grave.

The fresh earth was encrusted and hardening under the frosty atmosphere; but having been turned up so recently, presented but a slight obstacle to the determined resurrectionists.

The Jew now laid a sack at his feet, and pulled from under his coat a spade, pickaxe, and crowbar.

The night was pitchy dark.

The ivy-clad tower of the old village church could with difficulty be discerned through the gloom.

Midnight now chimed upon the air with a dull, solemn clang.

Scarce had the last note, dirge like, quavered away upon the stillness of the night, ere it was succeeded by a sound that was horrible and dreadful to be heard at that mystic hour.

The noise that awoke the before dead silence in the churchyard was the sound of iron striking into the hard, frozen earth.

A quarter of an hour passed, still the sound rose upon the crisp, frost-laden air.

With muttered oaths the body-snatchers proceeded in the execution of their horrible task.

"Give me the shovel, Ben; I'll soon unearth 'em, or I'll know the reason why. Curses on it, the frost has hardened the ground more than I thought; however, as the sawbones offered fifty goldfinches (guineas) for the job, Resurrection Bill warnt the cove to refuse, though he risked being topped (hanged) for the snatch. Light the glim (lamp), old 'un. I've got at 'em at last. Lower down the yarn (rope)."

Working vigorously at his task, the resurrection man had at length struck his spade upon some wood.

He had reached the coffin of the dead.

It was a wild scene in the lone churchyard that winter night.

The wind in hollow murmurs sighed and surged hollowly over the graves of the departed.

The bat, with its leathern wing outspread, hovered around the ivy tower, and roosted in the dark green foliage.

The moon, too, now emerging from the heavy clouds that had before obscured it, cast her pale rays upon the scene.

Enveloping church, tower, graveyard, all alike in a ghastly spectral glare.

"Confound it, Ben; our task scarce half over, and Oliver (the moon) showing his face. Haul away, old 'un. So, so! yo ho! easy does it. That's the ticket; now to prize open the meat-box. Shove the stiff-'un in the sack, and away to the sawbones."

Jumping from the grave, the resurrection man had handed a rope to his companion, who stood on one side of the yawning depth, and seizing another end of the thick cord in his own grasp, between them they hauled up the coffin from the dark recess; and in a few moments it laid upon the upturned earth beside the grave. The moon shone with her bright blue light full upon the black coffin, the white plate on the lid of which glittered in the pale moonbeams.

Sinking down upon his knees, the resurrection man examined the plate; then, starting up, seized the crowbar from the hands of the Jew, and prized open the lid.

"Its all right, Ben; this here is the young gal's coffin, and, right and tight, here she is, looking for all the world like a wax doll. Curse me, she must have been a stunner. Why, she looks beautiful even in death.

Beautiful, indeed, looked the corpse of the young girl, as she laid still and calm in the narrow box.

The lovely features, wax-like, livid, and fixed though they were, looked fair indeed, even in death. Bright golden hair could just be discerned beneath the shroud that enwrapped the face.

"She is a stunner! A splendid stiff-'un!" muttered the resurrectionist, as he gazed in admiration on the corpse of the unfortunate young victim.

The moonbeams played full upon the pale waxen face.

It was a strange scene, that villain standing beside the coffin of the disinterred dead, in rude admiration gazing upon the rigid corpse.

Near him stood the old Jew, sack in hand, ready to remove the body from the last resting-place that had held its cold remains.

"In with her, Ben; and now I think on it, we may as well have the other, if he only brings the price of his ivories. We'd better collar him; remove the girl, while I unearth the other. 'Twould be a shame to part 'em!" said the ruffian, with a rude laugh, jumping again into the grave.

The Jew, meanwhile, rolled the corpse of the young girl out of her coffin; and, opening the sack, prepared to thrust it in, first having removed the winding-sheet from the body.

Busily engaged with another coffin in the grave they had opened, and which was that of the poor girl, Bessie Templeton, and her brother, the resurrection man heard not a cry of alarm from the Jew, nor ceased in his labours to remove the second coffin, till, interrupted in his task by the appearance of the Jew's face looking down upon him, whilst the wretch exclaimed, with horror depicted on his features—

"Hist! hist! Bill! By de fiends, some vone ish in the churchyard. Py ma soul, ve shall be dishcovered."

With a curse, the resurrection man bounded up out of the grave; but, on glancing round, nought could be seen.

The bright moonlight shone in silvery rays upon the graveyard; but, save himself and his companion, the old Jew, it appeared deserted.

It was now past midnight, and, with an oath, Resurrection Bill again leaped into the grave, reminding the Jew, with a curse, that at that late hour no one could appear to interrupt them in their task.

The old Jew, trembling, once more prepared to put the corpse of the young girl in the sack, whilst his companion, using all his great strength, drew the other coffin out of the dark grave, and presently stood beside the Jew, the black receptacle of the dead resting beside the grim, darksome cave from which it had been drawn.

Prizing off the lid, Resurrection Bill was in the act of lifting the corpse out of the coffin, when his arm was clutched by his companion with a vice-like grip, whilst, incapable of speech, he mumbled indistinct words, and pointed to the form of the young girl.

"What the fiends do you mean, Abrahams, by mouthing and jabbering thus? Are you mad? curses on yer. You're not often frightened thus. This arn't your first snatch. What the —— do you mean?" said the villain, with a fierce oath. "Why do you point to the stiff-'un? Damme, you're not afraid of cold meat?"

"She—she—she's alive!" gasped the Jew.

"Pshaw! old man, you're dreaming."

"By my shoul, I'll swear it!"

"Hold the glim."

The ruffian now knelt beside the body of the young girl.

He lifted it up in his arms, and gazed into the livid face.

With a curse and cry of surprise, he dropped it to the ground, at the same time starting to his feet.

The moon's rays shone full and clear upon the livid features of the poor girl.

Resurrection Bill and his companion glared speechless upon the body.

The eyes of the disinterred body were wide open.

"Bill!"

"Abrahams!"

"Ish she alive?"

"Ten thousand devils, no! She's cold and stiff enough. Dead as a nut."

"But her eyes; mein Gott, her eyes!"

"Have not been properly closed. Hell furies! don't I know a stiff-'un when I sees it?"

"Bill, hark!"

"What is it?"

"There is someone near at hand, pa my shoul. I heard a footstep."

"Your imagination, Ben. There arn't no one here save me and you; but, howsomever, we'll make a bolt on it. I'll carry the other stiff-'un, while you vamoose (run on) with the gal. I'll make a few goldfinches out of this here cove." Turning round to the coffin containing the body of the young man; Resurrection Bill lifted the corpse up out of the receptacle, and the Jew, sack in hand, stood by his side.

An exclamation of horror and alarm now fell from the lips of both men.

Who stood glaring at the tombstone placed at the head of the grave?

Transfixed, the robbers of the dead, with widely expanded eyes, stared at the sight which they beheld.

The death-pale face of a man, white and ghastly, just appearing over the top of the tombstone before them.

The eyes of the watcher met those of the body-snatchers.

For a moment Resurrection Bill remained with the corpse still held in his arms, then letting it fall, with a horrible oath he darted forwards. There was the sound of a struggle, a single, shrill cry for aid, then a horrible, sickening blow, and all was still.

Resurrection Bill now appeared, dragging forwards the lifeless form of a young man, whom he, with a curse, flung into the empty grave; then seizing the body of the girl in his arms, and bidding the Jew place the other in the sack, he hurried from the churchyard, closely followed by his hoary companion, staggering under his grizzly load.

A few minutes afterwards the sound of wheels might have been heard, whilst the clattering of horses' hoofs rung on the still silence of the night, as the cart, driven by the resurrectionists, bearing its terrible load, left the spot.

An hour afterwards, a figure, with face streaming in blood, scrambled up out of the desecrated grave.

It was the unfortunate man who, watching the villain resurrection men in their task, had been discovered.

Pale, bleeding, and uttering shrill screams for aid, he staggered from the churchyard.

Taking a by-road which led to Holly-tree Farm.

The young stranger, the midnight watcher in the churchyard, who had near met his death at the hands of the resurrection man, was no other than the unfortunate younger brother of Bessie Templeton, he who, in the morning, had sworn to terribly revenge his sister's and his brother's deaths, as he knelt beside the new-made grave.

———

CHAPTER IX.

THE "DEVIL'S PUNCH-BOWL" IN RATCLIFFE HIGHWAY.—THE VIPER AND HIS COMPANIONS.—THE MURDER.—A ROUGH NIGHT.—THE COUNTRY ROAD.—HARROW IN THE EIGHTEENTH CENTURY.—THE DARK LANE, AND THE SHADOW BY THE COPSE.—THE MEETING NEAR THE "BOLD HORSEMAN."—THE DIAMONDS.—THE CONFLICT.—THE TIMELY ARRIVAL OF EUSTACE MALTRAVERS.—FURY OF THE VIPER.—THE THREAT AND OATH OF VENGEANCE.

IT is now many years since there stood in one of the dark, narrow, unpaved turnings off Ratcliffe-highway an old-fashioned, ruined tenement, known by the sign of the "Devil's Punch-Bowl."

It was a miserable, tumble-down house, falling every day more and more into decay.

Built of red brick, with red tiled roof, it was called by some the Red House, though the sign of the building was, as we have said, the "Devil's Punch-Bowl."

The name of the landlord of this ruinous public-house, placed over the door, had long been lost sight of by being covered up in a thick coating of dirt.

Everything in and about the "Devil's Punch-Bowl" was covered with black, grimly dirt.

The oil-lamp was an inch thick with grease and dirt, the glass having turned of a uniform dark brown or dull black.

There was a low doorway leading into the public-house; to reach this door the visitor had to make his way down two steps that opened out direct upon the footpath; pushing his way through this entrance, a stranger would then find himself in a large apartment, with seats all down one side, and a counter fixed at the end of the chamber, facing the doorway. This was the bar of the "Devil's Punch-Bowl."

And a motley crowd was oftentimes collected within its portals.

It was a house bearing an ill repute was the "Devil's Punch-Bowl."

A house that was watched by the Bow-street runners and others, but which it was dangerous to enter unless known.

It was a house known and feared by the myrmidons of the law.

Feared as a den of crime.

In which had been committed vile deeds of horror and violence.

Men had been seen to enter that house who had never emerged from its doors again.

Frequented by seamen, labourers of doubtful character, Lascars, Africans, river pirates, and others. It was a place well avoided by those who had anything to lose.

Amongst other things, the landlord of the "Devil's Punch-Bowl" combined the business of a fence or receiver of stolen goods.

Cracksmen and others visited the "Punch-Bowl" to dispose of their ill-gotten goods.

Joe Noggins drove a good roaring trade down the highway.

His public-house brought him a good income, though got by anything but honest measure.

But robbery and crime went on in the world of London a century ago as now; and so Joe Noggins flourished, and the "Devil's Punch-Bowl" drove a roaring trade.

It was on the night following the event upon the river when Eustace Maltravers was so hunted as to take safety in the river, that the three men, Bony, Nosy, and their companion, made their way down Ratcliffe-highway, and proceeding up a dark, murderous-looking lane or narrow street, at length stood before the door of the "Devil's Punch-Bowl."

"In yer goes, Viper; we'll follow arter," exclaimed Bony.

The three men, now pushing open the door, were presently in the bar of the public-house.

There was a rude assemblage—a motley crowd of fierce, savage-looking men.

Oaths, curses, and loud cries were strangely mingled.

For a few moments the three new visitors were unobserved.

A thick, heavy cloud of rank tobacco-smoke hung about the room, through which the single oil lamp behind the bar shone dim and indistinct.

It was a strange scene that in the bar of the "Devil's Punch-Bowl."

The hour was eleven.

A time when the frequenters mustered in strong force.

The oaths and execrations of the crowd, with the snatches of conversation held among them, told the calling of the London Night-Birds.

Two or three hands were held out to welcome the new arrivals.

"Ha! Bony, how are yer; thought yer was lagged; was told you'd collared a lifer (transported for life)!"

"No fear. Who told yer that?"

"Why, the Duffer."

"Then he told yer wrong."

Then, turning to the bar, and addressing a sleepy-headed, sullen-looking lad, who, with one eye kept blinking, owl-like, at the solitary oil lamp, the man, Bony, called for some drink.

"Now you Josephus, let's have a dash of brown (two glasses of gin and some porter)."

The fellow's companion, named by his comrades the Viper, meanwhile asked the lad if Joe Noggins was in?

"If so, Josephus, my beauty, just tell him as how I wants to see him wery pertickler," exclaimed the burly ruffian, the same at whose hands Eustace Maltravers had near twice lost his life the day before at the old house at Bankside, and at night upon the river.

"Do you and Nosy stay here, Bony, whilst I speak to the argler (purchaser of stolen goods)."

"What's the lay with Noggins, Viper?"

"A message from Captain Guy about them sparklers as he ain't yet collared the Stephen (money) for."

"What, the necklace?"

"The same."

"It will fetch a heap of canaries I should say, Viper."

"Ay, more nor old Noggins can stump up, I'm a thinking, although he's pretty well lined with the goldfinches."

"Does the captain think as Joe can tip the Stephen for the jewels?"

"Well, he asked me to sound him."

"As yer got the sparklers?"

"Yes. Guy knows me; besides, I daren't play no trick—the whole band would hunt me to the death," said the ruffian, returning the glance of his companion with a meaning look, as the other kept opening and shutting his hands, and gasping out the words—

"Viper, if we dared do it, we could bunk, and—and live in clover."

"Arn't to be done, Bony, nohow. But kious (softly), there's a sailor cove just come in, and I rather think as he's nobbling (listening), and here comes Joe. I'll be back in a minute, as we must be off on the crack afore twelve, and we've a good ten mile to go."

The ruffian, now beckoned behind the bar by the landlord, left his companions, who, finding the young sailor who had just entered inclined for conversation, unceremoniously thrust themselves into his company.

The result of this converse was that the young seaman, who had only the day before returned from a long voyage, was presently closeted with the two men in a large chamber at the back of the "Devil's Punch-Bowl," where, plied with drink, he promised soon to be quite oblivious of where he was or with whom.

The wretched young man was rapidly losing all consciousness under the effects of the deep libations, when the door of the chamber opened, admitting the form of the villain comrade of the two thieves, who were at the moment dexterously employed emptying the contents of the sailor's pockets into their own.

"Has yer sounded him?" exclaimed the Viper, with a cunning leer at his companions, as he pointed to the drunken sailor.

"All right, Viper; we've nicked (got) a turnip and trimmings (watch and seals), and a couple of flimsies, with half-a-dozen canaries, and if ye're ready, why, we'll bunk," exclaimed Bony, rising from his seat; then, followed by his companion, he left the table at which he had been seated, and exclaimed, "How about the necklace, Viper? Has Noggins offered the gilt for it?"

"He can't do anything. It's more than he cares for. He advises Guy to trip over to the continent; but curse me, if I wouldn't get summat for it in the long village, without going out on it. It is a rare article, arn't it, Bony? Makes one's eyes dance to look at it."

The ruffian here drew from his pocket the necklace of diamonds offered to Ralph Fairley, the money-lender of the Poultry, only a few days before.

It was, indeed, a rich and rare article of jewelry.

The stones glittered like stars in the thin rays of the oil-lamp that lighted up the chamber.

A thousand prismatic rays were thrown out by the large, sparkling diamonds.

The three villains were struck with awe at the sight of the costly jewels.

Weighing them in his hand, the Viper, with his comrades by his side, stood near the lamp that hung from the ceiling, gazing at the bright and glittering gems, lost in admiration at their size and beauty.

"Stunners."

"Beauties, and no flies."

"Sparklers of the first water."

"It were a lucky grab for Resurrection Bill and Abrahams, warn't it?"

"Yes; and has got them into favour with Captain Guy, who, cuss him, objects to snatchers, lowtobymen (footpads), long-shore prigs (river pirates), and such like, having the privileges of the band of the bonny Night-Hawks; howsumever, I advises another party. I've put it about, and by——," said the villain, with an oath, "ere another month is over, I'll be the captain of a band I'll call the Red Band, in which no one shall enter who arn't chived (stabbed) a cove, and made cold meat of his man. We'll be all red-handed, and we'll dare the Night-Hawks, these hightobymen, these knights of the road, and flash culls."

"Right you is, Viper. Resurrectioner will go in with yer."

"In course he will," echoed Nosy.

"Like a trivet."

"Down as a hammer."

"And no flies," exclaimed the ruffians, who gazed admiringly upon their superior in crime, Jem Vaughan, or Viper, as he was called.

And well the villain deserved the appellation, as the sequel will show.

Engrossed with the beauties of the diamond necklace, and conceiving the sailor who they had so daringly robbed to be unconscious of what passed, the three villains conversed aloud, nor noted the form of the seaman rise from beneath the table, and glare wildly round the room.

Some words falling from the mouth of the Viper had informed the sailor of all. Recovering suddenly from his drunken stupor, he now became aware that he was robbed and in the power of men capable of any crime. Incapable of calm reflection, the wretched man staggered to his feet and made for the door. Though not aware he was sober enough to leave the place, the sailor would have been allowed to escape had he not turned as he reached the door, and, beholding the diamond necklace in the hand of the Viper, darted forwards and seized him by the arm, exclaiming, in a thick, hoarse voice—

"Where, where, got you that necklace? Speak, you black-faced land-lubber, or, damme, I'll smash in your ugly figure-head." Wild fury replaced the drunken look upon the seaman's face. Some powerful emotion had, in a moment, completely sobered him.

"Let go yer hold, curse yer, or I'll knife yer."

"Villain, thief, murderer, where got you those diamonds? Tell me, or by the devil, your master, I'll down your house (knock you down), and smash in your face with the heel of my boot."

"Let go, I say."

"I'll hold on till I know the truth. That diamond necklace, when last I saw it, was in the hands of a man who I loved as my own brother. Nay, stand back, or curse me, if I don't let you have an inch of cold steel," said the determined man, as the other ruffians were about to dash upon him. "Stand back. If there were twenty of yer instead of three, Jack Marline arn't going to lower his colours. Now, you ugly, piratical hound, tell me where got you those diamonds? Speak, or, damme, I'll throttle you as I would a dog."

"Curses! Will you loose yer hold?"

"Give me the diamonds."

"Let go, I say."

"The diamonds, yer lubber."

"Knife him, Bony."

"Let him have it. Chive him."

"Slit his weazand."

"Knock out his brains."

"Down with him."

"Sleek the trap (lock the door)."

A fearful, desperate struggle now took place between the three ruffians and the brave sailor.

The Viper, suddenly writhing and twisting from the tenacious grip of the courageous tar, aided by his companions, had now grappled with and hurled the doomed man on the floor.

It was a terrible scene that followed.

Murder shone in the eyes of the three ruffians as they held the struggling sailor in their arms.

Fierce, dark looks of fury, of savage ferocity, lighted up their features as they lent over their victim.

Madly the victim fought to save that life which was doomed.

Passing a handkerchief round the neck of the struggling man, two of the murderers each seized an end in their hands, and, pulling with all their force, caused a strange gurgling sound to issue from the throat of the wretched sailor.

Kneeling upon the heaving chest of their victim, the Viper glanced, unmoved, upon the convulsed features of the dying man.

"Pull away, Bony," he ejaculated, with a horrible grin.

"Thugging is cursed easy, arn't it, Bony," exclaimed the wretch Nosy.

"And a devilish fine way of turning up your toes," echoed the Viper.

"Easy does it."

"Hold on."

"We'll soon make cold meat on him."

"He's getting blue on it."

"He'll soon be a kicker."

Convulsively the doomed man struggled in the hands of his murderers.

But the fiends held on, drawing, with savage ferocity, the fastening round the throat of their victim.

The face of the wretched sailor was now horrible to look upon.

Dark flecks of blood and foam darted from his mouth.

His tongue, a dull black, lolled out of his mouth streaming with blood, bitten completely through in dying agony.

The features, first of a crimson tint, turned to purple, then black and horrible.

The eyes stood right out of the head, looking as though about to start from their sockets.

A bubbling noise sounded in the victim's throat, succeeded by a stifled rattle. The legs were drawn up convulsively, then darted straight out. There was a sharp, convulsive jerk or shudder, then all was still.

Murder fell, and bloody work was over.

Still, horrible and ghastly, the corpse of the murdered man laid upon the floor.

A terrible, a fearful sight.

"He's done for."

"Dead as a doornail."

"Well, we were bound to make a stiff-'un on him."

"Or he'd have nosed about the necklace, safe as beans."

"And got us all topped, or sent to Botomy Bay."

"Safe as houses; but we warn't to be done."

"We've croaked him."

"He's a stiff-'un."

"And worth summat, if only for his ivories, which will fetch a couple of canaries (guineas)."

"Out with them, Bony," exclaimed the Viper, who, with his ruffian companions, had gazed cool and calm upon the horrible-looking corpse of the murdered man.

The wretch, Bony, now producing a couple of instruments he brought from a closet, knelt down, and with horrible coolness proceeded to extract the teeth of their victim.

In a few moments the hideous task was finished.

"The old spot for the stiff-'un, Viper," exclaimed the villain, rising to his feet.

"Ay, away with it! or Noggins will be here, and be down on us for some of the pewter (silver money)."

Going to the farther end of the room, the man, Bony, opened a door and disappeared down a dark passage. In a few moments he returned, and, seizing hold of the feet of the murdered man, exclaimed—

"Collar hold of his head, Nosy; it's all right; we'll be with you in a jiffy, Viper."

The two murderers, carrying the hideous corpse between them, entered the dark passage, at the end of which was a flight of stairs.

Descending these, the ruffians, with their horrible burthen, arrived at a large underground cellar that ran beneath the old house.

A strange, horrible odour hung about the place.

A musty, charnel-house effluvia.

The Viper, who had hastened after his companions in crime, had followed with a light, and now running forwards, opened a door in the corner of the cellar.

A door fastened by a long, rusty bolt.

With a creaking, grinding noise it revolved back on its hinges.

The horrible odour increased as the door was flung open.

"In with it, and let's begone," exclaimed the ruffian, Viper, holding up the light, which showed the recess to be a disused cesspool.

Laying down the dead body of their victim, the two villains entered the closet and removed three or four of the boards, which were unfastened and lifted up from the planks beneath.

A suffocating, horrible effluvia now rushed up from the black, yawning cavity.

Into the dark, hideous recess the murderers dragged their victim, and, with brutal oaths, hurled the disfigured corpse into the horrible pit.

There was a dull plash, as though the body had fallen into a thick, muddy stream; then all was still—awakened as the boards were replaced by a scratching sound, accompanied with strange, hideous screeches.

"They're at him!" exclaimed the Viper, with a grin of horrible meaning, as he left the hideous cellar, followed by his companions in crime.

An hour afterwards the three murderers were far away from the scene of their crime, driving through the town in a light cart till they arrived at Tyburn, from which place they made their way towards Harrow.

"Hadn't yer better have gone to the Mint and returned the sparklers to Guy afore yer came on this ere lay, Viper?" ejaculated Bony, as the vehicle in which himself and his comrades were seated rattled along down the Edgware-road, then all open country.

"It ain't no matter; he'll have it in the morning."

"Yes; but yer see, Viper, there's some bad characters about: we might be robbed, yer know."

A loud laugh here escaped the three ruffians.

"Does yer think we'll make much out of this lay, Viper?"

"Lots. Old Fairley's got heaps of swag."

"And he arn't at the Grange, yonder."

"No; the old bloak is in town."

"Good. Many slavies to tackle?"

"Three."

"Any animals about the crib?"

"Yes; a bloodhound. A fierce, savage brute."

"Whew!" exclaimed the other ruffians in a breath, as their companion gave them this intelligence.

"Why, Viper, it ain't no good going for to try to crack the crib."

"Yes."

"The devil! and tackle the dog?"

"Yes."

"Well, Viper, we gives in to you, I and Nosy, in course; though, curse me, if I see how the job's to be done."

"Easily. Jem Vaughan knows his game."

"Doesn't doubt yer in the least, Viper."

"What does yer intend to do?" said Nosy, vigorously puffing at a clay pipe, sending clouds of thin blue smoke into the night air.

"Why, in course I arn't come without a doctor (a piece of poisoned meat)."

"But does yer think the brute will collar?"

"In course; what dog wont?"

"And I sposes, Viper, that we needn't be partickler as to any bloak what interferes with us in the course of our business?"

"Not at all. You've got your barking irons, Bony?"

"Right and tight."

"And you, Nosy?"

" I'm all lively, Viper; I've my old pal the sticker."

" Then we can't fail to carry out the crack, and collar the swag; which I tell yer I were put up to by Captain Guy, who has got a mortal grudge agin old Fairley. Howsomever, here we is in the Harrow-road, not far from the 'Bold Horseman,' the roadside inn, kept by old George Watson, what were once on the hightoby lay. We'll call upon the old man, and get a nip of summat, for curse me, if it ain't cold."

The vehicle driven by the murderers, who, in their calling, combined body-snatching, river-piracies, and burglary, now entered a dark, narrow lane, lined on each side with thick, heavy copse.

This lane, turning off the high road, was taken by the midnight marauders to avoid a passing patrol, whom they observed as they drew near the turning, driving down the lonesome dark lane. The cart made but slow progress.

" Where does this ere place lead to, Viper? Yer knows the road, I don't," said Bony.

" It'll come out agin at the back of the 'Bold Horseman,' a few minutes' ride from the high road, Bony. But, hist! kious! what the —— is that in the copse?" exclaimed the ruffian, with a fierce oath. The vehicle was now stopped, and the villains, getting out of the cart, darted to the place where a moment before they had all discerned a dark figure stealing along by the thick woods.

" It warn't a patrol, Viper, were it?"

" No, Bony; but, by the fiends, we are watched."

" Oliver's lighting up; cussed if the lag won't be queered."

A thin ray of blue light now poured down into the lane. The moon emerging from the heavy clouds that had before enwrapped it.

The bright silvery light shone full upon the copse; whilst the hoar frost upon the bushes and trees glittered like silver in the pale blue rays.

For some minutes the companions in crime walked along the edge of the copse, peering into the thick-set hedges and wild woods.

But nought could they discover.

All was thick black darkness in the heavy copse.

" It's no go, if it were anyone, they have slung their hook (gone) into the cart with yer, Bony."

The three villains now returned to the vehicle, but all three started back with a curse as they beheld a tall figure standing by the horse's head, fully discernible in the blue, silvery rays of the moon.

A low laugh fell upon their ears.

The villains, with fury, gazed at the dark figure before them.

A man, shrouded with a black cloak, and with a cap pulled over his brow, so that his features were not discernible.

" How are you, gentlemen? Delightful night for a ride, is it not? Lady Blue shines out, and throws a silver radiance on the scene."

" Damn! enough of this. Upon him, Bony."

" Stay! Stand back, my friends, unless you wish to have a leaden pill in your bodies, which you will find rather hard of digestion."

" Curses, who are yer?" shouted the Viper.

" Your humble and obedient servant. By-the-bye, gentlemen, it's a rude question, but how are you off for cash?"

About to rush upon the stranger, the villains drew back, as, perceiving their intention, he pulled from his pocket a brace of pistols, and, cocking them, presented them at the heads of the three men.

" Don't disturb yourselves, gentlemen; don't get excited; it's a bad habit; it spoils the equanimity of the temper."

" Curses on him! Never mind his barking irons, but on to him, Bony."

" Bony had much better remain where he is. I have a steady eye, and am a sure aim. I've sighted yourself and friend, Bony, and my bullets will crash just between the eyes into your skulls. But there's no occasion for this. I only require the diamond necklace you have so carefully stowed away in your pocket. I mean the article you showed to Joe Noggins at the 'Devil's Punch-Bowl,' in Ratcliffe-highway, an hour or two back."

" Fiends and furies, who, what are you?"

" Ha! ha! ha! Would you know? Well, then, hark ye, I'm a knight of the road, and, by the devil, your master,

if you don't tip over that jewelled necklace, I'll place a couple of slugs in your veins."

The stranger stood erect by the horse's head levelling his pistols at the enraged and astounded villains.

The Viper, making a step forward, exclaimed—

" If you're a knight of the road and hightoby man, then we are pals."

" Not so, lad; I don't consort with padders, snatchers, murderers, area-sneaks, or buzmen."

" Curses!"

" You are all these; whilst I'm a knight of the road. I've only just come up to London. Dropped in at the 'Devil's Punch-Bowl;' heard about the diamond necklace; swore it should be mine; and, damn me, I'll keep my oath."

" We are three to one, though our barking irons arn't loaded. We can beat yer in a tussle, but we don't want to injure a pal," exclaimed the Viper.

There was a look about the eyes of the stranger that made the ruffian qail at the idea of an encounter.

" If you are a hightobyman, you have heard of the Night-Hawks of London," added the villain. We are members of the band."

" The diamond necklace which I have about me is the property of our chief, and could yer drag it from me, why, curse yer, it would cause yer to be hunted to the death."

" Well, I'll chance that; hand it over."

" The patrol are upon us, fly!" shouted the Viper, glancing behind the stranger. The ruse succeeded.

The highwayman turned his head.

There was a loud cry of triumph, and the three ruffians bounded upon him.

There was a fierce struggle in the dark lane.

Loud oaths and curses rung upon the air.

Deep-breathed execrations.

Wild shouts of rage and fury.

A loud report rung upon the night air.

With a yell of pain, the ruffian Nosy staggered back, his countenance smothered in blood.

It was a desperate struggle that took place in that dark lane near the Harrow-road.

A struggle of life or death!

" I've got him now, Bony. Give us yer knife, I'll soon chive him!"

" That's the hammer, Viper. Let him have it in his bread-basket!"

Powerless the stranger laid before his foes, his foot entangled in the fallen reins of the horse. He had stumbled, and was thrown at the very feet of his antagonists.

With a cool, devilish look of ferocity, the ruffian, Bony, opened a huge clasp-knife, the broad blade of which glistened in the moonlight. With a dark, murderous gaze he handed the weapon to his companion, who was kneeling upon the chest of the stranger.

With a chuckle, the villain clasped the knife.

Hissing between his teeth, "Will yer have the sparklers, my beauty, or shall I make cold meat on yer?"

The villain paused, and brandished the glittering blade of the knife before the eyes of the helpless man beneath him.

The delay lost him the advantage he had gained; for, unexpectedly rising upon his knees, with a terrific exertion of strength, the stranger hurled the wretch off, and, starting to his feet, was about to dash once more upon the two ruffians, when he was seized from behind by the wounded wretch who had been shot in the beginning of the struggle.

The stranger's fate seemed sealed.

The villain, Bony, knife in hand, rushed forwards; whilst the Viper, cocking a pistol he had just loaded, presented it at the head of their foe.

A stunning report rang upon the air, accompanied by a cry of fury from the lips of the foiled villain, the Viper, whose arm, as he raised the deadly weapon, was knocked violently upwards, the bullet from the pistol burying itself, not in the head of the stranger, as intended, but in the trunk of a blighted oak that stood at the edge of the copse.

A wild shout followed the report of the pistol, and the sounds of a renewed struggle, accompanied with horrid oaths and curses of rage.

In a few moments the struggle ceased.

The knight of the road, and his preserver, who had

THE DARK DEED IN THE CHURCHYARD—THE SECRET WITNESS.

dashed up the lane in time to turn the pistol of the Viper from its intended object, stood side by side, while the discomfited ruffians belonging to the cart were lying upon the grass at their feet, bleeding and panting from exhaustion in the fierce conflict.

"So, then," ejaculated the highwayman, stepping forwards, and bending over the senseless form of the Viper, from whose person he took the coveted necklace of diamonds; "so, my rumcull, the baubles are mine. You're tricked and sold. The trump card was in your hand, idiot, when your knife was at my throat; but you held it back, and lost the game."

Turning round, the stranger now addressed the newcomer, adding, "To you, sir, I owe my life. This diamond necklace is worthy the dower of an Indian princess. We will fairly halve the sum I may be enabled to procure for it, as without your timely aid I had ere now been a bleeding corpse upon the earth at our feet."

The Viper, returning to consciousness, glared wildly round him. Stunned by a blow from the butt of a pistol, given him by the young man who had rushed upon the scene as the highwayman was about to be destroyed, he had fallen, and for a few moments was oblivious of what passed, and now recovered to find himself and his companions defeated and helpless, and at the mercy of their foes.

Groans of pain and fury escaped the villain's lips.

Whilst a cry of astonishment burst from the young man who had saved the highwayman, as he beheld the face of the Viper in the bright blue rays of the moon.

"What, is it you! you murdering hound? Ha! ha! ha! Foiled again in a deed of blood, and mine the hand to stay you in your bloody purpose."

"A shout of fury escaped the lips of the Viper as he beheld, in the figure before him, Eustace Maltravers; he who had already twice eluded his vengeance.

Staggering to his feet, the ruffian, livid with rage, shook

his fist in the face of the young man, exclaiming, in a voice choking with rage—

"Look you, my swell, you are protected by Guy Essington, the leader of the Night-Hawks; but this shall not save you from my vengeance. You have procured the love of the girl who I vowed should be mine. For this I swear to pursue you to the death. You have twice escaped me, and for this I hate you with a hate that, curse ye, shall be satisfied alone with your death! I defy Guy Essington and all the band; and, I swear that they shall not save you from my revenge! You have triumphed to-night. Look to it, Eustace Maltravers, when next we meet, the cards may be in different hands, and I may hold the winning one; and you, too, my flash cull, you've bested me to-night. We shall meet again. When we do, beware the Viper's sting!" And muttering threats, the ruffian, followed by his companions, jumped into the cart, and, giving the horse the reins, made from the spot, a loud shout of jeering laughter ringing in their ears from the mouths of their conquerors, who had allowed them to depart unmolested.

"Well, we've routed the enemy, and have the field," ejaculated the highwayman.

"And you hold the spoils, do you not?" exclaimed Maltravers.

"Ha! ha! ha! Yes, and the buzman knows not yet of his loss," said the other, with a shout of laughter.

"The hound! 'tis not the first time we have met; and, had I done aright, I should have planted a bullet in his villainous skull."

"Thanks to your timely arrival," exclaimed the stranger, "you prevented such a catastrophy happening to me. Another moment, and a leaden pill would have entered my brains from the pistol of the ruffian leader of that crew of housebreakers and busmen (pickpockets). However, my time arn't come yet; and, for the future, you may command me to the death for the services you have rendered me this night."

"Speak not of it," exclaimed Maltravers. "I know the ruffians from whom I rescued you; they are villains of the blackest dye."

"Well, I owe you many thanks for your timely aid, and I am one not ready to forget a service. May I ask to whom I am indebted?"

"I am a stranger in London, having only recently come from the country, and my name is Eustace Richard Maltravers, known by my friends as Dashing Dick; and you, my friend, I know not why, but I seem strangely inclined towards you. I have no friend with whom I can entrust my secrets, and whose companionship I might enjoy."

"Then," exclaimed the stranger, "let me, Eustace Maltravers, be that friend, and, as long as life lasts, a real and true one; ever ready to assist in distress or aid in the hour of danger, you will find Dick Turpin, the highwayman."

Holding out his hand, the man whom he had rescued from the ruffians who had attacked him so shortly before advanced to Maltravers, who met his new-found friend by clasping his hands in his, and vowing to retain his friendship while he lived.

"You have heard of me, doubtless, Maltravers, and my bonny Black Bess, whose neigh even now rings upon the air? I have left her at old Watson's, of the 'Bold Horseman,' within a few minutes' walk of this. Come, we will hasten thither, and, on the way, you can recount to me the incidents of your early life, and what you purpose in your future career, and, be assured, whate'er your path through life, Dick Turpin is your friend for ever."

"Thanks, Turpin. I will with you to the inn, and, perhaps, this very night you may join me in an enterprise of no little danger, in which we may again encounter the ruffians from whom I rescued you so short a time back."

"I am with you. Here we are, at the 'Bold Horseman,' and over some steaming grog, some of old Watson's best, you can tell me your errand, and command Dick Turpin, whose very life is at your service."

Having left the lane where the conflict had taken place, Turpin, followed by Eustace, had hurried on, till at length they stood opposite a roadside inn, that, standing alone, some hundred yards away from the high road, looked cozy and cheerful, with its thatched roof and diamond-paned casements.

A large, old-fashioned, but comfortable looking place was the roadside inn, called the "Bold Horseman."

In front of the inn was an old oak tree, that towered high above the pitched roof.

From one of the lower branches swung the sign of the inn.

A large, flaring, yellow board, with the figure of a man on horseback, with indifferently-written in red letters, in the day time might be read, "The Bold Horseman. G. Watson. Best entertainment for man and beast."

As Eustace and Turpin arrived opposite the inn, the sign swinging backwards and forwards, gave out a creaking, grinding noise, which sounded strangely melancholy in the night air.

Rapping loudly at the door of the inn, Turpin shouted out—

"What, ho! house! house! Watson! house, I say!"

"Who's there?" replied a voice, whilst a head, covered with a mysterious nightcap, was thrust out from a window above.

"Zounds, George, you old fool! don't you know me, man? Damme, it's Dick."

"What, Turpin! All right, my tulip. I'll be down in a twinkling, my flower." The head now disappeared. A moment afterwards there was the sound of bolts as they were withdrawn from their sockets, and the rattling of a chain, followed by a lock-creaking noise, as the door was opened, discovering the figure of George Watson, the innkeeper, who, wrapped up in sundry garments, thrown on in a hurry, looked mysterious and outré, as he stood in the passage of the inn holding up a lantern, in which sputtered and flickered a piece of candle.

"Why, Turpin, my boy! my flower! my daisy! my daffydowndilly! what's brought yer back?"

"Oh! a little affair, George, prevented me stopping in town to-night; and now, show us in the parlour and brew some brandy hot, for me and my pal here, Eustace Maltravers. It's all right, George, he's one of us."

"All right! One of us! Why, of course he is," said Watson, who had made his way into a large back room of the inn, which at that late hour boasted a blazing fire on the hearth, the huge wooden log upon the dogs sparkled and sputtered, and gave out a ruddy glare through the dark-wainscoted apartment.

"And so you are Eustace Maltravers. Glad to see yer; and don't forget, young sir, that George Watson, of the 'Bold Horseman,' is yer friend. I have heard of yer before, young gentleman, though we arn't met till to-night. Yet, I'm sure your uncle, Guy Essington, would not wish to see yer in better hands than ye're in now. You'll find Dick there, a real downright trump, true as steel, and no flincher in the hour of danger. A hightobyman and knight of the road, of whom you may be proud and glad to call a friend."

"Then you are acquainted with my uncle?" said Eustace, staring with surprise upon the landlord.

"Acquainted with Guy Essington, the bold leader of the Night-Hawks of London! I should say I and Guy could tell yer some queer tales. Oh! the moonlight canters over Hounslow Heath, and jolly Bagshot too. Ah! well, all's over now; but I can't help thinking of my younger days sometimes. Now, Turpin, my flower, there's the brandy, and there's sugar and lemon. Now brew for yourself, and don't shirk the liquor. I'll be sworn it won't taste with a less relish when I inform yer it's duty free."

Placing bottles and glasses on the table, the landlord was about to hurry from the room, but was called back by Turpin, who insisted that he should join himself and Eustace in a bumper. In a few minutes the loud shouts of laughter, and clattering of glasses, told that the party were in high glee.

Glass after glass of the spirits disappeared, and, under the influence of the drink, Eustace had nearly forgotten the purport of the errand that had brought him into the neighbourhood; when, laying his hand upon the shoulder of Turpin, he informed him that he must away, or else he might be too late to accomplish his project.

"Have with you, lad; business before pleasure. As I understood you we were likely to have a brush, I'll just hand the sparklers I eased our friend the Viper of, over to George here."

Turpin then drew from his pocket the diamond necklace, and handed it to the jolly host, who received the glittering gems with a shout of surprise.

"Why, damn it, Dick, where got you this?"

"From a buzman (pickpocket) I happened on at the

road at the 'Devil's Punch-Bowl' in Ratcliffe-highway. I thought it was too good a concern to be in the hands of such sneaks as that, so took the trouble to ease them of it; though I was nearly done up over the job."

"Why, Dick, my flower, this is the property of Guy Essington; whom, by-the-bye, I must introduce you to. What will yer do with the jewels?"

"Get you to return them to the owner, George. Dick Turpin arn't the lad to prey upon a pal. I've only just come to London. Don't yet know all the fraternity or the different kens; but my reputation's gone before me. There are a few of the lads that know Richard Palmer *alias* Dick Turpin. The jewels are worth a tidy screw; but if they were ten times the value, I would return them."

"Spoken like yer, Dick, my flower. But I shall not rest easy till I've made yer join the band of the Night-Hawks, which will shortly consist of nought but high-tobymen, knights of the road, and tip-top cracksmen. Zounds and the devil! What's that?"

George Watson bounded from his chair as though he had been shot, as a loud bang! bang! sounded at the door of the inn.

Bang! bang! bang!

Turpin calmly dived his hands in his pockets, pulling out a pair of pistols; glancing meaningly upon the landlord, he exclaimed—

"Philistines, George; or I am cursedly mistaken."

Bang! bang! bang!

The door of the old inn fairly shook again under the violent hammering made upon it.

Bang! bang! bang!

"Dick, my flower, they're no friends that knock like that at this hour."

"No, George, they are runners, safe as the bank."

"What's to be done?"

"There is only one way of escape."

"And that"—

"Is by the Old Mill."

"True; I had forgot. Tip us the lantern, George, old boy, I'll be off. Black Bess in No. 2?"

"Yes. You'll find her all right."

Bang! bang! bang!

A loud voice now shouted from without.

"Open, open, in the King's name!"

"Off yer go, Dick."

"Maltravers, we shall meet again; for the present, farewell. The summoners at the door are Bow-street runners, who have been after me the past fortnight. Fare-thee-well, and remember, from to-night, Dick Turpin is your friend for ever."

About to dash away, Turpin was restrained by Eustace, who exclaimed—

"You are in danger. I am my own master, of bold, determined spirit. I love peril, and can grapple with it when I meet it. We are friends, Turpin. My uncle, Essington, not many days since, pointed out the path I must follow. As knights of the road we will work together.

"As you will, Eustace, lad, follow me."

"Open the door, George, old boy, but parley with the varmints till we are underground."

"All right, Dick, my tulip!"

With a bound Turpin now dashed from the room, followed by Eustace, who had taken a liking to the highwayman, who was of a daring temperament, akin to his own.

The hammering at the door increased as the two friends left the room, making their way to the back of the house.

The loud shouts of the myrmidons of the law were heard high above the din by Turpin and his newly-found friend as they descended a steep flight of stairs leading to the lower part of the old inn.

CHAPTER XII.

THE STABLES OF THE "BOLD HORSEMAN."—NUMBER TWO.—BONNY BLACK BESS AND HER MASTER.—THE APPROACH OF THE RUNNERS.—THE SECRET PASSAGE UNDERGROUND.—THE STRANGE JOURNEY.—THE ARRIVAL AT THE OLD RUINED MILL.—SUDDEN APPEARANCE OF MAD WILL.

FOLLOWING his companion Turpin, Eustace Maltravers descended the steep flight of stairs that opened at the end of the passage that ran outside the parlour in which they had been closeted with Watson.

"Hold on, Eustace; take the glim."

Turpin handed to his young friend the lantern he had received from Watson when leaving the parlour.

Eustace, taking the light, held it up, whilst Turpin unfastened a door that was at the bottom of the stairs.

With some difficulty it was forced back, a rush of air smelling as though rising from a stable saluting them as the door was thrown open.

A loud neigh and whinnowing noise now sounded from the passage.

"It's Bess; she hears my footstep," exclaimed Turpin.

Taking the lantern from Eustace, after carefully closing the door, the highwayman led the way down a dark, narrow passage, till they arrived at three doors on their left, numbered respectively 1, 2, and 3.

"Let me see No. 2."

"Here we are."

Turpin, unlocking the door with a key he took from his pocket, entered a large stall of the stable, followed by Eustace, who glanced round in surprise.

At the further end of the vaulted, but comfortable stable, was a fine handsome mare, with a coat that shined and glistened in the rays of the lamp.

As the two friends entered the stall, a low whinnowing attested that the beautiful steed knew that her master was in the stable.

Turning her head, she with her fore feet pawed the ground, and struggled to free herself of the rope that confined her, in her eagerness to reach Turpin.

The bright, full, large eyes of the faithful beast were turned upon the figure of the highwayman, nor could aught divert her attention from him.

Of symmetrical form, with a finely arched neck, broad forehead, small ears, slender limbs, deep chest, and her skin shining like the nicest silk, a splendid creature was the highwayman's mare, Bonny Black Bess, and well did she deserve the encomiums of her master.

"My faithful beast, my own Bonny Black Bess! how is it with thee, my lass?"

Patting her on the neck, the highwayman laid his face against that of the horse, the dumb brute pawing the ground with pleasure, rubbing her nostrils over the face of her master.

Struck with admiration, Eustace stood silent, his gaze fixed upon the beautiful animal before him.

The intelligent brute seemed in ecstacies that her master, who had been absent some hours, had at length returned.

Forgetful of the cause that had brought them hither, Turpin was eulogizing his steed to his companion, when he was recalled to himself by the sound of voices at the end of the passage that led to the foot of the stairs.

"Find the key and open the door, Watson, or, damme, we'll slip the darbies on you as an accomplice. We knows our man is here, and we must have him, 'cos we wants him."

"Gentlemen, it's all a mistake. Me have a highwayman in my house! not if I know it."

"Come, come, Watson, that sort of thing don't wash with us. Open the door, I say, or we'll bust it open."

"Well, gents, as yer will. It's hard lines, though, knocking a man up out of his bed. Me have a highwayman hiding? Ha! ha! what a hidea."

Another loud shout of laughter sounded in the passage, as the landlord adopted this means of warning his friends.

Meanwhile Turpin, who had not been idle, to the surprise of Eustace, had opened a secret door behind the manger or rack where the corn was placed for the horses. Pressing his heel upon a knob in the floor, and pulling a ring that was hidden in the wall, the door slowly swung back, revealing a dark cavity beyond.

The voices of Watson and the runners were now heard in the passage without.

Muttering a few words to his horse, who, bending her head without hesitating, as if aware of what was required of her, at once entered the passage, Turpin bidding Eustace follow him with the lantern.

No sooner were they with the horse well out of the stable, than Turpin pushed-to the secret door, that closed with a very slight snapping noise.

Taking the lantern from Eustace, the highwayman, holding the reins of his sagacious steed tightly in hand, slowly proceeded down a steep incline, that led far down into the earth.

Eustace Maltravers, casting his eyes round, by the dim

rays of the lantern observed that they were now in a wide passage, but with roof so low that the horse was obliged to sink down her beautiful head as she walked.

It was evident that the underground pathway had been traversed before by the highwayman and his steed.

As they proceeded onwards the ground became soft and damp under their feet, whilst the voice of the runners and Watson grew indistinct and inaudible in the distance. It was a gloomy, dark passage, that underground causeway, and seemed interminable in length. At one time the roof was high above them; at another, so low that, had not the horse been the docile and sagacious animal that it was, it would have been impossible to have proceeded onwards.

Asking his companion the general way of entering and leaving the stables, Eustace was told that there was a door in No. 1 that led by a circuitous path to the yard at the back of the inn.

"But we are near the end of our journey now, Eustace," exclaimed Turpin.

They were now ascending a steep incline. Painfully and slowly the little party toiled up the hilly passage, till at length they arrived at a door similar to that which opened upon the stable at the inn, called No. 2.

Pushing back a pair of huge rusty bolts, Turpin, with a good word of encouragement to his steed, led her through the doorway, and, to the surprise of Eustace, he beheld the sky high above them, but appearing only in one round mass of a few feet in diameter.

They were at the bottom of a deep shaft.

The moon, riding high in the heavens, shone like a ball of silver, her thin blue rays darting down into the pit.

"How are we to get out of this?" said Eustace, with a laugh, to his companion.

"Easily; and I think you'll confess that this way of escape from the 'Bold Horseman' is as good a double as any you'll find in the oldest kens in or out of London."

"Hold on, now, my bonny Bess! Steady, girl; steady, my lass!"

Bidding Eustace follow him, Turpin guided his mare to the end of the pit or shaft, and, stooping down, they made their way into another passage, and anon were scrambling up another steep incline.

As they pursued their way, the wind blew in biting chill gusts in their faces, making its way through an opening near, by which entered a thin ray of light.

Arriving at the end of the passage, Eustace observed that the place of exit was covered by a mass of brambles. These, however, Turpin quickly pushed his way through, and the little party presently stood once more in the open air.

They were in the centre of a little hollow that had once been a mill stream.

But all was now dried up. Brambles and wild plants grew in profusion.

It was a melancholy-looking place.

Before them the old mill reared its ruin, looking sad and dismal in the blue spectral rays of the moon.

The old wheel that had once worked the mill still remained, but fast rotting and falling to decay; brambles and wild tendrils clung to the intricacies of the ruined woodwork.

Leading his horse up out of the dried-up mill-stream by means of a rude bridge that, overturned, had once led into the mill, Turpin and his companion reached the open ground.

A quarter of a mile off, in the bright moonlight, Eustace discerned a house standing alone; overtopping the roof he beheld the branches of a giant oak.

"That building is the 'Bold Horseman,'" said Turpin, as he observed his companion's eyes fixed upon it.

"I thought so, Dick. Well, this is certainly one way of getting out of danger and fogging the Philistines. But what do you propose now?"

"To enter the old mill for a quarter of an hour. Let my foes get well away before I venture any further."

"As you will; but where will you put the mare whilst you go with me?"

"Where is your destination? How far from here?"

"Oh! half an hour's walk."

"The place?"

"The Hemlock Manor House."

"The Hemlock Manor House; why, that's the residence of old Ralph Fairley, the miser."

"Zounds, Eustace, lad, are you going to crack the crib?"

"No, but others are."

"What mean you?"

"You remember the ruffians who attacked you in the dark lane?"

"I guess I don't intend to forget them awhile."

"Well, these men are going to break into Hemlock Manor House to-night."

"The devil!"

"And I!"

"And you intend to spoil sport by trying to be beforehand with them? Not a bad lay. And it's for this you require my services? As you will, lad, though in-door business is rather out of my line. I prefer a dark night, an open heath, a stage coach, and stand and deliver."

"You mistake me, Turpin! burglary is not my object."

"The devil it ain't! Why, damn me, you arn't going to carry off old Fairley, are yer?"

"No; but I wish to prevent harm to the old man or his child."

"His child? Ah! yes, I see—a daughter, of course."

"Well, yes."

"Hum! Take care, Eustace; beware the petticoats; they are brittle ware."

"The miser's daughter is a lovely young girl, I am told."

"The devil! what, haven't you seen her? Why, damme, lad, this is the very romance of love."

"I have not seen her, Turpin; but I've heard my uncle speak of her in terms of the highest praise for her beauty and her goodness of heart. Guy Essington owes a deadly enmity to old Fairley. I heard that a burglary was to take place at Hemlock Manor. I found that old Ralph Fairley and his daughter had left only to-day for the Manor. I knew the ruffians who were going to break into the house, and I determined to save the miser's daughter, for whom, strange as it may appear to you, I feel drawn by some irresistible impulse. Laugh, jeer me as you will, I have told you all. I intend to visit the Manor, though I peril my life in so doing."

"Well, lad, you know best; I'll not be one to dissaude you from your purpose. From to-night I'm your sworn pal. Dick Turpin is yours till he's lagged or topped (hanged); only Tyburn Tree shall part us; but, if you intend to visit the Manor, we had best begone; time passes. Come, I'll leave Bess in the mill till our return; she'll be safe enough."

"But, suppose anyone happened to pass and enter the old mill?"

"Never fear, Bess can take care of herself. Though so tame with me, she can show her temper to others. Besides, the old water mill is haunted; 'tis avoided by all after dark."

"Well it looks, I confess, a dark old ghostly ruin," said Eustace, glancing at the decaying structure, that reared itself up in the bright moonlight.

A dark object at that moment circled round and round the summit of the old ruin, causing Eustace to start and draw nearer to his companion, who laughed loudly at his alarm.

The creature that had startled our hero was a huge bat, that, with leathern wing and unsightly form, appeared whirling and circling in the air.

Leading his horse to the back of the mill, Turpin passed with her through a large opening that had once been a door.

And now the two friends stood in the silent old ruin.

It was a ghastly structure was that old mill.

A shudder darted through the frame of Eustace as he stood beneath the dismantled roof.

The thin, pale rays of the blue luminary above darted in between the interstices of the old, rotting woodwork of the mill.

A large white owl flapped its wings and hooted in the faces of the two friends as they entered the place.

Leaving his mare, muttering a few words by which the sagacious animal was made aware she was to remain for awhile, Dick, followed by Eustace, made for the opening by which they had entered the ruin, and was about to leave the place, when such a piercing shriek, or yell, rang upon the night air, that the companions drew back in alarm.

"Curses, what is that?" said Turpin.

"'Twas like the yell of some incarnate fiend," ejaculated Eustace, who shuddered as he remembered the story Turpin had told him as to the old mill being haunted.

"Damnation, we're beset to-night!" said the highwayman, with a curse, as again the horrible yell or shriek of laughter rang on the night air.

"Let us leave the place at once, Turpin."

"Hold on, lad; I arn't to be done this night by a trick of my foes. But, stay. God of heaven! Look at that, Eustace!" The bold, daring highwayman drew back into the mill, as he shudderingly pointed out to his companion a gaunt, giant-like human form standing in the moonlight without.

Of gigantic proportions was the strange, weird-looking figure, that, motionless and erect, stood in the broad, pale, blue rays of the moon.

Again came the horrible, startling yell upon the night air.

Turpin pulled a pistol from his pocket, placing it on half cock.

"I don't want to hurt you, my friend; but, if you go on like that, I shall certainly quiet yer with a leaden pill you won't find easy of digestion."

The blood of Eustace Maltravers, though we have seen he was a bold, daring young man, curdled, and grew icy cold as that maniac yell sounded again in his ears.

Turpin, with a curse, raising his pistol, prepared to leave the mill, followed by his companion.

In another moment they emerged from the ruin.

Their appearance was the signal for another wild shout of maniac laughter.

"Curses on him! Be he man or devil, I'll fire."

The weapon was raised as the huge gaunt form darted forwards, but the arm of Dick Turpin was held back, as a young man who had, unseen, approached the spot, exclaimed—

"Nay, don't fire, Mr. Turpin; he won't do any harm; it's only poor Mad Will."

Turning round with a start, Eustace stared in surprise upon the person of the new comer.

"What, Hugh, lad, is it you? What's the news?"

"The runners have gone, cursing and swearing like blazes. Ha! ha! ha! Father can double on 'em. Oh! you and he be 'cute fellows. Cuss me if I wouldn't like to turn highwayman, if it was only to torment the damned Bow-street runners. The devil seize them!"

"Well, Hugh, lad, since the coast is clear, take my bonny mare back to the inn till I return. And now, Eustace, have with you, and hey for cracking a crib and the miser's daughter."

Hugh Watson, bringing the mare out of the inn, was about to depart, and the two friends were on the point of wending towards Hemlock Manor, the roof of which could just be discerned in the moonlight, some half mile off, when they were stayed by the ungainly spectral form of the idiot, who, bounding forwards, peered into the faces of Eustace and Turpin, and, giving utterance to another of his hideous yells, exclaimed—

"Ha! ha! ha! Whither would you go? Leave not the old mill. Will-o'-the-Wisp bids you stay. There is danger abroad. A dark cloud passed the moon's disk an hour back. It was spotted with specks of blood. There is murder in the air—grim murder! Look not thus amazed. I know; I know. You cannot deceive Will-o'-the-Wisp. Ha! ha! ha! You are young, bold, but go not hence, unless you wish for death—ha! ha! ha!—unless you wish for death."

Then, with another wild yell, the gaunt figure of the maniac bounded from the spot, and, in a few moments, was lost to sight in the distance.

"A handsome young gentleman, I must confess. However, his prophetic warnings won't deter such men as you or I, Maltravers; so let us away. And now, Eustace, ho! for the Hemlock Manor House and the beautiful Sybil Fairley."

Hurrying from the mill, the two friends made for the highroad, and, at the end of half a mile, halted at the corner of a country lane that, bordered on each side with a row of wych elms, looked drear and gloomy in the wintry night.

"At the bottom of this lane is the Hemlock Manor House," said Turpin. "Have you your barking-irons all right?"

"I have."

"Then let us on."

The two friends proceeded cautiously down the lane till, at length, when near the end, each paused, and gazed, first at a dark object drawn up at the side of the road, and then at each other.

"They are here, then."

"Well, I reckon we'll spoil their sport. I should have fancied they had had enough of it for one night. Why, damn it, lad, they have collared some of the swag and gone back for more."

Turpin had looked in at the back of the little cart that had attracted their notice as they arrived at the end of the lane, and, with a grin, pulled out a sack, which, on being opened, proved to be half full of silver plate.

Eustace, scarce noting what his companion said, hurried on, whilst Turpin, with an oath, exclaimed—

"Well, as I am in for cracking a crib, damn me, I'll have this pewter for my pains, and serve out my sweet friends, who, in that cursed lane, would have chived (stabbed) me like a sheep in a slaughter-house."

With a low laugh, Turpin, seizing the sack, hurled it with the contents into a thicket of hawthorn and brambles that grew by the wayside; then, hurrying from the spot, reached Eustace Maltravers as he had, after passing through the grounds, halted in the front of Hemlock Manor House.

The unclosed shutters of a large bay window pointed out the way by which the burglars had entered the house.

Silently and cautiously Eustace and his companion made their way to the window.

One half of which they now discovered was open.

"Well, it seems they're determined to get plenty of the loble (plate) while they are about it. How they'll stare when they get back to the rumbler (cart) and find the swag has gone; but in with you, Eustace, and let us finish the job."

Scarce waiting to hear his friend out, Maltravers had forced his way through the casement.

Following him in, Turpin stood by the side of the young man, listening breathlessly for the sound of an alarm.

But all was quiet in the old Manor House.

Not a sound could be heard.

"Curse them, what are they after?" exclaimed Turpin, who, with Eustace, approached the door of the apartment that opened out into the hall.

Groping their way blindly forward, for all was pitchy darkness, the two friends passed out of the parlour into the hall; from thence they made their way up a flight of stairs. All was quiet—still as death—in the old house.

Groping his way forwards, Eustace, who could not discern his hand before him, so pitchy dark was all around, was suddenly startled by a cold hand being laid on his, whilst a voice close behind him exclaimed—

"Bony, does yer think the swag safe in the lane? Sposes a trap (constable) or patrol passes, we should be caught like rats in a cage. Hell devils! vot is the Viper arter? Let us enter the gal's room arter him, and tell him we're tired of vaiting on the ladder (staircase) vile he collars the swag."

Drawing his breath short and thick, Eustace Maltravers followed noiselessly by the side of the burglar, leading him to suppose it was his comrade he had addressed; but where was Turpin? he asked himself, as, with the ruffian by his side, he passed through a door on the right, leading into a large and lofty bed-chamber.

A faint ray of light played upon the floor in the middle of the room.

It was the dull glimmer from a dark lantern.

Two dark, shadowy forms appeared kneeling on the ground.

Eustace felt the hand of the ruffian by his side tighten on his arm, whilst a deep-breathed curse escaped his lips, causing the two burglars before him to start to their feet.

"Dowse the glim, Viper! The game's up. Collar the swag, and let us away."

About to dash to the door, the ruffians started back, as they beheld the form of Eustace Maltravers, who a moment afterwards was struggling in the grasp of the burglar by his side.

"Trip him up, Nosy!"

"Sleek the gate (shut the door), and let us be off."

"Give him one! That's the ticket!"

There was a momentary struggle. Eustace was then

thrown to the ground. There was a loud cry of murder from some occupant in the bed that stood in the corner of the chamber. Then the ruffians bounded from the room, and a few minutes afterwards loud shrieks were heard in another part of Hemlock Manor House.

'Twas the cry of women in dire distress.

With mad fury, Eustace, only for a few seconds stunned by the fall he had received, now staggered up to his feet, and darted from the room.

Shriek followed shriek in rapid succession.

Arriving at the door from whence the sounds proceeded, Eustace found it locked.

At the bottom of the stairs was his companion, Dick Turpin, in fierce conflict with one of the ruffians, who kept him from rushing up to join his friend. Armed with a formidable crowbar, the ruffian kept the highwayman at bay.

Loud oaths, shrieks, and cries of murder echoed through the house.

The dull clang of an alarm bell sounded in the air.

The inmates of the house were thoroughly aroused.

Cries of servants were now heard.

Loud shrieks for help rung on the night air.

Again the shrill cries of frightened women sounded through the house.

With a fierce oath, Eustace darted a few paces back.

Then with all his force dashed himself against the door.

Locked from within, the strong oaken structure remained fast on its hinges.

It would not give way.

Again and again, Eustace dashed himself at the doorway.

While the shrill screams from the chamber rung through the house.

Dick Turpin now bounded up the stairs, for the moment having disarmed the ruffian with whom he had been in conflict.

Seizing the iron bar that had been wielded by the burglar, Turpin joined his companion above.

With a blow he sent the heavy weapon crashing against the strong oak door.

For a moment it withstood the attack.

But when again brought down with fearful violence, the iron bar crashed against one of the panels and splintered it to pieces, the door flew open.

Eustace, with a loud cry, dashed in, leaving Turpin engaged with a ruffian without.

On entering the chamber, two young girls darted from the arms of the two midnight marauders, the Viper and Bony, who had held them in their grasp, and rushed to Eustace for protection.

There was something about the young man's appearance told them the stranger was a friend.

"Upon him! It's the flash cove, Maltravers."

"Let's have his blood."

"By the powers of darkness, you don't escape us now, lad!" exclaimed the Viper, darting forwards with upraised knife.

The two young girls, cowering behind Eustace, shrieked with affright as the ruffian made a step forwards to their protector.

Wild shouts of conflict sounded from without.

With a smile of defiance, Eustace coolly pulled a pistol from his pocket, and pointed it at the ruffians before him.

"Don't be alarmed, ladies. Now then, my friends of the society of ugly mugs, perhaps you will, without ceremony, take your leave. I should be very sorry to have to quicken you with two bullets from these barking-irons of mine; but if you will compel me, why, I must oblige you."

"Curses!"

"Yes, just so; rather vexing, ain't it? Are you going, Viper, my beauty? I'll have to draw your sting before I've done with you." The ominous click of the pistol warned the burglars that in another moment Eustace would fire? Despite his careless manner, there was a lurking devil in his eye boded them danger.

"Once more it's your game, Eustace Maltravers; but I will yet show you the Viper can sting, sting yer to the death. I owe you a debt, and, curses on yer! I'll pay it."

"Don't trouble yourself; but, before you go, perhaps you'll take this for a keepsake." There was a loud report and a howl of pain, as the two ruffians dashed out of the room through the door, and, falling in the arms of Dick Turpin, who had for ever ended the career of their com-

rade, Nosy, by breaking in his skull with the iron bar, they were aided in their descent of the stairs by a vigorous kick, savagely and heartily delivered by the enraged highwayman.

On entering the chamber, Turpin found the young girls at the feet of Eustace, with clasped hands and eyes bedewed with tears, thanking their preserver, who had rescued them from the ruffian burglars.

About to raise them to their feet, Eustace and Turpin started as a tall, well-built, hale old man made his way into the chamber. With a wild scream of joy, one of the young girls started up and threw herself in his arms, exclaiming, with hysterical sobs—

"Father! father!"

Eustace and Turpin drew back as the old man bent his keen gaze upon them.

Each guessed before whom they stood.

The old man was Ralph Fairley, the miser and money-lender.

CHAPTER XIII.

THE DOCTOR'S SHOP IN THE TOTTENHAM-COURT ROAD.—THE EARLY MORNING.—THE SUMMONS AT THE NIGHT-BELL.—THE MYSTERIOUS LOAD.—THE HORRORS OF THE DISSECTING-ROOM.—THE RETURN TO LIFE.—TERROR AND FLIGHT OF THE DEAD ALIVE.

MANY years ago there stood a little tumble-down, dirty, dilapidated doctor's shop near the Oxford-street end of the Tottenham Court-road.

The other end of this bustling thoroughfare was not then, as now, peopled with the residences of thriving tradesmen.

Kentish Town and the surrounding neighbourhood was all open fields.

Tottenham Court-road, one hundred years ago, was as unlike the present well-known spot as the new Mint-street in the Borough is to the old.

Time, and the master hand of improvement have made vast changes in our good city of London.

Our iron roads, our miles of rail, were at the time we are writing of unknown.

London and its environs have strangely altered since the last century.

A hundred years have made wonderful changes.

The environs of Hackney, Dalston, Islington, Camberwell, and others of our now thickly-populated environs, were all open fields at the time the incidents occurred which we are now relating.

Tottenham Court-road, as we have said, was far different then than now.

The shops, few and scattered, were all dirty and dilapidated.

The thoroughfare, long, straggling, with uneven roadway, and ill-lighted at night with but a few oil lamps, was a darksome, gloomy place.

At an early hour of the morning, when the resurrectionists hurried in alarm from the scene of their unhallowed task, a light cart drew up outside the shop of a Doctor Appleby, in the Tottenham Court-road.

Doctor Silas Appleby was well known in the neighbourhood.

By some he was called the mad doctor.

Devoted to his profession, he neglected all else to follow up his beloved pursuit of science.

A ruinous, seedy-looking habitation was that tenanted by Silas Appleby.

A dirty-looking, dingy green door was surmounted by a huge yellow pestle and mortar, with large letters written beneath, "Silas Appleby, Doctor of Medicine."

The mad doctor, as he was called, had a very extensive, though not very remunerative practice.

Exceedingly clever at his craft, he scarce ever asked for payment.

Possessed of a competency, he cared not for money.

He pursued his calling in mere love of science.

On the matter of science Silas Appleby was mad.

From morn to night Silas Appleby received visits from his numerous patients.

On arriving at the door of the mad doctor, Resurrection Bill and the Jew hastily alighted from the cart, and gave a vigorous summons at the night-bell.

A few moments only elapsed, when the sound of a falling chain and rattling of bolts was heard from within.

" It's all right, the doctor's up. Out with the stiff-'un, Ben."

With evident reluctance, the Jew, obeying his companion's orders, went to the vehicle, and drew from it a large sack containing their horrible spoil.

At the same moment the door of the doctor's shop opened, and the face of a middle-aged man appeared, peering into the darkness.

" Have you the subject ? " he exclaimed.

" Right and tight, Master Appleby."

" Managed without interruption ? "

" Leave me alone. I've done the job as I always does, neat and clean. Resurrection Bill, as you knows afore to-day, never bungles a snatch."

" You were not seen ? "

" Not we ! The parson's lodgings (graveyard) was silent and deserted. It were as fine a place for a snatch as ever I'd wish to be in."

" 'Tis well. Follow me."

Resurrection Bill, who, aided by the Jew, had conveyed the horrible load from the cart into the house, now proceeded after the doctor up a flight of stairs, whilst his companion hastily left the house, and departed with the horse and cart."

On reaching the summit of a steep staircase, Silas Appleby unlocked a door facing them, and, followed by the resurrection man, made his way into a gloomy-looking apartment. Closing the door, he bade his companion place his load upon a long table that stood in the centre of the chamber.

With a raven-like chuckle, the man obeyed, exclaiming—

" There yer are, doctor; and as fine a corpse it is as ever I seed in my life. She is a rale right down beauty. Cuss me, if she arn't as fine a stiff-'un as ever I've clapped eyes on, and I've unearthed a few. There, arn't she a stunner ? "

Ripping open the sack with a pair of scissors, the resurrection man exposed the corpse at length upon the table, casting an admiring eye upon the still, rigid, livid form.

With eager gaze the doctor bent forwards, and examined the body before him.

" A lovely girl," he murmured. " How calm and still she lies in her death-sleep ! "

" Yes, she is a perfect stunner," exclaimed the ruffian body-snatcher.

" She is beautiful, indeed," murmured the doctor.

" Ah ! she is so. A right down handsome subject as ever I seed."

For a few moments Silas Appleby kept his eyes fixed on the corpse, then, turning to his companion, exclaimed—

" Your task is done. Nought now remains but the payment of your work. Here is the sum I promised you. I would now be alone. Leave me."

" All right, doctor. I doesn't want to intrude; but, afore I goes, I wants to tell yer summat."

" Say on."

" Well, yer must know, when I was earthing up the body of that there young gal, thinking to bring it away, 'cos why I thought it were a shame to part 'em, I left Ben Abrahams, my pal, to shove her blessed corpse into the sack and convey it to the cart; but, hearing a cry from Ben, I jumps out of the grave, and, on looking at the stiff-'un, curse me if the peepers warn't wide open."

The resurrection man gazed round nervously, and shuddered as he looked at the pale, rigid form upon the table, and then at the hideous collection of skulls, bones, and surgical instruments gathered together in wild confusion in various parts of the room.

A smile wreathed the features of the surgeon.

" You imagined this. The unfortunate girl now lying so still and calm before us is dead. The breath of life hath left her frame, and nought but matter now remains. The soul, the spark of existence, has fled."

" Maybe so, doctor; in course you knows. Howsumever, I've got the rowdy, and I'll leave yer with the blessed corpse; and, when yer wants the services of yer humble and obedient servant, a note will always find me at the " Fox in the Hole," in the Mint, or the " Devil's Punch-Bowl," in Ratcliffe-highway. Good morning, Doctor Appleby ; you is a downright trump, you is," ejaculated the resurrectionist, weighing the gold given him by

the doctor; " and curse me if I won't always do a snatching job for you for half I'd charge anyone else ! "

With renewed rough thanks, and farewells, interspersed with original oaths, Resurrection Bill left Silas Appleby alone ; the jar of the door below giving note of his departure.

Silas Appleby, the mad doctor as he was called, was now alone.

Alone with the body of the unhappy girl, Bessie Templeton.

A strange scene was it.

That man, standing in that grim chamber, beside the table upon which rested the corpse.

The rays of an oil lamp, hanging from the ceiling, cast but a faint light through the apartment.

Strange shadows were cast around.

The skulls, lying in the corners of the room with heaps of bones, looked hideous and ghastly.

The wintry wind, sighing without, added to the grim horrors of that darksome chamber, the dissecting-room of Silas Appleby.

" Strange fate, unhappy girl, was thine. Doomed to die so young ! " murmured the doctor, as he bent over the corpse, and gazed fixedly upon the waxen features of the dead. " Beautiful she is, e'en in death. Found without life in a lone copse some distance from her father's farm. 'Twas supposed horror, a broken heart, and exposure to the winter weather had caused her death. In vain I begged to be allowed to open the inanimate corpse. I was refused. What might science gain by discoveries I might make ? What might it have lost had the body remained in the grave ? Determined to investigate the matter—to learn the cause of death—I called in the aid of the wretch who left me but now. Ha ! ha ! ha ! She is mine ! But to my task—to my task ! "

Silas Appleby now left the room, carefully closing the door.

Some few moments elapsed; then a low moan sounded through the apartment.

A low, stifled, gurgling moan.

As of one in extreme bodily pain.

A horrible scene now took place.

The lamp suddenly, with a bright flicker, flared up and then expired, enveloping all in darkness.

Save a dim, uncertain shadow of light from a small casement at the further end, all was thick darkness.

The strange, moaning noise now ceased, and Silas Appleby, returning, opened the door and entered the room.

" Confusion ! the lamp out ! The boy, then, has neglected to replenish it with oil, as I desired him to do ere he left. No matter; a wax taper stands in the closet. I cannot wait the light of morning for my task, but will at once to my purpose. 'Twas a strange, mysterious matter, this poor girl's death; and I have sworn to learn the secret, and I will." Stumbling across the dark chamber, the doctor passed the side of the bier on which rested the body he was about to anatomize.

Groping his way forwards, his hands suddenly seemed as though clasped by others formed of ice.

With a shudder, he drew back.

" The hands of the corpse," he muttered. " Her arm has fallen from off the table. It must be my imagination, but I could have sworn the ice-cold fingers of the corpse clasped mine in their chilling grasp."

Leaving the side of the bier, he now made for a closet, opening which, he took from a shelf a small hand-lamp in which was a waxen taper. By the aid of a flint and steel, he at length procured a light.

But the faint, thin rays from the little lamp served but to increase the gloom and horror of the apartment.

Turning from the closet, Silas Appleby made a step towards the bier in the middle of the room.

Holding above his head the taper, he, at first, did not behold a sight that, now as he drew near, caused a cold chill to dart through all his frame.

" Gracious heavens ! what, what is this ? " he gasped.

Rooted with horror to the spot, Silas Appleby remained, the lamp still retained in his shaking hand.

The thin, faint light shone upon a strange, wild scene.

Sitting half up, on the table, was the body of Bessie Templeton, her long, fair hair hanging in showers down to her waist.

The face, a livid white, was turned full upon the surgeon.

The eyes seemed to dart fire as they were fixed upon him.

A strange moaning noise fell from the lips of the living, corpse-like figure.

About to dart forwards, Silas Appleby was withheld from his purpose by such a dreadful, fearful shriek of agony and horror pealing through the chamber, that it froze the life-blood in his veins to hear.

With a cry, he drew back, letting the lamp fall from his nerveless grasp; then, as a loud crash sounded close beside him, accompanied by another wild shriek, he dashed forwards.

But as he made his way to the door of the room a dark shadow rushed past him, whilst such another yell rung in his ears that he staggered back, struck with horror and alarm.

For a few moments he lost all consciousness.

On recovering his dazed senses, he once more procured a light.

Casting his eyes round, he beheld the table overturned and the door of the room wide open, whilst the body of the young girl was gone.

Dashing out of the apartment, he made his way below.

The house, a small one, was searched through in a few moments.

Silas Appleby at length returned to the dissecting-room.

A wild, unsettled look upon his brow.

"I never thought of this. I suspected foul play. I thought poison might have hurried the young girl to her grave; but I now see it all. She was not dead; she was but in a trance. My love of science, that urged upon me to find out the cause of death, has, on this occasion, led me to rescue the living from the grave of the dead. How wonderful and inscrutable are the ways of Providence! Through me has the living been rescued from death. But I must hence, and learn whither the frantic creature has bent her steps, or even now may she perish."

The gray light of morning was stealing over all, as Silas Appleby hurriedly left his house in pursuit of her who had so strangely returned to life, and who, awakening from her death-sleep, in maddening horror had flown from the spot.

CHAPTER XIV.

THE CEDARS, KENSINGTON.—THE OCCUPANT OF THE WALNUT-WOOD CHAMBER.—RECOLLECTIONS OF A NIGHT OF HORROR.—VISIONS OF THE PAST.—TERROR AND MADNESS.—DESPAIR OF THE VICTIM OF FATE.—CAPTAIN LESLIE AND THE FAIR STRANGER.—THE MEETING.—THE RECOGNITION.—THE CURSE OF THE BETRAYED.

THE Cedars was an old, red, brick-built house, with a little square, turretted clock-tower on the roof.

Large gardens were at the back and front of the Cedars.

Standing some little way from the high road the roof of the house could be just discerned amid the branches of the trees that surrounded the building.

Ivy grew, in wild luxuriance, up the walls of the tenement, trailing and clinging round and about the little clock tower.

It was a pretty, romantic, rural retreat, was the Cedars.

Standing some half mile from any other residence, it looked a sweet, cozy, retired habitation.

Even in the winter time of year everything about the Cedars bore a pleasant aspect.

The cheerful, ruddy glow of huge fires could be discerned through the diamond-paned casements, some of which, consisting of coloured glass, looked bright and beautiful in the rays of the sun, or the flash of the fires within.

It is early morning; the sun, with cold, wintry glare, darts his rays upon the roof of the Cedars and the trees and shrubberies around, glittering with pretty effect upon the veil of hoar-frost that rests on everything around.

The robins twitter merrily in the morning air, circling round the ivied tower, and anon swooping down to flutter in and out of the brushwood below.

Eight o'clock has just chimed out from the bell of the Cedars.

The sun, like a ball of burnished copper, rises high in the east, gilding the frost-laden scenery with beautiful effect.

Though 'tis the winter time of year, all is bright and joyous round and about the villa known as the Cedars.

A flood of light darts through a casement at the back of the house, pouring its rays full into this upper chamber. The sun gilds everything in its mellow lustre. It is a richly furnished apartment, that upper room in the Cedars.

The blinds, drawn back, allow the orb of day to pour his rays through the glass full into the chamber.

Everything in and about the chamber bespeaks the wealth of those who own the Cedars.

The back room, through the casement of which the sun stole that winter morning, was fitted up with lavish richness.

In one corner of the chamber was a beautiful, highly-polished walnut-wood couch, filigreed with gold; the hangings of dark brown satin, were trimmed with gold lace; the quilt of the couch, of dark brown velvet, also being laced with gold. All the furniture in the bed-chamber was of the same costly material, whilst the wainscot reached high up round the room; the walnut-wood so richly polished that it glistened in the rays of the sun. Soft Turkey carpets lined the floors, while on the walls hung several fine oil-paintings. Statuettes and articles of rarity and beauty, in porcelain and ivory, stood upon the tables and the mantelpieces.

It was as the clock was giving out the half hour after eight, that a slumberer in the gaudy bed-chamber of the Cedars stirred upon the couch; and anon a white hand drew back the curtains. The jingling of the rings connected with the hangings seemed to startle the occupant of the bed, who, uttering an exclamation of alarm, sank back.

The sun now poured a flood of light upon the couch.

A young and lovely girl, lying in the bed, glared round the room, and then at the casement, through which stole the rays of the sun.

Beautiful, too beautiful, was that young girl; like a bright, lovely seraph of the other world she looked as she reclined at length upon that rich couch.

A round, white, and polished arm, soft and plump, rested on the coverlid. The snow-white sheets seemed dark beside the lovely neck of the beautiful girl; her round, white, and heaving bust rivalling in shade the Parian marble. Beautiful features did the young girl possess; but pale, livid pale, were they. Wildly she looked about, as she now rose up in the bed. Whilst drawing her soft white hand across her brow, she glared round the apartment, low murmured ejaculations escaping her lips.

"'Tis all then a dream; but, oh! how terrible! how like reality! My brain turns to madness when I recal the past. Where, where am I, too? This chamber—I remember it not." At this moment the occupant of the bed was startled by the opening of the door. A slight scream escaped her lips; but, on perceiving only the form of a female, she gasped out, at the same time clutching the hand of the visitor, who had approached the bed—"Tell me, tell me, where, where I am! I know you not. I recollect nought but my hideous, terrible dream."

"Nay, my dear child, give not way to your terror thus. All is well. You are in good hands."

"But who are you?" gasped the trembling girl, her pallid, corpse-like features bent eagerly forwards as she awaited the other's reply.

"I am a friend."

"A friend?"

"Aye, a friend—a friend that will never see you want. I can guess your story, my poor girl. When my carriage nearly dashed over you in Oxford-street, as I returned from a rout, that I now thank heaven I visited, I said to myself, this is some poor unfortunate who, deserted by her destroyer, has determined on death, to end her sorrows; but so young and lovely a girl must live— live for happiness and joy. Place yourself under me, my dear girl, and you shall have wealth — all you can desire."

"Oxford-street! carriage! death!" exclaimed the beautiful occupant of the bed, as she glared wildly at her companion, "what mean you? But stay, I remember me. My dream! Listen, and I'll tell you. You guess my story. Perhaps you can explain the vision I have seen,

THE NOBLE HIGHWAYMAN TO THE RESCUE.

or unravel to me the secret of my hideous dream, that haunts my recollection with life-like reality."

Eagerly the woman bent forwards as the young girl seized her arm.

"See, see, the bright sun! Thus it shone when last I met him; he for whom I would have given life, but who proved himself a villain! I loved—oh! how I loved him. At first all was sweet delirium, till at length he rudely broke the spell by casting me off. I learned he was about to wed another. Driven to fury, I upbraided my seducer. Then, choking with passion, fell at his feet, and, for a time, lost all recollection of my situation. Now comes the strange portion of my story—my fearful, terrible dream!"

The woman who sat by the bedside—a fine handsome matron, of perhaps forty years of age—gazed scrutinizingly upon the features of the pale, shivering girl before her, who, continuing her relation, exclaimed—

"When I returned to consciousness, all was dark, pitchy dark around. I could see nought, but heard the sobs of a man near me. This grief-stricken person seized my hands in his, and muttered words over me that were inexplicable, but horrible to my ears in their hideous meaning. That which struck me with such horror was that in the tones of the bereaved man's voice I recognised my father's. It was he who stood beside me.

"'What means it all?' I asked myself. God of heaven! what a thrill darted through my frame as I said to myself, 'Why is it I hear my dear parent's voice, but can see him not?' I guessed the terrible truth—I was blind!

"For some minutes I lay stricken with horror, as I thought upon cruel fate.

"Blind! blind! No more should I gaze upon the bright glorious sun and the green fields; all was now enwrapped as in a funereal pall. I tried to shriek, but with horror I found I could not give utterance to a sound! My blood seemed all turned to ice in my veins. I now tried to move, but discovered that I was bereft of all motion. Oh! how I offered up prayers to be released from my hideous and terrible dream. I now heard my father quit my side. I felt myself seized in the grasp of two men, and placed in a shallow box. I now listened to their conversation. I could hear the least sound in my terrible dream. What they said drove me into madness. I discovered my eldest brother had perished by the hand of my seducer. I heard these men screw him down in his coffin, and then I heard them screw me down in mine."

The face of the woman who sat listening to the young girl's strange story grew troubled in expression, whilst she muttered to herself—

"Would that Doctor Henderson were here. She still wanders. Something terrible has happened to her. But if she can be saved, he can do it. Her beauty is such 'twere a pity she should die. Do not think upon your misfortunes, my dear girl," she exclaimed, aloud. "My medical attendant will be here anon; he shall see and prescribe for you."

"I thank you kindly, generous madam; but, I pray you, hear the finish of my dream of horror."

"I fear that it may increase the indisposition that preys upon you."

"No, no, no! That which preys upon me is the uncertainty as to whether I really have been in a dream."

"Why, my dear young lady, how could it be aught else? What could it be but a dream?"

"Might it not be death?" The young girl glared wildly into the disturbed features of her companion.

"Alas! my dear, you know not what you say. I beg of you to endeavour to seek repose. The doctor that attends me will soon be here, and he shall see you."

"You are stricken with horror at what I have disclosed, but the remainder far outvies the first portion of my terrible narrative. Let me see," she exclaimed; "I told you I heard the two men fasten my brother in his coffin. So they did me, and by this I knew that I was dead. So lost in terror was I that recollection left me, and when I again recovered, I heard voices close beside me, but not the same as before. I seemed to have been asleep a long time, but I felt cold—oh! so cold. My eyelids were closed as before, but now, with a superhuman exertion, I was enabled to force them open, though still my whole body was rigid as a corpse, and without life or motion.

"A wild scene appeared before me. Was I, indeed, dead? and was this some terrible phase in an after existence? Yet no, I seemed still on earth.

"Above me rode the bright blue moon, silvering all around in a heavenly lustre. But how my heart grew ice-like in my frame as I beheld the little village church into which I had been wont to go with my dear parent. I heard a strange sound close beside me, as of the digging up of earth, accompanied with the voices of two men, who, giving utterance to dreadful oaths, were busied close at hand. I looked again around me. With a chill of horror I discovered I was lying upon some fresh earth in the churchyard. Then, as my senses were about again to leave me, I discovered the hideous features of a man bending over me. Then all was a blank. One more scene of my wild dream is soon told—a dark room, a footstep, a flash of light, the power of my limbs once more restored. Mad with horror, I dashed from some house, out, out into the air! I saw or heard not the approach of a vehicle, but felt myself reeling and falling to the earth. When I returned to consciousness, an hour back, I gazed round me, fearing once more to meet some terrible sight that would drive me into madness. But you came in, and I said, 'Thank heaven! the horrible dream—if dream, indeed, it be—is over.'" With a moan, the young girl sank back in the bed, relapsing into a heavy sleep. Rising from her seat, the woman was about to leave the chamber, when a slight tap was heard at the door. Hastening forwards, the female opened it, and admitted a tall, dark, elderly man.

"Good morning, Mrs. Somers. You wished to see me?"

"Yes, doctor; I have a strange patient here—been wandering terribly."

Walking to the couch, the medical man gazed at the young girl, who, still livid pale, lie in a death-like sleep. Taking up the little white hand, he felt the wrist, exclaiming—

"Care must be taken of your young friend, Mrs.

Somers; her pulse is so slow, it scarce gives signs of life. She must be bled immediately. And now tell me what you know of your new protegé. By heavens! she is very beautiful—too beautiful to be seized upon by the king of terrors; and I'll do my best to call her back to life."

Whilst unfastening a case of instruments he drew from his pocket, Mrs. Somers related to her medical friend all that had passed with the unfortunate girl who now lay in such a death-like sleep.

The features of the medical man grew thoughtful and serious as the woman proceeded with her relation, but as she told him how the unfortunate girl had informed her, with an air of truth, of the scene at the churchyard, he seized her hand, and, drawing her from the bed, exclaimed—

"Mrs. Somers, all that that girl has told you has really happened."

"Good heavens! doctor; what mean you? Do you mean to say the poor creature was dead and buried?"

"Not dead, Lucretia Somers; not dead, though buried; the girl was in a trance."

Such a wild shriek now rung through the chamber, that the medical man and his companion fairly started with horror and alarm.

Turning their eyes, they beheld the face of the unhappy girl looking wildly out from between the curtains. Blood was bubbling from her mouth, whilst with another shriek she exclaimed—shouting with hysterical laughter—

"Ha! ha! ha! my dreadful fate is told. Buried alive! Ha! ha! ha! Buried alive! buried alive!" Then, with a groan of anguish, she fell back insensible.

"Hot-water bath directly. Don't stand amazed, Somers; she'll recover it. Now a reaction will take place; but we must lose no time in the application of restoratives."

Lifting up the slender form of the young girl in his arms, the doctor bore her from the chamber into a bath-room. Placed in hot water, she was then, by his directions, placed between some blankets, and, lancing her fair, round arm, a slow, sluggish stream of dark blood issued from the puncture—at first drop by drop, and then in a continued spurt. For three hours Doctor Henderson remained by the couch of the invalid. At length he rose and left the room, joining Mrs. Somers in the parlour below.

"Well, Henderson, how is she?"

"As well as we can expect."

"Will she recover?"

"Yes."

"Think you I can bend her to my purpose?"

"'Tis impossible to say; she is very young."

"She has been deceived."

"Therefore, will the more readily accede to our plans, you think; but may it not cause her to be wary, and reflect upon her future course?"

"You know not woman, Henderson; once she falls, all is lost."

"Maybe so. If you are right, then will you have done well in bringing this young girl here."

"Save her life, Henderson, and, mark my words, she will well repay the debt she owes us. She is young and beautiful. We want a fresh face. There is one who would give thousands to call her his."

"You mean Lord Arlington?"

"The same."

"Comes he not to-day?"

"Aye, to-night."

"Let him know, then, of the young beauty, Lucretia. Fire his imagination with a description of her charms—her matchless loveliness; then let him see her to-morrow, and we may demand a goodly sum for our lovely prize, for lovely she is, and worth a fair price to those that care for such things, but I care only for gold, Lucretia—gold, the bright, sparkling, red gold. Beauty affects not me. I thirst only for the world's dross." The doctor here rubbed his hands, and chuckled as he gazed into the face of his companion.

"You are a strange man, Henderson. I can remember the time when you were not so indifferent to female charms. 'Tis not fifteen years since you near lost your reason for love of one who rejected you for another."

"Lucretia," ejaculated the doctor, fixing his keen, piercing, hawk-like eyes upon her, "Lucretia, you know all the incidents of my past life; recall them not to me;

I wish that to which you refer buried in oblivion. 'Tis a dark spot in my life I would fain drive from the tablet of my memory. I said you knew all, but I remember me; there is an incident connected with that business with which even you are unacquainted; but let the matter be dismissed from our minds. And now for the girl whom you have so strangely lighted on. Use every care as regards her. Any sudden excitement might kill her. We must not lose her now; her beauty must repay us for the saving of her life. I will now go, returning hither in an hour." Shaking hands with his companion, Doctor Henderson left the room, paid another visit to the young girl above, and, finding her still wrapped in repose, quitted the house.

A grim smile crossed the features of Mrs. Somers as the door of the house closed upon the doctor, whom, from the parlour window, she discerned making his way along the gravel walk towards the large white gates leading to the high road that faced the Cedars.

"So, then, I don't know all, James Henderson. I thought I was well acquainted with the whole particulars of that affair with Edith Lester, but it seems I've been mistaken. My secrets are all known to you, and, by heavens! I'll find out the mystery in connexion with that affair that occurred so long ago with yourself and the pretty Lester, or I've lost all my usual woman's wit and cunning; but who is this?" ejaculated the handsome owner of the Cedars, as she observed the figure of a young man approaching the hall door. "Captain Leslie, as I live." A deep flush settled on the face of the handsome Mrs. Somers as she heard a loud rat-tat at the door. Presently afterwards a man's footstep sounded without, and in a few moments Captain Leslie stood before her.

Rising, and stepping forwards, Mrs. Somers hastened to meet her visitor.

"Well, Lucretia, how fares it with you? How is pretty Maude, and Lady Bell, and my favourite, the fair Fanny Hemmings? is she still rosy, plump and saucy?" The captain here threw himself on the couch beside the buxom Mrs. Somers, and, placing his arm round her waist, imprinted a kiss upon her still ruby lips.

"Lord, Leslie, you wretch! What, the same as ever? Has not your trip out of London improved you at all? What, still the same audacious scamp? Oh! captain, you have much to answer for." Mrs. Somers, who, though forty years of age, possessed a plump, full figure, a handsome, well-developed bust, soft white hands, with a pretty face and dark, flashing eyes, bent her lustrous orbs full upon her new companion, and kept them fixed upon his handsome features till her look was returned with a gaze so full of meaning that the hardened woman dropped her eyes, her face flushing a deep crimson.

"Ha! ha! ha! What, Lucretia able to summon up a blush? devilish good, 'pon my soul! But come, tell me, how are the girls?" Captain Leslie here drew the handsome woman to his side, and again and again pressed his lips to hers; the hectic flush on his face proclaiming that, early as was the hour, he had been indulging in wine.

"Cease your nonsense, do, Leslie; and if you'll sit quiet I'll tell you a strange story about a young girl I have in the house."

"A young girl, hum! Let us hear it. Let us hear all about her. Is she pretty?"

"Oh! she is a lovely young creature, not yet eighteen."

"And in the house?"

"Yes; she is now asleep in the walnut-wood chamber."

"I must see her."

"Nay, my dear captain, not to-day. She is very ill."

"But, zounds and the devil! am I not even to see her, just to have a glimpse of this new paragon of female loveliness?"

"First hear her strange and terrible story."

"Say on, thou angelic fair one," exclaimed the captain, as, leaning forwards, he seized a decanter of brandy, and, pouring some out in a goblet, drank it at a draught, and then threw himself back on the couch beside his handsome companion.

Mrs. Somers now proceeded to relate to the captain the strange, wild incidents connected with the young girl, who lay in a room above, but just recovering from her terrible trance.

At first little attention was paid by Captain Leslie, who kept freely helping himself to the brandy that stood before him; but, as Mrs. Somers went on, he set down the glass and listened eagerly to the story. Once or twice his features grew deadly pale, whilst his fingers clutched nervously his companion's arms.

"Go on; go on," he gasped, as Mrs. Somers gazed in surprise at his contorted features.

"Why, Leslie; how is this? The story appears to affect you deeply."

"Yes. 'Tis a dreadful tale. I pray you, finish it."

In surprise and astonishment at the strange demeanour of her companion, Mrs. Somers related how the young girl had been saved by Doctor Henderson, and at this moment lay slowly recovering from her dreadful trance.

"And her name?"

"I know it not, Leslie."

"What is your purpose with her?"

"Why, of course, I shall introduce her to the girls, and then she will learn the exact state of things. She is very beautiful; besides that, she is young, and though having fallen a victim to her lover's passion, is still artless and innocent."

"Your purpose, then, Lucretia, is to make her like the rest, to condemn her to a life of sin and shame?"

"Why, Leslie, what is this? The roué Captain Leslie turned moralist?" Mrs. Somers, gazing at her companion with a look of astonishment, burst into a merry laugh. Then, as she observed a frown gathering on his brow, she exclaimed—

"Ah! ah! captain, I see you wish to take my young protegé from me, as you did pretty Kate Simmons. But this cannot be. The girl is beautiful. Lord Arlington will pay nobly to call her his."

"She shall never be his," said Leslie, his voice hoarse with passion.

"And pray, who will prevent it?" exclaimed Mrs. Somers, whose handsome features now kindled with indignation at the stern and determined manner of her visitor.

"I will."

"You? Ha! ha! ha! Why, Leslie, you are mad."

"You will be, Lucretia, if you attempt to thwart me in this. That girl must leave this house to-morrow, and with me."

"Indeed. To-night Lord Arlington comes hither, and I shall speak of this young beauty to him. He will pay nobly to procure her to his arms."

"She shall never be his. I swear it. Lucretia, you know me. Attempt to thwart me in my purpose of removing the girl from the house, and you shall rue it."

"I care as little, Captain Leslie, for your threats as I do for your friendship; and from this time forth the doors of the Cedars shall be shut against you."

Furious with passion, the woman stood before her companion, at the same time pointing to the door.

The face of Captain Leslie grew livid with rage. Stepping forwards, he seized the arm of the enraged woman, and, leaning his head down, hissed between his set teeth—

"Lucretia Somers, you do well to defy me. Do'st forget that night—three years ago—when the poor girl Ada Hellsby" ——

A shriek burst from the lips of the beautiful woman, who, falling on her knees, sobbed wildly and hysterically, exclaiming—

"Oh! no! no! no! Remind me not of that, Leslie." Then, starting to her feet, she added—"Besides, if you recall past events, so can I. Shall I tell you? Shall I remind you that I am aware by what means you gained your present wealth?"

Recovering from her momentary alarm, Mrs. Somers now glanced scornfully and defiantly at her companion.

"So, then, you brave me?"

"Since you drive me to it, yes."

"But you are in my power."

"So are you in mine."

"Lucretia, listen to me. 'Tis vain for us to quarrel."

"I think so."

"Let us understand each other."

"I am perfectly agreeable we should do so."

"The girl whom you now have in the house, respecting whom we have had words, can remain."

"I had determined she should remain."

"I had wished to convey her away with me for certain reasons."

"What were they, Leslie. Do you know aught of the stranger?"

"I do."

"Indeed! Who and what is she?"

"I can explain all if I can see her. Till I do so, I'm uncertain."

"You shall do so. You shall see her."

"When?"

"Now; within the hour."

"'Tis well. Follow me into the chamber, and you will be answered why I wish to take her hence."

"Am I to understand, Captain Leslie, that, for the future, whate'er our disagreements, you will not allude to any secret of mine, I making the same compact as regards your past career. Remember, if I am in your power, you are in mine!"

Captain Leslie gazed fiercely upon the female who thus defied him. An unscrupulous, bold, reckless *roué*, holding men and women alike in scorn and contempt, he was furious at thus being held in check by the mistress of the Cedars.

A woman of strong mind, and bold, bad passions was Lucretia Somers.

The two thus at war, it was the one with superior wit and cunning would overthrow the other.

There were some dark secrets between Captain Leslie and Lucretia Somers.

Strange scenes had passed from time to time at the Cedars.

Scenes of horror and crime.

The Cedars was a house in which resided some six or eight young girls, kept by Mrs. Somers, who was patronized by several aristocratic individuals.

The young ladies of the Cedars were always fine young girls of the greatest beauty.

Gentlemen of the highest rank in the fashionable world visited the Cedars.

Captain Leslie had been acquainted with Lucretia Somers for some five or six years, constantly visiting at her house, the Cedars, at Kensington.

Finding that she was determined to brave him in respect to the young stranger whom he wished to take from the house, Captain Leslie dissembled, resolving in his own mind to be even with the woman who dared to thwart him in his plans.

"She shall repent the day she thus set me at defiance," he murmured to himself, as he quitted the room, following Mrs. Somers, who led him to the walnut-wood chamber in which reposed the young stranger.

On entering the apartment in which slumbered the young girl who had gone through such a terrible ordeal as that of being buried alive, Captain Leslie made his way to the couch, and, drawing aside the curtains, gazed upon the beautiful features of the sleeper.

For a few seconds Leslie remained motionless and spell-bound, glaring upon the lovely form of the young girl as she lie in her balmy sleep. Mrs. Somers cast a scrutinizing and keen glance upon the working of his features.

"It is her. 'Tis, indeed, her. How lovely, how beautiful she looks!" he muttered.

At this moment the sleeper, disturbed by the drawing of the curtains, or the low tones of Captain Leslie's voice, started and awoke.

With a wild, frenzied stare, she turned her eyes upon the countenance of the man beside her couch.

"I dream, I dream!" she gasped.

"No, dear Bessie, you dream not; 'tis I, your lover, Arthur Leslie. Will you not forgive the past?"

Wildly the young girl glared upon the features of her seducer—he to whom she owed all her sorrow.

Fearing a relapse, or that the scene with her betrayer, if prolonged, might kill her, Mrs. Somers seized the arm of Leslie, exclaiming—

"Come away, captain; if she is excited in her now weak state, it may cost her her life. Come away, I say."

"Nay, Lucretia; loose your hold. I do repent me of my conduct with this girl. I will make reparation for the past. Bessie, dear one, say, oh! say, do you forgive me? Say you will forgive me, sweet love, and all may yet be well."

Unable to draw him from the bedside, Mr. Somers stood gazing upon the two figures of the seducer and his victim.

Pale—ghastly pale—was the face of Bessie Templeton, for it was indeed that unfortunate girl who had been rescued from her living grave. Her eyes, blazing with a fierce, unnatural light, glared wildly upon the features of Captain Leslie. Leaning forwards, she seized his hands in hers, and exclaimed, in a thick, husky voice—

"Arthur Leslie, your hands are stained with blood."

"What mean you, dear girl? Look not on me thus; 'tis I, your lover. Say you will forgive the past, and all will yet be well."

"Your hands, Captain Leslie, I tell you, are stained with blood!"

"Nay, dear one; you wander. My hands are as yours, white and spotless."

"Liar!"

The eyes of the young girl fairly blazed as they glared upon her seducer.

A hectic flush replaced the pallid hue that had before rested on the cheeks of Captain Leslie. Drawing himself back, he exclaimed—

"Bessie Templeton, I came prepared to redeem the past. You know me—have given proof of that—and are evidently determined to insult me. I will go, but had hoped to procure your forgiveness."

"What, with the blood of my brother on your hands?"

Leslie started, and his countenance again assumed an ashy tint, as Bessie Templeton glared wildly upon him.

"Your brother, Bessie! the blood of your brother on my hands? What mean you?"

"Did you not slay him, accursed wretch?"

"By heavens, no! His blood rests not upon my head."

"Liar! thrice accursed liar! your pallid cheek gives the lie to your quivering lip. You slew my brother; basely shot him; laid him a corpse at your feet."

"We met in fair and open duel. He forced the meeting on me; but how know you this?" ejaculated Leslie, glaring nervously around him, and turning his face away from the couch. He could not bear the fixed stare of his victim.

"I know all, Captain Arthur Leslie! all! I heard how you had stained your hands in my poor brother's blood. When I laid beside him in my coffin, in my deadly trance, that I then thought a hideous dream, I became informed of the extremity of your villany. I then vowed, should I live, to be to you your bitterest foe. I have returned from the grave, Captain Arthur Leslie; returned to revenge upon you my brother's death! My bitterest curse upon you! Through life I'll follow you like your shadow. You shall shed tears of blood for your accursed crimes. See there! There, beside you! my poor brother, pale and bleeding. He points with his bloody hand to you! you, Captain Leslie! Ha! ha! ha! your cheeks grow livid with fear; you tremble at the curse of the betrayed." With a wild shriek the wretched girl fell back senseless, whilst the guilty seducer, in fear and horror, dashed from the room, and left the house. Cold drops of perspiration trickled down the brow of the man of crime, as he hastened from the Cedars.

He remembered, whilst his blood ran with icy chill through his veins, that this was the second curse of an injured one invoked upon his head.

Only a short time before had the unfortunate Lizzie Heywood called God's curse on the head of her destroyer.

In after years Captain Arthur Leslie remembered with a shudder the curses of his victims, when, through them, an All-wise Providence fearfully punished his former crimes.

CHAPTER XV.

THE OLD MINT AGAIN.—THE "FOX IN THE HOLE."—THE MEETING OF THE NIGHT-HAWKS. — THE VIPER, THE RESURRECTION MAN, AND THE JEW. — THE QUARREL.—EUSTACE MALTRAVERS AND THE CLOAKED STRANGER.—THE INTRODUCTION.—DICK TURPIN, THE HIGHWAYMAN, AND THE BOLD NIGHT-HAWKS.

IT was a dark, murky night, a week after the above incidents, that two muffled figures turned off the High-street, Borough, and boldly entered the murderous-looking thoroughfare known as the Mint.

The rain, that had threatened throughout the day, was falling in torrents.

In mimic streams the muddy waters rushed along the broken, uneven roadway.

The wind in wintry gusts tore along, howling shrilly,

and dashing the heavy rain hither and thither in misty clouds.

Not one lamp remained alight in that dark thoroughfare that wild winter night.

The clouds in black, inky masses rolled overhead, the rain pouring down in torrents.

The rush of the waters as they plashed on the pathway from the eaves of the houses or broken pipes, and the howling of the wind, sounded grim and horrible that dark night.

Occasionally the loud shriek of a woman rung upon the night air.

Accompanied ever and anon with the cry of murder.

These alarms, however, were of frequent occurrence in the Mint.

In the last century, scarce a watchman ventured after nightfall to enter its purlieus.

Only in open day would a strong party of runners, when hunting for some daring criminal, dare to make way into the old Mint at Southwark.

Unheeding the wild cries that fell upon their ears, or the fury of the tempest, the two muffled forms hurried on along the dark, gloomy turning, conversing in a low tone as they pursued their way.

"Nice night, Dick."

"Charming."

"Plenty of the family out on the lay."

"Certain. Well, it arn't a nice night for a canter."

"Capital weather for buzmen (pickpockets) and cracksmen (housebreakers), though—but, hallo! here we are at the 'Fox in the Hole,' Dick, so cover up your frontispiece and follow me."

Boldly pushing open the door of the public-house, the two friends made their way into the bar.

It was past ten o'clock, so there was a riotous and motley crowd collected together in the bar of the "Fox in the Hole."

Pushing his way through the drunken, swearing crew, the foremost of the two strangers beckoned to the landlord. Busied at the other end of the bar, the summons was not noted by Josh Jordan; but, upon the stranger tapping loudly on the counter with a pewter pot, he hastened forwards.

"Well, lads, what can I do for you? Some brandy? I've some rare old stuff; will scent your breath like a nosegay. Pardon me, gemmen, I doesn't know yer; and, as you're swells, why, I'd advise yer to cut from the crib. Mayhap you'll find it difficult to get out of the Fox's hole if you stop too long."

The latter part of this speech was said in an undertone, whilst Josh Jordan cast his eyes meaningly upon the motley crowd in front of the bar.

The elder of the two strangers now leant over the bar, and, with a low laugh, let fall his cloak from his face, exclaiming, in a low voice—

"Well, Josh, my rum cull, how are yer?"

"What, Dick Palmer! Damn it, tip us yer flipper, lad! Well, this is a surprise!" The landlord, finding he had drawn the attention of several of his customers to the two visitors, lifted up a portion of the counter that admitted them behind the bar, and the three were presently seated in a cozy little snuggery behind the bar-parlour, a huge, herculean fellow being left to wait upon the orders of those without.

Whilst the landlord was conversing with the two muffled strangers, and the noisy, ruffianly crowd were drinking and swearing in the bar, a strange scene was taking place in the large underground chamber beneath the "Fox in the Hole."

A couple of dozen men were seated round the long table that stood in the centre of the apartment.

Some fierce, murderous-looking ruffians, with countenances bearing the index of their brutal passions.

Others there were, fine, handsome, dashing men, but of rakish bearing that well accorded, however, with their flash, showy attire.

Some of the men round that table were dressed in coarse fustian and rough woollen clothes, with gaudy handkerchiefs wound round their necks. These bore upon their features the marks of desperate conflicts. All alike were stamped with the impress of ruffianism and crime.

Two or three of the better looking were habited in rich velvet surtouts, with deep cuffs edged with gold and point lace. High jack boots reached to their knees, while round their necks they wore rich lace cravats. These men were highwaymen, the others footpads and housebreakers, while all alike were members of the formidable band of the Night-Hawks.

All were in high glee. Glasses were raised, and as soon emptied, whilst loud oaths, obscene jests, and shouts of laughter echoed through the chamber.

It was just as one of the company had finished a song, that the sound of three loud knocks was heard without.

An herculean ruffian, stationed at the further end of the room, pulling aside some drapery, disclosed a door, and leaning forwards, exclaimed—

"Who's there?"

"Friends," replied a gruff voice without.

"The pass!"

"'Hawks are out and want to nest.'"

"'Tis well. Enter."

The door was now thrown open, and three dark figures entered the room.

Rising from his seat at the head of the table, the leader of the band exclaimed—

"How now? Who is that?"

"Who is it, Guy Essington? why it's Resurrection Bill, Ben Abrahams, his pal, and Jemmy Vaughn, the Viper; and we wants a reckoning up from you, to-night, and curse me if we don't have it!"

The ruffian, whose flushed face gave token of inebriation, glared savagely at his leader.

"What mean you, you drunken hound?" exclaimed Essington, starting from the table, and coming forwards.

"Why, I means wot I says. Now, Burker and Coffin, don't hang back, and turn lily-livered, but, damme! stand up and speak your mind. Curse yer! who's afraid? Resurrection Bill arn't!" Such a volley of oaths now fell from the villain's lips, that the words of the men he had called upon were drowned and not heard. Rising up from the table, however, they crossed over to the ruffian, and ranged themselves beside him.

Glaring with rage and fury at the resurrectionist, Guy Essington thrust his hand into his bosom, whilst choking with passion, and in vain attempted to speak. The veins in his forehead now swelled up like knotted cords, while his face grew of a dark purple tint.

All gathered in silence near their chief, awaiting the finish of the scene.

Resurrection Bill, with his friends, stood near the door, which in the confusion was left ajar.

Smiling grimly and scornfully at his leader, the resurrection man exclaimed—

"Look here, Guy Essington, yer big looks arn't no good with me. I arn't to be scared by the living or the dead! Now, all I wants is our rights; and if others is afraid to ask for 'em, why, curse me! I ain't. I'm Resurrection Bill. I doesn't care a curse for the downiest runner out. I laughs at the beaks, and I'll dance myself out of the world at Tyburn Tree! Don't keep fingering your barking-irons, governor, but get cool and listen to me."

"Say on; but, by hell, you shall suffer for this!" ejaculated Essington, at length forcing his tongue to utterance.

"Now, what I and my pals here—Coffin, Burker, Ben, and the Viper—want to know is, what has come of those sparklers, the diamond necklace? It's time they were sold, and divided among the band."

"Right you is, Bill."

"Just the identical."

"The very hammer."

"Couldn't be plainer."

"Not a ha'porth."

Whilst uttering their thoughts aloud, the companions of the resurrection man glanced nervously at the other members of the band standing near their chief. But there was no sign of approval. All stood mute, awaiting the finish of the scene.

"What if I refuse any account of the necklace, which, by-the-bye, was lost by Jem Vaughn, though returned to me by those into whose hands it fell."

"Well, look yer, Captain Essington, if yer refuses to give me my share of the sparklers, curse me! if I don't nose on the gang."

A loud yell here broke from the group near the captain, whilst pistols and knives flashed in the rays of the lamps.

"Lynch him, Essington!"

"No bodysnatchers among the Night-Hawks."

"Down with him."

"Hang him."

"Give him a dose."

"Kick out the Churchyard groveller."

These and like cries resounded through the apartment. Whilst there was every indication of a conflict between the two parties, three more figures appeared upon the scene, darting through the half-closed door.

"Curses on yer all! Stand back, or by ——," said the resurrection man, with a horrible oath, "I'll save the topsman a job! And since yer defies us, and refuses our rights, why, curse me if I don't snitch on yer all afore the clock strikes twelve, and get yer all a lifer (transported for life), or a dance upon nothing beneath Tyburn Tree. Come on, pals! Curses! we'll nose on the Hawks and blow the gaff!"

"No, you won't," said a loud, clear voice just behind him. A dark figure, standing by the door, here stepped forward, and, as the resurrection man turned, gave him such a terrific blow between the eyes, that like a log he fell, doubled up in a heap upon the ground.

A cheer rang through the apartment, whilst letting fall the cloak that concealed his features, the stranger revealed the countenance of Essington's nephew.

Eustace Maltravers!

Another loud cheer rung through the underground chamber.

Accompanied by rude oaths and execrations from the mouth of Resurrection Bill and his friends.

"Those who dare Guy Essington, and are ready to join the Red Band, follow me," yelled the resurrection man, as, with a loud yell of fury, he dashed from the chamber through the still half-open door.

There was a brief struggle by the opposing parties, and at length, with yells of defiance and threats of revenge, the friends of the resurrectionist made good their escape after their companion.

"Let them go," said Essington, as Eustace and the cloaked stranger were about to follow in pursuit of the ruffians who had fled. "Let them go. The brave band of Night-Hawks are well rid of such carrion birds. And now hear me, all," exclaimed Essington, who, his eyes flashing with fury, stood amidst the company who surrounded him; "hear me, all. Let my words be well remembered. For the future, I place a ban upon the men who have dared this night to rebel and mutiny against my authority. Let it be a task undertaken by all to hunt down James Coffin, Burking Sam, Jem Vaughn, the Viper, the Jew Abrahams, and their ringleader, Resurrection Bill. To execute a terrible vengeance on the latter be your task, Eustace. You owe him a heavy debt of vengeance. See it paid, or thou art unfit for the leadership of this noble band. That, from henceforth, I entrust solely to thee. Pals, knights of the road, lightobymen, rum culls, and padders, behold your future captain, who, by his maiden deeds, has proved himself capable and worthy the onerous leadership of the brave band of the Night-Hawks of London."

With a smile of joy, Eustace bowed his head in acknowledgment of the loud shouts that greeted him on all sides.

"Long live the captain of the Night-Hawks!"

"Three cheers for the veteran, Guy Essington!"

"Hurra!"

"A groan for the topman (hangman), all beaks, spies, and runners!".

"Another cheer and a bumper for Eustace Maltravers, our dashing captain, fearless and bold!" exclaimed the highwayman, Gentleman Jack.

"Hurra! hurra!"

The shouts sounded clear and hollow in that underground chamber.

Seating themselves at the table, wine and spirits again circulated freely among the daring band, toasted by numerous members of the company.

Maltravers now rose, renewed shouts saluting him as he returned his thanks.

"Pals, freemen, and dashing knights of the road, I beg to thank you sincerely for your kind welcome. Believe me, I shall never disgrace my uncle Guy Essington's encomiums. I have already, since my short visit in town, gone through dangers, and escaped them, as only a bold, daring, courageous man can. I evaded the murderous attempts of the ruffianly, mutinous hound, Resurrection Bill, and the villain, Viper, who, with two companions, hunted me, a few nights back, upon the river; but I eluded them by dashing into the rolling tide. I shall ever, in my career, prove myself a fast friend and a dangerous enemy. And at the same time that I become your captain and leader, allow me to introduce to your notice an esteemed friend, and a stranger who wishes to enrol himself in our brave band, Gentleman Jack; and you, Flash Harry, may, perhaps, be acquainted with Richard Palmer, better known as Dick Turpin."

"Dick Turpin?" exclaimed the band, in one voice.

"Aye, Dick Turpin, pals," ejaculated the cloaked stranger, starting up and throwing aside his disguise.

A loud shout greeted his appearance, for though then in the early part of his career, Turpin was well known by several of the family in London.

"Knights of the road, rum culls, cracksmen, buzmen, lowtobymen, buskers, bushcoves, and bred cracksters, I'm proud to become a member of your band; for your captain here, he has rendered me his debtor for life. He aided me, a few nights back, in a set-to with two of our amiable friends, who have just departed. Through my new-found pal, I escaped their murderous intentions. I got away without a slit-weazard or a bullet in my brainpan; and, curse me! if ever I forget the service. And here, before all, I swear to ever remain a fast pal to our captain, and will follow to the death any cove that noses on him or deserts him in the hour of danger. An old pal of mine, one George Watson, of the 'Bold Horseman,' at Harrow, well known to you all, was to bring me hither among you, but your captain volunteered to introduce your humble servant—pal that is—and fast friend that will ever be. Dick Turpin is a lad that will never snitch on a comrade in the hour of danger, though it saved him from a dance upon nothing at Tyburn. And now, pals, I have a toast. Fill glasses to the brim—bumpers, and, mind, no heeltaps. Stand up, all. Here is long life to Captain Maltravers. May he never want a friend in need, or turn pale at sight of Tyburn Tree."

Such a shout, such a loud, ringing cheer followed this toast of Turpin's that the men in that underground chamber scarcely heard a loud, angry summons at the door.

Bang! bang! bang!

Followed by a thundering crash, as though an attempt were being made to force the door.

In a moment there was complete silence in the chamber that a minute before had rung with loud shouts and noise of rude mirth.

The Night-Hawks well knew the meaning of that imperious summons.

Officers of justice were without.

Someone within the secret and underground chamber was, in the phrase of the runners, wanted.

Bang! bang! bang!

"Open! open! in the King's name."

Motioning for silence, Essington stepped forwards, and, placing himself by the door, exclaimed—

"Is that you, Geoffery Newton?"

"Curses! yes. Open the door."

"Are you in a hurry?" ejaculated Essington, with a low laugh.

"Come, no nonsense, Captain Essington, but let us in at once, or it will be worse for yer."

"Who do yer want?"

"A stranger, who we know is concealed in the house, and Gentleman Jack, for that affair of his at the Hollies, last week."

"Oh! is that all?"

"Yes. Open the door."

"Will you nammus quietly if Jack and the other submit to the darbies?"

"Yes."

"You swear it?"

"Damn it! yes. Geoffery Newton arn't the man to break his word."

"Well, I would let you in, but 'tain't of no use."

"No use? Confound it! what do yer mean?"

"Why, the men you want. Let me see; who was it?"

"Gentleman Jack, and a stranger; one Dick Palmer."

"Well, they arn't here."

A loud curse escaped the lips of the leader of the thief-takers without, who dashed with all his force against the door.

"All ready?" said Essington, glancing round.

"Yes; the birds have flown," said a tall, lantern-jawed fellow standing in a corner of the chamber.

"Gone to nest?"

"Yes; and are now at roost."

"'Tis well, Black Will. Open the door, and let those barking hounds in."

Bang! bang! crash!

The strong oaken door seemed about to give before the assailants from without.

Black Will, the tall, herculean ruffian who generally guarded the entrance to the underground chamber, now shot back the huge bolts, and the door, swinging open, five or six Bow-street runners burst in, headed by a stalwart, rough-looking man, who, with huge black whiskers, and his face seamed with scars, bore a fierce, bold, determined appearance.

With oaths of rage and fury, the leader of the runners searched through the apartment in vain.

The men he wanted were not to be found.

Dashing up to Guy Essington, and glaring upon him with eyes that blazed with passion, he exclaimed—

"You are tricking me, Captain Essington; but, by the fiends! you had best take care, or you may find yourself, some morning before the next month is out, journeying to rope. By the devils below! I'll help yer to a hempen necklace, if yer play with me."

"Softly, Geoffery Newton, Bow-street runner, and late convict of Botany Bay. Remember to whom you utter your threats. A word from my lips, Geoffery Newton, and some fine morning you would be found with your throat cut from ear to ear. You understand. Come, come; 'tis useless you or I trifling with each other. I have admitted you here, you find the men you want are not to be discovered, so away with your men, or I won't answer for what may happen. There are some rough hands knocking about the Mint to-night. If you value a whole skin, take my advice, make yourselves scarce; it were best, and safest."

Whilst Essington was speaking, Geoffery Newton, a daring and well-known Bow-street runner, glared savagely round the chamber at his men, who were carrying on a fruitless search for the missing ones.

In vain every corner was scrutinized by the runners. The men wanted could not be found.

"It's no use your hunting about, lads; your men arn't here," exclaimed Guy.

"Essington," ejaculated the leader of the runners, hoarse with passion, "it's your turn to-night; the next time 'twill be mine. Look to yourself! for, curse me! if I don't lodge yer in the stone jug, come what may. Come on, Smithson, let us away. We're done to-night; the birds have flown."

Followed by his men, Geoffery Newton now prepared to leave the place, a loud yell of derisive laughter ringing in their ears as they quitted the apartment.

On reaching the door, Newton, hoarse with rage, hissed from between his clenched teeth—

"Remember, Guy Essington, I owe you one, and will not fail to pay it!"

Then, as he cast a last glance round the chamber, his eye lighted up, whilst his features, before a livid white with passion, now turned a dark crimson. About to make his way back with his men into the room, he was pushed forwards by the members of the Night-Hawks that crowded upon him; and with loud yells, and exulting shouts of defiance, was thrust from the place. When fairly over the threshold of the door, the latter was shut to with a loud slam, Geoffery Newton, with his runners, being left in the dark passage without.

CHAPTER XVI.

GEOFFERY NEWTON AND THE NIGHT-HAWKS.—THE CUNNING OFFICER AND HIS PLOT.—THE DEPARTURE.—THE SPY.—EXULTATION OF THE RUNNER.—THE PISTOLS AND THE LIFE-PRESERVER.—A COLD HAND AND A DEATH GRIP.—THE STRUGGLE.—THE OLD WELL.—TERRIBLE FATE OF THE SPY.—THE ESCAPE OF THE HIGHWAY-MEN.—THE MEETING WITH THE RUNNERS.—THE CONFLICT.—A SCENE OF HORROR IN THE OLD MINT.

"HIST, Jones!"

Geoffery Newton spoke cautiously and under his breath, as, with his men, he pursued his way down the dark passage.

The runner named stopped, and halted as his leader called him aside.

"Jones, a word with you. Hold on, my men, a minute or two."

In obedience to the order of Newton, the runners paused, and all halted in the centre of that dark passage beneath the old inn of the "Fox in the Hole."

"Now, look here, Jones. You are one of my most experienced and boldest men. I have a dangerous task for you."

"All right, Mr. Newton. Only say what you want, and I'm your man."

"Have you your barking-irons?"

"Yes, Mr. Newton, and a nutcracker as well, loaded with lead." The runner here pulled from his pocket a little staff or life-preserver.

"'Tis well. I, with the rest, am going to leave the inn. But you, Jones, must remain."

"As yer like, governor; but I don't see yer game in that. What am I to do?"

"Watch, spy, and find out how we've been tricked."

"But how am I to do it?"

"By remaining here."

"Where?"

"Why, in this passage. Make your way back, hide behind the door, and listen to what passes within."

"I see the dodge! You cut with the rest; I remain, and smoke the trick?"

"Exactly."

"I'm your man! I arn't afeard on 'em; not while I has my barkers and my cocoa-nut crasher."

"Now, listen. When you have learnt all you can, make good your way out of the inn, and you'll find us without."

"I see. Then we all returns, nabs our birds, and the trick's done?"

"Precisely. We must now leave you. Our stay will be noted. Act with all your cunning and bravery, Jones, and remember your life is the hazard of the die!"

"Never fear, Newton, I am up to my work."

"'Tis well. I must now away." Followed by the others, Geoffery Newton proceeded up the stairs leading to the house, and, shortly after, left the inn. The man Jones returned down the dark, gloomy passage, bent upon his dangerous mission.

A task endangering his very life.

Though a bold, fearless man, and one who had gone through some terrible scenes of danger in his perilous calling, the runner felt his blood run cold as he beheld the last of his companions disappear from his sight.

He returned down that gloomy, underground passage, not exactly with a feeling of fear, but with a strange, terrible foreboding of an impending ill.

On reaching the strong, oaken door leading into the chamber himself and his companions had left a little time before, the runner sank down upon his knees, and listened intently to what was passing within.

The voices, though dull and partially indistinct, could occasionally be distinguished by the spy.

Well he knew that warning from above would be sent to the chamber that the officers had gone.

Nor was he mistaken; whilst kneeling beside the door, the sound of a footstep behind him sounded on his ear.

It was a messenger from above.

Now was a dangerous moment of peril to the runner.

His life hung upon a thread.

If discovered there alone, his life would doubtless pay the forfeit.

He would not be allowed to escape.

The spy would be condemned with one voice.

Starting up from his knees, the daring runner who had accepted the dangerous task of spying upon the Night-Hawks, drew himself up against the wall, flattening his figure as much as possible.

The heart of the officer beat thick and fast as the heavy foot of a man approached the spot on which he stood.

Fortunately for the runner, the messenger carried no light; had he done so, with one spring the officer had determined to strike him to his feet with the weapon he held ready in his hand—the deadly staff loaded with lead.

Halting at the door, the unsuspecting messenger gave three loud knocks, noting not the dim, dark outline of the figure close behind him.

"Who's there?" exclaimed a voice within; a low murmur that had before rung upon the air being hushed.

"A Hawk."

"What news?"

"All's clear. The hounds are off the scent."

"'Tis well. Enter."

The door was thrown open; the stranger darted through the heavy hangings into the chamber.

The entrance being left partially ajar.

A loud shout now fell upon the ears of the runner.

An uproarious shout of triumph.

"Newton's done!"

"We've sold him again!"

"Come on out, boys. The game's up!"

Throwing himself on the ground, the runner drew nearer to the door, and, underneath the hangings that hung over it inside, he was enabled to gain a partial glimpse of the scene within.

To his surprise, he now beheld the forms of two men, one of whom he recognised as Gentleman Jack, emerge from what appeared to be a deep pit in the corner of the apartment.

This hole the runner remembered to have discovered some months before when on a visit to the "Fox in the Hole," after a man who it was known was secreted in the house.

That very night Geoffery Newton had thrown aside the boards that covered up the opening, and which appeared to be an old well-hole. The rush of water could be heard beneath, and they were told that it was a portion of a deep ditch that ran under the house and led to the river.

That there was deception in connexion with this well-hole, it was now apparent. Here lay the secret of the disappearances of everyone that was wanted when the inn was searched by the officers.

News, indeed, for Newton.

Forgetful of his perilous position, the runner lay peering into the apartment, by the conversation that ensued, apprised of the secret of the well-hole, and who the stranger was that issued from its depths with Gentleman Jack.

"Well, my worthy knight of the road, what do you think of the old well?" exclaimed Essington, with a loud laugh.

"Infernally cold," answered Gentleman Jack, with an oath.

"But better than a lodging in the stone-jug or a dance at Tyburn."

"Right you are, Guy; and I trust, when hunted by the Philistines, you'll never have a worse hiding-place than the well-hole in the meeting-chamber of the Night-Hawks; and now fill glasses, lads. Here's to our new comrade, Dick Turpin! and death and confusion to all runners."

"Death and confusion to all runners!"

There was a loud jingling of glasses as they were thumped on the table after they had been drained of their contents, accompanied by shouts of laughter and rude oaths.

The Night-Hawks exulted over the trick they had played the wily and astute officer, Geoffery Newton, a man feared and hated by them all, as a clever and unscrupulous agent of the law.

"Well, Newton's done this time."

"Right and tight."

"He's a downy bird; but he is to be sold."

"Safe as beans."

"Ha! ha! ha! we've done him to-night."

Loud shouts of laughter rung through the chamber.

"Laugh on while yer can. Perhaps you'll change your tune afore morning. Let me see. I thinks, thanks to the wit of clever Geoff. Newton, that we shall cage our birds after all; and now, as I know all, I'll see to my barking-irons and my skull-cruncher, in case of accident, and take my hook." Muttering his thoughts half aloud, Jones, the runner, rose to his feet, and was about to turn round and make his way down the passage, when he felt a pair of cold hands clasp him round the neck; and with a smothered cry he fell to the earth, borne down by the herculean form of a man who had come down the passage unseen by the unfortunate runner.

"Easy does it, my boy. No, you don't."

The wretched man had made a desperate effort to wrench a pistol from his belt.

No cry escaped the officer, only a strange, gurgling, smothered sound.

Gripped round the throat by the man who had surprised him with a death-clutch, he lay, incapable of uttering a word.

"How are you, my flower? So you staid behind to spy on the Night-Hawks, did yer? You wouldn't have been so close agin the door, mark yer, if Black Will had been on guard in the council-chamber. What, yer don't like it, my daffydowndilly, don't yer? Does I hurt yer? Beg yer pardon, but I can't help it. No, you don't."

Again the wretched officer strove with frantic efforts to hurl off his enemy.

Remorselessly the other held on with a death-grip, clutching his foe round the throat.

The doomed man at length, with a last exertion of dying agony, released his neck from the other's grasp, and a shrill, piercing cry escaped his lips.

"Murder! help!"

But no help was there. The runner-spy was doomed.

The door now thrown open, a glare of light flashed upon the scene.

Whilst such a yell burst from the crowd that hurried forwards, that the unhappy runner, who had wrenched himself from the grasp of the man Black Will, fairly staggered back, and, incapable of flight, stood glaring upon the enemies that surrounded him.

"A runner, by all the fiends!"

"Bill Jones, that got Jim Dyson a lifer!"

"Chive him!"

"Give him a dose with his own nut-smasher!"

A ruffian here snatched from the wretched, dazed officer the staff he had clutched nervously in his hand.

Guy Essington now stepped forward, and pointing to the doomed man, exclaimed—

"Away with him, lads; his pals are back upon us. Hark to those shouts."

Oaths, shrieks, and cries, mingled with the sound of conflict, were now heard above.

Alarmed at the non-appearance of Jones, Geoffery Newton had returned.

The runner, hearing the noise, and distinguishing the voices of his comrades, yelled aloud for help.

"Stop his 'tater-trap. Away with him!" said Essington.

"He knows the secret of the well, captain," exclaimed the man Black Will.

A dark cloud gathered over the brow of Guy Essington, who, pointing to the corner of the chamber, ejaculated—

"Then must the well silence him for ever. Be yours the task, Will. But see, our foes return. Away with you, Turpin; and you, Eustace, follow your pal. Gentleman Jack, come you with me, and we'll yet give them the double."

A terrible scene now took place.

Screaming wildly for help, the unfortunate runner was dragged into the dark corner of the chamber, in which was situate the old well-hole.

Desperately the doomed man struggled with his powerful adversary.

"Help! help! help!"

"'Tain't no use, my tulip. You're booked for the long voyage! Easy does it. I thinks that's a settler!" With a curse, the ruffian, Black Will, brought the loaded staff of the officer full upon his head.

With a low, gasping sob, the doomed wretch sunk at the feet of his remorseless foe.

Again the hideous weapon descended.

There was a dull, sickening crash of splintered bone; a convulsive shudder through the frame of the runner, who, then, with a gasping sob, fell as if dead.

The shouts and cries above now increased.

A moment afterwards, Black Will hurled the body of Jones into the dark chasm that yawned at his feet.

Such a horrible, piercing scream of death-agony issued from the officer's lips, that the ruffian, Black Will, shuddered as it rung in his ears.

With his skull beaten in, consciousness had returned as the doomed one was hurled over the side of the old well-hole. For a moment his blood-stained face appeared to his assassin, as despairingly he clung to the edge of the horrible opening. Then, letting go his hold, with a last, dying yell, he disappeared from sight.

There was the sound of a loud plash, the gurgling of water; then all was still.

The murdered runner lay a bleeding corpse in his horrible grave.

THE MYSTERIOUS VISITOR IN THE KEN.

Stooping over the black hole, the murderer now, holding a lamp down, gazed into the darksome depths.

But nought could he discern.

All was black, inky darkness.

The gurgling rush of water falling on the ear.

"He's gone his road, and is food for the rats. Now to draw up the ladder."

The murderer of the wretched runner, leaning over the well-hole, put his hands down and pulled up a rope ladder, the top of which had been hooked on to a large iron nail, driven in the brickwork that lined the well.

The ruffian shuddered as he observed some dark crimson stains upon the top part of the rope.

It was the blood of the officer, whose crushed and bleeding skull had struck against the side of the well in the descent of the body.

"It arn't a bad dodge, hanging on to the ladder when there's grubs (officers) above hunting for a cove, but, cuss me! if I should like an hour in the well-hole," muttered Black Will, as he moved away.

The hardened villian could not dismiss from his mind the agonized, blood-stained face of his victim, as it had appeared to him when falling down the dark abyss.

Meanwhile, Guy Essington, followed by Eustace and Turpin, made his way along the passage till they reached the stairs.

Loud shouts and rude oaths now sounded from above.

"Come on, lads. One rush out into the Mint. 'Tis but a run to Jack Redfern's, where you say you've left your horseflesh, and all's right."

The three men now reached the summit of the stairs, and, pushing their way through the door at the top, entered the passage leading to the bar. Here they were met by a crowd of dark forms, that were swearing and fighting like demons.

"Down with the grubs!"

"Knife them!"

"Down with the runners!"

These and such-like cries rung upon the air, mingled with the noise of the conflict.

With a dash, the three friends for whom the runners were in search, made their way through the fighting crowd, dexterously avoiding the efforts of the officers to secure them, and making their escape into Mint-street.

Here, however, they were met by some more of the runners, and a fierce struggle took place in the street.

"Ware Hawks! up, boys! the Philistines are upon us," shouted Essington, with stentorian lungs.

In a moment, as if by magic, a hundred dark figures rushed from the different courts and alleys in the Mint.

The loud clang of a bell now rang upon the air.

Whilst the glare of some torches lit up the wild scene, fearful, murderous-looking faces appeared among the crowd, to which reinforcements were added each minute.

The runners drew back and commenced to retreat.

A rather difficult task, as dozens of their enemies kept coming up behind them every minute.

Geoffrey Newton, a bold, daring, and expert officer, began to feel alarmed.

His only object now was to draw his men out of the crowd of savage foes that surrounded them on all sides.

The men, to secure whom he had ventured into the purlieus of the Mint, had, he knew by this, made good their escape. He had discerned the figures of Eustace and Turpin, as, darting through a line made for them by the mob, they had disappeared, making their way towards the Borough.

Newton's efforts now were solely those of self-preservation.

Escape for himself and his men.

The whole of the Mint was aroused.

Links flashed in the thick, murky darkness of the thoroughfares.

It was a strange, wild scene—that reckless mob shouting and uttering yells of fierce defiance at the officers of the law.

But Geoffrey Newton was a bold man, and one not easily frightened at a sudden danger.

"Back—back, men! use your staves and your barking irons on the curs if they won't give way!" shouted the daring, courageous leader of the runners.

"Let 'em have it! Down with the blues!"

"Ware Hawks! death to the grabs!"

"Down with the runners!"

"Privileges of the Mint for ever!"

"No quarter!"

"Cut 'em up! Give it to 'em!"

The loud screams of women now added to the strange, wild, horrible scene, one not readily forgotten by those who were the victims of the rioters.

One of the wretched runners was borne away from his comrades and dragged through the mire—kicked and torn by a hundred savage hands.

Battling his way down the street, Newton slowly drew near to the end opening out on the Borough.

Riots were of frequent occurrence in the Mint; therefore, the few watchmen who passed the murderous thoroughfare hesitated to enter its precincts, that were as jealously guarded by the inhabitants as the Alsatia of Whitefriars years before.

With numerous bruises, his face streaming with blood, Newton and three of his men at length made their way from the scene of horror, pelted and yelled at to the last.

Shaking his fist with impotent fury, the thief-taker breathed a fearful curse of future vengeance upon his enemies, and turned from the spot.

The mob, retreating to their dens, a partial quiet fell upon the scene, occasionally broken by the loud shouts of drunken revelry.

CHAPTER XVII.

THE MIDNIGHT RIDE.—THE ROBBERY OF THE YORK MAIL ON THE HARROW-ROAD.—THE HAUNTED MILL.—THE WHITE FIGURE IN THE MOONLIGHT.—A PISTOL-SHOT, AND ITS RESULTS.—TERROR OF BONNY BLACK BESS, AND DEPARTURE OF THE HIGHWAYMAN.

AN hour after their escape from the runners in the Mint, Dick Turpin and his companion were cantering along the Edgware-road.

Both mounted on good steeds, they cantered onwards at a gallant pace.

Though not quite equal in beauty and grace to the splendid mare bestrode by Turpin, yet the steed mounted by Eustace was a noble-looking animal.

A beautiful bay, with long, streaming mane, a white spot upon the centre of her forehead, and a coat shining and glossy like silk, the mare upon which our hero was seated was well matched with Turpin's bonny Black Bess.

Gracefully the beautiful steeds trotted along the lonely road, the shadows of their riders thrown far behind by the bright rays of the moon, that, now the clouds had dispersed, shone with a silvery glare upon all around.

"Well, Dick, we got well out of that," exclaimed our hero, as he rode by the side of his friend; "but I wonder how Gentleman Jack got on."

"Made his escape out at the back, so I heard. That's a fine mare he has given you, lad; a fit companion for my bonny Black Bess."

"Yes, she's a fine creature. I fancy Guy Essington gave a trifle for her though. She has been, so they tell me, on many a journey on a dark night, standing Jack in good stead when pursued by his foes, the Philistines; but I think the steed he now calls his even more graceful and suited for the road than the one I now bestride. But, however, I'm well content with Starlight Sue, and trust that, in company with bonny Black Bess, she may go through many adventures with her new master in his career as a knight of the road."

"Well, we are now sworn pals, lad; and, in danger and difficulties, I swear you'll never find a truer friend than Dick Turpin."

"I'm sure of that, Dick; nor shall you find Eustace Maltravers ever desert his pal in the hour of need. And now to business. What do you propose as regards the old miser, Ralph Fairley, of the Hemlock Manor House—he whom we have so egregiously gulled? Do you return to his house in the morning?"

"That I most certainly shall. We must not let the old Crœsus slip through our fingers. By-the-bye, Eustace, that girl Sybil is a fine creature; and, for beauty and grace, worthy the coronet of a duchess. Pity she should be the daughter of such a miserly old hunks as old Ralph Fairley, the money-spinner."

Turpin noted not the strange look that stole over his companion's face, or the deep flush that crimsoned his brow, as he praised the beauty of Sybil Fairley; but, with a laugh, continued commenting upon the loveliness of the miser's daughter. "Beshrew me, Eustace, do you know I've half a mind to make strong love to that girl and carry her off."

"Dick Turpin, I know you but jest."

"Jest be ——," exclaimed the highwayman, with a gay laugh. "I was never more in earnest in my life."

"Then you must abandon your project."

"The devil!"

Turpin looked in amazement upon his companion.

"You must not dream of destroying the poor girl. 'Twould be a base act, under the guise of a rich and titled gentleman, to secure her affections, and cause her to give herself to a highwayman—one hunted by the laws, and an outcast to society. A strange fate has thrust me in my present position, but still, Turpin, I feel I am but a knight of the road, a victim of fate, scourged by evil fortune; but, though a wanderer of the night and a robber, still I would give up life ere I deceived a young and spotless girl, such as she you have named."

Seizing his comrade's hand as they rode along, Turpin, dismissing the smile that had before rested on his features, exclaimed—

"Eustace, my friend, my pal, the preserver of my life, I confess I was wrong, but I had no serious intention of fulfilling my project with regard to the miser's daughter; and, had I, indeed, been bent upon following up the young girl, I fancy I should have met with one great impediment; for, if we both entered the lists, and made a siege upon the young girl's heart, yourself, Eustace, I suspect, would be the favoured swain, or I mistake the looks she cast upon you yesterday as you sauntered by the old mill near the Hemlock Manor House."

The before somewhat pale features of his companion now flushed a fiery red, as Turpin, with a smile, made his friend aware that he had watched him and Sybil Fairley the day before.

"You do not mean, Turpin, to say that the lovely Sybil cast a glance of friendship upon me during our walk yesterday from her father's house?"

Eustace grasped the reins so tight, that his steed was on the point of drawing up.

"That is just what I do mean. Give Sue the reins, lad, or we shall not reach the 'Bold Horseman' by sunrise." Turpin, in surprise, noted the excitement of his companion, and added, "But, zounds and the devil, Eustace, lad! what do you look so scared for? Surely not at the idea that you have unwittingly made a conquest, and secured the heart of the pretty Sybil Fairley?"

"Turpin, if I could think that that poor girl cast eyes of favour upon me, I'd never enter the doors of the Hemlock Manor House more."

"Pshaw! you talk wildly. Now, I'll tell you candidly, I think, under your assumed character of the Hon. Frank Hartland, you have but to ask the young girl's love, and 'tis yours."

A wild gleam of joy darted across the handsome features of Eustace, succeeded by a deadly pallor, as his companion's words fell upon his ears.

"You think, Turpin, that I might secure her love, then?"

"Of course. Did you not save her and her parent from the brutality of the burglars? Of dashing person, and easy suavity of manners, you have everything in your favour. The old miser, ever ready to extend to you the hand of friendship. Listen to me, Eustace. I am a few years older in the world than you. Let me give you some advice. Let not this opportunity of enriching yourself, and securing a handsome bride, pass you. Her father is old, and cannot last long. His wealth is enormous. We may as well share it as let it fall into other hands. Woo, then, and win this golden bride. I am your sworn friend, and advise you to your own benefit."

In silence his companion listened to Turpin, whilst their steeds trotted along the moonlit roadway, nor attempted to interrupt his speech; but now, as the highwaymen paused, Eustace turned round, gazing earnestly into the features of his comrade, exclaiming—

"Your counsel is given with all good and friendly feeling, Turpin, I am assured, but I cannot do as you advise. Though the wealth of the Indies were secured me by the deed, I could never deceive the fair and virtuous Sybil Fairley."

A grim smile crossed the face of Turpin.

"Shall I tell you why you talk thus? because, unhappily, you are in love—bewitched by the maiden's charms. Come, rouse thee, Eustace. Remember, lad, you are a knight of the road, and sworn pal of Dick Turpin. Pshaw! lad, we can secure the smile of a pretty wench where'er we go. Then give not way thus, but at once make up your mind to woo the girl. Secure her, and the old miser's wealth, or think no more about her."

"Think no more of her, Dick? Impossible. Her beauteous image will be ever before me."

"Ah! I see, lad, you are hopelessly in love. But come, I suppose you will not adhere to your resolution of not visiting, with me, the Hemlock Manor House in the morning. Remember, there is to be some business transacted. On the morrow the old man goes to London with some gold he purposes stowing away at the office in the Poultry."

"Well, what then?

"What then? Why, curse me, Eustace, this love has lost you your wits. Why, the gold taken away by the old man must be ours."

"How—how, will you secure it?"

"By e'en taking it from him."

"Robbing him?"

"Precisely."

"But will he not discover us?"

"Ha! ha! ha! And do you think, with craped faces, and as knights of the road, the old man will recognise me, Richard Palmer, gent., and the Hon. Frank Hartland? No—no, Eustace; that's right enough. Leave all to me; I'll warrant there's no mishap. Money we want, and money we must have; and I see no reason why we should hesitate to ease old Ralph Fairley of some of his superfluous cash."

"As you will, Dick. As an older and more experienced hand, I leave all to you; and I will own that I feel a strong and sudden attachment for the miser's lovely daughter, but cannot force myself to win her young heart by a false and cruel act, such as you advise. But, hark! what is that? Is it not the rattle of wheels?"

"Ay; and, by heavens! the sound of a horn is carried on the wind."

"What do you take it to be, Dick?"

"The York coach, my boy; and to-night you can show your friend your mettle by letting him hear you cry, 'Stand and deliver!'"

"You surely do not think of stopping the mail?"

Eustace, though a bold, daring young man, had not yet attained that cool impudence and scorn of danger possessed by his older and more experienced companion.

"Not intend to stop the mail? don't I; and, with your help, 'tis hard if we don't pretty well skin the passengers, some of whom I will wager carry full purses and pretty trinkets. But hark! she comes. Get ready your barking irons. Shove this crape on your frontispiece, and when I cry 'halt!' do you seize the reins of the horse on the off-side, and leave the rest to me. But see, they are here."

The mail could now be discerned whirling along the road, the lamps throwing a yellow glare upon the hedges by the wayside. The horn of the guard sounded loud and clear, whilst the driver smacked his whip through the air with a sharp crack.

On came the coach, the roof of which was crowded with passengers.

Eustace, backing his steed to the side of the road, and grasping his pistols with a firm clutch, awaited the moment for action.

Turpin, as the mail came bounding on, put spurs to his mare, and, giving a shout to Eustace to follow him, met the coach as it dashed on.

"Clear the road, damn yer, or I'll drive over yer!" yelled the coachman, who perceived the glitter of the barrels of Turpin's pistols, as he darted forwards to meet the coach.

Slashing at the horses, the mail was crashing on, when Eustace, touching his mare on the flank, arrived by the side of the mail, and, seizing the reins, stopped the animals in their flight. In another moment Turpin severed the leathern thongs that confined the horses' heads, and the York mail was, for a time, prevented from prosecuting its journey.

Loud shrieks burst from the mouths of the female passengers, mingled with oaths from the male portion of the travellers in the coach.

"Sorry to inconvenience you, ladies and gentlemen, but necessity compels." Turpin here raised his hat, and approached the side of the coach. "Eustace," he added, "tell that fool of a guard to drop that blunderbuss of his, and if he refuses, oblige him with a two-ounce bullet."

Having severed the reins, and prevented the mail proceeding on her journey for a few minutes, Eustace left the horses' heads, and cantered, pistols in hand, to the side of the coach.

It had been arranged that Turpin should rob the passengers, whilst Eustace guarded against surprise.

Scarce had Turpin directed his companion's attention to the conduct of the guard, ere the latter, bending over the dickey, presented a wide-mouthed piece at the highwaymen, and, with a loud laugh, exclaimed—

"Yer wants summat, don't yer? Take that!"

There was a stunning report, a yell of triumph from the guard, and then the coach was dragged a few paces by the frightened steeds, at length upsetting by the wayside.

Screams, oaths, and prayers for mercy escaped from the lips of the passengers, some of whom were much hurt by the overturning of the coach.

Two figures busily engaged themselves assisting the inside passengers to extricate themselves from their unpleasant position.

These were the companions, Turpin and Eustace, our hero cleverly avoiding the discharge from the weapon of the guard, by spurring his steed aside and getting in the rear of the mail.

"Now, ladies and gentlemen, pay the toll, please," said Turpin. "Eustace, that serious-looking individual in the white choker wants to decamp. Hold him back."

With a laugh, Eustace dragged back the portly figure of a clerical gentleman, whose rubicund visage purpled first with rage and then paled with fright.

Leaving the outsiders to themselves, as pigeons not worth plucking, they being all of the poorer class, the two highwaymen proceeded to inspect the inside riders of the York mail, of whom there were four; one was the stout clerical gentleman; another was a fashionably-dressed young man, who, with diamond rings on his fingers, appeared a person likely to reward the robbers for their daring by a goodly sum; the others were two ladies—a mother and her daughter, a fair-haired English girl of seventeen or eighteen. Both the ladies were elegantly attired, the mother of the young girl carrying a richly-jewelled watch, that, in the overturning of the coach, had escaped from the bosom of its wearer.

"Ladies, your rings and watches; sorry to deprive you of the gems, but really, such charms require not trinkets. Eustace, see to our portly friend—he appears impatient. The gentleman, too, beside you looks mischievous; just let him know you carry barking irons; tap him on the head."

Bowing and smiling to the trembling women, whilst he robbed them of their money and jewellery, Turpin left his companion to do the same by the men.

The outside passengers, in a terrified group, congregated near the roadside. Coachee and the guard, lying under the horses' feet, were strongly bound by the highwaymen; they had been thrown, and rendered helpless.

"Now then, reverend sir, your watch—money. Quick!"

"Profane wretch! wouldst thou commit sacrilege? I have nothing for thee."

"Haven't you? Hem! that's a pity; for as I never put up with disappointment without having revenge. I must blow your brains out—that's if you have any."

Eustace here cocked his pistol, the lock giving an ominous click, that caused the clerical gentleman to fall on his knees and pray for mercy.

"Mercy! Mr. Highwayman. Slay me not! Spare, oh! spare a pillar of the church!"

"Well, I really don't think the church will be the gainer if I do, as it is evident you are a very rotten pillar. But, come! shell out; tip the rowdy—pay the fees of the road, and be off. I'm poor. Remember, 'he that giveth to the poor, lendeth to the Lord.'"

"Indeed, I assure you, Mr. Robber, I've very little; positively, very little."

In terror and rage the clergyman glared round him, while Eustace, with a loud laugh, proceeded to turn out the contents of his pockets.

"Why, you lying churchman, what do you call this?" Eustace here held up a canvas bag, that, on being shaken, emitted a jingling noise.

The perspiration, in beads, poured down the features of the unfortunate parson, as he beheld his gold torn from him.

"My gold! my gold! Give me back my gold!" Fury nearly choked the utterance of the churchman, whilst Eustace, yelling with laughter, and shaking the bag in his face, exclaimed—

"I have but a little—positively very little! I will take your little, my dear friend, and accept it as the widow's mite!"

Shouting with laughter at the furious looks of the parson—who muttered something very like an oath—Eustace now turned to the young man who, livid pale, stood by the coach door.

He was a young man of about the same age as the highwayman—perhaps a year or so less. A very effeminate look rested about the not bad-looking features; a sinister expression hung about the brow, that was added to by a low and receding forehead.

Dressed in the height of the fashion, it was evident the stranger moved in high circles; his rich velvet coat was fringed with gold lace, whilst the rings upon his fingers glittered with diamonds of the first water.

Chuckling at the rich harvest before him, Eustace demanded the stranger to hand over his money and his trinkets. For a moment the stranger hesitated; then, livid with rage and fear, he pulled the rings off his fingers, and, with a richly-jewelled repeater and a heavy purse, handed them to Eustace, who, with pistols ready cocked, stood before him.

Lifting his hat courteously from his head, the highwayman was about to join his companion, who, with a loud whistle, gave warning of departure, when the young man suddenly darted upon him, and, with a small knife he drew from his breast, attempted to stab him.

Ever alive to danger, Eustace was prepared for the attack, and, with the quickness of thought, stooped down, and as the stranger lunged at him, knife in hand, seized his wrist, and, twisting it round in his iron grasp, caused his assailant to drop the weapon with a yell of pain.

In the struggle, however, the crape fell from the countenance of Eustace, whose features were thus revealed to the other's gaze in the broad glare of the moonlight.

Picking up the knife, the handle of which was of mother-of-pearl inlaid with gold and jewelled with turquoise, Eustace noted not the start and look of wonder and astonishment that rested on the other's features as his own were revealed in the pale, silvery rays of the moon.

"Bullet the cur, and mount, Eustace; the game is up," shouted Turpin.

About to rush upon the cowering form of the young man, Eustace curbed his anger at the other's treacherous attack, and calling upon his steed, that, at a word, trotted to his side, leaped into the saddle, exclaiming—

"Look you, my young friend, that was a cowardly attack. Don't try it on another time. A less-merciful knight of the road may scatter your brains to the four quarters of the wind. I will keep your pretty sticker for a keepsake. Farewell! Au revoir, ladies! Heaven bless you all! You will soon be again upon the road. You can tell our friends that are coming to your assistance, that if they want a canter we are ready for a race. Hillio! ho! away! Go on, Sue!"

Followed by Turpin on his bonny Black Bess, Eustace, giving his mare the rein, bounded away from the scene of their exploit; the loud cries of the parson, who yelled for help, ringing upon their ears as they galloped off.

For some minutes the two friends, giving their horses the reins, dashed along the road at a terrific rate.

At length, at a turn in the road, they drew in their reins, and, pausing for a moment, bent their heads down towards the ground; then, gazing into each others' faces, they both exclaimed—

"We are pursued!"

"Ay, Dick, and our enemies are mounted on good pieces of horseflesh. Hark! how plain the sound is now. We must make speed. Where shall we go—to the 'Bold Horseman?'"

"No, Eustace, it won't do. George's place will be well searched; besides, 'twill be out of our road."

"What are we to do then—ride on?"

"Yes, until we reach the Hemlock Manor House."

"The Hemlock Manor House! Good heavens! You do not think of visiting the residence of Ralph Fairley to-night?"

"That's just the thing I do intend. We couldn't find a better hiding-place."

"But the old man. What will he think? what will he say?"

"Why, that he is glad to see the Hon. Frank Hartland at any hour."

"How will you account for our appearance at such an hour?"

"No room at the inn, so we cantered on."

"'Tis a daring expedient."

"And, therefore, will succeed. We shall throw our enemies off the scent, and be regaled with a good supper; for the old miser has good cheer ready for people of money and rank, such as you and I."

A low laugh escaped the lips of Turpin as he winked at his companion; then, giving the animals the rein, the highwaymen once more rushed along the road at lightning speed.

A warm glow diffused throughout their frames by their midnight ride.

At length the sound of pursuit ceased, and the two friends, having distanced their enemies, proceeded at a slower pace.

The moon, bright and clear, shone with a silvery light upon the scene.

Some tall wych elms, that lined the road they were now pursuing, looked like grim, giant spectres in the pale moon's rays.

Congratulating each other on the success of their first exploit together, the two friends proceeded onwards, till at length, on raising their heads, they were startled by a large black mass, that reared itself up a short distance from the road.

Black, grim, and horrible looked that dark mass in the light of the moon.

"What the devil's that place, Dick?"

"Don't you recognise it?"

"No."

"Still you have been within the place. 'Tis the haunted mill, in the dried-up stream of which is the secret passage leading to the 'Bold Horseman.'"

"Would it not be advisable to make our way into the passage?"

"No, Eustace, it ain't to be done. Starlight Sue might object, not having travelled that road before."

"True! Then there is no help for it but to hasten on to the Hemlock Manor House."

The two friends had now drawn close to the mill.

The ruin looked grim and ghastly in the pale moon's rays.

"It is a ghastly-looking place, Dick. Do you place any credence to the ruin being haunted?"

"No, Eustace, I don't believe in spirits or beings of the other world. The legends about them are but tales to frighten children; men of sense are above such trash. I'll tell you some time or other the story connected with this old ruined water-mill, and all about the ghost said to haunt the place, not a word, mind you, of which do I believe."

"Hush! hush! Dick. What's that?"

A long sighing sound was now heard on the night air. The horses at this moment betrayed, too, a feverish impatience to be off."

"Pshaw! Eustace. You are, I suppose, a believer in supernatural beings, and my making you acquainted with the fact that the old mill is said to be haunted has caused you to fancy you heard an unearthly noise. Those are the only ghosts that haunt the ruined mill, I'll swear!"

Turpin, with his riding-whip, here pointed out a huge bat, that rushed out of the ruin blindly in the night air, spreading out its leather wings.

"You say, Dick, the place is haunted, and that you don't believe in supernatural beings. God of heaven! then, can you explain that?" gasped Eustace, clutching his companion by the arm, and pointing to a white, shadow-like figure, that appeared stepping through the doorway of the mill.

Turpin, speechless with amazement, returned no answer to his friend, but gazed steadfastly upon the tall, shadowy figure that emerged from the old ruin.

Pacing up and down in the blue rays of the moon, the two friends both alike beheld the strange form.

It bore the appearance of a human figure, but so shadowy and ill-defined that the sex could not be determined.

A horrible chill crept through the frame of Eustace as he gazed upon the strange sight.

Fascinated with awe and terror, the highwaymen remained seated on their steeds, gazing upon the strange sight.

Up and down in front of the old ruin the shadowy figure kept pacing, not appearing to walk, but to make a kind of spasmodic jerk at each step, and at times to hover two or three feet from the ground.

At length it paused. White and ghastly, shadowy and spectral, it appeared stationed in front of the mill.

"That is no human form, Dick. By the heavens above us, 'tis a being of another world!"

"That I will ascertain," muttered Turpin, with a curse. "By the fiends! I'll not be juggled with."

At the instant that he pulled a pistol from his pocket, both the highwaymen were startled by the sound of someone on horseback close behind them, whilst a cold wind, as of ice, rushed by them. Both turned their heads at the same instant expecting to behold a horseman.

A thrill of horror darted through their frames as they found they were alone.

A moment after, Turpin, with a deep-breathed curse, raised his pistol, and, pointing it at the shadow by the mill, fired.

There was a sharp, clear report; then all was still.

With a cry of horror, Turpin, on looking forwards, discovered the figure still standing, fully revealed in the spectral rays of the moon.

"By the foul fiend, I'll know what this means," said Turpin.

Then, patting his bonny mare, that snorted and shook with terror, he leaped to the ground.

Eustace also dismounting, each made for the old mill.

Clear, distinct, and with a kind of mist around it, stood the strange figure before them.

Weird and horrible it looked, in the pale blue rays of the moon.

Slowly the two friends made their way towards the mystic appearance.

Both alike determined to unravel the mystery of the apparition.

In silence, they bent their steps to the front of the ruined mill.

The highwaymen were bold, determined, fearless beings, but each shuddered with strange awe and terror as they drew nearer to the mill.

The loud neighing of the horses, as they impatiently pawed the ground at their feet, and the sighing of the chill night wind, alone broke the stillness of the scene.

"Dick, let us return. I fear no man on earth, but by the heavens above us, it is no human figure that is now stationary before us by the old mill."

"Do you stand back, Eustace. By all the fiends below, I'll not be juggled with."

"Where you go, Dick, I follow; and be yonder form fiend or spectre of another world, I care not; together we will approach it."

Nearer and nearer they drew to the mill.

The dim, shadowy form, enveloped in a thick mist, remained where first discovered.

Turpin, pulling a pistol from his vest, cocked it, the lock making a loud click upon the silent air.

"My eye may before have deceived me; I'll fire again."

"Nay, Dick; by heavens! discharge not your weapon, unless we are the victims of a vision. The figure before us is that of a young and lovely girl."

"You are right. I will not fire; yet will I find out the mystery of this appearance, and if we are made the fools of stupid jest, let the perpetrators beware."

The companions had now reached within four or five feet of the figure.

Both started and shuddered with horror as they gazed upon the sight before them.

The figure of a slight young girl stood motionless by the entrance to the ruined mill.

The white cloud, or mist, that had before enveloped the strange form, had now dispersed.

Ahead of his companion, Turpin was nearest to the girl, and, suddenly darting forwards, the highwayman grasped at the figure.

The moon shone bright, clear, and beautiful overhead, pouring a silver radiance on all around.

As if by enchantment, turned into a block of marble, Turpin stood beside the figure, rooted to the spot.

With a thrill of horror, Eustace beheld a strange, wild sight.

A sight that made his blood like ice course through his veins.

A sight long remembered—never forgotten.

He beheld his friend stretch forth his hand to clutch the young girl.

The mystic form, at the same moment, heeded not the man beside her, but bent a fixed, wild stare upon the countenance of Eustace, and stepped in front of Turpin.

The eyes of the strange figure shone upon him with a cold, meaningless, metallic stare.

A look that seemed to freeze all the blood in his body.

But that which struck Eustace with such horror, that caused his blood to crawl ice-like through his veins, was that he could see his friend's body through that of the young girl!

He beheld the glitter of the pistol held in the right hand of his friend, as the moon poured down upon him.

And yet erect before him was the form of the girl.

At length, with a wild cry of horror, Eustace dashed forwards.

With a bound, he was upon the spot upon which stood the strange figure.

Darting right through the mystic shadow.

A deep-breathed curse escaped the lips of Turpin, who now seized the hand of Eustace in his own, dragging him from the spot in frenzied haste.

Wildly the friends bounded to their steeds, and, mounting them, were presently borne with lightning speed from the mill.

Turning their heads as they galloped off, they discovered that the figure had vanished.

But neither doubted now the truth of the report as to the haunting of the old ruin.

Either they had been strangely juggled with, or 'twas the spectre of the mill they had seen that night.

Without a word, the highwaymen galloped on.

A bend of the road at length hid the haunted ruin from sight.

And at the same moment each drew up.

Their steeds panting from the race.

Eustace was the first to break the silence.

"Well, Dick, what do you think of what we have seen?"

"Why, that we have both been the victims of a cursed delusion, or that we have indeed beheld the spirit said to haunt the mill."

"Well, Dick, I shall never forget the sight I've seen to-night."

"Nor I. When I grasped at the figure, my hand met nought but empty air. I clutched but at a shadow, though I felt as if I had plunged my hand into a sea of ice; I stared right through the spectral form, as though it were a sheet of glass."

"'Tis very strange. You know the story of the old mill, Dick, do you not?"

"Well, no, not exactly; but George Watson, of the 'Bold Horseman,' can tell you all about it. But we have forgotten our friends. Hark!"

Raising his hand, Dick pointed down the road.

Loud and clear upon the night air came the ringing clatter of horses' hoofs.

"We are still pursued. What's to be done, Dick?"

"Why, we must house ourselves for the night."

"But where?"

"At old Fairley's."

"But we shall be tracked."

"Not if we act with caution."

"And the horses?"

"Must be placed in the stables of Hemlock Manor."

"Well, Dick, as you will; I care not. I begin to imbibe your dauntless spirit and defiance of danger and detection. Lead on! 'tis fearfully cold; and by all the demons below in the fiery regions, I should be glad of a warmer berth."

The companions once more gave their steeds the reins, and soon reached the lane leading to the entrance-gates of the Hemlock Manor House.

The sound of horses' feet, clattering along in the distance, ringing plainer upon the air.

"Well, Dick, 'tis our first adventure together. We have well lined our pockets, and have passed through strange scenes to-night. We have secured a good round sum in bright guineas and costly trinkets; but the Philistines are upon us, and we are about to seek safety in a house where I'd give up life itself sooner than be discovered."

"Have no fear of that, Eustace. Leave all to me. Your pal will pull you through. There, the gate is unfastened. Bring the horses in; we'll soon have the bridles off, and have them snug and warm in old Fairley's stables."

Turpin, who had dismounted, and had managed to open the gates of the Manor House, made his way along the gravel walk, followed by Eustace, a moment afterwards, with the horses.

Slowly, cautiously, they made their way along the drive in front of the manor.

At length Turpin proceeded down a narrow path in the garden, lined on either side with thick shrubbery.

At the bottom of this walk they came to a door.

This was the side entrance to the Manor House.

With little difficulty Turpin opened this bar to their progress, and they were presently, with their horses, making their way through the grounds at the back.

At the other extremity of the gardens was situated the stables.

Into these, in a short time, Turpin had safely housed his own and his friend's steed.

"Now our bonny mares are right for the night, Eustace, let us look to ourselves."

"What do you propose to do?"

"Why, to make my way to that delightful apartment, placed at our disposal by the most lovely of her sex, the beautiful Sybil Fairley."

"But to do this you must break into the house."

"Precisely. We shall thus effectually throw our enemies off the scent if they call hither, which is not to be supposed. Why, old Fairley's servants will pretty soon acquaint our friends with the fact that they have made a slight mistake, whilst, in the arms of Morpheus, we can enjoy ourselves in the oak chamber."

"How will you get into the bedroom?"

"By aid of the vinery that grows against the walls we can reach the window. See, the moon throws her rays full upon the casement.

Turpin pointed to a large window that, overshaded by a thick vine, was some twenty feet from the garden below.

"I will admit, Dick, that our entrance to the oak chamber is easy. By the way, you proposed also that we shall find a safe haven from our foes; but how about our appearance to old Fairley in the morning? How shall we account for our presence? The least suspicion aroused, and all is discovered."

"Leave all to me, and fear not for the result."

Followed by his companion, Turpin, by means of the thick vinery that grew against the wall, made his way to the casement above, that overlooked the gardens of the Hemlock Manor House, and, in a few moments, the highwaymen were safely lodged in the residence of the miser.

CHAPTER XVIII.

THE MISER'S DAUGHTER AND THE HIGHWAYMEN.—THE CONFESSION OF LOVE. — SYBIL FAIRLEY AND HER NOBLE-HEARTED ADORER. — THE DISGUISE THROWN OFF.—LOVE AND HONOUR.—THE DECISION OF A FOND HEART.—THE TROTH-PLIGHT BENEATH THE BLIGHTED OAK.—THE ALARM.—SUDDEN APPEARANCE OF RALPH FAIRLEY.—FURY OF THE MISER.—LOVERS' VOWS AND A FATHER'S CURSE.

THREE months passed away. 'Tis now the bright and happy spring time.

Winter, with its frosty breath and cheerless aspect, its bleak winds and storms of snow, has gone.

'Tis bright, joyous spring.

Spring, with its warm breezes from the sunny south, and its glinting flowerets and green foliage.

How changed the aspect of the country!

'Tis a lovely scene. The open meadows; the bright, green fields; the thick copse, with its glorious garb of approaching summer; all looks gay and beautiful.

But few changes have occurred to the different characters in this our drama of real life.

Crime still flourishes in the world of London. The wealthy and the indigent still run on their course side by side, playing their parts in the drama of life on the world's stage.

The scene of our story again takes us to the country residence of Ralph Fairley, the Hemlock Manor House.

It is a lovely morning; the bright and glorious sun in golden rays pours down a flood of light on all around.

The dewdrops, like crystals, hang upon the shrubs, glittering in the light of the sun.

The hedge-sparrow, the trilling lark, and warbling linnet skim joyously in the air, waking up the echoes with their sweet notes.

The breeze sighs with a gentle murmur through the thick copse that lines each side of the lane leading to the Hemlock Manor House. All is silent, save for the twittering of the feathered songsters and the tap-tap of the woodpecker, that sounds with a somewhat pleasant noise upon the air that spring morn.

'Tis a beautiful rural scene that lane near the Hemlock Manor House. Near one end is the highroad leading to London, at the other is the residence of Ralph Fairley. The roof of the money-lender's dwelling can be just discerned through the topmost branches of some giant oaks.

Slowly wandering down the lane on this lovely morning are two figures.

One that of a young and beautiful girl, the other a dashing, well-built, handsome young man.

Side by side they wander on. Soft words are breathed by the companion of the fair girl, who, with downcast head, trembles as she listens to his honeyed accents.

'Tis a lovers' meeting. A fond lover is pleading his suit. Nor could a more favourable spot have been chosen for such a purpose than that pretty rural lane.

The birds, billing and cooing in the hedgeside, are envied by the young man, who, with death-pale face and sinking voice, urges on his suit, breathing out for the first time his vows of love.

"Oh! hear me, sweetest Sybil; turn not from me thus. I love you, dearest; love you to madness. Say but that I may hope. I have a secret, a terrible secret to reveal, but dare not let it pass my lips without I receive token from yours that you do not hate me."

"Hate you, my Frank? Oh! no! no! no! But this sudden declaration. Should my father know ought of this, I know not what he might say; though I think your rank and noble birth would secure his friendship. But he is a strange man."

The young girl, the beautiful Sybil Fairley, bending her graceful head from her lover's gaze, began to pick to pieces a lovely bouquet of choice spring flowers she held in her hands.

The face of her lover grew dark and clouded as Sybil mentioned her parent. Drawing to her side, he now seized one of her soft, white hands in his, and, with a face that was crimson and pallid by turns, exclaimed—

"But you—you, Sybil! Say your father for some reason spurned me from him, should I possess your love? Speak, dear girl; let me know if I have read aright your dove-like eyes. Sybil Fairley, I would lay down my life for you. Do you love me?"

There was such an earnest, impassioned tone in her lover's voice, such a look of dark despair and sorrow upon his handsome features, that involuntarily she clasped his hand in hers and sank her head upon his shoulder low sobs escaping from her coral lips whilst she tremblingly clung to his side.

There needed no words to tell her lover that he held possession of her heart.

Convinced that she loved him, the young man gazed with a fond look upon the lovely girl he held in his arms, but his brow was still clouded with a dark shade of sorrow —of despair.

Raising her blushing face, Sybil Fairley started as she gazed upon the pallid features of her lover.

"Frank, dear Frank, oh! tell me what means that look of trouble? Know, since you have wrung the secret from me, that I long have loved you. Can I ever forget," murmured the lovely girl, "that, but for you, my father and myself would have fallen victims to the murdering housebreakers, months back? Frank Hartland, that service can never be forgotten. Besides, I love you fondly—dearly."

Hiding her flushed face in her lover's bosom as she uttered this avowal, the beautiful Sybil beheld not the look of pain and misery that rested upon his singularly handsome features.

Drawing her gently forwards from the glare of the sun beneath the shade thrown on the path from the huge trunk of a blighted oak, the lover untwined the girl's arms from around his neck, and exclaimed—

"Sybil Fairley, I have won your love, but under a disguise. I must now, though it cause your love to turn to hate, reveal a secret that has for weeks preyed upon my mind."

"A secret! What mean you, dear Frank?"

"Nay, call me not by that name. Sybil, dear Sybil! the time has arrived to throw off the mask. I am not he for whom you take me. The young gentleman, whose name I have borrowed, is now in France, and I—I, the man who, by a villainous fraud, hath gained your virgin heart, am an outcast."

"An outcast!" The cheeks of Sybil, before flushed with crimson, now turned deadly pale as she reiterated the words of her lover. Staggering back, she leant against the trunk of the blighted oak tree beneath which they stood, and with eyes of alarm gazed upon the livid, convulsed features of her lover.

"Who—who and what are you?" at length gasped the trembling girl.

"My name is Eustace Maltravers, and I am"—— Such a look of agony here stole athwart her lover's face that Sybil, tottering forwards, seized his hands in hers, and gazing fondly into his eyes, exclaimed—

"Hear me, dear Eustace, since such be your name. 'Tis now above four months since that night that, passing the Manor with your friend, Mr. Palmer, you heard a cry of murder, and entering my father's residence saved us both from the hands of the assassin. My father is a cold, stern, money-loving man; but still he will not forget the debt he owes you—the debt of a life. From the first hour of our meeting, dear Eustace, I felt drawn towards you. Your eyes spoke your thoughts; from the first I saw you loved me. Eustace, you have this morning wrung from me the secret I have kept hitherto hidden in my bosom—that your love is returned."

With a deep blush crimsoning her face, the lovely girl now drew a locket from her bosom, and, holding it out to her lover, she murmured—

"Eustace, to prove how I love you, know that I have kept this portrait since the morning I discovered it on the floor of the oak chamber in which you slept with your friend. I expected at each fresh visit that you would ask for it, but you failing to do so, I have kept it. When you have been absent I have often gazed upon the picture so like my Eustace. Can you now doubt that you have won my heart? I care not if indeed you hold no rank; I can as fervently love Eustace Maltravers as the Hon. Frank Hartland; but if you belong not to noble family, might I ask, dear Eustace, how you own a portrait so richly set with gems?"

A half-smile rested on the features of Sybil, as pressing a spring of the locket she held in her hand, she revealed the portrait of a young man studded round with brilliants and emeralds.

The paleness that had left the cheeks of Eustace as Sybil had fondly avowed her love now returned—his countenance becoming even more livid than before. Taking the jewelled locket from Sybil, he gazed with staring eyes upon the portrait.

Wildly Eustace glared upon the miniature, the features of which were the counterpart of his own.

"Where got you this?" gasped Eustace, whilst convulsively he clutched the locket in his grasp.

"I found it on the floor of the oak chamber," exclaimed Sybil, in alarm, gazing at the pallid features of her lover.

"Have you shown it to your father?"

"No eyes have seen it save mine."

"Sybil, there is only a wonderful resemblance in this picture to me; 'tis nothing more: 'tis not mine. I tell you this lest you should imagine I am still of a rich and titled family."

"Dear Eustace, I care not for wealth or titles; gain but my father's consent to our union, and I am yours."

The fair girl fondly approached her lover, and once more encircled his neck with her soft, round arms.

"Sybil, your father will never give your hand to me."

"Never? Oh! say not that: my father loves me, Eustace; besides, he owes you his life. I feel certain that in time he will consent."

"Never, Sybil; and I will tell you why. Know that your wretched lover is not only an outcast, but a hunted felon."

A wild, piercing shriek rung upon the air, and, staggering back, Sybil appeared as though about to fly madly from the spot; but hesitating, she glanced upon the agonized features of her lover, whose heaving chest gave token of the emotion within.

Transfixed, the beautiful girl, pale as a lily, and her eyes beaming with pity, gazed upon the wretched man before her. Looking up, and with his hand brushing off a tear from his face, he, in a hoarse voice, husky with suppressed emotion, exclaimed—

"Sybil Fairley, I have long looked for this. The bitter hour has come—the hideous truth is told. I saw and loved you. Like a moth, I fluttered round the flame kindled to destroy me. When I found my earnest attentions rewarded with smiles, I said to myself, she loves me. To-day I wrung the secret from your lips. Had you made known to me that I was held in your affections, I should have pursued a far different course; but when, dear girl, you told me I possessed your sweet love, I felt in honour bound to reveal my terrible secret. Sybil Fairley, I was a castaway from my birth—never knew a father's or a mother's care. My only relative is a man of crime; I have been tutored to vice from my childhood; I have embarked in a course from which there is now no return; I am an outcast, a man at war with society and its laws! Sybil Fairley, curse me! curse the man who has won your fond heart under a villainous disguise! Sybil, Eustace Maltravers, the man to whom you have rendered up your virgin heart, is a villain and a robber!

Curse me! and fly me as though I were infected with a pestilence!"

"For heaven's love talk not thus, dear Eustace! You know not what you say. Your acts, your past conduct to me bespeak a different being to that you would paint yourself; and be you what you may, I could never hate or curse the man I once loved!"

Choked with her tears, Sybil paused, and gazed in alarm at the contorted features of her lover.

Starting forwards, and placing his hand upon her shoulder, he exclaimed—

"Sybil, my poor, pale, deceived victim, you know not what you say. I tell you, girl, you will curse me, and fly from me, as from a leper, when I tell you all!"

"You mistake me, Eustace Maltravers. You know not woman once she loves, or you would not talk thus. Your terrible secret—whate'er it be—will never rob me of your love. Oh! say, dear one, you did but jest—you have uttered these terrible words to test your Sybil's heart! Is it not so?"

Beautiful Sybil looked, as, pale and trembling, she stood before her lover. The crystal tears, like rain, bedewed her lovely features. With head bent, like a drooping lily, she stood by the ruined oak, the sun shining on her rich tresses and white and plump shoulders.

With wild, frenzied gaze, Eustace bent his eyes upon the lovely figure before him, a storm of passion raging in his bosom. Had he carried out his act of treachery, the miser's daughter would have been his; but a spirit of honour was possessed by the young highwayman, that rebelled at the thought of gaining the fair girl to his arms by a deed for which he would deserve her bitterest curse.

"Sybil, this scene were best ended for both our sakes. Strive to forget one who, it were well, had never crossed your path. I shall leave this neighbourhood to-day, and—and"—the voice of Eustace here grew thick and indistinct—"and we shall never meet again!"

With a sob, he murmured the last words, and was about to hurry from the spot, when he was restrained by Sybil, whose pale face was turned beseechingly upon him.

"Do not leave me thus, dear Eustace, but tell me who and what are you?"

"Sybil Fairley, your lover is a highwayman—a knight of the road! Now, curse me, and bid me quit your sight!"

With a low moan, Sybil fell into the arms of her lover, murmuring—

"'Tis not your fault, but a cruel fate, dear Eustace. The soul of honour is the man who could proclaim this to one he loved as you do the unhappy Sybil; and though you are that you say, the heart of poor Sybil is still your own!"

A shout of joy escaped the lips of Eustace, who clasped the fainting girl in his arms, pressing his mouth madly to hers. With tears of joy he kissed her lips, brow, and snow-white neck. He knelt upon the soft sward, and vowed to give up his present course, and endeavour to make himself worthy of her hand. Lost in joy, as he gazed upon the beautiful features of his mistress, Eustace heard not the noise of a stranger crashing through the copse, and was only aroused by a hand being placed upon his shoulders. Starting up, he let the senseless form of Sybil, who, overcome with emotion, had fainted, resting upon the gnarled root of the blighted oak; and, turning round, was astounded to find himself face to face with Ralph Fairley, the money-lender.

There was a dark look of rage and fury upon the features of the old man.

For a few moments passion choked the miser's utterance. At length the words that fell from his lips made Eustace acquainted that the father of his beloved knew all.

"Thief! robber! scoundrel! I will drag you to the scaffold!" hissed Ralph Fairley, between his clenched teeth. "I see it all! 'Twas your companion robbed me of my gold two months back, as, following your advice, I conveyed some of my jewels to London. The account that, in the early morning, a second time, you surprised some housebreakers, was a lie to account for your presence in my house. I have been your dupe; but, by the fiends! you shall surely swing upon the scaffold! You shall hang at Tyburn, dog! I have over-heard all. You have, with the cunning of a fiend, won the love of my child; but did she perish at my feet for the act, I'll send you to the gibbet! Ha! ha! you have breathed your vows of love beneath the blighted oak. The warning is prophetic. A murder was committed in this lane years back, and the assassin was hung in chains from the boughs of this aged oak; and you, Eustace Maltravers, highwayman! thief! robber! you shall hang at Tyburn!"

His face, livid with fury, and the veins of his forehead standing out like whipcord, the old man poured out his threats and vows of vengeance.

Meanwhile, the unfortunate Sybil, recovering from her swoon, rose to her feet, and casting her eyes in dismay upon her parent, drew to the side of her lover.

With a howl of rage Ralph darted forwards, and dragged her back.

"Approach him not, girl, unless you would have me breathe my bitterest curse upon your head!"

"Father! father! dear father! look not on me thus! What means this terrible scene?"

"It means, girl, that I have heard all. I have been the dupe of that man, the thief! the highway robber! whom I will bring to the scaffold, for he has robbed me of my gold, and I will have revenge! I will have his life!"

"Oh! no—no—no! Father, say not so! He saved yours, you will not betray him to his foes!"

Madly the distracted girl clung to her parent, who, in savage fury, hurled her from him with such force that she fell to the ground at her lover's feet. About to raise her in his arms, Eustace was prevented by the fury of the old man, who, rushing forwards, raised his clenched fist, and struck him in the mouth. Stung to madness by the blow, Eustace was about to raise his hand against Ralph Fairley, when Sybil, rising, threw herself in his arms.

"Hold! hold! Eustace; he is mad, and knows not what he does. For my sake, forgive that blow and harm him not!"

"Sybil, dear one, for your sake, I would cheerfully meet the doom your father threatens me with—death upon the gibbet! Ralph Fairley, I excuse your fury. Do as you list. As regards me, pursue me to the death if you will I can never turn against you, for you are the parent of the one I love as I love my life."

"She shall see you swing, swing at Tyburn!"

Wild screams pealed from Sybil's lips, as her enraged father tore her from her lover's arms.

"Heed not his threats, dear Sybil; we shall meet again."

"Yes, when you are led to execution; for I will hang you, Eustace Maltravers! By the Being above that made me, I swear it!"

"Nay, father, for heaven's sake! stay your oath. Spare, oh! spare him. Pursue him not with your fearful vengeance!"

"Curses upon you, girl, for your infamous passion! He shall hang, hang, I tell you, for he has duped and robbed me of my gold, and I will have revenge!"

Hoarse with rage, the white foam gathering in flecks upon his lips, the old man now staggered back, leaning for support against the old oak.

With a wild look of entreaty, Sybil motioned her lover to go.

Seizing her hand in his, and thrusting the jewelled locket he had held into hers, Eustace, first pressing his lips to her marble brow, bounded from the spot, followed by the curses of the enraged Ralph Fairley, distracted with grief.

An hour afterwards the unhappy Sybil was alone in a large, deserted chamber of the Hemlock Manor.

Alone, and a prisoner.

Placed in the chamber, and locked and bolted in by her enraged parent, who, with a fearful oath, registered a vow that she should not leave her prison till he took her from thence to Tyburn Tree to witness the execution of her lover, Eustace Maltravers, the knight of the road.

THE ESCAPE.

CHAPTER XIX.

THE OFFICE OF THE MONEY-LENDER. — THE YOUNG
CLERK AND THE WAITING-MAID.—DISTRESS OF NANCY
WATSON.—NAT. STEVENS AND HIS FELLOW-CLERK.—
THE QUARREL AND THREAT OF EPHRAIM RASSELTON.
—THE VISITOR.—EPHRAIM AND THE STRANGER.—THE
CONFERENCE. — DEPARTURE OF NAT. STEVENS, AND
STRANGE RENCOUNTER WITH EUSTACE MALTRAVERS.
—THE WARNING.

THE bright midday sun shone with glorious radiance upon
the good city of London, causing the thronged and bustling
business-thoroughfares to look gay and cheerful.

Even the gloomy, dusty office of Ralph Fairley, in the
Poultry, looked bright and homely in the rays of the
summer sun; true the blinds and windows looked more
dusty and dirty, but still, on the whole, the darksome
office wore a more cheerful aspect.

Sitting, gazing dreamily out into the street, through
the wire blind, was our old friend Nat. Stevens, the
younger clerk of the money-lender. A troubled expression rested on the features of the young man.

"Confound it! what's up, I wonder? It ain't a trifle
that causes a cloud to rest upon the pretty face of my
sweet Nancy, bless her bright eyes and rosy cheeks. Law,
how I do love that girl, and yet," muttered the young
clerk, as he nibbled the end of a pen, every now and then
giving it a savage bite, "and yet, what a fool I am! What
is the use of me falling in love? A fellow that earns
nothing a year, and has to live on it, arn't got no business
to fall in love; though, for the matter of that, as Jem
Stacey, the chairman at the 'Magpie and Stump,' justly
observed the other night, a poor man has as much right to
love and be married as a rich one. I think it's very hard
for one man to have thousands for doing nothing, and his
fellow-man dying of want. Well, it gets over me."

Poor Nat Stevens had imbibed some radical principles
at the "Magpie and Stump," and could not understand
the right of the Hon. Augustus Fluff having twenty
thousand a year, whilst he, Nat, hadn't as many shillings.
With a puzzled, disturbed air, Nat remained seated by
the window, gazing out into the street. The cause of the
young clerk's distress was, that on his arrival at the office
that morning, he found that Nancy Watson had come up
to town from the Hemlock Manor House without her
master or mistress; the money-lender would come up

during the day, but Sybil Fairley would remain at the manor house. In a few disjointed sentences Nat had gathered this from Nancy, who, hurrying from him, sobbing violently, had gone to her chamber. Now, as the young girl never, by any chance, came down into the office, poor Nat knew that he could learn nothing till one o'clock, when he would have to go into the kitchen for his dinner. Moodily he sat, paying no heed to the scowl that gathered over the features of the head clerk, who several times hemmed and hawed as a gentle hint to the young man that he was doing nothing. At length, indignant at Nat's non-attention to business, Ephraim hobbled out of the inner office, and, coming forwards, tapped the absorbed Nat upon the shoulder.

"Eh! eh! eh! Fine morning, Mr. Nat Stevens. Perhaps you would like to go for a walk. You seem to have quite forgotten that there is such a thing as business to attend to in this office. Other people may work while you skulk."

"Look here, old dot-and-go-one; you go and stick to your work and leave me to mine."

Turning coolly from his companion, Nat again looked into the street, as he whistled a popular air of the day, quite ignoring the presence of the head clerk.

Had Nat seen the evil scowl, the look of fury that darted athwart the features of the deformed clerk, he would have been startled and warned against him. It was the first time that Nat had in any way alluded to the other's misfortune. Rasselton noted, with fury, the contemptuous glance the young man had cast upon his deformed person.

"Eh! eh! eh! Perhaps you have forgotten that in the absence of Ralph Fairley, I am your master."

"You my master? Ha! ha! ha! Come, that's good. Let us hear it again, old humpy. Look here, you owl-faced, deformed, evil-disposed cur, I'll just speak out."

Bounding off his chair, Nat, his face red, and looking as though he was about to inflict chastisement upon his fellow-clerk, let his indignation have full sway. He long had hated the man who, by every means in his power, had imposed upon him; and, enraged at his helpless position with regard to the fair Nancy, and also remembering a conversation he had held the night before with his friend Jem Stacey, at the "Magpie and Stump," who had advised him to leave the money-lender for a situation where he would be paid well for his services, Nat was determined to speak his mind, as he said.

"Look you here, you cursed ugly dot-and-carry-one; you humpbacked, weazened-face, club-footed, ferret-eyed monstrosity. I don't care for you. I don't care for old miser Fairley. You can both of you go to the devil. You can tell the old hunks, whose crawler you are, that Nat Stevens ain't going on any longer working for nothing. I can have a pound a week at Snatchems, Grinder, and Co., the lawyers in Swithin's-lane, and I won't stop here to be bullied by a monstrosity for nothing a year. There, old boy, you can put that down in your note-book, and if you want anything else, why I can tip you one on your cheese-cutter of a smeller in about a minute. Oh! you need not look surprised, I mean it; just that, and nothing else."

Speechless with rage, Ephraim scowled savagely upon the antics of Nat, who kept dancing round him, flourishing his fists in the most approved style of boxing, ever and again making a feint as though about to let his companion have one in the eye or the ribs, yelling with laughter as the dwarf started back, uttering a cry of alarm.

"Look here, old dot-and-go-one. That's the style; gently, feint with the left, and prop the right well upon the smeller; the claret is tapped, and you draw first blood. Won't you have a round?"

Amused at the other's rage and alarm, Nat kept on dancing round Ephraim, who expected each moment to receive the right upon the smeller, and behold his own claret. At length, with a howl of fury, Ephraim rushed to the inner office, whilst laughing till the tears came in his eyes, Nat danced towards his furious fellow-clerk, who, unable to close the door of the little office, rushed all round the outer one, Nat following, making sundry feints with his clenched fists; in darting after Ephraim sent his left full into the chest of a burly man, who at that moment entered the office. The stranger, with an audible curse, halted by the door, glaring first upon Nat,

and then upon Ephraim, the latter with bloodshot eyes and livid face, the features contorted with rage, glaring with wild fury upon Nat, who, apologizing to the stranger, burst into shouts of laughter.

"Well, gemmens, you is practising for a bruising-match, I suppose, and it are very apparent to me that little 'un don't like it; and, curse me! if you don't hit hard, too, young feller. But, howsomever, let's to business. Which of you two can introduce me to your master?"

"He is not in town, but will be here late to-day."

"Hum! Perhaps you can tell me summat of this?"

The man here pulled out a dirty, crumpled paper, and pointed to an advertisement, headed £100 reward. Nat, about to take the sheet in his hands, it was snatched away from the stranger by Ephraim; who, beckoning the man to follow him, entered the inner office, darting a scowl of malicious fury upon Nat, who returned it with a smile of contempt.

Impelled by irresistible curiosity to learn the purport of the stranger's visit—a man evidently of the lowest orders—the young clerk noiselessly stepped up to the door of the small apartment in which were closeted Ephraim and the stranger.

Low muttered sentences, however, could alone be caught up by Nat.

"Ralph Fairley—reward of £100—Eustace Maltravers—'Fox in the Hole,' Mint-street, Borough—that night—money down!" followed by a low chuckle from the lips of Rasselton.

"Mischief brewing anyhow, since old Fairley offers a hundred merely for revenge against someone, and that someone is evidently this Eustace Maltravers. I'll mention this to Nancy, perhaps she may know something."

Hearing the handle of the door turn, Nat darted to his desk, and appeared to be busily engaged as Ephraim and the stranger came out.

"Well, then, the old man will be here by five?"

"Certain."

"And you think the coin is right?"

"As if you had it now in your possession."

"Good! Then I will be here."

The stranger now left the office. Hobbling up to Nat, Ephraim hissed out between his clenched teeth—

"Nat Stevens, you have defied me, made me your jest, your scoff! Look to yourself! I'll follow you through life, till I have upon you a fearful, a terrible revenge! Eh! eh! eh! you shall rue the day you defied Ephraim Rasselton. If I wait for twenty years I'll have revenge!"

"Oh! go to the devil."

Nat snapped his fingers contemptuously at his fellow-clerk, who, with eyes burning like live coals, with fury and malice in his looks, went into the other office, just as the clock struck one. Nat jumped off his chair, and in a few moments was seated in the kitchen below, by the side of the pretty Nancy Watson. Asking the cause of her distress, at first Nat could gain no reply.

"Don't ask me, Nat. 'Tis a horrid story. Oh! my poor dear mistress, we shall never see her again. I know she'll die! Oh! that wicked old man."

Here Nancy burst into a fit of weeping.

At length, her sex's love of imparting news got over her sorrow, and she proceeded to inform her companion as to the cause of her distress.

"You remember, Nat, dear, my telling you that a lord had fallen in love with Miss Sybil?"

"Perfectly; and also that he was a deuced good-looking fellow. Well, it ain't anything about him, is it? I don't suppose money-grubbing old Fairley can have any objection to a lord."

"But Nat, dear, he ain't a lord."

"What?"

"No; it appears that he is a highwayman!"

"The devil!"

"Yes, and my lady loves him, and the poor fellow loves her. But it's all over. Ralph found it all out, and he has offered £100 reward for the capture of the highwayman, and has locked up poor dear Miss Sybil in the deserted chamber of the Hemlock Manor House, and has registered an oath that she shall not be released till her lover, poor Eustace Maltravers, is hanged at Tyburn."

"What name was that you mentioned, Nancy, my darling?" exclaimed Nat, starting from his seat.

"Eustace Maltravers, the highwayman! He will be hanged, and he is so handsome. It will kill Miss Sybil."

Oh! dear, oh! dear." The young girl here sobbed violently.

"Nancy, listen to me. You say that Miss Sybil and the highwayman love each other?"

Oh! yes; and I'm sure it arn't his fault that he is a robber; but Ralph has sworn he'll hang the poor, dear fellow, and, of course, he will."

"No, he shan't."

"Who's to prevent it?"

"I will."

"You, Nat, dear? Impossible."

"But I tell you yes." Nat now made Nancy acquainted with what he had overheard between Rasselton and the stranger in the morning. "Now, it is evident," he added, "that that fellow has come for the reward. The place where they are to capture the highwayman is 'The Fox in the Hole,' in Mint-street. Now, Nancy, I must go there."

"Go to that horrible spot! What for?"

"Why, to meet this Eustace, and tell him of the plot laid to capture him."

"But, perhaps, you will be murdered. You know, Nat, they are awful people that live in that place."

"Oh! leave me alone. I'll manage it all right; and, do you know, I fancy I shan't stop much longer with old money-grubber. I spoke my mind to dot-and-go-one Ephraim this morning."

"And you think of leaving Mr. Fairley? Why, Nat, whatever will you do?"

"Go to Snatchem and Grinder's, the attorneys, in Swithin's-lane. They will give me a whole pound a week, and then you know, Nancy, we can bring off that little affair." Nat, with a grin, looked lovingly upon the blushing face of the pretty Nancy. The clock now striking two, warned Nat to make his way to the office. Bidding Nancy dry her tears, he left the kitchen, and a few minutes afterwards was at his desk. Instead, however, of sitting down, Nat put away all the papers, took his hat off the peg, and prepared to go. Ephraim, with astounded and enraged looks, glared upon the young man, who, coolly whistling and humming a tune, made for the door. Speechless with rage, Ephraim beheld Nat's figure disappear out into the street.

"He has gone. He means to leave Ralph Fairley. Eh! eh! eh! The fool! the idiot! that he has not done so before; but go whither he will, like his shadow my vengeance shall follow him. I will have his life—his life! Eh! eh! eh! I will have a sweet revenge upon him yet, or Ephraim Rasselton has lost his usual cunning." With a fierce scowl upon his hideous features, the clerk hobbled into the office.

Meanwhile, on gaining the street, Nat Stevens made his way towards London-bridge, and was soon threading the mazes of the Mint, undaunted by the scowls and looks of dislike cast upon him by several dirty hags and fierce, ruffianly-looking men. Nat pursued his way, eagerly watching for the sign of the "Fox in the Hole."

When half-way down the gloomy thoroughfare, that even in the rays of the bright summer sun looked horrible and hideous in its squallor, Nat was stayed in his course by a fashionably-dressed and handsome-featured young man, who, tapping him on the arm, exclaimed—

"Are you aware where you are, stranger? Excuse me, but I fancy you have lost your way."

"Not at all, sir; but at the same time that I thank you for your civility, may I ask if you can direct me to 'The Fox in the Hole?'"

"'The Fox in the Hole?' 'Tis a house of ill repute, stranger. Unless your business is urgent, I would advise you not to venture within its doors."

"Oh! I know what I'm about. My business is urgent. I think the name of the party I am in search of will protect me from rough usage."

"And may I ask who it is you would seek at 'The Fox in the Hole?'"

"One Eustace Maltravers. Do you know him?"

A start and a cry of surprise from the stranger caused Nat to peruse his features more attentively.

It scarce needed the words of the young man to tell him who he had addressed.

'Twas Eustace himself who had warned Nat Stevens as to the nature of the place he was in. Won by the good looks and careless demeanour of the young clerk, our hero had hurried forward to protect him from harm.

In a few moments Nat's errand was explained. A dark look of anger crossed the handsome features of Eustace as he heard of the imprisonment of the unhappy Sybil.

"So, then," he muttered, "the old man is determined to pursue me with his malice. 'Tis evident naught but my death will assuage his fury. For your kindness, young man," he added, "I can return you but my poor thanks. Possibly some day I may be able to requite the favour in another manner. I am warned in time, and to-night will be prepared. Get you back to the money-lender's, and pray accept this as a token of friendship from one who is pursued by a cruel fate—a destiny over which he has no control. Nay, refuse not to take the gift; 'tis not the proceeds of robbery. For the present farewell. We shall meet again, and remember that Eustace Maltravers is your debtor for ever. Darting down a narrow court, he then disappeared. Half an hour afterwards Nat, with a smile of triumph, was seated at his desk, listening to the converse of old Ralph Fairley, who had come to town, and the burly, ruffianly stranger that had had the interview with Rasselton in the morning.

CHAPTER XX.

THE FLASH KEN IN ST. GILES'S.—THE RATS OF RATS' CASTLE.—BURKING SAM AND THE LEADER OF THE RED BAND.—EXULTATION OF THE VIPER.—THE BURKER AND HIS MISTRESS.—THE DEPARTURE.—THE CELLAR OF THE OLD HOUSE IN THE ROOKERY.—JEALOUSY AND MURDER.—CAPTURE OF THE ASSASSIN.

STANDING in the dirtiest and most ruined part of the horrible neighbourhood of St. Giles's, many years ago was a large, red-bricked, red-tiled roofed building known as "Rats' Castle."

Part public-house and part boarding-house, it was frequented by all the dissolute outcasts of society.

The Bow-street runners and other officers of the law were especially careful when visiting "Rats' Castle."

The most horrible murderers, the most daring criminals, always sought refuge from justice in "Rats' Castle."

All the windows of the building were covered with such a thick coating of dirt, that it totally precluded a sight of the tenement within to those without.

One large lamp swung over the door, from which at night a pale, dull, yellow flicker was cast upon the dingy doorway.

"Rats' Castle," was one of the vilest dens in that vile neighbourhood.

It was on the evening of the day that saw the interview of Ralph Fairley with the stranger who came for the promised reward, that the same man wended his way from the Poultry, and after a sharp walk reached the neighbourhood of St. Giles's.

Walking hurriedly along he bent his steps in the direction of "Rats' Castle," and, as twilight began to fall upon the scene, entered the dark, gloomy-looking building. Proceeding down a dark passage, the man then descended a flight of stairs; thence he passed through two small chambers, and thence into a large underground apartment, fitted up as a huge kitchen.

Although so early in the evening, there was a goodly assembly in the dining-room of "Rats' Castle," and every minute added more to the number.

Making his way towards an immense fire at the extreme end of the chamber, Ralph Fairley's visitor seated himself beside the huge grate, and casting a glance round, nodding in answer to two or three salutations, pulled a pipe from his pocket, and waited patiently the arrival of one who he found was not yet there.

Though the middle of spring, the evening was a cold and chilly one, so that the huge fire in the grate of that vast kitchen looked cheerful to those congregated in the chamber.

A strange set of beings were they who held levée in the kitchen of "Rats' Castle."

Criminals of every class.

The veriest outcasts of society.

Wretches who gained a living by every conceivable dishonesty.

Here was a fellow smoking a pipe and playing at pitch and toss with another, who, during the day, walked along with a board upon his breast, on which, in rude characters, was written "pity the poor blind."

Another beside him, a blear-eyed-looking drunkard, in the daytime enacted the starving schoolmaster.

In another part of the chamber, alone at a side-table, was a mild-looking, genteel young fellow, who gained his living by begging-letter writing.

In addition to these, pickpockets, housebreakers, shop-lifters, low gamblers, and all the lower class of London thieves, made up the company of "Rats' Castle."

An hour passed away.

The fellow by the fire began to show symptoms of impatience, when, catching sight of the face of a new-comer at the further end of the room, got up, and hurried forwards to meet him.

"You're late, Viper; 'tis gone eight."

"Lots of time, Burker. Have yer collared the rowdy?"

"Half on it—yes. 'Tother handed over when the capture has come off."

"Couldn't yer get the whole of the swag?"

"Warn't no go."

"All right. Well, we must keep it quiet for the present, that 'twas us as nosed on the bird, or Guy Essington might be one too many for us. Have yer seen Jem Coffin and Resurrection Bill?"

"No; but they come here to-night."

"Do they know that we takes the oath and inaugerates the band?"

"Yes; and Resurrection wants to know if he can't act as captain with you; so that any time you are lagged he can take the command."

"Oh! yes; Bill is one of our best hands, and don't fear nothing. But mind, no one joins the Red Band as can't prove he has, one time or other, made cold meat of a cove."

"They all understand that, Viper; and now, as time passes, hadn't we better go and see how that affair of the old money-lender's comes off?"

"Yes, Sam, we'll be off. Ha! ha! ha! I told my downey peach, my flash young rum cull, the young knight of the road, to beware the Viper's sting. By all the devils, I'll go and see him topped; he'll look mighty pretty in his fine duds as he swings on the leafless tree! But, come, we'll begone, and at midnight return for the meeting of the bold hands of the Red Band; and, by the fiends! we will war to the death with the cursed Night-Hawks."

Followed by his companion in crime, Burking Sam quitted the kitchen of the "Castle," and the two made their way to the residence of Ralph Fairley.

Here the exultation of the Viper was stayed by the information that their victim had escaped. 'Twas ascertained that he had been during the day at the "Fox in the Hole," but from some source had gleaned information that an attempt would be made for his capture, and had made good his escape.

Furious at the loss of his money and the escape of the victim of his hate, Ralph Fairley could scarce be pacified by the promises of the men, Jem Vaughan and Burking Sam, that Eustace Maltravers should yet fall into his power.

Enraged at the loss of the remainder of the reward, the companions in crime, with oaths and curses, quitted the miser's house, nor noted that they were followed by two tall, dark figures, who, with stealthy gait, tracked their footsteps.

The day, that had been so fine a one, was followed by a dark, gloomy night.

Not a star was visible in the sky.

No moon was up to light the dull scene.

All was thick darkness.

Slowly wending their way back, the two ruffians, with horrid oaths, cursed the ill-fortune that had enabled their victim to escape.

"But I will be down on him yet, Sam. I've sworn to follow him up, and curse me, if I don't yet be the means of sending him to the scragging post. I hate his cursed uncle, I hate him, and I hate all the band. By the devils! I'd send them all to Tyburn if it were possible. We arn't had no reckoning up as to those diamonds, and now we are scouted out by this Eustace Maltravers. Resurrectioner and Ben Abrahams owes him one. He has twice escaped me; but, by ——," ejaculated the Viper, with a brutal oath, "if once I lays my mawleys on him, I'll hold on like a leech; I'll knife him and slit his weazand. By the fiends! he shan't escape the Viper's sting."

Loud footsteps close behind them caused the two ruffians now to turn their heads. They had entered a dark, narrow court that led into St. Giles's. Not a single lamp hung in the place. All was dark—black as ink.

Scarce had the two men halted, ere they were hurled to the ground, uttering fierce oaths as they struggled with their assailants.

"Curses on yer! let go yer hold. If you're on the lag, you've collared hold of the wrong game," gasped the Viper, as he struggled desperately with his foes.

Not a word was uttered by the strangers, who proved to be both strong, powerful men.

Desperately the struggle went on in that dark, murderous court.

The companions, so savagely attacked, giving utterance to oaths and curses of fury.

At length the assailant of Burking Sam slipped and fell to the ground. The latter, released of his foe, with a howl of rage, made one blow at the stranger in the dark, and then bounded off, leaving the Viper to effect his own escape.

For a few minutes the struggle was prolonged.

There was the sound of a crushing blow, a moan of pain—then all was still.

The Viper was a prisoner in the hands of his mysterious assailants.

When, eluding the grasp of his adversary, Burking Sam had dashed through the court at a terrific pace, he feared a second encounter with a man of such amazing strength as the one he had coped with, nor paused in his headlong flight till well in the rookery of St. Giles's.

Entering the first public-house, he called for half-a-pint of brandy, and drank the fiery potion at a draught. The villain was unnerved by the strangeness and suddenness of the attack made upon himself and his companion.

Calling for fresh liquor, the ruffian drained it off as he had done the first. Then, leaving the house, made his way towards "Rats' Castle;" but, retracing his steps, muttered, as he walked along—

"No! no! I'll go home to Bet, she'll cheer me up. Curses on it! I feel as though I was going to be scragged. Poor Jem! I wonder how he got on. 'Twarnt no manner of use my stopping the devil that had me in his iron grip— could have throttled me as easy as put on a glove. He had a wrist of steel. Who—who the devil could it have been? By ——!" added the ruffian, with an oath, "I have it. We've been watched. The party as warned the cove we nosed on put our enemies on our track. Lord! what will they do with Viper?"

The villain staggered and leant against the wall of a public-house, as he, with his brain in a whirl, thought of the incidents of the past hour.

"It is so! That's it," he muttered, "and poor Jem is doomed. By the fiends! I've made a lucky escape."

The villain's teeth chattered as he thought upon the fate of the ruffian comrade he had left behind, and how near he, too, had shared his ill-fortune.

About to hurry on, he started back as a young woman and a man emerged from the public-house. The tones of the female's voice was familiar to him. With a deep-breathed curse, he hung back, and, like a cat, stole after the two figures as they walked on.

"Well, Bet, my flower, you'll think the offer over, and let me know. You oughtn't to hesitate a moment. I knows how Burker treats yer. I makes twice as much coin, and in a more respectable way. I reckons a clever forger afore a housebreaker or burking cove any day. Such a pretty gal as you, Bet Simmons, is thrown away on such an animal as Barney Samuels, alias Burking Sam. But come, you will meet me to-morrow and decide?"

"Yes, Harry; but you must get him in quod or he'd have my life," said the woman, in a voice husky with terror and emotion.

"All right, leave that to me. Burker once nosed on a pal of mine who was topped. I'll now return the compliment. He is a sneaking, murderous hound. I know Geoff Newton is arter him, and if you decide to-morrow, why, he shall be in the hands of the runners afore night."

The two had now arrived at an old ruined house, the windows of which were all beaten in, and were stuffed with paper and old rags.

Ruined and dilapidated as this house was, it was inhabited; Burking Sam and his mistress living in the cellar, and families of seven and eight on each of the different floors.

Halting in the front of the ruined house, which was situated in the centre of St. Giles's, the man and woman, whose converse the Burker had overheard, remained with each other for a few moments; the man, then, bidding her good night, hurried from the spot, the woman entering the house.

There was a solitary oil lamp over the door of the old house. As the Burker stepped forwards from an abutment, behind which he had been concealed, and stood in the dull glare of the light, a stranger would have been struck by the fiendish look that rested on the livid features of the man.

The face of the ruffian was the livid hue of a corpse; the lips were open, pale, and destitute of colour; the heavy, beetling brows were knit in a terrible frown.

Wildly he glared round him; up at the dark sky, and out into the murky air.

He was alone.

Diving his hand into his pocket, he drew forth a large clasp-knife, the blade of which darted out with a sharp click, as the villain pressed a spring at the back of the handle.

It was a murderous-looking weapon, the keen blade glittering in the thin, pale flare of the oil lamp.

With terrible ferocity and coolness, the wretch drew the edge of the knife across his fingers.

"Yes, that will do—'twould split a hair. So! so! Harry Hewsen, you'd send me to the topsman, would yer?" muttered the villain, as he glared round him in revengeful fury. "You would have my Bet, would yer? So yer shall when she is a corpse. I'll have her blood this night! How dark it is? Shadows seem to gather all round me. Poor Jem Vaughan, too! it's all up with him. What a night this has been! I seem as in a dream. But let me to my task."

With a fearful curse, the Burker now entered the ruined house, and in a few minutes reached the cellar. The woman, who had been sitting by a small fire, the smoke from which found its way out by the grating into the street, now rose, and exclaimed—

"How is this Sam? you have returned soon."

"Ay, too soon for you, Bet Hawkins."

"What do you mean, Sam? have yer come home in one of yer devil's humours, curse yer?"

"Yes; and I means to take a devil's vengeance on yer to-night."

"Oh! I see how it is; disappointed of a lay; lost a haul, so you've come home drunk. Well, I'll go, and return when you've slept off the fit."

The woman stepped to the door, but the Burker, thrusting her back, exclaimed, with a curse—

"No, yer don't."

"Stand aside, Sam. I won't be used by you like a brute. Let me go out."

The woman now grew pale and frightened, as the fire, breaking into a flame, revealed the contorted, hideous features of her paramour.

"Bet Hawkins, you'll never go out of this cellar alive."

"Never go out alive?" gasped the wretched woman.

"Never, Bet. When next you leave here they'll carry yer out in a box. You understand?"

Tottering back, the woman, pale and trembling, gazed round with a look of wild despair. She needed no words to explain the scene. She knew she had been followed by her paramour; knew his fierce, savage disposition. With a freezing, ice-like feeling at her heart, knew that she was doomed; she saw it in the deadly, savage glitter of the man's eyes; in the nervous twitchings of his muscles, and savage, determined aspect.

"You won't murder me, Sam?" gasped the wretched woman, as she glared wildly round.

"No; I'll let yer go; and with Harry Hewson, the forging cove, yer can nose on me to-morrow, and get me topped."

Paying no heed to this sneer, the unhappy woman staggered forwards towards the stairs, and attempted to pass her revengeful paramour.

"Let me go? pray! pray! let me go, Sam."

"In course, my beauty. That's jest it. But wait a bit; what's yer hurry?"

"Stand aside, monster, and let me go."

The woman now gave utterance to a shrill scream.

Seizing her in his powerful grasp, the ruffian, with murder in his soul, exclaimed—

"Bet Hawkins, did I not tell yer that yer would never quit this cellar in life again. In another five minutes you'll have ceased to live. I've sworn to have your life, and I will, if I'm scragged at Tyburn for the job."

The ruffian, with a savage yell, here drew forth his glittering knife.

Loud, shrill screams pealed through the cellar, mingled with prayers for mercy and deep curses.

"Help! help! help!"

Wild, thrilling, horrible shrieks escaped the doomed victim of the murderer in that horrid, darksome cellar.

"Curse yer! call on yer Harry Hewson now; see if he'll save yer. That's the ticket; now I'll stop yer."

With a horrible oath, the villain drew the knife across the wretched creature's throat, as she lay beneath him. With savage ferocity, he buried the weapon deep into the neck of his victim, the blade cutting through to the spine, and the blood, in a shower, spurting out upon the ruthless murderer.

For a few moments he seemed to experience a horrible delight in gazing upon the bleeding form of the wretched woman. At length, rising to his feet, he wiped his hands upon the shawl of his victim, and, by the light of the fire, stood glaring upon the blood-stained body that lay so still at his feet.

"Curse her! she's gone, and I'm revenged. Now, I must next see to my friend Harry Hewson. The knife that has drunk her blood shall also have his, or my vengeance is but half-sated. How still and quiet she lies! what strange faces, too, seem to start up all round me! What the —— is this?" muttered the murderer, with a dreadful oath. "This arn't my first deed of blood; and yet I feel I know not how!—horrible mouthing faces appear to gather round me!—thick shadows seem to enwrap and compass me! By the fiends! I shall go mad. I must leave this cellar; 'tis tainted with her blood. Curses on it! how my hand shakes. I—I cannot find the door. Now, too, the fire is out. The cellar is full of those horrible shadows; and she—she, Bet Hawkins is among them. She points to me with her bloody hand. She approaches me. Keep back! keep back!"

With a wild yell of horror, the murderer dashed to the door leading from the cellar, but staggered back with a cry of terror, for as he approached the door he was seized by a human hand. Loud voices now sounded through the place, followed by the noise of a desperate struggle. Anon, the light of three or four lanterns cast their rays into the cellar. The struggling ceased, and helpless, and securely bound, the murderer lay upon the ground, beside the blood-bedabbled corpse of his victim.

In the cellar stood some five or six Bow-street runners.

It was a horrible scene lighted up by the rays of the lanterns carried by the officers.

Upon the ground, in the centre of the murder-den, lay the corpse of the unfortunate woman, her head nearly severed from the body.

A pool of blood had collected around the corpse, that looked grim and ghastly in the rays of the lamps.

His hideous face, smeared with the blood of his victim, but otherwise of a livid hue, the murderer looked like some fiend from the regions of the accursed, as he glared with a wild stare upon his captors.

Horrible oaths and curses escaped his vile lips, as he was borne from the cellar. His victim was placed in a shell, and conveyed to a neighbouring public-house, there to await an inquest.

That night, Barney Samuels, *alias* Burking Sam, the murderer of his paramour, was confined in the cells of Newgate.

CHAPTER XXI.

THE MIDNIGHT MEETING. — THE PRISONER AND HIS JUDGES.—THE SENTENCE OF DOOM.—FEARFUL PUNISHMENT FOR A LIFE OF CRIME.—THE VIPER ROBBED OF HIS STING.

TWELVE o'clock! the dreary, weard, and mystic midnight hour chimed out with dull clang from the bells of St. George's and St. Saviour's, in the Borough.

The moon shone bright and clear upon the now deserted

streets, casting a light upon spots that at other times, when clouds gathered in the firmament above, were enveloped in darkness.

Pale, flickering oil lamps cast fitful gleams here and there, looking strange and ghastly in the silent night.

Save the footfall of a solitary watchman, nought sounded on the air.

Honest traders, worthy artizans, and the busy bees of the hive of London were all now wrapped in repose.

'Twas the silent midnight hour. The streets had ceased to resound with the hum of toil; the clatter of horses' hoofs, the whirl of wheels, and sound of voices no longer rung upon the ear.

All was quiet; all was still; 'twas midnight. The weary workers were at rest.

But some there were at that drear hour of night who sought not the couch or sweet repose, but who gloried, revelled in the shadows of the midnight hour.

The robbers prowled about the deserted streets like foul night birds, watching for their prey.

The burglar, the churchyard desecrator, the resurrectionist, the coiner, the river pirate, all were at work; as the veil of night fell upon the town, each had departed on his errand of plunder.

Murder, too, with grim visaged front, now stalks abroad. The knife of the assassin is reeking with the blood of the doomed.

Dark shadows hover in the air.

Whilst death, with pale visage, calls upon those whose fate is sealed—whose time has come.

A dreary sound is the chimes of the midnight hour.

What aching hearts in the city of London, as the last note rings upon the air are called to rest.

Now the weary and desponding, the wretched and frantic, seek refuge from their sufferings in death, voluntarily plunging into eternity and the other world.

What is that dim, dark figure prowling on the bridge that spans the darkly-flowing Thames? 'Tis a shuddering female form.

The moonbeams glint upon her pallid features; they are pinched and sunken with want—so thin, so livid. Starvation has done its work. That young girl was once beautiful, timid, virtuous, and lovely. She is now a wreck. Vice and crime have done their work.

Hurriedly the pale, shrinking figure pursues her way upon the bridge. She approaches the balustrade. She places her hands upon the edge, is about to give a spring over into the watery gulf below, when a strong hand is laid upon her shoulder, and she is stayed from her suicidal act, whilst the stranger who had deterred her from her purpose exclaimed—

"Why, how now, girl! tired of life? About to take your leap into the dark before your time? Pshaw! you are too young to die."

"Let me go. In Heaven's name! would you rob me of the last means of procuring forgetfulness of the past? Loose your hold, man! I will not be stayed!"

A wild shriek now rang from the mouth of the maddened female, as she beheld the scowling, evil features of a man who was held in the firm grip of the stranger beside her.

"Ha! ha! ha! And have you come here, James Vaughan, to triumph in the dying agony of your victim? Ha! ha! ha! Monster, parricide, incestuous hound! Has not thy master-fiend, Satan, yet called thee to him? But thy time is near, the hour is at hand. I saw you, Vaughan, in a dream last night. You were led to my bed-side. Your face was convulsed with torture; and I said to myself, 'the murderer has been punished. The fiat of doom has gone forth!' Ay, turn livid; glare, savage as you are, upon me. I care not; but, mark me, your doom is near at hand."

"Accursed hag, thou liest!"

There was a deep-breathed curse, a momentary struggle, a shrill scream, and then the sound of a heavy blow, followed by a few instants of silence, at length broken by the stranger, who exclaimed—

"Hold on to him, Eustace, lad! or, curse me! if he won't escape."

"Not if I know it, Dick! See to the poor girl. I fear the villain has done for her."

Dick Turpin—for he and Eustace it was who were passing over London-bridge at the time of the young woman's attempt at suicide—turned from his companion,

who was securing the ruffian Viper, whom they held prisoner, and directed his attention to the unhappy wanderer of the night.

Staggering against the stone-coping of the bridge, the girl waved him back, whilst pointing her finger to the fierce, vindictive features of the Viper, she exclaimed, in a choking, gasping voice—

"Let him not escape. 'Tis well I should perish by his hand! But I fear not death, and die content that I know his doom is near. See how livid pale he grows when I foretell his fate! Ha! ha! ha! Jem Vaughan, parricide! murderer! the hour of divine vengeance is at hand. I can see it in the stars, I can read it in the black cloud that now hangs above your head. You are doomed! whilst I may yet be saved!"

With a piercing shriek, ere a hand could be laid upon her to draw her back, the wretched woman now bounded over the coping of the bridge, and disappeared in the rolling waters below.

Turpin and Eustace, witnesses to the strange scene, shuddered as they glanced at the ruffian Vaughan, who, with livid face and eyes of horror, glared up at the sky above.

Directly over the villain's head hung a thick black cloud.

A convulsive shudder shook the ruffian's frame, as he glared wildly at the sky.

"So! so! Kit Carson is rubbed out—gone her road. Curse her! What did she mean by mouthing her trash to me?" muttered the villain.

Then, turning to the two friends, who held him firmly in their grasp, he added, with a rough oath—

"Now, then, lead me on. But, by the devils in ——! you shall repent this night's work, or the Viper has lost his sting!"

"Indeed, we shall see. Come on, Dick. I owe him one," said our hero, "and this night it shall go hard but what I'll draw the Viper's sting!"

"Well, I reckon he won't have a chance of nosing on friend or foe after to-night."

"Not he, Dick. The Night-Hawks punish treachery with deadly vengeance."

The two friends, with the villain Viper between them, now made their way over the bridge, and anon reached the Borough. Hurrying on, they at length turned off into the narrow, ill-paved, half-lighted Mint.

As they entered the darksome thoroughfare, the ruffian Viper made a last effort at escape, but was secured by Turpin, who gave him a blow with the butt of a pistol, that stretched him nearly senseless at his feet.

"No go, lad; it's all up, Viper. You're booked this time for something worse, I take it, than a trip across the herring-pond. The varmint has nearly slipped the darbies. Let us at once to the house, Eustace; time's up, and the Hawks await our return," ejaculated Turpin, as he dragged their prisoner to his feet.

"Ay, Dick, you are right. But here we are at the 'Fox in the Hole.' And, confound me!" said our hero, "but I could almost pity the wretch's sufferings; his encounter with the unfortunate girl has quite unnerved him."

The two friends, with their prisoner, had now halted by the door of the thieves' ken—the "Fox in the Hole." As they were about to enter, the Viper, with a frenzied look, glared up at the sky.

He started, and gave utterance to a horrible oath; then shook his fist with fury at the vault above.

Just over his head hung a huge black cloud.

Black and dark as ink.

"It is there, there still!" gasped the villain. "Curse her croaking! How black and grim it looms over my head! Ten thousand devils! Why did she cross my path to-night? and I in the power of the accursed Night-Hawks. But, by ——! I'll not be dragged to doom!"

There was a brief struggle; some loud oaths rung upon the air; the thick, heavy cloud crossed the moon's disk; for a few moments the Mint was enveloped in thick darkness. When the pale moon again burst forth, all was quiet.

The three figures had disappeared!

Sounds of drunken revelry issue from the bar of the "Fox in the Hole;" but all is still, silent as death in the underground chamber, in which assemble the band of the Night-Hawks.

'Tis a strange, wild, horrible scene, that midnight meeting.

No rude shouts of laughter echo through the chamber.

There is a terrible stillness in the vault-like apartment.

The chamber is draped around with black.

Twenty-four men are seated round the large table, whose appearance is sombre and terrible.

They are all masked, and wear large black cloaks, upon the left shoulders of which are the horrible insignia of a skull and cross bones.

At the head of the table is seated a tall, majestic figure, who, with a parchment laid out before him, glances from the paper, ever and anon, at the dark curtains at the end of the apartment.

"Time passes; they should be here," muttered the muffled form.

Three loud knocks now sound from without.

"'Tis they!" said the tall, cloaked figure. "Admit them."

The drapery is drawn back, a door is opened, and three men enter.

One is manacled by the wrists, and is led forwards to the foot of the table.

The cloaked, masked form, seated at the upper end, now rose, and exclaimed—

"How is this? There were two marked out for judgment; here we have but one."

"The Burker has escaped us for a time, captain; but the master-fiend, Jem Vaughan, the Viper, is here!"

"'Tis well, Eustace. Bring the prisoner forwards."

The Viper, livid with fear and rage, was led up to the head of the table by the man who had secured him.

Throwing off the black mask that had concealed his features, the cloaked form started up, and, glancing sternly upon the ruffian Viper, exclaimed—

"James Vaughan, do you know me?"

"Ay, Guy Essington, and though a prisoner here before yer, curse yer! I fear yer not. 'Tis your turn to-night; my time will come."

With looks of fury and malice the prisoner glared around him.

Not one of those masked figures moved in their seats; but dark eyes could be perceived darting out piercing rays upon the features of the villain Viper.

"James Vaughan, you formerly belonged to this band of Night-Hawks. You, with others, deserted your comrades, and yesterday gave information where, and at what hour, two of them might be secured. You, however, were foiled, and the men whom you had condemned to the gallows were by me, their captain, deputed to capture you this night. Your companion, Barney Samuel, or the Burker, has for a time escaped us; but to-night, ay, within the hour, James Vaughan, you shall receive the reward of your villainy," exclaimed Essington.

Then turning, and glancing round the table, he held out the parchment, adding—

"Night-Hawks, there are two modes of punishment decreed in our rules for such a villain as the man who now stands before you. Say, what shall it be. Shall I condemn James Vaughan, otherwise the Viper, to the extreme penalty of death?"

The deadly pallor that had stolen across the features of the captive now deepened. The face of the doomed ruffian grew livid; cold, bead-like drops of fear started out upon his brow, and a half-shriek escaped his lips, as the dark, cloaked forms rose up, exclaiming, in one voice—

"Death! death! Nothing but death!"

"James Vaughan," ejaculated Essington, "you hear your doom."

"No—no—no! I cannot die! Curses on yer, I will not die!"

"Red Judas, prepare to carry out the sentence that has been passed."

One of the masked figures bowed to Essington and left the vault, presently returning with a coil of rope and a huge hook, that he fixed to a beam that ran above, near the ceiling of the apartment.

Meanwhile frantic prayers for mercy, mingled with horrid oaths, curses, and yells of savage fury burst from the lips of the condemned man.

"Essington! pals! you will not let me hang. Curses on it, give me to the law. Let me stand my chance. You, Bill Redmund, say a word for me. Remember, 'twas my hand saved you from the bullet of a runner a twelvemonth back. Curses on you all, I will not die!"

Wild yells pealed through the apartment from the lips of the maddened wretch, as he perceived the rope being fastened to the hook that was fixed in the solid oak beam above his head.

"Curses on yer all, loose your hold! By the fiends! I'll be revenged for this. Beware, Guy Essington. You may find the leader of the Red Band avenge this. I won't die. Curses, I say, I won't die!" yelled the ruffian, struggling fiercely with his captors.

Then, as the rope was placed around his neck, in terror and wild agony the Viper fell upon his knees, and clasping his hands, prayed for mercy. The wretch who had so oft bedewed his hands in innocent blood, now uttered shrill screams for that life which was doomed.

"Will no one speak for me? Bill, Bill Redmund, say a word! Only let me live, and I care not." Wildly the miserable villain whined and prayed for mercy.

About to jerk him from his feet, the man, Red Judas, was stayed in his purpose by a sign from Guy Essington.

"Hold!" exclaimed the stentorian voice of the leader of the Night-Hawks. "Take the rope from off his neck."

The halter was removed. A grim smile flitted athwart the features of Essington as he beheld a look of furious malice wreathe the face of the Viper.

"James Vaughan, you have prayed for life; you shall have it, but at such a price that you will curse the hour you stayed the fulfilment of my first sentence. Red Judas, bring in Yellow Jack."

The man left the room.

Presently returning with a thin, cadaverous-looking fellow, who, with sharp, piercing glance, stared at Guy Essington, and, immovable, remained standing where he had been left by his conductor. Beckoning the strange being to his side, the leader of the Night-Hawks whispered a few sentences in his ear, at the same time pointing to the prisoner.

With a grim smile, the new comer exclaimed aloud—

"All right, Guy Essington, it shall be done; in five minutes he shall stand powerless before you."

The Viper stared round him with a horrible fear of some impending ill, a terror of he knew not what. The fixed, motionless forms of the Night-Hawks, in their black cloaks and masks, awed and frightened the murderer. "What—what!" he kept asking himself, "were they going to do with him?" He ground his teeth savagely, with impotent fury, as he felt how helpless he stood amidst his foes. The wretch was at length aroused from his reflections by Yellow Jack, who, assisted by two of the Night-Hawks, drew him to a corner of the chamber.

Turpin and Eustace went over to Essington. There was a few words between them, then the two friends, with a start, turned round and glanced at the corner of the apartment, where the Viper had been conveyed by his enemies.

The two friends were very pale. A look of horror rested on their features.

'Twas a strange, wild scene, in the gloomy-looking, vault-like chamber.

All was silent as death.

Grim and stern, the masked forms stood around their chief.

The lamps cast a flickering yellow light upon the scene, casting strange shadows on the dark drapery.

Anon, the silence in the apartment was broken by a piercing shrill scream of direst agony, followed by horrible oaths and blasphemous curses.

Then the three dark figures that had gathered round the Viper drew back.

The ruffian staggered forwards, uttering fierce oaths and threats of vengeance.

"Curses on yer all! Why have you tortured me thus? My brain is on fire! my blood runs ice-like through my veins! And what is this? Curse yer? why don't yer speak? Tell me why have yer put out all the lights?"

Staggering forwards, the villain stumbled and fell. Then, rising to his feet, with howls of rage, and threats of future vengeance, he made for the door.

"Judas, take him out, place him in a vehicle, and see him to his home. His punishment is effected; the Viper is robbed of his sting! James Vaughan, let your fearful fate serve as a warning to others who would dare to cope with the Night-Hawks. Away with him! All is over!"

In a moment every man removed his cloak and mask; the drapery was removed from the walls, and, uttering hoarse oaths of vengeance on his enemies, the Viper was conducted from the chamber.

In a few minutes the ruffian was standing without the inn.

"The moon shines bright, Jem Vaughan," ejaculated his conductor, "but 'twill never be revealed to you again! Yours is a fearful punishment."

The man shuddered as he grasped the arm of the other, who stumbled as he stepped forwards.

"What mean you, Judas? Curses on yer! why do you keep me thus in the dark?"

"You are not in the dark, Viper. We are out in the open air, and Oliver shining bright and blue overhead."

A terrible shudder shook the frame of the miserable victim of a fearful punishment, as the truth began to reveal itself to him.

"But I—I—cannot see, Judas! All is dark, black as ink! A veil is over my eyes—I cannot see!"

"Viper, you will never see again! You are blind!"

A moan of intense anguish burst from the lips of the wretched villain. Low, gasping sentences escaped him, as he was led into a vehicle.

"Blind! God of heaven, blind! The curse of Kit Carson rings in my ears! the black cloud! the agony of the past hour, and I cannot have revenge!"

Oaths and tears by turns escaped the frantic, doomed wretch, who beat the edges of the seat on which he sat with his fists, in impotent fury and despair.

'Twas a terrible night for Jem Vaughan.

A fearful puhishment had been inflicted.

A terrible sentence carried out.

The Viper had, indeed, been robbed of his sting.

He was totally, hopelessly blind!

By a fearful human agency *his sight had been destroyed for ever!*

CHAPTER XXII.

ARRIVAL OF THE STRANGER. — GUY ESSINGTON AND GALLOPING DICK.—THE COMPACT.—THE OATH.—THE PROJECTED ROBBERY.—SUDDEN APPEARANCE OF THE RED MASK.—THE THREAT.—FURY OF THE NIGHT-HAWKS. —THE PISTOL-SHOT, AND MYSTERIOUS ESCAPE OF THE RESURRECTION MAN.

SCARCE had the door of the secret chamber of the "Fox in the Hole" closed behind the forms of the man, Red Judas, and the wretched villain, the Viper, than Guy Essington bade his companions forget the dreadful scene that had just passed, and in the wine-cup drink success to the bonny band of which they were members.

Loud cheers greeted the chief as, with our hero and Turpin by his side, he seated himself at the head of the table.

"Long life to the Night-Hawks of London!" exclaimed Essington, raising high a goblet of rich, red wine, and then, placing it to his mouth, draining it to the dregs.

"May the knights of the road never fail to win a prize in a moonlight canter over Hounslow Heath, or a kiss from the pouting, cherry lips of a pretty maid," ejaculated Turpin.

Renewed shouts and jingling of glasses echoed this speech.

"Here's to Eustace Maltravers, the future captain of the brave Night-Hawks," said Essington. "Drain your glasses all to the health of the dashing knight of the road, who, in his maiden trip, secured a prize worthy of the oldest hand."

"Hurrah! hurrah!" shouted the members of the band, who, in the rich wines and ardent spirits, soon forgot the terrible incident that had occurred so shortly before.

Suddenly all were startled by three loud knocks on the door without.

"Who's there?" said the watcher at the entrance of the secret chamber.

"A friend," replied a voice.

"The pass?"

"Night is on the wane. Hawks, to your nest."

"'Tis well; enter!"

The curtains were now drawn back, the door opened, and a tall, herculean fellow entered the apartment, followed by a young man—the latter possessing a tolerably good appearance, but bearing about him an unmistakable rakish look.

Both advanced boldly forwards — the younger man gazing around with an air of some surprise upon the scene before him.

"Ha! Ned Wildgrave, my prince of hightobymen, is it you?" exclaimed Essington, holding out his hand to the eldest of the two visitors; "and how fares it with you, Ned? Has dame Fortune, that fickle jade, met you fairly in your excursion to the north? Have you a well-lined purse to show us on your return?"

"Yes, captain, I've been pretty busy; have collared a tidy amount of ready Stephen (money), in white and yellows (silver and gold), and have also in hand some wedge (plate), and flimzies (notes), that we must ding (dispose of) quickly, afore the runners is put on the scent; but afore we goes into business, allow me to introduce a pal of mine, who wishes to join the band, Richard Ferguson, *alias* Galloping Dick, knight of the road, and tip-top rum-cul. Come forwards. Duck your cocoa-nut, tip the captain your flipper, and he'll pretty soon enroll yer in the bonny band of the Night-Hawks of London."

With some little hesitation, awed somewhat by the throng of strangers around him, the young man stepped forwards, and bowing to Essington and Eustace, who stood at the head of the table, exclaimed—

"Captain Guy Essington and gentlemen all, I beg to ask the favour of becoming a member of your society. You'll never find Galloping Dick flinch in the hour of danger; and should I join I'll prove a true Hawk, and always strike my quarry."

"You swear to serve faithfully, as a member of this band; never to peach on a pal, though to save your own life; to make a comrade's enemies yours; to laugh to scorn a death at Tyburn Tree; and never to swerve from duty for the smiles of the fair. Swear this, Galloping Dick, and become from this hour one of the Night-Hawks of London."

"I swear," exclaimed the young man in a firm voice.

"'Tis well," ejaculated Essington. "Prepare the ordeal."

Scarce had the last words left his lips ere all the lights were extinguished. There was then a dead silence in that underground apartment, followed by a strange clicking noise. In a few moments the lights again cast a glare through the chamber, and the young man, Richard Ferguson, started, giving utterance to a slight cry of terror, as he discovered that he was surrounded by a group of figures all attired in black cloaks, and wearing half masks upon their faces. Each held a pistol, ready cocked, presented at his head. Startled at first, he quickly recovered himself, and smiled as he cast his eyes upon the grim, dark forms around him, one of whom, stepping up, pointed a pistol at his head and fired. There was a sharp, clear report, and a thin wreath of smoke curled through the air. But erect among the dark forms stood Galloping Dick, unmoved or frightened by the discharge of the weapon.

A murmur ran through the apartment. At a sign from Essington, the dark cloaks and masks were thrown aside, and all gathered round and shook hands with the young stranger, who had shown himself possessed of cool courage and daring during the recent ordeal.

"Richard Ferguson, *alias* Galloping Dick," said Essington, "you are now one of the Night-Hawks. Remain firm and true, and in the hour of danger your comrades will rally round you, and protect you from your foes; but turn traitor, and death will be your portion, each and all hunting you down till your treachery is avenged. But come, we will now drink to your future success, as one of the bold Night-Hawks of London."

Loud shouts and cheers greeted this speech of the chief. Eustace, Turpin, Gentleman Jack, and others, warmly welcoming their new comrade.

At length order being a little restored, Galloping Dick craved speech with Essington.

"Captain," he exclaimed, "now that I am duly enrolled, I would have a few words as to a project I have in hand."

"Say on."

"I have been for some weeks serving with one Jack Hopcroft, landlord of the 'Three Tuns,' in Piccadilly. Now, this house is frequented by merchants, bankers, and lords, who happen to be leaving London or returning

THE GHOST AT THE OLD MILL.

from the country. The inn is the best patronized at the West-end. The cause of my accepting a berth as servant was a *penchant* I had for a pretty little maid. Losing the object of my passion last week, who unromantically bolted with one of the waiters, I was about to quit my place, that without the sight of my charmer became somewhat irksome, when I bethought me of a plan that would enrich me and others who might join me in my scheme."

"I read your purpose, Galloping Dick," exclaimed Eustace with a smile; "you propose to remain at the inn, and give information of the movements of all its frequenters to your comrades, the Night-Hawks."

"A capital plan," said Turpin, glancing approvingly upon Dick Ferguson.

"He is a down pin."

"A real cute 'un."

"One of the right sort," ejaculated others, elated at the plan proposed.

"I am glad you approve of my project, comrades," exclaimed Ferguson; "you have guessed aright," he added, turning to Eustace. "As a spy at the inn, I can give note of the departure of any pigeon whom we may think worth plucking. I can receive my reward for the information, and rest in security at the inn until such time as accident, or a wish for change, may cause me to leave; and, to prove that I mean business, I have come here to-night with news that may be worth a trifle to us. To-morrow evening a party of three will leave the inn in a carriage and four. The trap will be driven by four postilions; in addition to these there will be two men-servants and two women."

"You would have the carriage attacked?" exclaimed Eustace.

"Yes."

"Who and what are the persons whom we are to assail?"

"Those well worth the plucking. The riches that may

be secured will be worthy the ransom of a prince. They must be ours if half the band make the attack."

"Indeed ? This is a prize we must certainly not let slip," said Essington, "if you are rightly informed, Ferguson, as to the booty that may be secured."

"Oh! that is all right; but the treasure will be well guarded. The party in the carriage will consist of Lord Walsingham, his only son, and a fire-eating military officer, a Colonel Moreton, owner of some estates in Gloucester, known as Moreton in the Marsh."

"A nice little family party, namesake," said Dick Turpin, with a laugh. "But what is the rich treasure guarded by these swells, whom, by the devils, I'll be one to pluck of their feathers ?"

"The booty to be secured is a wedding present from Lord Walsingham to his only daughter. The bridal gift consists of a coronet of diamonds and pearls, bracelets and armlets to match, and is worth, from all I have heard, not less than ten thousand guineas."

"Whew! What a haul!" said Turpin, giving a loud whistle, and then smacking his lips with delight as he thought of the prize."

"Well, Turpin, we must secure this treasure," said Eustace.

"Right, my bonny one; and if the captain, your uncle, is agreeable, why, damme, we'll do the job alone."

"No! curse me if you do! I'll have a hand in this," ejaculated Gentleman Jack.

"And I!—and I!" echoed others, pressing round Dick Ferguson, eagerly questioning him further as to the prize.

At length it was decided that the party to attack the carriage of Lord Walsingham on the morrow should consist of Eustace, Turpin, Gentleman Jack, and a strong, daring member of the band, known as Black Will. Gathering round the table, the Night Hawks filled their glasses to the brim, and, draining them of the fiery spirits, drank success to the projected exploit of the next day, the more pleasing to them from the danger that might be expected to attend the enterprise. All had once more relapsed into conviviality, when they were suddenly startled by three loud knocks at the door. The pass was given, the entrance opened, a cry of surprise escaping from the lips of all present at the appearance of a tall form, enveloped in a large red cloak, and wearing a mask of the same colour.

"Close the door," shouted Essington, with a fierce oath; but the intruder started back, and, standing just at the opening, his form partly enveloped and shrouded by the heavy curtains that hung before the door, with a hoarse laugh, drew forth a pair of pistols, and presented them at the head of the man who would have made him a prisoner.

"No you don't, my tulip," muttered the stranger, in a thick, guttural voice, evidently disguised; "not if I knows it."

In a moment the barrels of twenty pistols were presented at the daring stranger by the enraged Night-Hawks.

"Ha! ha! ha! Curses on yer! Fire away. Lead's cheap. But yer don't fluster me."

"Seize him!" shouted Essington.

"No yer don't," ejaculated the stranger, with a low laugh.

"Brain him!"

"Down with him!"

"Bullet him! Down with the spy!"

"Hold and hear me, brave Hawks, that are thus cowed at sight of one vulture."

The voice of the stranger sounded mockingly in the ears of the enraged band, who, at a sign from Essington, threw themselves in their seats, eying the daring intruder, however, with looks of fury.

"Who and what are you?" ejaculated the captain.

"That yer shall soon know. I'm the leader of a bonny band, the brave Blood Boys. I've sworn by all the fiends in the infernal regions to have the life of one Guy Essington, and curse me if I don't keep my oath. I'm the leader, the captain of the Red Band. I've come here to-night to tell you that I've sworn to hunt yer to the death. Yes, Guy Essington, I'll have your blood. I've sworn it by the bones of my father rotting on the gibbet, and I will keep my oath. You have robbed the viper of his sting, but you have now to battle with his mate. Guy Essington, the day shall come that I will convey your lifeless body to the Sawbones or swing myself upon the gallows. The churchyard robber, Resurrection Bill, tells you this, and by —— he will keep his oath."

A yell of rage burst from Essington and his companions as they gazed upon the daring ruffian before them—no other than Resurrection Bill.

A loud, exultant laugh escaped the villain as Essington's shout of rage fell upon his ear. There was then a stunning report as the leader of the Night Hawks fired at his foe.

A dozen figures dashed to the door to seize the intruder.

There was a cry of rage and astonishment.

The resurrection man had disappeared.

He had strangely avoided the bullet from the pistol of Essington, and made good his escape.

From that night a ban was set against the resurrectionist and his companions.

The Night Hawks being bound by a fearful oath to pursue them to the death.

The oath was kept.

Strange, wild scenes took place between the Night-Hawks and the murderous assassins of the Red Band.

CHAPTER XXIII.

A DARK NIGHT, AND A NIGHT OF MYSTERIES.—THE ROBBERY ON BAGSHOT HEATH.—LORD WALSINGHAM AND THE BRIDAL GIFT.—THE CONFLICT WITH THE HIGHWAYMEN.—FURY OF COLONEL MORETON.—THE RECOGNITION OF EUSTACE, AND THE YOUNG LORD.—THE MOONBEAMS, AND THE SHADOW ON THE HEATH.—THE WARNING, AND THE OATH OF VENGEANCE.

THE night following the incidents related in the preceding chapter was a dark and wild one.

The sun had sunk to rest tinging the clouds with a coppery blood-red hue, that betokened a storm ere many hours passed.

It was unusually cold, too, for that summer night, the wind howling bleak and shrill over the busy-peopled town or wild deserted country roads.

It was, as darkness fell upon the earth wrapping all nature in the sable mantle of night, that four horsemen cantered along the high road in the direction of Bagshot, their loud voices and bursts of laughter ringing on the ear.

The road at that part which the horsemen were now traversing was singularly wild and gloomy.

Dwarf oaks, the ghostly wych elm, and the tall poplar, reared their heads by the roadside, the wind soughing and singing in their leafy branches.

Over head all was thick black clouds, behind which ever and anon could be traced the light shadow of the moon's rays, as the leaden canopy crossed its disc.

It was a wild dark night.

And the road along which the merry party proceeded, in its dreary loneliness accorded well with the gloomy, threatening sky.

"Well, Dick, it's a fine night for our plant; Lady Blue is surrounded by the heavy clouds, and bids fair to hide her face for some hours," ejaculated our hero; for it was Eustace and his companions who were so merrily cantering along that darksome road, and who were pursuing their project of stopping the coach of Lord Walsingham, on his journey to his ancestral home.

"How long do you take it, Turpin, we'll be getting on the heath ?"

"Well, Jack, I should say half an hour."

"And from the intelligence given us by galloping Dick, the coach of his lordship will pass over the heath of Bagshot at ten."

"Just so."

"Then we must hasten on, Turpin," ejaculated Eustace, "for 'tis now near the hour, and, by heavens, I could almost fancy I heard the sound of wheels."

The highwaymen paused, and with their steeds reined up in the middle of the road, listened intently as they sat motionless in their saddles.

"'Tis but sighing of the wind through the branches of the trees," muttered Turpin; "but come, we will on, as 'twere best we made our attack upon the travellers in the centre of the heath."

Giving their horses the rein, the highwaymen, who were all well mounted, galloped on till at length they caught sight of a dark, drear, wild, and open plain, or immense common, before them.

This was Bagshot Heath.

Wild and sombre it looked, as for a moment the pale sickly rays of the moon, bursting from the clouds, cast a gleam upon the open tract that, without tree of any kind, presented nought but an uneven mass of black frowning furze.

"A delightful spot for our labours, Dick."

"Yes, Jack. I think old Bagshot is rather the ticket, and fit scene for the cry of stand and deliver."

"What the devil is that strange noise that appears to sound in advance of us, Dick?" said the highwayman Black Will, as he peered into the thick darkness before him.

"Oh! that's the skeleton of an old farmer hanging in his chains. Old Bolus they call him. He committed a horrible murder, and, after execution, was hung upon the heath here in chains, to fright all evil-doers. By-the-bye, I can relate you an anecdote about old Bolus as we canter across the heath."

Receiving the assent of his companion, Dick Turpin then told them the following story :—

It appeared that some ten years before an old farmer, residing near Bagshot, had murdered his wife and only son, together with the child of a neighbour. The reason of his crime was not thoroughly understood. Drink and madness, it was thought, had had something to do with it. The spot upon which old Bolus was hung in his chains was always carefully avoided by all travellers crossing Bagshot Heath.

One dark winter's morning, when the snow lay thick upon the heath, and the moon shone with cold, dull glare upon the scene, two countrymen, with a waggon loaded with hay and straw for the London market, made their way over the dreary track. Each knew that on the heath over which they passed hung the murderer in his chains. One of the men, too, laughed and jested his companion upon his terror at their close proximity to the gibbet of old Bolus.

"Thee mayst laugh as thee loikes, Toby Cornflower; but, dang my buttons, I'll bet three half a gallon o' yale thee daresn't go to the gibbet of old Bolus, and ask him how he does."

"Dang it ole man, whoy shouldn't I?"

"Cos yer daresn't, Toby. Wi' all yer laughing at I, thee daresn't to go to old Bolus and ask him how he do."

A chuckle escaped the lips of the speaker, as he fancied he had frightened his companion.

"Look yer, Billy Freckleton, don't e' go to laugh at I; don't hallo afore thee is out o' the wood. Nay, dang ma buttons and ma ole man, if I doesn't show thee whether I cares for ole Bolus. I'll pretty soon ask him how he do; and here goes."

Enraged at the grin upon the face of his companion, the man bounded off in the direction of the gibbet, that could just be discerned rearing its hideous height up in the pale blue rays of the moon.

It was a bitter morning; the wind, laden with the icy breath of the north, whistled across the open heath in keen and wintry gusts.

The snow, three feet thick, lay upon the ground, glistening in the rays of the moon.

Hurrying on, though with fear now knocking at his heart, the waggoner presently reached the gibbet.

The clank, clank, of the chains jarred rudely on the ear, whilst the hideous skeleton of the murderer looked ghastly horrible, as it swayed gently to and fro in the wintry blast.

Taking a pull from a flask he drew from his pocket to revive his drooping spirits, the waggoner, shivering with terror at his own hardihood, at length halted beneath the gallows, and, in fear and trembling, exclaimed—

"Well, old Bolus, how dost do?"

"It's very cold," replied a hoarse voice; the skeleton at that moment swinging towards the unfortunate country-man, as though about to descend from its iron shroud, and grasp him in its terrible embrace.

A wild cry of terror escaped the lips of the horrified Toby Cornflower, who, with frantic speed, bounded from the spot, followed by a loud peal of yelling laughter.

At length, reaching the waggon he had left guarded by his companion, the countryman related to the other what had passed, nor ceased to look behind him with horror and affright till they had crossed the heath.

The ale was lost by Billy Freckleton; but he did not acquaint his terror-stricken comrade that he it was who had answered his query at the gallows.

Making his way by another path, the waggoner had concealed himself behind the gibbet, and had answered his comrade's salutation to the murderer in his chains.

To his dying hour, Toby Cornflower believed old Bolus had replied to him. Even when made acquainted by his friend of the trick he had played upon him, Toby refused to believe it.

Loud laughter greeted the anecdote related by Turpin, who had just finished the relation as the rumbling of wheels sounded behind them on the open heath.

"The carriage of Lord Walsingham," said Eustace.

"Gentleman Jack," exclaimed Turpin, "do you seize the horses' heads on the off side. Black Will, to you belongs the task of intimidating the postilions. Ready, ready, gentlemen. See to your barking-irons, but use them not if you can avoid it. Hark! our friends are approaching. Act determinedly, and with caution; and remember the bridal *trousseau* must be ours."

"And for my share of the spoil, comrades," said Eustace, with a laugh, "I claim the jewelled bracelets; the rest will go for the benefit of the band. But see, his lordship approaches. Prepare to pay the aristocrat all due respect."

Excited by the scene and the companionship in which he found himself, our hero lost all thought of danger in the prosecution of their task.

Drawing up on the heath, at each side of the rude carriage road, the highwaymen awaited the approach of their victims.

All was thick, black darkness.

The heavy clouds, in masses, rolled overhead; the wind sighing with a mournful sound over the open heath.

Approaching each moment nearer and nearer to the spot on which they stood, the highwaymen beheld two dancing stars of yellow light.

Brighter and brighter grew this ball of flame.

It was the lamps belonging to the carriage of Lord Walsingham.

Nearer and nearer came the vehicle.

The smacking of whips now sounded on the air, together with the heavy grinding noise of carriage-wheels rattling over the gravelly road.

The lamps cast a broad yellow light on the heath, whilst the carriage, black and looming like a moving tower, appeared in the gloom of that dark summer night.

The forms of the postilions, bending over the necks of their steeds, could now be discerned by the highwaymen, whilst the voices of those within the carriage could be heard urging on them to increase their speed.

Bagshot Heath was the known resort of the knights of the road, and however valourous the traveller, it was generally arranged to hasten across the dreary track.

"Boot and spur, lads! Get over this confounded heath!"

"Hold! On your lives!"

"Ha! we are attacked."

"Your money or your lives! Be not foolhardy—take it easy. That's the ticket. Dick, cut the traces! I'll see to his lordship and his companions."

"Help, Eustace!" gasped Turpin, who was struggling in the grasp of a tall, powerful man who, at the first alarm, had leaped from the carriage and seized upon the highwayman as he knocked a postilion over and cut the traces of the horses.

Screams, oaths, and curses rung in the air.

The sharp crack! crack! of pistols awakened up the echoes around.

A fierce struggle took place between the robbers and their victims.

For some minutes the *melée* continued; the sound of angry voices ceased, and were replaced by deep breathings and the noise of feet upon the gravelly road. The carriage, in the early part of the affray, had been over-turned, and the horses, freeing themselves from the harness, had darted from the spot.

A thin, pale ray of moonlight now lighted up the scene.

A strange and wild one!

The noise of conflict now ceased.

The struggle was at an end.

For a few moments nought but the deep breathing of the vanquished and their assailants could be heard.

Desperately the travellers had defended themselves from the attack of the robbers, but notwithstanding their superiority in numbers over the highwaymen, Eustace and his companions had conquered Lord Walsingham and his servants.

"Bring that carriage lamp here, Will, and let's see what's up with Dick," exclaimed Eustace, who now took the command.

The lamp wrenched from the vehicle was brought forward by Black Will in obedience to the order of our hero.

"Hand me the glim, Will. Now, Dick, old boy, what's up?"

"A sprained ankle, Eustace, nothing more. See to our enemies, or by the devils we may even now lose the prize for which we have dared so much. No yer don't, my gray-headed Trojan," ejaculated Turpin, who, limping forward, pounced upon an elderly stern looking-man, who, rising from the ground with looks of rage, had cocked a pistol, presenting it at the head of Eustace. Knocking the weapon from his hand, Turpin now proceeded to rifle the pockets of his victim, who, unarmed, was awed by the loaded pistols held to his head by the highwayman.

The moon now having struggled from a mass of clouds cast a white thin light upon the wild open waste.

Lying on its side, in the centre of the roadway, was the vehicle in which the unfortunate travellers had been attacked.

Browsing upon the soft sward, some yards off, were the horses, as they roamed about at will, the broken harness trailing behind them on the ground.

By the side of the carriage were thrown the affrighted postilions, bound hand and foot. Near them were the two young women who had ridden outside with their two fellow-servants. The latter, with pale, bleeding forms, leaned, shaking with terror, by the carriage, watching with dismay the actions of the robbers.

Upon the heath, by the roadside, were stretched two figures—one, that of a slight young man; the other, that of a dashing-looking military person, whose undress uniform of an officer in the army bore tokens of the fierce part he had taken in the recent conflict.

"Now, then, Eustace, lad, let us pluck our pigeons, and make ourselves scarce."

"All right, Dick; I think we were best away, for I fancy I heard the sound of horses' hoofs a few minutes since."

"So also did I. But, see! the moon is again enshrouded by a heavy cloud. Under cover of the darkness we'll mount and away."

Despite the anger and struggles of their victims, the two friends plundered them of all the valuables they possessed, first securing the costly diamonds forming the wedding present of the Lord Walsingham.

"Come on, Eustace, we had best away, and hasten our return to the Long Village" (London).

Having mounted his bonny mare, Dick Turpin awaited impatiently the arrival of his companion, who had been detained by the young Lord Walsingham, who, as he was about to start away, had seized him by the arm.

"Hold!—a word with you, highway robber. 'Tis the second time we have met—the second time I have been plundered at your hands; beware our third rencontre, for you or I shall perish."

Laughing scornfully at the words of the enraged young man, Eustace was about to join Turpin, when he was restrained by the voice of Lord Walsingham, who, stepping forwards, exclaimed—

"Listen to me, thief, assassin, and midnight marauder! You triumph now; but, by the heavens above us, I will pursue you to the death for the outrage of this night. I will bring you to the gallows, if 'twere only for your mystic resemblance to one whom I always held in my deepest hate."

The moon at this moment again burst from the clouds, throwing, for a few seconds, a broad flood of silvery light upon the scene.

A dim, dark shadow now appeared behind the overturned carriage, and then was lost to sight as the blue luminary above again became curtained by the clouds.

A gleam of triumph shone in the eyes of Lord Walsingham, as he caught sight of the shade.

"Ha! ha! ha! See the shadow of your doom! Your victory is short-lived. Already do you stand upon the brink of the precipice down which you shall be hurled!" shouted the nobleman, rushing with fury upon the astounded Eustace.

Wheeling his horse round, Turpin was about to dash forwards, when his bonny mare was startled by a flash of light in her eyes, followed by the stunning report of a pistol.

Loud shouts rang upon the air, mingled with the discharge of firearms.

A second conflict took place upon the wild heath.

A desperate and savage one.

When the sounds of the struggle ceased, the pale, blue rays of the moon shone upon a group of dark figures, in the centre of whom lay a young man, who, bound and helpless, looked with bold defiance upon the forms that gathered round him.

Far away, scouring wildly and with lightning speed across the heath, was a solitary horseman.

A few moments elapsed; then two tall, fierce-looking men mounted a couple of steeds, and darted in pursuit of the flying figure that bounded over the heath.

The solitary horseman was Dick Turpin, the highwayman.

The young man bound and helpless in the hands of his foes, no other than our hero, Eustace Maltravers.

Surprised by a couple of passing patrol, who had stole upon them in the darkness, our hero and his friend had been overpowered by the officers and their former victims.

One bloody and grim-looking corpse lay stretched upon the roadway; dark and fierce looked that blood-stained body as it lay where it had been shot down.

A bullet-hole in the centre of the forehead made the features of the robber Black Will look yet more ferocious and horrible.

The murder of the unhappy runner, Jones, in the well-hole of the flash ken in the Mint had been avenged.

His assassin, Black Will, had perished in his encounter with the officers on Bagshot Heath.

Disdainfully Eustace glanced upon the features of his enemies, who, gloating in his capture, vowed to journey with him to the gibbet, that they swore should be his doom.

The last words of Turpin rang yet in the ears of our hero.

"Fear not, Eustace, you shall be rescued, or your pal shall perish on the same tree."

It was a sad night for the young highwayman, who was accompanied on his return to London by the relentless nobleman, who breathed his incessant vows of vengeance in his ears, nor left him till they arrived at their journey's end.

It was many hours ere Eustace, with his captors, halted before a dark, drear, and sombre-looking pile, standing in the heart of the town.

All was bright and sunny without this grim pile.

But within was a dark, heavy, funeral gloom.

A gloom that weighed upon and depressed the buoyant spirits of our hero.

For the first time Eustace Maltravers entered the dark portals of the celebrated London prison-house, before the doors of which so many had perished a disgraceful death upon the gallows.

Eustace Maltravers, the young highwayman, was now a prisoner.

A prisoner in Newgate.

CHAPTER XXIV.

THE CAPTIVE IN THE HEMLOCK MANOR HOUSE.—THE MISER AND HIS DAUGHTER.—EXULTATION OF RALPH FAIRLEY.—DISTRESS AND DESPAIR OF SYBIL.—MAN'S HATE AND WOMAN'S LOVE.—THE OATH.—HORROR OF SYBIL.—FURY OF THE MISER.—THE VOW OF VENGEANCE.—THE DARK FIGURE AT THE CASEMENT.

THE sun rose bright and beautiful upon the red-bricked building of the Hemlock Manor House a few days after the events related in our last chapter.

It was a lovely morning, the warm, genial rays of the sun shining with golden lustre upon the scene.

Without the residence of Ralph Fairley, the miser, all was joy and happiness.

The birds fluttered, and winged their way in the air, twittering merrily their morning song.

The trees, looking bright, green, and beautiful, waved gently their leafy branches in the night breeze, singing a gentle lullaby in the air.

The gaudy butterfly hovered in the air, darting from flower to flower, and fluttering its tiny gossamer wings in the sun's rays.

All was bright and beautiful without the Hemlock Manor House that summer morning.

But within was nought but storm and passion.

Terror and distress.

Captivity and despair.

In a lone, deserted chamber of the old house was the miser's daughter held prisoner by her enraged parent, who had never forgiven her vows of love to the man whom he hated, and followed up with determined vengeance.

Ralph Fairley never forgave the imposition practised upon him by Eustace Maltravers, and for the robbery of his gold swore to see him hanged upon the gibbet.

It was as the clock of the Manor was giving out the hour of eight that bright sunny morn, that, with a smile of joy irradiating his features, the miser proceeded to the chamber in which he held prisoner his child.

Entering the lone room that stood by itself in a neglected wing of the old house, Ralph Fairley surprised his daughter engaged in prayer.

A grim smile wreathed his features as he glanced upon the kneeling form of his child.

"Well, Sybil, fair and obedient daughter, I have news—oh! such brave news for you this morning. But come, first tell me, are you still obstinate in your determination to resist my will?"

"If, to still feel love for the unfortunate man who, by his honour and nobleness of soul, has won my heart, then I am still your disobedient child."

"You persist, then, in your attachment to this thief—this assassin?"

A purple shade of passion crossed the features of the old man, succeeded by a grim smile as his daughter started forwards.

"No—no, father! Assassin he is not, nor ever will be. A fearful, horrible fate has plunged him into crime. He wants but a hand to rescue him from the abyss: be yours the one to save him. Believe me, he is all nobleness and truth, and though leagued with outcasts to society, and a man upon whose head the law has set its ban, yet is he all honour and truth. Say, dear father, you will aid him to leave England? In another clime he may by virtuous industry make amends for the errors of his youth."

"Ha! ha! ha!"

Shouts of derisive laughter fell upon the poor young girl's ears; then, starting forwards, the miser seized her wrist, and with his right hand pointed to the casement, through which poured a flood of light.

"Sybil Fairley, behold yon shining orb of day! After to-morrow it's golden lustre will be no more visible to Eustace Maltravers, the highwayman!"

"What mean you?"

A deadly pallor stole across the face of the unhappy girl, who shuddered as she caught sight of the grim smile upon her parent's features.

"I mean that your robber-lover's doom is fixed. In two days he hangs—hangs at Tyburn Tree!"

A shriek of anguish rang through the apartment, accompanied by a hideous low chuckle from the lips of the miser, then there was the sound of a heavy fall, and all was still.

With folded arms and stern, relentless visage, Ralph Fairley beheld his only child sink with horror in a death-swoon at his feet. Like a beautiful corpse the young girl looked as the warm sun poured its rays upon her pallid, upturned face.

"I could almost find it in my heart to wish she might never rise in life again," he muttered. "To think that she should cherish love for a thief, a robber on the highway, a man who now, in the condemned cell of Newgate, awaits his execution! At Tyburn Tree will he perish, and I will be there; for, curses on him! he has robbed me of my child; but, by the fiends, I will crush her stubborn spirit or break her heart! I will follow to the execution of her accursed lover, and gloat with joy upon his death agony!"

Another wild shriek rang through the chamber as, returning to consciousness, the latter part of his speech was heard by the unfortunate Sybil.

"Father! father!" gasped the wretched girl, "speak not thus! Say, oh! say 'tis but a cruel jest! He, the man whom I love—whom you hate! Oh! tell me not, in your anger to fright me with horrid terror, that he is doomed to death! I will not—dare not believe it."

"Believe it or not, as you will. Again I tell you, in two days from this the man who you love will perish at Tyburn, and his body will be hung in chains upon Bagshot Heath, the scene of his last exploit."

With a deep curse, throwing her from him as she clung to his knees, Ralph Fairley left the chamber, his wretched daughter convulsed with grief at the cruel intelligence of her lover's fate.

"To be hanged—hanged at Tyburn!" she gasped.

Wildly the poor girl glared round the room when once more left alone.

"To be hanged—strangled out of life! Oh! 'tis horrible! But can I not save him from this terrible doom? I have gold unknown to my father. My jewels may procure assistance to rescue my dear Eustace from death. Yes—yes, it shall be so. I will away, and gain an interview with he whom they have doomed to perish. With gold I will procure his release, and together we will fly this hated land for ever."

Then, darting to the door, she placed her hand upon the lock, but started back with a cry of despair.

The poor girl had forgotten that she was a prisoner.

A prisoner in her father's house.

How could she aid her lover in his hour of peril?

No; she was a captive; and sick and faint she grew as she reflected upon her lover's fate.

When next she passed the threshold of the door of the chamber in which she was imprisoned, her lover, the unfortunate Eustace, would have ceased to exist.

The inexorable law would have carried out its fiat.

The highwayman would expiate his venial crimes upon the scaffold.

Bitter, scalding tears chased each other down the cheeks of the unhappy Sybil as she thought upon her lover's wretched fate.

Was there no hope?

None.

No means of flying from her prison-house.

Could she escape, she would to London, and endeavour to aid her doomed lover.

Gold would do much. Her lover might yet be saved.

But how was she to leave the chamber in which she was imprisoned?

With wild, despairing gaze, Sybil again looked round the lone room, and, with a burst of grief and despair, acknowledged to herself that, without aid, she could not escape.

And what could aid her?

She was hopelessly a captive till the terrible death of her lover procured her release.

"There is no hope. None—none," she moaned.

A slight shriek now escaped Sybil.

The shadow of a man who was clinging to the ivy without.

Tap! tap! tap! There was the sound of knuckles upon the glass of the casement, followed by an earnest ejaculation.

"Open! open! 'Tis a friend!"

The dark figure at the casement was now fully revealed in a broad glare of moonlight, that flooded all without in a silvery lustre.

With pallid features and tottering limbs, Sybil staggered to the casement.

The figure of the stranger drew closer to the window, as the terror-stricken Sybil drew near.

"Who—what are you?" she gasped, looking wildly at the dark form without.

"A friend. Have no fear. If you would save the life of one you love, admit me."

With bewildered brain, and in nervous terror, Sybil drew back the fastening of the casement, and in another moment the dark form bounded into the chamber.

Noting the alarm of the miser's daughter, the stranger darted forwards, and, seizing her hand in his, exclaimed—

"Nay, be not terrified, sweet Miss Sybil. To allay your fears, I will at once inform you that I come from the unhappy Eustace Maltravers. If you would save his life, hear me. Do not be alarmed. On my soul, I come not to harm you, but to aid my friend."

"Say on; I would gladly assist he of whom you speak.

But hasten to let me know what you have to say ere it be too late, for at any moment my father may be here," ejaculated Sybil, breathlessly awaiting her companion's reply.

"You, doubtless, are aware that your lover and betrothed now lies a prisoner in one of Newgate's dreary cells?"

"Yes—yes. Would—would it were in my power to aid him!"

"You can do so."

"No, no. You know not, stranger, what you say. I am myself a captive in my parent's house, and could I escape from hence, how could I render assistance to the unfortunate being upon whom I have bestowed my love?"

"I will tell you. Eustace Maltravers has friends without his prison-house who will risk their very lives to save him from a death at Tyburn Tree."

A convulsive shudder shook the frame of the unhappy Sybil, as the stranger reminded her of the fearful doom to which her lover would be condemned.

"Alas! how can I aid him?" she murmured, weeping bitterly.

"Listen. Sybil Fairley, your father is rich; gold is needed to enable the friends of the poor captive to render him assistance. Jailers are but men, gold may do much; and remember, whate'er the sum advanced by you, it will be faithfully returned ere a month is out."

"Talk not thus. All I have, my very jewels will I part with to save him I love from a horrible death. Well assured am I that a terrible fate, over which he has had no control, led him to adopt a course of life that has thrust him to the edge of the abyss on which he now stands. To rescue Eustace I will give all I possess, but know not how to lend my help unless I can quit my own prison house, for all I have—my jewels and a little gold—are at my father's house in town."

"I will assist you to leave this house if you will place yourself under my guidance. You forget the companion of Eustace Maltravers. I am he!"

The stranger, letting fall the cloak that he had before held up to his countenance, now exposed features well remembered by Sybil, who, however, still paused irresolute by the casement.

Turpin, for it was he who had thus made his way into the old Manor House, now advanced, and exclaimed—

"Well, Miss Sybil, if you cannot render the aid I require without going to town, and also refuse to join me in quitting this house, then must I return alone, and seek another method to procure the gold that is required."

Turpin then made for the window. In another moment he was making his way out of the chamber, when his arm was clutched by the hapless Sybil, who, with white pallid face, and with nervous, trembling accents, ejaculated—

"Stay! stay! I will go with you. Heaven forgive you if you mean me harm! But I will not pause in this dread peril; he, Eustace, must be saved. But, tell me, how are we to quit my father's house?"

"I have come prepared for your flight, knowing you were held a captive by your parent. See, I have here a strong ladder of silk. By its aid you may reach the ground below. I can descend by the thick branches of the ivy that assisted me in my entrance here."

Turpin, whilst speaking, had drawn from his pocket a strong ladder made of twisted silk, which he now made fast to the casement, the lower portion of this means of descent trailing on the ground some feet below.

Recalling to her mind the recent interview with her stern and cruel parent, Sybil, who loved the object of her passion, Eustace Maltravers, with all the affection of her young virgin heart, cast aside all feeling of fear at the undertaking before her, and boldly placed herself in the hands of Dick Turpin. The latter, with the utmost ease, lifted the sylph-like form of the miser's daughter in his arms, as though she had been a child, and whispering words of encouragement and friendship in her ears, aided the terrified girl in her descent of the silken ladder. Clinging to the ivy, the highwayman, with Sybil close beside him, with little difficulty at length reached the ground.

Taking the hand of the young girl in his, Dick Turpin hurried across the moonlit gardens, and in a few minutes sood in the lane that led to the high road and faced the Hemlock Manor House.

Giving a low whistle, the highwayman, with his fair charge, waited a moment at the end of the lane. Sybil, who had been unable to speak in the excitement of the scene through which she had just passed, now tremulously inquired the cause of the delay.

"I but await the arrival of bonny Black Bess, who must with all speed convey us both to London. Ah! see, she is here."

The glossy, raven-coated mare, the loved steed of the bold highwayman, now appeared, as she dashed from the thick, dark coppice that grew on either side of the lane, giving expression to her delight by a low whinnying noise, and rubbing her superb head upon the face of her master, the noble and sagacious brute stood in the lane silently awaiting his bidding.

Lifting Sybil on the saddle, Turpin then himself mounted his brave steed, at the same time praying the betrothed of his friend to excuse the grasp he gave her slender form to hold her on her novel and precarious seat.

"In an hour, Miss Sybil, you shall be at the door of your father's residence in London. Hillio! Away, Bess! Away, lass! The moon shines bright—'tis a cloudless night. You must carry double, and not halt on the road. Hillio! hillio! Away, away, Bess!

With a spring, the brave beast bounded off, and in a moment was out of the lane, dashing along, a few minutes afterwards, on the high road to London. For a few seconds the sound of the horse's hoofs could be heard. Then all was silent, still as death—a silence, at length, broken by horrid oaths and dreadful curses of impotent rage.

In the broad, white, and silvery light of the summer moon stood an old man, leaning on the gate of the Hemlock Manor grounds that opened on the lane.

Without covering on the head, his hoary locks were tossed about his brow by the breeze.

A look of fierce rage, of wild demoniacal fury rested on his features.

With clenched fists he stood, trembling with passion, and uttering horrible curses on the heads of those whom he had discerned issuing from the grounds that night.

Fearful vows of vengeance were registered by Ralph Fairley against his child and the man upon whom she had bestowed the affection of her fond young heart.

Truly and terribly he kept his oath.

CHAPTER XXV.

THE "DEVIL'S PUNCHBOWL." — THE COMPANIONS OF THE RED BAND.—THE CONSULTATION.—THE BAN OF BLOOD.—SUDDEN APPEARANCE OF THE BLACK MASK. —THE WARNING. — THE ATTEMTED CAPTURE. — THE ESCAPE.

It is night.

A dark and lowering one.

Huge black clouds hovered in the firmament above.

Not a star was visible in the skies.

All was thick, heavy clouds, and inky darkness.

An oppressive heat hung in the air.

Whilst the angry winds threatened a coming storm.

"We'll have rain to-night, Coffin; let us get under cover."

"All right, Cherry-nose. I can sight the glim outside the 'Punchbowl,' and here we is."

The two men, who had been hurrying along the dark streets, now entered the den of horrors and the resort of crime situate in Ratcliffe Highway.

Pushing their way through the bar, the two men made for the little room at the back, the same in which the unfortunate seamen had been so foully murdered by their comrades some months before; ordering some spirits and water and tobacco, the two ruffians prepared to pass away an hour whilst awaiting the arrival of some of their companions.

The two villains, when pursuing their path down the Highway, noted not a dark muffled form that followed them, warily and closely watching their every movement; the figure, that of a female in a dark cloak that muffled and concealed her features, boldly entered the "Devil's Punchbowl," and as the men made their way into the room at the back, darted into a little recess that concealed her from those who made their egress or ingress to the chamber, whilst, through the thin laths and plaster that formed the walls, all could be heard that passed within the chamber.

" And so then, Coffin, they tops poor Burker for that affair of slitting the weazand of his blowen ? "

" Just so. The wery identical Barney Samuels is booked at last for a leap in the dark from the leafless tree. Next Monday, at twelve, the scragging match comes off, and cuss me if I don't go and see if my old pal dies game."

" So will I ; but I rather think that Burker won't do other than die like a brick. But, howsomever, what is this you tell me about this little affair that's to come off at Kensington ? When is the lay to take place ? "

" To-morrow night, arter twelve o'clock."

" How many on us ? "

" Three : Resurrection Bill, myself, and you. If, Cherry, yer likes to join us, there'll be plenty of wedge (plate), only a gal to carry off, and fifty goldfinches paid for the job."

" Wery good. Who puts yer on the crack, and pays the gilt ? "

" One of the right sort ; a downright trump, and no flies ; no other than Captain Leslie. We've done business for him afore. He's a rare cove for the blowens, and is a good 'un at parting with the ready stephen (money). In course, Cherry, you'll join us ? "

" In course I will. Let me see, Burker were with you on the last lay, warn't he ? "

" No ; Jemmy Bullfinch, wot was lagged 'tother day for nailing a reader (pocket-book) and fogle (handkerchief) ; an' it were rare fun that night at Soho-square. I and Finchy set the blessed crib on fire afore we started, and a fine blaze it made, I can tell yer. But, come, as yer joins us to-morrow, Cherry, I can give a goldfinch (sovereign), and we'll have some more liquor in."

Hammering rudely on the table, upon the appearance of the slatternly wench who acted at the " Punch-bowl " as waitress, Coffin, the burglar, ordered some more of the fiery spirits of which himself and his companion had already imbibed a liberal allowance.

" Has yer heard about that there nevy of Guy Essington's what they say is stowed away in the stone jug ? Is it true as he's lagged, Coffin ? "

" Yes, he is caged safe, hard, and fast, Cherry ; and, mark me, if he wasn't, or were to escape a trip across the herring pond or a dance at Tyburn, why, he'll have to keep his blinkers well open, 'cos as how there is a ban set agin him by our blessed leader, Resurrection Bill. All on us as is members of the Red Band are under oath to pursue the Night-Hawks to the death. I for one has my knife in a few on 'em, and blowed if I don't mark 'em afore I'm much older."

About to speak to his companion, the man, Cherry, and his comrade, the Coffin, started in their seats as the form of a woman appeared before them.

Holding out her right hand, and with her fine figure drawn to its full height, the female, whose features were concealed by a black mask, exclaimed, in a firm, cool tone—

" A word or two with you," pointing to Coffin, she added. " I have overheard your project respecting a burglary at Kensington. You mentioned the name of one, whom I would give much to see. Tell me, then, where I may meet with Captain Leslie—he who has employed you to carry out his purpose to-morrow. Nay, start not, nor draw your knives. I fear you not. I am a bold, determined woman, and fear neither man nor Satan. I am armed ; and, if you attempt to move from your seats, will plant a bullet in your brains."

Placing her hand in her bosom, the daring woman drew forth a pair of pistols, that she now presented at the heads of the astonished ruffians before her.

" Well, I'm blowed, Cherry ! arn't she a stunner ? "

" Right you is, Coffin. Look at her sparklers. Doesn't they glitter rather ? "

" But we isn't going to be cheated like this, Cherry, by a blowen, is we ? "

" I guess not. Calculates as how we must ease her of those pop-guns. Tip up the barking-irons, my gal. We doesn't want to hurt yer ; but they might go off."

Both the ruffians started to their feet and made a step towards the intruder, who, with steady hands and glittering eyes, remained motionless. The villains, awed and struck by her bold demeanour, stood in mute surprise before her, whilst she exclaimed—

" Stand back, or by Heavens I'll fire. Tell me, as you value life, where—where may I find Captain Leslie ? "

" We don't know, my beauty."

" Liar ! where are you to meet your employer to-morrow night ? Attempt not to deceive me, for I will shoot you with as little remorse as I'd plant my bullet in the skull of a mad dog or ravening wolf. Say where you are to meet Captain Leslie after you have executed his mission at Kensington ? "

" Well, I doesn't suppose it much matters. Don't expect the captain will care for a blowen ; and, if yer must know, why we carries our prize to him directly we collars her. He will be waiting till the trick is done. Now yer knows all about it ; and Jem Coffin, who, mind yer, arn't frightened at the sight of a barking-iron in the hands of a woman, only tells yer cos he admires the pluck of the blowen who has boldly defied him within the walls of the ' Devil's Punchbowl.' On to her, Cherry."

With a shout, Coffin dashed forwards, as, taken off her guard during the ruffian's speech, the daring woman had relaxed her watchfulness.

There was a volley of curses and rude oaths. A bottle containing a piece of candle—the only light in the apartment—was knocked off the table, enveloping the room in darkness.

" Hold on to her, Cherry. I has her ! "

" Never fear, Coffin. I'll stick to the blowen like a leech. Light the glim."

For a moment there was a dead silence, broken in a few seconds by a renewed struggle, and a fierce oath from the mouth of the ruffian Cherry, followed by the opening and slamming to of a door. The glimmer of a light then threw its rays in the chamber, disclosing the form of the man, Coffin, at the table, and his companion standing at the door, with a look of rage and fury on his features, holding a large black cloak in his hand.

" Fiends and furies ! Cherry, where is the vixen ? "

" Escaped ; slipped like an eel out of her disguise. But she can't be through the bar. We may nab her yet."

Turning round, the ruffian placed his hand upon the handle of the door.

It was fast locked.

Fresh oaths of fury burst from the lips of the discomfited ruffians, who were maddened at the idea that they had been defeated by a woman.

Bursting the door from its hinges, they made their way to the bar.

All had seen the muffled form of the female enter, but none had noticed her departure.

The inn and the neighbouring courts and alleys were strictly searched.

But the mysterious, masked female had disappeared.

CHAPTER XXVI.

NEWGATE IN THE EIGHTEENTH CENTURY.—THE HIGH-WAYMAN IN HIS CELL.—THE VISITORS.—THE LOVE OF A GOOD WOMAN.—THE FAREWELL.—THE WONDERFUL PIE. —THE APPROACH OF NIGHT.—LOCKING UP THE CELLS.— ESCAPE OF THE DASHING YOUNG KNIGHT OF THE ROAD. —THE PURSUIT.—THE RACE FOR LIFE.

ON the same night that saw the visit of the mysterious female at the " Devil's Punchbowl," some strange incidents took place at the dark, dreary London prison-house known as Newgate.

The moon, riding high in the heavens, threw a silvery light on the old gray pile.

The dark, dismal, horrible-looking building was made, if possible, more drear and terrible in the whitish, ghostly glare of the luminary of the night.

Had those solid blocks of masonry power to speak, what hideous scenes would be related. The stranger, gazing upon the gloomy and terrible prison with a shudder, hurries on, fancying that dark, weird, mystic forms hover in the air about the precincts of the gaol. How many miserable criminals, with throbbing hearts and dizzy brains, turned almost to madness at a near approach to a terrible death, have passed beneath those dismal portals.

Led forth to suffer a dreadful doom.

A fearful, hideous death by strangulation on the gallows.

The gallows, whose black, frowning front met the last dying gaze of the doomed one.

What hideous scenes have taken place in the dismal, terrible prison !

May not the shades of those whose mouldering bones

lie rotting to decay in the darksome passage of the fearful building haunt its precincts?

On the night when Eustace was led a captive into the prison-house, a convulsive thrill, a terrible shudder of fear darted through his frame, as he passed from the outer world into the silent winding passages and dim corridors of Newgate.

A weary, restless night was passed by our hero; on awaking from his troubled repose, he started up to his feet, glaring wildly round his darksome cell.

An exclamation of terror escaped him, as he was thus reminded that he was a captive in the walls of Newgate. A few moments, however, served to dispel the grim feelings of awe and terror that oppressed him.

When visited shortly after by the thief-taker, Geoffery Newton, Eustace laughed to scorn his predictions of a near approach to death.

Three days passed away.

Eustace Maltravers was committed for trial upon the charge of highway robbery, Lord Walsingham, his son, and Colonel Moreton vowing to pursue him to the end for the attack upon Bagshot Heath.

From muttered sentences dropped by the jailers, and the exultation of Geoffery Newton, little hope was left in the bosom of the captive of escape from transportation or the gibbet.

But with his usual daring and confidence, our hero treated the matter with the utmost indifference.

As the silent hours of the night flew by, would he sit up when all was quiet in that dreary prison-house, thinking over two subjects ever in his mind.

His love of Sybil Fairley.

And a means of escape.

On the morning of the day that beheld the scene between the vengeful miser and his unhappy daughter, Eustace received at the wicket of the corridor, which he was permitted to traverse with other captives, a strange missive.

An apple was handed to him by his visitor, a young woman, no other than Brown Bet, she whom Eustace had saved from the violence of Resurrection Bill at the ken in Mint-street.

"Eat the fruit when you are alone, and don't swallow the pips," murmured the young girl. Then, bursting into a merry laugh, she began to rally one of the captives upon his downcast looks.

At length, retiring to his cell, Eustace, who felt convinced some hidden meaning was in the words of Gipsy Bet, took the apple, a large one, from his pocket, and found it had been divided in the centre, he then discovered a scrap of paper. Tearing it open, to his joy he found it was a note from his friend Dick Turpin. Listening for a moment at the door of his cell, and finding all was quiet without, he went to the grating, through which a ray of light darted into the dungeon, and ran his eyes over the few lines.

"DEAR EUSTACE,—*You must not wait a trial. 'Twill go against you, and I fear you'll be booked by the beak for a ride to Tyburn. But the Hawks are out. Fear not. You will receive a visit to-night from one who will tell you all.—Yours,* DICK."

Here was news indeed. Never, for one moment, had Eustace fancied that his friends would leave him in his peril, and now it was evident that they were exerting their utmost in his behalf.

Scarce had he torn the note into minute fragments ere he was startled by the rattling of keys, and, in another moment the door of his cell was thrown open, and two female forms were ushered in, the jailer giving notice that only a quarter of an hour would be allowed for consultation.

The door had hardly closed, the sound of the man's steps still echoing in the passage without, when the foremost of the two females, darting forwards, sank sobbing in the arms of Eustace.

The words, "Eustace! Eustace! is it thus we meet?" then struck upon the ear of the astounded captive, who was as one in a dream at the sound of a well-remembered voice.

The veil then falling from the features of the visitor, now revealed to the prisoner a face, the lineaments of which were engraven in the tablet of his memory.

With a cry of joy he wound his arms around her slender, yielding form.

"Dear, dear girl! my own, my best beloved! this is generous, kind, and true. My own sweet Sybil, this delicious moment that I hold you thus in my embrace, that I feel your dear breath fanning my face, you repay me for all. Dear girl, this is happiness that I dreamt not of."

At length, withdrawing herself from his arms, Sybil, who had contrived to gain a meeting with her lover, drew back, and, with her fair features flushing crimson at the remembrance of how she had thrown herself in his embrace in the excitement of again beholding the one whom she had thought lost to her for ever, now told her lover in faltering accents that they had but a few minutes to spare.

"Listen, dear Eustace; the jailer will return anon. That I have to say must be said at once. I have seen your friend, who aided me to escape my father's house; but all this you shall know hereafter. The purport of my visit is to tell you that to-night you must endeavour to escape your cell. This dungeon, we have learned, opens out upon a court-yard; gain that, ascend a high wall, and you are free. Outside the prison to-night you will meet George Watson, of the 'Bold Horseman.' He will conduct you to a place of safety. Hark! the foot of the turnkey sounds in the passage without. I must begone. Remember, dear Eustace, to-night you must escape from hence."

"But how, dear Sybil? The grating above is high and strong. Could I reach it, I have nought with which I could remove the iron bars."

"You will be furnished with all you require, and heaven aid you in your task. But, hush! the jailor returns!"

Drawing a thick veil over her features, Sybil now seized the hands of her lover in hers ere she prepared to depart. The door now, with a grating noise, was opened, and the turnkey, a bluff, herculean-looking fellow, stepping forwards, exclaimed—

"Sorry to interrupt you, marm; but time's up. I've delayed as long as it were possible, but I daresn't wait no longer; so bid good-bye to your jolly knight of the road, and, perhaps, we may manage to leave yer a little longer with the bold highwayman on your next visit."

Convulsive sobs shook the frame of Sybil as she drew herself from her lover's arms. Then, murmuring a last farewell, and the words, "Remember! to-night—to-night!" drew from his embrace and tottered from the dungeon, followed by her companion.

Eustace breathlessly stood listening to the dying footsteps of his betrothed; then, as they ceased to sound upon his ear, he sank into the only seat the cell contained, exclaiming—

"She's gone—gone! When, oh! when, shall we meet again?"

"Well, lord knows, Mr. Eustace. You is in for your trial to-morrow, and I expects yours will be a topping affair; a dance at Tyburn on the leafless tree. But, never mind, we must all go the road to the other world some time or other; so, if yer is to be scragged, yer may as well die game."

Bounding from his seat, Eustace, who had recovered from his former depression of spirits, exclaimed, with a loud laugh—

"Never fear, Smithson. I shall die game when my time is up, but it has not arrived yet. Present my compliments to Geoffery Newton, who exulted over his prisoner yesterday, and tell him the knight of the road, Eustace Maltravers, will yet give him trouble, and pay him for his one or two acts of kindness and attention for my welfare. Believe me, Smithson, the rope ain't spun that will croak your humble servant."

"Indeed. Well, blowed if I'd like to change places with yer any how. But, come, I'll do all I can for yer while you're here. That pretty little bloomer asked me to let you have this pie for your supper; and, as she rubbed my hand with some palm oil, why I consented to break one of the rules, though it's a risk that might cost me my berth, but, as there can't be any harm in letting a cove have a feed, why, damme, there it is."

The jailer here handed to Eustace a pie he had received, he said, from the female who had attended his sweetheart, and, with a knowing wink, and a joke about the late visitors, left the cell.

A smile wreathed the features of Eustace as he gazed upon the dish placed upon the table by the turnkey.

THE MURDER IN THE KEN.

"Hem! a good meal for a starving man. I am much mistaken if Mr. Dick has not had a hand in this affair," muttered Eustace, as he proceeded to cut open the pie that stood before him.

On removing the top crust, a low laugh escaped his lips. In place of fruit, our hero beheld a coil of silk with a hook at one end. On unrolling this, he found it was an ingeniously-contrived ladder. This, together with a small file, a knife, and a pair of minute but exquisitely silver-mounted pocket pistols, made up the interior portion of the pie.

"A bold device and a successful one, friend Dick," ejaculated Eustace.

Hiding these articles about his person, he now impatiently awaited the fall of night.

The hours flew by wearily and slowly to the captive.

Twelve o'clock at length chimed from the prison bell.

The noise of bolts, rattling of keys, and murmuring voices of the warders died away, and all was silence.

Every cell was locked up for the night.

All was quiet—still as death—in the dreary prison-house.

Barely had the last note of the midnight hour ceased to ring upon the air, before Eustace, who had been listening at the door of his cell, started back and prepared to carry out his task.

The grating, some ten feet from the ground, he found he could not reach, save by the aid of his rope ladder. The only table in the cell was insufficient for his purpose, and would not bear his weight.

With some trouble, he at last, after repeated attempts, contrived to catch the hook at the end of the ladder on the coping-stone of the grating. Then, mounting the silken ladder, clinging with one hand to the stonework, he, with his right, filed away at one of the iron bars, that, with joy, he discovered were rusted and in much decay.

Obliged to pause for rest from his labours, and working slowly so as to make as little noise as possible, it was some two hours ere he had contrived to remove two of the bars.

Mounting higher up the ladder, he now thrust his head through the grating, and then, with a deep-breathed curse, drew back, and slid down the rope into his cell.

A dark look of vexation—of despair—rested on his features.

When, glancing out into the courtyard, he had perceived the figure of a man pacing up and down in the moonlight past the cells.

There was a watch, then!

Here was an obstacle not foreseen by himself or friends.

For a few minutes Eustace stood irresolute in the centre of his cell; then, with a smile upon his face, he drew near the grating, murmuring—

"No matter; worse dangers than this have been surmounted by Eustace Maltravers. I must, I will escape. Let me see, I have to cross the courtyard, mount the wall, and then all is over; but to do this I must avoid being seen by the watcher below, and in the broad glare of the moonlight know not how 'tis to be accomplished. There is one way."

A dark look gathered over the brow of Eustace as he furtively handled the knife he had drawn from his pocket, then, replacing it, he muttered—

"No, no! I must not do that. I must not have the poor wretch's blood upon my hands; his life must be spared. I must at once to my task. A struggle with my man will soon finish the matter. 'Twill be hard if I cannot render him unfit to raise an alarm, or follow me in my escape."

Raising his lithe form up the ladder, Eustace clung to a bar that yet remained, and lowered the silken ropes out into the courtyard. The man had left the vicinity of his cell, and was some hundred yards from the scene of Eustace's labours.

The moon rode high and bright in the horizon.

Flooding the whole area of the prison in a silvery light.

"Would Lady Blue were under a cloud. Confound it! 'tis as light as day. Well, here goes. My usual luck may yet aid me."

He now drew his supple figure through the little space he had made by the removal of the two bars; then, sliding down the ladder, stood in the courtyard of the prison. His next proceeding was to unhook the ladder. This he effected with little difficulty. He had just accomplished this when he was startled by the watchman, who had turned in his walk and discovered the strange form beneath the cell.

In another moment a loud spring of a rattle rung upon the night, followed by the deep-breathed curses of the watchman, who was struggling fiercely with Eustace, who, darting forwards, had seized him in his powerful grasp, first wrenching the rattle from the man's hands, thus stopping the alarm from that source.

Desperately the two men struggled in the courtyard.

The moonbeams throwing their shadows in gigantic size upon the walls of old Newgate, Eustace, with a nervous thrill, discovered that the officer was a match for him in point of strength, though not so quick and agile.

"Help! help! help! Up, lads, up! a prisoner would escape."

"Hold your tongue, you fool, or, by heaven! I'll stop your tongue for ever," exclaimed Eustace.

Then, suddenly shifting his hold from the man's shoulders to his waist, he, using all his strength, hurled him off his feet, and sent him a dull, heavy thud to the earth.

There was a deep groan, and then all was still.

Falling on his head, the officer was struck senseless, lying stunned and helpless at the feet of his adversary.

But the first alarm had aroused those within the jail.

Lights could be seen flashing through the gratings and windows.

Flying to the wall, Eustace threw up his ladder till the hook caught in the iron spiking that ran along the top.

Just as this was done, a side door of the gaol at the east end of the courtyard was opened, and half-a-dozen officers rushed out, pointing and shouting at the figure of Eustace that was fully revealed in the broad glare of the moonlight.

"Ha! the bird not yet flown?" shouted Newton, who headed the warders. "Upon him, lads; let him not escape. Fire upon him! Dead or alive, he must be ours."

"Not this time, Geoffery Newton. Ha! ha! ha! Catch me who can?"

Climbing the ladder with the agility of a squirrel, Eustace reached the top of the wall as the officers were but half way across the courtyard, and as they fired their pistols at his form, with another shout of derisive laughter, disappeared over the side, falling at the feet of the bluff George Watson, who was standing in the street below.

"Welcome, welcome, Eustace! So you've done the trick, and slipped the grabs? But, hark! by the devils, there goes the alarm-bell! We must make ourselves scarce."

The bell of Newgate now, with a loud clang, rang upon the night air.

Hurrying along, Eustace and Watson were about to dive down a narrow turning, when they were suddenly faced by some four or five Bow-street runners.

"We have him! Lads, upon him!"

"Drag him back!"

"Down with him!"

"Slip on the darbies, Owen."

"Here comes Newton. We've got him, Geoffery!"

"Then mind you keep him!" shouted Eustace, who, suddenly and dexterously slipping from his coat, left the garment in the hands of the officer, and, like a hare, bounded from the spot, followed by Watson. The enraged officers, with loud shouts, pursued the flying form of the highwayman.

"Watson, do you leave me. Tell Dick I'll meet him at your inn. I must double like a fox upon the yelling hounds behind. Nay, do not follow me, George. I would rather be alone, as I can the better evade my pursuers."

"All right, Eustace, lad. Cuss me! I can't run as I did. I'll shoot down the next court. Good-bye! luck go with yer." Puffing and blowing with the unusual exercise, the bluff and jolly innkeeper disappeared down a narrow court.

The officers, in a yelling pack, followed after Eustace; their numbers increased by one or two pedestrians that happened to be out.

"Stop him! stop him! Stop thief! stop thief!"

With the speed of a hare, Eustace bounded on; he had now reached the bottom of Snow-hill, and, turning to his left, made for the top of Holborn-hill. There were scarce any passengers abroad at that early hour; but here and there a solitary watchman crossed his path. These Eustace either evaded by a feint, darting past them like a hound, or else with his clenched fist striking them to his feet, and then again dashing onwards.

The top of Holborn-hill was gained.

Eustace paused to catch his breath. The perspiration in beads trickled down his brow.

Half-way up the hill were a dozen Bow-street runners, accompanied by perhaps a couple of dozen people.

Rattles sprang loudly on the air, mingled with shouts and wild cries from the excited pursuers.

"Stop him! Twenty pound to he who brings him back!" yelled Newton, who headed the officers in pursuit of the escaped highwayman.

A man—a tall, herculean-looking ruffian, a butcher—darted upon Eustace, as he once more dashed on.

"No yer don't, my hearty! Hold still, or curse me if I don't throttle yer like a rabbit!"

"Let go your hold!" said Eustace, with a muttered curse, striving to free himself from the iron grip of the butcher.

"Not if I knows it. Yer friends is coming, and, cuss me, I'll collar the rowdy!"

"Let me go! Release me, I say!"

"In course I will, presently. Here they is."

There was a rush of officers who had reached the spot, a loud cry for help and heavy groan, then a fierce struggle. A few minutes after our hero was again dashing with the speed of a fawn along the road, followed by his enemies.

A group stayed behind gazing upon the form of the butcher, who had been struck down by a fearful blow received in his struggle with Eustace.

"Stop him! stop him!"

Rattle, rattle, rattle! How the silence of the morning was awakened by the shouting, yelling crowd!

Bravely the highwayman sped on in his race for life!

Wildly, madly our hero dashed on.

Followed closely by his pursuers.

The cries of "Stop him! stop thief!" ringing in his ears.

Looking back once or twice, Eustace discovered the

foremost of his pursuers to be the thief-taker, Geoffery Newton. Fleet of foot, and with vengeful feelings urging him on, the runner still kept close on the track of the flying highwayman.

Up one turning, down another, Eustace kept on at his fearful speed in the direction of the North road.

His pursuers still kept up the race, some few falling back from sheer exhaustion; others, however, taking their place, the crowd increasing as the morning advanced.

With a chill feeling of rage and despair, Eustace became aware that he could not much longer elude his enemies, unless some means of escape presented itself to him.

His limbs were stiff and cramped; his hair, in dark wet masses, clung to his brow, whilst his breath came short and thick, his chest heaving with the effects of the fearful race.

He clutched the knife and pistols concealed in his bosom with the firm grasp of fury and despair.

Hunted thus like some beast of prey, a feeling of revenge against his foes took possession of our hero.

He vowed, as he ran panting on, not to be taken with life; he would escape or perish.

Turning round once more, he discerned far behind the yelling, shouting crowd, and within two hundred yards was the officer Newton and two others mounting horses they had secured at an inn.

Here was a danger quite unlooked for.

His enemies would now run him down in a few minutes.

There was no chance, no hope of further escape.

In a few more moments he would be struggling in the grasp of his foes.

Words of despair issued from his lips.

Wildly he glared round to discover if there were any means of eluding his enemies.

For a moment he was about to give up all as hopeless.

Still racing on, he had arrived at the corner of a narrow street, turning off the Oxford road, up which he had been racing, with a cry of joy he dashed off the high road into the narrow street.

He would elude his enemies yet.

He might even now foil them, at the moment when they had him all but in their hands.

The shouts and cries of the officers, and the clattering of the horses' hoofs, now sounded close upon him.

They were within a few yards of the street, as Eustace turned off the road.

Five doors down there was a cart loaded with hay.

The little door, or opening of a loft, for straw and hay, was standing open, whilst a pig-headed lout, with a red flannel cap on, and a face as red as his head-dress, was pitching in, by means of a huge fork, the trusses of hay from the cart into the loft, that belonged to the corn-chandler, whose shop stood by the shed, the bottom of which were used as stables, and the upper portion as a loft.

Without a moment's hesitation, Eustace mounted the cart.

He had, with the quickness of thought, resolved on a means of escape.

With his usual daring, the plan was no sooner conceived than carried out.

"Domn thee, were beest thee cooming? Get out, or, by ma ole man, I'll gie thee summat!"

The country lad, with a threatening look, raised the formidable fork to strike the daring intruder down.

Wrenching the implement from him, and seizing the astounded chawbacon in his arms, Eustace hurled him, like one of the hay trusses, into the loft.

To jump in himself was the work of a moment.

Gagging the terrified lad, and stripping from his back his gray smock, and tearing off the red cap, arraying his own person with them, was the work of a few seconds.

Seizing the helpless youth, whom he bound with a rope he found in the loft, he then hurled him to the extreme end, and threw over his body some loose hay and straw, then, leaning over him, he exclaimed,—

"Lie there quiet, lad, or damme, I'll cut you up into mincemeat, or make you swallow your own pitchfork!"

Loud voices sounded without.

"He's in the hay-loft; we've run the fox to earth."

Stepping from the back part of the loft, Eustace now boldly made for the entry.

A loud shout greeted his appearance.

Standing by the cart were the officers, Newton and his men, whilst at the end of the street were some portion of the yelling mob who had followed in the pursuit.

"Hallo! who the —— are you?" said Newton, staring with rage and fury at Eustace, who munching away at some bread and bacon he had found upon the person of the red-faced one, stood calmly looking at the mob below.

"Eh! eh! eh! I be Giles Jolter. Get away from ma cart; thee'll frighten ma mare."

"Damn your mare!"

"Well, if it be all the same to you, I won't. She be a good 'un in harness, and a danged sight prettier nor you to look at, old pimple feace!"

"Look you here!"

"'Ess, I'se looking; and I can't zay as I thinks much on it. Thee be'est an ugly cove, anyhow!"

Bridling his rage, Newton exclaimed—

"Have you seen a man pass here?"

"A mon?"

"Yes."

"What sort of a mon?"

"Why, a dashing-looking fellow, without a coat or hat."

"Were he a tall mon?"

"Well, yes."

"Good-looking—reather loike me?"

"Well, he is not bad-looking. He is a devil-me-care-looking man; a young fellow."

"Oh! I understand; he be a Lunnun chap, a cute cove. Did he coom down here?"

"Yes."

"He had gotten noa coat, noa hat on?"

"No."

"Were he running?"

"Yes, he was. Where did he go?"

"Well, I doan't know, for I arn't seen him."

With a curse of rage, Newton turned away, whilst Eustace, cramming the bread and bacon into his mouth to prevent himself from laughing, stood gazing at the crowd below, chuckling at the rage of the infuriated officer.

"Well, lads," exclaimed Newton, "our man has out-witted us. I can make nothing out of that bacon-eating lout, curse him! Yet the highwayman cannot be far off. Owen and you, Hartley, guard the end of the street here. It has no thoroughfare; we may catch our bird yet."

"Well, he has given us a run, Newton. He is a downy bird."

"Ay, Owen. But, by the devils! he shall not readily get the best of Geoffery Newton. I'll have him! I'll pursue him, like a hound as he is! I have sworn not to rest till he swings upon the gallows; and, by the fiends! I'll keep my oath. But come, let us search the houses in the street. He must be lurking somewhere, and cannot be far off."

"Help! Dang moy buttons, ah woan't be robbed! Help! help!"

Newton started, and hurried back to the hay-cart.

The countryman had disappeared from the opening of the loft; and from the loft was it came these sudden cries for help.

"Our man, for a thousand pounds!" ejaculated Newton, clambering up in the cart, and from thence making his way into the little shed.

Followed by his men, the runner searched the loft. At the further end one of them discovered a human figure cowering in some hay and straw. To drag him forward was the work of a moment.

With an exultant shout, Newton seized the figure, that of a man without coat or hat.

"Ha! ha! ha! clever Eustace Maltravers! So, then, the fox is run to earth at last!"

"Let I goo! let I goo! Help! help! help!"

"Ten thousand devils! What is this?" exclaimed Newton, releasing the struggling form at his feet. "Fiends and furies! who have we here?"

"Speak, fellow! Who and what are you?" ejaculated one of the officers, as Newton, speechless with rage, stamped the flooring of the loft with passion.

"Why, I be Farmer Jenkins's mon. I ah been robbed and murdered! Somebody ah stolen moy cap an' moy smock, together with ma bread and bacon. Dang moy buttons! I'll be revenged on 'em."

Guessing how the matter stood, Newton stepped forwards, and turning to the bumpkin, exclaimed—

"Look, my lad ; you shall be paid for what you have lost, and something besides, but first tell me where the man has gone that has robbed you ?"

"Dang ma buttons ! that's more nor I can tell. He stole ma things, knocked I down, bundling I in the straw, and then disappeared. Domn him !"

"Is there any means of getting from here save by that place ?" said Newton, pointing to the way they had entered.

"Yes. Thee can goo doon trap into Measter Muggins's stables."

"Ten thousand devils ! Owen, the bird has flown !"

"Safe as the bank, Newton."

In another moment they were busily searching for the trap which they found open. Followed by his men, Newton descended into the stables below, but the highwayman was nowhere to be seen.

As Geoffery Newton said, the bird had flown.

———

CHAPTER XXVII.

THE PURSUIT.—THE STRUGGLE IN THE YARD.—THE FLIGHT OVER THE HOUSE-TOPS.—THE BED-CHAMBER AND ITS INMATE.—THE YOUNG SERVANT-MAID AND THE HIGHWAYMAN.—THE OFFICERS OUTWITTED.—THE FIGHT ON THE STAIRCASE, AND ESCAPE OF THE KNIGHT OF THE ROAD.

UPON the officer, Geoffery Newton, turning away for a moment with his men, Eustace, aware that every moment might reveal the trick that had been played upon them, prepared to fly. Scarce had he discovered the existence of the trap leading to the stables below, ere with a grunt and a moan of pain and terror, the country-lad, managing to free himself of the gag and his bindings, started up, and was about to cry for help, when Eustace, driven to extremities by the urgency of the moment and his danger, darted forwards, and, with a blow in the stomach, sent the unfortunate youth, howling with fright and pain, into the straw from which he had risen.

Lowering himself down the trap, he found he was in a small stable ; hiding-place in this there was none. Hearing the exulting cry of Newton and the officers, and finding them close upon him, he darted from the stable by a door at the back ; he then found himself in a large yard, surrounded by a high wall.

A servant wench, with a scream at his appearance, dashed from the yard into the house, slamming-to and bolting the door after her.

"Pleasant, very !" murmured our hero, glancing round the yard. "Like a fox in a hole, I seem run to earth. Confound it ! to be caged like this, after escaping thus far, is maddening. Ah ! that ladder must aid me to quit this infernal yard."

Eustace, who had discerned a ladder in a corner of the yard, rushed forwards, and endeavoured to remove it ; it resisted, however, all his efforts. Placed there by some workmen who were repairing the roof, it had been fastened at the top, and could readily be moved. Time was precious ; already he could hear the voices of his pursuers ; he must away, or he would again fall a captive in the hands of his foes.

About to mount the ladder, and make his way to the roof above, he was foiled in his purpose by receiving a fearful blow at the back of the head. With his brain in a whirl, and the feeling as if the whole place were swinging round with him, Eustace sank back upon the ground. Still clinging to the ladder with a nervous grip, in that moment of pain and rage, against his foes he retained sufficient consciousness of his peril to grasp at the only means that offered him for escape.

"We have him now, lads. That was a clever trick of yours, David. Owen, and the stone was cleverly thrown ; he's stunned and helpless by the blow. On with the darbies !"

"Not yet, Master Newton. You don't drag me back so easily to the stone jug."

With a shout of defiance, Eustace, who had returned to thorough consciousness, as the officers were about to slip the handcuffs on his wrist, wrenched himself from their grasp, and endeavoured to mount the ladder. One of the runners, perceiving his intentions, rushed upon him

to drag him back, receiving a fearful blow between the eyes from the clenched fist of Eustace that sent him reeling to the ground like a drunken man.

Newton and another officer now dashed at the highwayman, and the three were presently engaged in a terrific struggle.

Oaths, curses, and cries of fury echoed through the yard.

"Crack him on the head, Owen. On with the bracelets."

"Curses on him, he has a wrist of iron ! he has twisted my arm from its socket," moaned the officer, staggering back, limping with pain, from a fearful kick received from the heavy boot of Eustace in the struggle.

"Down with him !"

"Stun him !"

"Shove the darbies en him !"

"Drop a bullet in his skull !"

"No, he must swing at Tyburn !" yelled Newton.

A moment after the report of pistols sounded on the air, and one of the officers, pale and bleeding, sank back fainting to the ground ; whilst Eustace, who had thus for a moment freed himself of his assailants, rushed up the ladder, a crowd of people from the stable shutting out means of escape by a return that way.

"After him, my men ! Fifty guineas to he who drags him back !" shouted Newton.

One of the officers who had followed Eustace up the ladder, now paused and shuddered with horror. Glancing up, he perceived the hunted man unfastening the rope above.

In another moment the ladder would be unloosed.

The house was a high one. The ladder hurled back, would doubtless cause his death.

There was no escape. His victim even now places his hand upon the frail support to push it back.

"Help—help ! Mercy—mercy !" gasped the terrified man.

"What mercy have you shown to me ?" ejaculated Eustace, about to hurl the ladder from the house. He then looked down once more into the convulsed and pallid features of the miserable officer.

"Make your way down, you cowardly hound ; and don't forget that you owe your life to the man whom you have assisted to hunt to the death !" ejaculated our hero.

Needing no second bidding, the terrified runner, pausing not to descend by the rounds, slid down the frail support ; scarce reaching the ground, ere, with a crash, the ladder was hurled back, falling upon the wall of the yard below, but the man was uninjured as Eustace had hoped.

Pausing not to look back, Eustace made his way over the roof of the house.

It was a dreary prospect before him.

A row of houses, some four stories high, and with no possible or apparent means of descent.

With haste, and in desperation, Eustace made his way over three of the roofs.

As he stood taking a survey, and irresolute as to his further course, he discerned the figures of his implacable foes following in his dangerous path.

Eustace, glancing round, coolly proceeded to load his pistols, murmuring—

"At least they shall join me in my journey of death. But I will not pause until I can go no further. At the last moment some means of escape may open to me."

He now hurried on, followed by the shouting officers.

The sun, now fairly in the horizon, threw a golden lustre upon the scene.

Heeding not the beauty of the summer morn, or the ruddy, golden-tinted clouds, the runners, like ill-omened birds of prey, hurried over the roofs in pursuit of their victim.

Eustace proceeded on till, at length, he arrived at the last house of the row.

Behind him were his foes, following like bloodhounds upon his track.

In front was a depth of many feet to a street below.

Eustace, with a feeling of despair, made for the back of the house.

With a sigh he turned aside.

There was no possible means of descent. Like a caged tiger he was at the mercy of his foes.

With bated breath, and flushed cheeks, he awaited the coming struggle.

He registered an oath not to be taken with life.

He would escape or perish.

Already he could perceive the features of the foremost of the runners.

The man, Geoffery Newton.

About to take aim with his pistol at the officer's advancing form, Eustace was diverted from his purpose by catching sight of an opening in the roof.

He might yet escape.

He would beat through the trap below, opening upon the garret of the house, and, perhaps, evade his pursuers now when all hope had left him.

In another moment, he had squeezed his slim, agile form through the opening in the roof.

Replacing the trap he found in the loft, to hide from his enemies his lurking-place, he now searched for the other trap that opened upon the upper landing of the house, or one of the garrets.

In total darkness, Eustace groped about the loft in search of the inner trap.

Anon he heard the tramp of feet upon the roof above.

His pursuers had arrived.

Were searching for him on the roof.

At length, with a thrill of joy he discovered the trap for which he was in search.

He pulled at it with all his force.

It resisted his utmost efforts.

With a muttered curse, and exclamation of despair, he sank back.

The trap was fast secured, the bolts refusing to give way.

Eustace gnashed his teeth with rage and fury at the helplessness of his situation.

He heard the officers conversing on the roof.

In a few more moments his retreat would be discovered.

With the last effort of despair, he knelt down, and, using all his strength, essayed to move the trap. For a few seconds it resisted his attempts, then suddenly, with a loud snap, the bolts that fastened it gave way, and the trap, torn from its place, was in his hands.

With a murmur of joy, he lowered himself into a sort of lumber-room.

Seizing an old pair of steps that rested against the wall of the apartment, his first business was to place the piece of wood in its original position. Then, shooting one of the bolts back, first driving in the nail that held the staple, he jumped down, and surveyed the apartment in which he stood.

It was evidently used as a lumber-room, but was filled with a heterogeneous collection of goods that fairly surprised the intruder. Old helmets, swords, foils, gauntlets, faded velvet finery, paint pots, and lumber of every description met the eye.

With a smile, and a look of wonder, Eustace picked his way through the rubbish that filled the chamber, and boldly opened a door that he discovered led to the landing of the stairs without.

Fancying that he heard the officers trying the trap upon the roof, Eustace was about hurriedly to descend the stairs that faced him, when he was startled by beholding a young girl ascending them.

To make his way down without being seen was impossible.

Should he attempt it, and boldly descend, an alarm would be raised that would lead his enemies to the spot immediately.

They had not yet made their way into the room he had left, for a few moments longer he was safe.

The young girl ascended higher and higher, in a few seconds she would face him.

Starting back, Eustace retreated to a door that was opposite that which opened upon the apartment in which was stowed the mysterious assortment of goods.

The door was unlocked, and yielded to the touch.

With a smile at the novelty of his position, Eustace glided in.

He found himself in a neat and comfortably-furnished bed-chamber.

Articles of female attire were scattered about the room, telling at once the sex of its occupant.

A large four-post bedstead stood in the centre of the apartment, hung round with coloured curtains.

The room, neat and comfortably furnished, looked out upon the front of the house.

Darting to the window, Eustace opened it, and gazed out into the street.

On the other side of the roadway he perceived four or five stalwart, stern-looking, ill-favoured men.

They were Bow-street runners—one of them no other than he whom Eustace had spared when clinging to the ladder at the back of the corn-chandler's house.

"They are on my track, and are, it seems, determined to follow me to the death. Well, we shall see; I have baffled them yet. My usual good fortune may not desert me, and once I elude them and reach the 'Bold Horseman,' I care not. But," ejaculated Eustace, a dark frown gathering on his brow, "from this night I swear I will pursue the path I have hitherto trodden. I am a marked man—a hunted felon. Be it so. Geoffery Newton, the wily thief-taker, is my sworn and bitter foe. He has sworn to see me swing at Tyburn Tree. Let him look to it; for, by the heaven above me, I will spare him not should he cross my path. From this hour I am his determined foe, as he is mine."

A light footstep sounded on the landing.

Recalled to himself, and without pausing to close the casement, Eustace darted behind the bed, the curtains of which he found would effectually conceal him.

Scarce had he sought this refuge, when he heard the door open, and the young girl, the same that he had beheld ascending the stairs, entered the room.

"Dear me! I have left the window open. How careless, to be sure."

With a smile upon his face, Eustace saw the young girl close the window.

At present he was very well pleased. The female was young, plump, and pretty. His foes, the officers, had not yet entered the house.

For a time, therefore, he was safe.

Securely hidden by the bed-curtains, he beheld the young girl unseen.

Singing a snatch of a song, she gazed for a few moments furtively out of the window, but suddenly paused and started, looking round the room with alarm.

There was a strange noise in the other room.

The murmuring of voices and trampling of feet.

A deadly pallor gathered on the young girl's cheeks.

About to totter towards the door, she staggered back with a half shriek, as Eustace appeared, darting forwards and turning the key in the lock.

"Pardon me, my dear girl; be not alarmed. But, if you would save the life of the unfortunate man that stands before you, hear me. By those bright eyes and pouting lips, I know you are one that will listen to and aid me in my peril."

"Who—what are you?"

"One who is pursued by the myrmidons of the law; even now they have burst their way into the house, to drag me from my hiding-place to imprisonment and death. But you, sweet girl, will save me! You have but to deny my presence here, and all is safe!"

A crimson flush suffused the cheeks of the young maid as Eustace knelt at her feet, pressing her soft, plump hand to his lips.

We have said our hero was of handsome form. His rich chestnut, curly hair resting on his open brow, his dark and sparkling eyes, and the smile upon his handsome features as he gazed into the face of the young servant-maid, won upon her to listen to his entreaties.

"I don't know what Mr. Avery would say. Dear me! the idea of a young man in my bedroom!"

"And a very pleasant place, too, my dear, for a young fellow to be in. But, hark! my enemies are even now at the door. Say, dear girl, where can I conceal myself?"

Eustace glanced hurriedly round the room, but no hiding-place could he discover.

The officers now hammered at the door of the chamber, demanding, in authoritative tones, to be admitted.

"Open! Open the door in the king's name!"

The young girl, motioning Eustace back, gave utterance to a shrill scream.

"A gal is there, Newton. Our cove has gone below."

"Girl or no girl, I'll search the room. Now, then, young woman, open the door, or I'll burst it open!"

"Murder! Go away, you horrid wretches! Come in my room, indeed! I see, I see! Here's some house-breakers want to murder and ruin me!"

"All right, Jane I'm a coming. Now, then, Mr. Blackmuzzle, what's your identical little game?" a rough voice ejaculated without.

A moment afterwards there was an animated and not very amicable conversation going on between the fresh arrival and the officers.

"It's Joe. He'll give it to them!"

"And who may Joe be, my dear? Not the possessor of the heart that beats in that dear bosom, I trust!"

Master Eustace forgot himself whilst gazing into the bright eyes of pretty Jane, who, as the dashing young stranger gazed into her features, pouted and blushed the hue of the damask rose.

Jane was a young girl from Somersetshire, and not accustomed to the honied accents of the gay deceivers.

Poor Jane, she learnt too soon the falsity of man!

Scarce could pretty Jane keep from shouting with laughter as Eustace, who had discovered a wardrobe in a corner of the room, proceeded to array himself in some female apparel.

In a few minutes the costume was arranged.

Stepping, then, to the toilet-table Eustace busied himself at the glass, as the door, with a loud crash, gave way to the repeated attacks of the officers.

A crowd of four or five poured into the room, notwithstanding the expostulations and struggles of Joe, who, in no measured terms, railed at the men of the law.

"Damn yer! What does yer mean? Step out, and cuss me if I don't box any two on yer. Get out of the gal's room!"

Jane now shrieked loudly, whilst Eustace stood by the table, prepared for any sudden emergency should his disguise be discovered.

Joe, who had been engaged struggling and cursing with the officers, now started as his eyes fell upon the form of Eustace.

"Why, Jane, who the devil's that?"

Despite the frowns and mute cautions of Jane, Joe, who was not in the secret, gazed in undisguised astonishment at the figure of our hero.

"I say, Newton. I thinks as we're on the right track."

"So do I. Owen, get the darbies ready."

"I smell a rat," muttered Joe. "Damme, I've done it!"

"I say, my dear," exclaimed Newton, turning to Eustace, "would you like a walk? No reply. Poor thing, she's shy; ashamed like. She a strapper, too; not very delicate looking, ay, Owen?"

"Not exactly, governor. Now, then, marm, come along with us, and we'll give yer a ride in a coach, free, gratis for nothing."

"And lush yer in the bargain."

"And won't take not no liberties."

"On no account."

"We'll treat yer like a lamb."

"Just so. Behave to yer like gemmens."

Low chuckles and smothered laughter issued from the mouths of the officers.

Poor Jane, who had taken a fancy to the dashing, handsome person of Eustace, stood pale and trembling gazing at the scene, whilst the redoubtable Joe, with clenched fists, eyed the officers in no friendly manner.

"Let us have no more delay, Owen; on with the darbies."

Newton, with two officers, here darted forwards, when Eustace, throwing off his disguise, drew forth his pistols, and with one bound reached the door."

"Seize him! Let him not escape!"

"We are too many for you, Maltravers; you had better yield yourself a prisoner. You can't escape."

"You lie! Geoffery Newton. Stand back, or I'll plant a brace of bullets in your skulls," exclaimed Eustace.

Jane shrieked loudly, whilst Joe, astounded by the scene, stood gazing on with a bewildered air.

Just as the officers were about to dash at Eustace, a tall, handsome-looking young man appeared, and, with a half laugh, and a smile upon his features, exclaimed—

"Zounds and the devil! what frights the house from its propriety? Jane, what knaves are these?"

"No knaves, please you, sir, but officers," exclaimed Newton.

"Officers! And pray may I, in a gentlemanly manner, ask what the devil you are doing here, in my house?"

"We came hither to secure an escaped felon."

"Indeed! And where is the unfortunate breaker of the laws?"

"There, beside you."

The young man, taking a survey of Eustace, who remained, without attempting flight, amused at the scene, then turned to Newton, ejaculating—

"Well, really Mr.—Mr."—

"Newton. Geoffery Newton, Bow-street runner, at your service," ejaculated the officer, bowing.

"Well, Mr. Geoffery Newton, Bow-street runner, allow me to observe, in the most gentlemanly manner in the world, that you look more like a thief than an honest man; and just allow me also to observe that if you don't instantly quit my house, I shall do myself the pleasure of kicking—yes, kicking—you down stairs. Joe, show these black-muzzled gentlemen out."

"Oh! this won't do."

"Won't it? Will this?" exclaimed the young man, as Newton stepped forward, delivering him such a blow that he reeled back and fell to the ground.

This was the signal of a general assault.

In another moment there was a *melée* between the officers. Eustace, the belligerent Joe, and his master, the latter an expert boxer, soon settled the matter, bruising the frontispieces, as he facetiously termed it, of the runners to such an extent that they were presently in a blissful state of ignorance as to their whereabouts, groping blindly about and seizing hold of each other in the confusion of the fray.

With a loud laugh, the eccentric young man seized hold of Eustace by the arm, and dragged him from the room, leaving Joe with the bewildered officers.

"Now, I think the best thing you can do is to get away from the house as fast as you can. I do not know if you are what the officers say, nor do I care," ejaculated the young stranger. "But I found four on to one; and Herbert Clavering always sided with the weakest party. Farewell! I hear the men coming down the stairs. Away with you!"

"Stay one moment! Where may I see you again?" said Eustace, who, struck with the friendly manner of the young stranger, wished to give him some substantial proof of his thanks for the service he had rendered.

"Glad to see you any night at the 'Magpie and Stump,' near the Mansion House, old fellow," replied the young man; "but away at once—your foes are here!"

Even as he uttered this warning for Eustace, the form of Newton appeared dashing down the stairs.

Shaking hands warmly with his preserver, Eustace turned from the door, and was soon far from the house.

"Damned nice fellow!" muttered Herbert Clavering, as he entered the house.

"A strange young man, but a kind-hearted one. Perhaps some day I may be able to return the favour he has rendered me," murmured Eustace, as he hurried away.

The day did come. The fates of Herbert Clavering and Eustace Maltravers were strangely interwoven.

CHAPTER XXVIII.

THE CEDARS AND ITS INMATES.—LORD ARLINGTON AND THE BEAUTIFUL VICTIM.—THE MIDNIGHT HOUR.—THE DARK SHADOW AT THE CASEMENT.—THE LORD AND THE BURGLAR.—THE SHRIEK FOR AID.—HORRIBLE DEATH OF THE ROUÉ LORD.—LUCRETIA SOMERS AND THE MASKED STRANGER.— THE THREAT.— THE DEFIANCE.—BESSIE CARRIED OFF. — RENCONTRE WITH THE BLACK MASK.—FURY OF CAPTAIN LESLIE.

In a large drawing-room at the Cedars, at Kensington, the residence of Lucretia Somers, she who it may be remembered had rescued the unfortunate Bessie Templeton from her fearful trance, are seated three lovely young girls.

It is a warm summer evening, the light breeze waving the rich muslin curtains that draped the windows to and fro, and sighing with a soft murmur through the branches of the trees without.

The occupants of the drawing-room are seated at the casement, gazing dreamily out into the grounds that surrounded the house.

All are young.

Young and beautiful.

Fair and lovely, and in the full blush of youth were

they, but yet with a certain air of *abandon* about them that told of a life of luxury and dissipation.

The eldest, a fair, dashing-looking girl of some eighteen or nineteen years of age, turning from the casement, and looking round at her companions, exclaimed—

"Heigho! this is very dull. What say you, Bell, to a walk? Who knows, we may happen to meet that graceless fellow, Leslie, who has held himself aloof from us for the last month."

"I am agreeable for a stroll, Maude, dear, if Fanny here will join us."

"With all my heart," exclaimed the youngest of the three girls, a fair, rosy-cheeked, plump, saucy-looking little creature, whose dimpled features, and dancing curls of light brown hair, likened her to some mischievous, merry little fay.

The lovely companions were about to issue from the chamber, when they were stayed by the entrance of the mistress of the Cedars, Mrs. Somers.

"How now, my dears—whither away?"

"We are going for a walk, Lucretia, darling," ejaculated the youngest of the girls, in a coaxing tone, as though fearing she and her friends would be stayed in their purpose. A cloud gathered athwart the features of the before-smiling Fanny, as Mrs. Somers exclaimed—

"Not to-night, dears; not to-night. I expect a visitor every moment, and you must all be here to receive him."

"There's always something to keep us in-doors," ejaculated Fanny, with a pretty pout of her rosy lips.

"Who is it you expect?" said the eldest girl, called by her companions Lady Bell.

"No less a person than Lord Arlington," replied Mrs. Somers.

Looks of disgust rested upon the faces of the girls, which left them, as she reminded them that Lord Arlington always left a handsome present for each on his departure.

"Now get ready, dear girls, and look all nice to receive him," she exclaimed; "and to-morrow you shall all three go for a drive to Hammersmith."

A shout of joy greeted this promise, and the young girls at once left the room to arrange their toilet, and prepare for the arrival of the expected Lord Arlington. Scarce had they gone, ere Mrs. Somers was startled by the sudden entry of the servant, giving the announcement of the presence of James Henderson, the doctor following upon the heels of the lackey.

"James Henderson! Is it you? I did not expect you to-night."

"Nor would you have seen me, Lucretia, but for strange news I have to tell."

"Strange news! What news?"

"Listen. You have resolved that to-night you will give the young girl, Bessie Templeton, to the arms of Lord Arlington?"

"Well?"

"This must not be."

"And wherefore not, wise and discreet doctor?" ejaculated Mrs. Somers, with a dark shade of ill-humour on her brow.

"Because I will it, and I command it!"

"You command it, indeed! We shall see. But why this sudden change?—you were yesterday as eager as me for the business."

"Circumstances have occurred, Lucretia, that has made me resolve on another course."

"What are they, and what do you propose?"

"You shall hear. 'Tis now near four months since the girl Bessie fell into our hands. During that period her health has been such that it would have been dangerous to have subjected her to any sudden emotion."

"Well?"

"You would tell me that the money and trouble the girl has been to you must be returned?"

"Just so."

"To this I agree; but it must not be by giving the girl over to Lord Arlington."

"And why?"

"I will tell you. Because the horror of the scene would cost the girl her life."

"Pshaw! Henderson, you are mad. The girl is well enough now."

"Possibly; but a sudden emotion may cause a relapse of her dread disease, another trance may congeal the

life-blood in her veins, and keep her senses wrapped till death really seizes upon her frame."

"You talk wildly. The girl is young and beautiful, and may prove to us a mine of wealth," exclaimed the fiendly woman, coolly determined to sell the wretched victim in her power to the highest bidder.

"Hear me, Lucretia. I act not in this matter upon my own judgment. I was with old Silus Appleby to-day."

"Hem! The mad doctor of Tottenham-court-road?"

"The same; but mad he is not, save in the absurd practice he has of giving to every one, and of taking from no one. But to continue: for the first time I mentioned to him the strange matter of the girl Bessie's trance, relating her story to my brother of medicine, I then, to my astonishment, learned that he it was who had received the body of the young girl; nay, had paid the resurrection man to bring it to him. I told him I had saved her life and kept her for four months, and asked him if he thought her now strong enough to go through any trying ordeal, as I feared that something would occur that would much excite her. He then told me any unwonted scene of terror, or anything likely to cause emotion, would probably cause her death."

"And this is all!" A smile of contempt wreathed the handsome features of the female fiend as she gazed upon her companion.

"No, not all."

"What more remains? What else? What other news?" muttered the daring, merciless woman, in a tone of the utmost contempt.

"Other news, that will cause you to alter your plans in respect of the girl Bessie Templeton. There are two men on their way to the Cedars who will give up their lives to save the girl."

"Who are these champions for virtue in distress?"

"Captain Leslie and the girl's only brother."

"Her brother!" Lucretia Somers now started and gazed uneasily upon her companion.

"How knows he she is here?"

"I know not. For three months he has been seeking the lost one. He beheld the wretched girl torn from the grave, and vowed to know no rest till he had discovered whither the body had been conveyed. He has, it seems, learned that she lives, and is here in the neighbourhood of Kensington."

"And how did you learn this?"

"From my faithful servant and spy, Will Digarde, who is ever on the watch for his master's interests. He chanced upon the brother of this girl, and has given me note of what we may expect."

"This news, indeed, troubles me. For Leslie I care not—I defy him. He dare not interfere in this, though I well know only the girl's ill health has saved me from some rash attempt on his part to take her from this house; but, however, let me hear what you would advise."

"I think, Lucretia, 'twere best to be prepared for a visit from this young man, and would advise you to let the girl depart with her relative, upon you, of course, receiving an equivalent for your services in her behalf."

"I thought so. And you would have me, then, give up the young beauty, for whom Lord Arlington would give half his wealth? He has seen her, and has conceived for the girl a passion that resembles madness rather than sanity in its intensity. He will bring a sum to-night that I cannot—will not refuse, though I peril ruin in the securing it. The girl shall be his, Henderson, though a thousand brothers stood forth to save her."

There was a dark, evil expression in the eyes of the bold, unprincipled woman, that bespoke her well prepared to carry out her threat.

"You are resolved, then, Lucretia?"

"I am."

"Despite of my objections?"

"Yes."

"Remember, should this affair become public, you are ruined—may meet with fearful punishment."

"I care not. I will run the risk. There are two reasons to urge me on."

"And they?"

"Are money and hate; for know, Henderson, I hate with a fierce, undying hatred this scornful and proud beauty."

" And why ? For what do you hate the girl ? "

" Because Leslie loves her ! Because of her beauty and her honour ! I would see her as the rest ! Now you know why I am determined to give this sample of chastity to the arms of the hoary *roue*, Lord Arlington."

A deep flush rested on the face of Lucretia Somers ; then, subduing her momentary passion, she added—

" But enough of this. I am fixed in my resolve, Henderson ; to-night I will receive from Lord Arlington the price for all my troubles and annoyances of the past four months in connexion with this girl, Bessie Templeton."

Without awaiting her companion's reply, she then hastened from the room.

Shortly after, Doctor Henderson quitted the house, murmuring as he went—

" She is too bold—too bold ! I must leave her, or she will drag me with her to the abyss of doom."

A smile of contempt and scorn wreathed the features of Lucretia Somers as she beheld from her window the departing figure of her companion in crime.

" He grows old and cowardly—lacks his former nerve ! We must part, or he will, in his coward fears, betray all."

It was some two or three hours after the interview of the doctor and Mrs. Somers in the drawing-room, that a carriage rolled up to the Cedars, and an elderly man alighting, dismissed the vehicle and made his way into the house, admitted by Mrs. Somers herself, who had hastened down to the hall.

The visitor was ushered into a large room overlooking the gardens at the back.

In this chamber, hung with costly prints and paintings, was seated the three young girls, who on the appearance of the stranger rose from their seats and hurried forwards.

Glancing at the three beauties with a bold lascivious gaze, the visitor threw himself upon a luxurious couch, exclaiming—

" Come hither, Lady Bell, and sit beside me. You, my pretty little romp, Fanny, place yourself on that settle near me ; and for you Maude, my bright-eyed Maude, what better place than at my right hand ? "

Wine was brought in as the *roue* nobleman, Lord Arlington, for he it was, drew the fair girls around him.

Shouts of merry laughter rang presently through the chamber as a contest and struggle took place with the bevy of damsels and the lord, for the possession of a pair of diamond earrings he had held temptingly before them.

It was a strange scene.

That white-haired man, panting, struggling, and toying with those fair young girls, who were all full of health and youthful glee.

Lord Arlington was about fifty years of age. Originally a handsome man, age and dissipation of every kind had not quite robbed his features and form of their prepossessing appearance.

He was still a fine-looking man, though the *roue* was plainly perceptible in that lustreless eye and shaking voice.

Joined by Mrs. Somers, the party passed away the time in singing and dancing, Lord Arlington draining glass after glass of the generous wines, and listening to the dulcet notes of the piano and the harp, both of which were skilfully played by the girls, Lady Bell and Maud. At length, twelve o'clock striking from a time-piece in the room, Mrs. Somers motioned the girls to leave the chamber, and a few moments afterwards the mistress of the Cedars and Lord Arlington were alone.

" Well, Lucretia," exclaimed the nobleman, " am I this night to call your new and peerless beauty mine, or am I to endure still the tortures of suspense ? "

" My lord, you will find the door of the walnut-wood chamber unlocked. The beautiful Bessie is in your power," murmured the guilty woman, sinking her voice, and gazing uneasily round.

Starting to his feet, Arlington thrust a bundle of notes into the hands of Mrs. Somers, and staggered from the room.

A gleam of triumph lighted up the features of Lucretia Somers, as she beheld the *roue* stagger from the chamber. Then, placing the notes in her bosom, she also left the room.

The midnight hour had scarce ceased to chime from the little clock tower of the Cedars, before the dark,

muffled forms of three men entered the garden in the rear of the premises.

Slowly and cautiously they made towards the house.

The moon, high in the heavens, threw the dark shadows of the three figures full upon the broad walks.

Presently, arriving at the house, the three men paused.

A few moments afterwards, the silence of the night was broken by a strange grinding noise and the murmuring of voices.

This at length ceased, and one of the dark figures began to swing itself up by means of the ivy that grew thickly against the walls of the house.

Reaching a casement, through which streamed a thin ray of light into the garden, the figure paused.

" Are yer all right, Coffin ? "

" As a trivet, Bill. I can sight the woman on the bed, and a rale stunner she is, and no flies," said the ruffian to his companions, who stood in the grounds below.

" Kious (softly—be quiet), or the woman will awake, and you'll be piped (seen), Jem."

" It's all right, Resurrectioner ; she doing a dorse (sleep). The blinkers (shutters) arn't closed, so I can see into the box stunning. Kim up ; the ivy's strong, and by the devils ! we'll soon do the trick ; collar the woman, the wedgelob (plate), and get back to the long village afore Lady Blue hides her face."

A few minutes afterwards, the companions of the midnight marauder were by his side.

All three now peered into the room.

A strange scene met their view.

One that kept them for a few moments forgetful of their task.

A fierce oath and cry of astonishment escaped from one of the men.

" Damn it, Resurrectioner, you'll blow the gaff. What's up ? "

" Why, as I live, Coffin, if that gal arn't the one as I unearthed three months ago for old Sylus Appleby. Ten thousand devils ! I see it all ; the gal warn't a stiff-un, by the ——," added the ruffian, with a horrible oath. " She is a stunner, and does credit to the taste of the captain as put us on the lay to carry her off ; but, kious, see an old bloak (man) has entered the dossing apartment. See, he fixes his eyes upon the piece of female furniture as though he'd eat her."

Peering over the edge of the window-sill, the housebreaker and his companion gazed intently upon the scene within.

A large lamp upon a side table shed a glow of light through the chamber.

The rich silk curtains of the bed drawn back, exposed the lovely form of a young girl, who, in a deep sleep, was unconscious of the presence of an intruder.

With flushed features and satyr gaze, Lord Arlington stood by the bedside of the sleeping girl.

His bold hand drawing down the coverlid, the daring intruder exposed the lovely bosom of the unconscious girl.

White as Parian marble and smooth as ivory was the beautiful bust of Bessie Templeton.

With gloating gaze, the licentious *roue* remained rooted to the spot.

About to seize the form of the unconscious girl in his arms, a sudden noise at the casement started the guilty nobleman from his purpose.

Turning round, and casting his eyes upon the window, a cry of rage and alarm escaped his lips.

Where the blind was drawn aside he discerned, flatly pressed against the glass without, the forbidding-looking countenance of a man.

Scarce had he recovered from his astonishment ere there was a crash of glass, and, following each other, three men made their way into the room from the open casement.

A wild shriek of terror escaped the lips of the wretched Bessie Templeton, who, starting up in her bed, glared wildly at the figures of the housebreakers.

Wild shrieks and cries for help echoed through the apartment.

" Seize the gal, and leave the bloak to me, Coffin !" exclaimed Resurrection Bill, with a fierce oath, rushing upon the enraged Arlington, who, upon the first appearance of the burglars, had seized the heavy steel poker from the fireplace, and prepared to attack the ruffians before him.

Cowardice was not one of Lord Arlington's failings.

THE SENTENCE OF DOOM—TERROR OF THE VIPER.

A hideous scene now took place.

That before silent chamber resounding with the noise of a terrific struggle, accompanied with rude oaths and blasphemous curses.

"The old reprobate shows fight. Chive him, Cherry," shouted Coffin, who, despite her cries, had seized upon the person of Bessie Templeton.

"Help! help! help!"

Madly the poor girl struggled in the powerful grasp of the ruffian, Coffin.

The villain, Cherry, with a broken arm, from a blow given him by the enraged Arlington, now staggered back towards the casement, Resurrection Bill alone remaining to combat with the determined man.

"Where's yer barking-irons, Bill?"

"Close with him, and chive him in the ribs."

"Wrench away the poker, and beat the ——'s brains out."

These and other ejaculations issued from the mouths of the murderous ruffians.

Meanwhile Arlington beat back his assailants with his formidable weapon.

Calling loudly for help, the shrieks of the terrified Bessie, the curses of the burglars, made up a Babel of sounds, the noise of the conflict ringing with terrible din on the night air.

Voices sounded in the apartments, and a few moments after the clang! clang! of an alarm-bell added to the horror of the scene.

Turning the key of the door in the lock, Cherry made the wretched nobleman, Lord Arlington, a prisoner, while he and his companions were safe from a surprise.

Coffin, with the screaming, terror-stricken Bessie, had now made his way to the casement, and was half through as the dark figure of a cloaked and masked stranger appeared at the window.

"The girl—have you the girl?" said the new comer.

"She's here, all right and tight, captain."

"Give her to me, then, and haste away. A passing patrol may arrive and spoil all."

Dragging the now senseless girl from the other's arms, the stranger slid down from the casement, and a minute afterwards was hurrying across the grounds.

A fearful scene now took place in the walnut-wood chamber of the Cedars.

A scene of horror and of blood.

Furious at being kept at bay by Lord Arlington, Resurrection Bill had determined on taking the wretched man's life.

With the idea of murder in his brain, he heeded not the warnings of his companions, but remained behind as they disappeared through the casement.

He grated his teeth with savage fury as a fearful blow from the dangerous implement wielded by his assailant left his right arm dangling useless by his side.

With a howl of demoniac rage and pain, the ruffian, stooping to avoid another blow, closed with the doomed man.

There was a short struggle, ending in the defeat of the unhappy Lord Arlington, who, exhausted by his former efforts, soon succumbed to the strength of the younger and herculean resurrection man.

There was a loud hammering at the door, as the ruffian ruthlessly dragged the struggling noble to the fireplace of the chamber.

"Mercy! mercy! mercy!" gasped the choking and terrified victim, with freezing horror noting the murderous look upon the other's visage.

"Oh! yes; I've always lots of that commodity on hand, curse yer. Take that—and that."

There was a gurgling sob of dying agony from the lips of the doomed man, as the ruffian, with fiendish glee, dashed the head of his victim against the carved steelwork of the stove.

There was a horrible, dull, sickening crash, and a shower of blood that spurted up in the demoniac face of the murderer.

Then all was still within the chamber.

Murder had done its work.

The wretched man had perished a horrible death in the pursuit of his passions.

Starting to his feet, the resurrectioner and housebreaker made for the window, as the door of the chamber gave way from the repeated attacks from without.

A crowd of servants and shrieking women poured in as the murderer, with a chuckle and a horrible oath, disappeared through the casement.

Shots were fired after his retreating form, but without avail, his burly figure being discerned hurrying on in the moonlight till it was lost in an avenue of trees.

Meanwhile, the cloaked stranger, bearing the sylph-like form of Bessie Templeton in his arms, bounded from the house, nor paused till he reached a low door in the garden-wall that opened upon a lane without.

Dashing through this opening—the door hanging wide open on its hinges—the stranger, with his senseless burthen in his embrace, stood for a moment irresolute, gazing up and down the lane.

"Curses on him! Where can he be? Simpson, where are you?"

"Where he can't answer; and where, perchance, you may have to go to meet him."

A dark, masked figure stood forth from the shadow of the wall.

A female form, that stood erect and motionless in the thin rays of the moon.

A start and an oath escaped the stranger.

"Who—what are you?"

"One who has sworn to thwart you, Captain Leslie, in all your villainous projects!"

"Curses!"

"You called but now upon your tool and slave, the villain Simpson; shall I send you to him?"

An oath and cry of alarm issued from the lips of Leslie, for he indeed was the midnight abductor, as he perceived the blue, glittering barrel of a pistol, the weapon held presented at his head by his daring aggressor.

"Who—what are you? Where—where is Simpson?"

"Supping with the fiends below! The tool of your base passions is dead! And I—I—woman as I am— struck the blow! But, enough of this; release the form of that senseless captive you hold so firmly gripped in your embrace, or, by the master whom you serve so well, I'll place a bullet in your skull with as little remorse as

I'd remove a deadly serpent from my path! No parleying, Captain Leslie, but at once release the girl!"

"Stand aside, idiot! Did the foul fiend himself bar my path, I'd not give up my prey!"

"Spoken like you, fiend and monster as you are! But I give you three minutes to decide; if you then refuse to yield up the girl, your blood, libertine and reprobate, be on your own head, for, by the supreme power above, I'll stretch you a corpse at my feet!"

"Indeed! Call now upon that power to save you and the girl, for both are at my mercy! Seize her, my man!"

"All right, captain; I as her like beans!"

There was a cry of fury, a brief struggle, and, a moment afterwards, bound and helpless, the masked female lay at the feet of the man she had dared so shortly before.

"Tear off her mask," exclaimed Leslie.

The ruffian who, unperceived by the strange, bold woman, had crept behind and secured her, now stooped down and dragged off the black mask that concealed her features.

The housebreaker and Leslie started back with a cry of surprise as the moonbeams revealed the face of the captive woman.

"Lizzie Heyward!" ejaculated Leslie.

"The blowen as bilked us at the ken," muttered the ruffian, Coffin, gazing with an admiring eye at the helpless figure of the bold young girl, and then murmuring— "A downright plucky crittur, and no flies."

"So, then, 'tis you who have dared to follow thus in my path! I sought you not when you made your escape from the Red Grange, nor thought to see you more! You are now in my power! You boasted, a few moments back, that you would plant a bullet in my brain with as little remorse as you would tread on a dangerous reptile. 'Tis well. I know you, and will effectually prevent any further interference with my projects at your hands. Gag and convey her to the carriage, Coffin, and haste away, for the alarm-bell of the Cedars now rings upon the air; the patrol will arrive and prevent your escape."

Obedient to his orders, the ruffian burglar seized the unresisting and helpless girl in his arms, and hurrying from the lane, followed by Leslie, at length halted beside a carriage, that, drawn up by the side of a thick copse, was hidden from the sight of casual passers by the lonely road.

Placing the senseless Bessie upon the seat of the vehicle, Leslie then dragged in, with no gentle force, the person of the defeated but daring Lizzie Heyward, she who had vowed her existence to the pursuit of one object.

Revenge upon her destroyer.

Vengeance upon the ruthless cousin who had sent her parents in poverty and sorrow to the grave, and robbed her of her honour.

Captain Leslie had changed, by his base acts, this young and lovely girl into a being of hate and vengeance.

Her existence—her youth was blighted.

She lived but for one object—revenge.

Terribly in after years did Captain Leslie suffer for his crimes of early youth.

Hurrying away, at the request of Leslie, the burglar, Jem Coffin, disappeared; and the postilion, then lashing the horses, the carriage rolled from the spot.

Passing into the high road, however, its course was stayed by three or four persons darting from the front garden of the Cedars into the centre of the carriage-way.

With a jerk that sent them on their haunches, the postilion drew up the horses, whilst, furious with passion, Leslie thrust his head out of the window, exclaiming—

"On with you, Smith! Drive over them! Ride down all who stop our way!"

"Hold, Captain Leslie!" shouted the shrill voice of a woman. "You leave not this spot till you have heard what I have to say! You have torn from my roof one whom your former cruelty sent into her grave! The ruffians who have aided you in your task have left the house with blood upon their hands! Lord Arlington is murdered! You! you have done this! and Lucretia Somers will yet drag you from your height of prosperity to beggary and want!"

Livid with passion, Leslie shouted to the postilion to drive on.

Obeying the commands of his master, the horses, lashed by their rider, dashed away from the spot, the enraged mistress of the Cedars nearly meeting a sudden death beneath the carriage wheels.

Half an hour after, a patrol reached the lone house.

But the burglars had escaped; their victim, Lord Arlington, lying a stark and rigid corpse in that abode where he had been wont to gratify his basest passions.

The bright and golden sun threw its rays upon the house on the following morn.

The feathered songsters whirled as before through the air, or twittered merrily among the trees.

But an air of gloom hung over the Cedars.

Not a blind was up in the villa.

For grim death was there; the victim of black-visaged murder laid in the house, and all within was darkness and horror.

CHAPTER XXIX.

THE ARRIVAL AT THE "BOLD HORSEMAN."—STRANGE NEWS.—THE SUMMONS FROM THE MISER'S DAUGHTER.—THE MEETING AT THE HEMLOCK MANOR HOUSE.—A FATHER'S TYRANNY AND A CHILD'S DESPAIR.—LOVE AND HONOUR.—THE RESOLVE OF A FOND HEART.—SYBIL ACCEDES TO HER LOVER'S PRAYER.—SUDDEN APPEARANCE OF RALPH FAIRLEY. — FURY OF THE MISER.—A PISTOL-SHOT AND ITS RESULTS.—STRANGE AND TERRIBLE DENOUMENT.

ON the evening of the day that beheld his escape from Newgate, weary and exhausted, Eustace sought shelter at the inn kept by George Watson, on the Harrow-road.

The sun was just sinking to rest as our hero entered the doors of the "Bold Horseman."

George Watson, who was busily employed at the bar, left the work he was engaged upon, and coming forwards to meet Eustace, led him at once to a private apartment. In a further corner of the chamber was the form of a man who was peering anxiously out of the window into the high-road, the chamber being a front one in the old inn.

Scarce had the landlord and his visitor entered the room, and closed the door behind them, ere the stranger, turning round, uttered an exclamation of astonishment; and, darting forwards, seized both the hands of Eustace in his own.

"At last! at last! Zounds and the devil! Eustace, I began to fear the grabs had laid hands upon you again, after all. I trembled for your safety when I heard from George there how closely you were hunted by the accursed runners."

"It was a sharp chase, Dick, I can assure you," replied Eustace to his companion, Turpin, for he it was who had been so anxiously awaiting his arrival at the inn. I gave the hounds a good run, and, like a clever fox, doubled on them at last. Some other time I will tell you my adventures. But now, tell me, how is Sybil? When and where can I see her?"

A cloud gathered over the brow of Turpin, who, in answer to the eager query of his friend, exclaimed—

"I have no cheering news for you on that point, my dear boy. The foolish girl, notwithstanding my earnest request for her to await here your arrival, would return to her father's roof."

"Well, Dick. Pause not. Let me know all. What else?"

"Why, from what George has been enabled to gather, it seems there was a fearful scene between the miser and his daughter on her return to his roof. In his fury, it appears the old man gave the poor girl a blow that stretched her senseless at her base parent's feet."

"The hoary villain! Were he not her father, I would have ample revenge for the dastard, coward act. But I will tear her from him! Surely after this, she, my Sybil, will scarce refuse to leave her base and tyrannical father."

About to reply to his friend, a tap at the door startled the highwaymen, who glanced uneasily at each other.

"Nay, it's all right, lads," ejaculated Watson. "It's my son, Hugh; I know his knock."

The landlord then, opening the door that he had locked after the entrance of himself and Eustace, admitted a young man, who, handing a letter, exclaimed—

"A letter, father. From Miss Fairley, of the Manor, to Mr. Eustace."

Darting forwards, our hero, with feverish haste, snatched the note from the young man's hand, and tearing it open, ran his eye over the few lines it contained.

The letter was brief, and the writing scarce legible; written evidently in haste and under powerful emotion.

DEAR EUSTACE,—*Come to-night to the Manor. I am confined a prisoner in a chamber next to that in which I was secured when rescued by your friend. I have much to say; my heart is nearly broken. God forgive me! I could almost wish I'd ne'er been born. I cannot, after to-day, reside beneath my parent's roof. I must escape. Death were preferable to imprisonment in this my father's house. Come to-night. You will best know how to reach my prison.—Yours till death,* SYBIL FAIRLEY.

The letter here was blotted and blurred with tears. Pressing the paper to his lips, with sparkling eyes, Eustace exclaimed, whilst seizing his companion by the hand—

"To-night, Dick, to-night you must with me to the residence of the miser!"

"All right, brave heart! What is your purpose there?"

"To bear my Sybil from her parent's accursed roof."

"You mean, then, to crack the crib, and, for your booty, to carry off the old man's daughter?"

"Ay, Dick, and by this time to-morrow we will be far from hence."

"What time shall we make the crack, Eustace?"

"To-night at twelve."

"We must go prepared for a warm reception; for, doubt not, the old man will expect our coming."

"I care not. I will not rest till I have torn his daughter from him!"

"All right; leave all the preparations to me. Watson, let me have those barking-irons of mine. I may require the nuts that are in the barrels for a hungry one to-night. Now then, Eustace, as we've settled business, let us clink glasses, and drink confusion to all misers and success to the crack to-night."

Urged upon by his friend to throw off the gloom that weighed down his spirits, Eustace endeavoured for a time to forget his sorrows in the ruby wines of old Watson's cellar, for the best of cheer was kept at the "Bold Horseman."

It was as the hour of eleven was chiming from the bell of the Hemlock Manor House, that the two highwaymen made their way cautiously through the grounds of the miser's residence.

Impatient to behold his beloved one, Eustace, despite his friend's solicitations to wait a little longer, had left the inn an hour before the time agreed upon in the earlier part of the evening.

"Eustace, dost see that light in that chamber there to the left?"

"Ay. What of it?"

"'Tis a proof that some one has not yet gone to rest; and I shrewdly suspect that 'tis the old man himself who is sitting up."

"By heavens, your are right, Dick! See, there is his figure upon the blind! I know his shadow by his stooping gait."

Eustace halted in the garden and gazed steadfastly at the chamber in which burned the light.

All the other casements of the old Manor House were involved in impenetrable darkness.

"Well, Eustace, what do you intend to do?"

"Break my way into the house."

"But the old man is evidently on the watch."

"I care not. I will rescue Sybil this night or perish."

"All right; I'm your man to join you. But, hush! Death and the devil, what is that?"

There was a crashing of twigs close beside them, and, the moment after, the companions were startled at the sight of two burning balls of fire, that flashed upon them from some shrubbery about five yards ahead.

The night was a dark one.

Thick, heavy clouds hung in the horizon.

'Twas a night well fitted for the purpose the two friends had in hand.

Nought had happened to interrupt them till now; but, at the mystic appearance of those two gleaming sparks of fire, the friends shuddered and started back in terror.

"Dick!"

"Eustace!"

"We are lost."

"Not yet; stand aside. Have ready your barking-irons in case I fail. We must not mind an alarm. 'Tis a matter perilling our lives."

Scarce had these words issued from the lips of Turpin, ere the silence was broken by a fierce yelling bay of a bloodhound.

Then followed the sounds of a brief struggle, a bark of agony, a sobbing, moaning noise, then all was still.

Eustace darted forwards as a dark figure leaped up from the ground before him.

"It's all right, Eustace; I have only got a scratch. My knife settled the business in a moment."

"Good heavens, Dick; are you safe?"

"Yes, sound wind and limb. I thought we might meet with a dog in the grounds, so I came prepared. I have a doctor (a piece of poisoned meat) in my pocket, but that was no good with my friend there, so I dashed at him and knifed him. But, see! his dying howl has alarmed the old man in the house."

The casement from which Turpin and his friend had beheld the light was now thrown open—the figure of a man appeared for a moment—then there was a loud, stunning report, and the casement was closed.

"That's cool, Eustace."

"What does it mean, Dick?"

"Why, that old Fairley politely informs anyone who may think of poaching in his preserves, that he is well prepared to greet them with some leaden pills for supper."

"'Twas certainly the old man that fired that shot."

"Of course it was. He thinks it very possible that I may give him a look in to-night; for yourself, of course, he imagines you are safely lodging in the stone jug. But, come, let us on. I'm now bent upon cracking the old fellow's crib; and, while you see to the daughter, damme I'll rake up some of the old man's gold."

The two friends now hurried on, and presently stood at a lower casement of the Manor House.

"Light the glim, Eustace, and I'll have these shutters open in a very short time."

A moment afterwards, a thin, pale ray of light stole out from the darkness.

There was a low murmuring of voices, followed by a subdued, scraping, grinding noise.

This continued for some time; there was then the crash of broken glass and a smothered curse, and the two dark figures standing by the casement disappeared.

Turpin and Eustace had succeeded in forcing an entrance into the miser's house.

"Curses on that window! I fear the breaking of the glass will arouse the old man. Let us await here, and if in half an hour all is still, we will pursue our way to the chambers above."

"As you will, Dick; but I am all impatience to hold my fond Sybil once again in my arms; but if I slay the old man in the accomplishment of my object, I swear to bear my loved one from beneath this hated roof to-night."

In a thick, hoarse whisper Eustace muttered these words to his friend, whilst they stood like statues in that dark chamber of the old Manor House.

A horrible nervousness crept over the two highwaymen as each listened intently for any sound that might come from above. But none came.

Only a horrible tick! tick! tick! in the room they were within.

A sound that caused the blood in their veins to rush through them like threads of ice.

Tick! tick! tick!

Tap! tap! tap!

"Dick, let us leave this accursed room. I feel I don't know how. I, that am a stranger to fear, feel a horrible sensation of impending ill. Some terrible scene is about to take place. I know not what to do. My Sybil must be taken hence to-night, and yet I want not her parent's blood upon my hands. Hark! how that fearful sound continues, with its horrible monotony, to wake up the silence of this lone chamber."

Tick! tick! tick!

"Pshaw! Eustace! 'tis but the tick of the death-watch. Be assured 'tis not you or I will be called hence to-night. But come, we will to the rooms above; and whilst you are arranging an escape with Sybil, I'll see if I can't lay hands upon some of the wedge (plate) and hidden treasures of the miser. But come; hark! the midnight hour rings from the tower above; let us to our work; and, oh! for the lovers' meeting and the bright red gold of Ralph Fairley."

Followed by Eustace, Turpin now left the chamber in which they had been concealed, and presently afterwards, stealing slowly and cautiously up the wide oaken staircase.

All was thick darkness.

Well acquainted with the old house, the two friends lost no time in their task.

The room in which Sybil was confined they knew to be in the east wing, a part of the Manor House seldom used by the miser.

To reach this chamber they were obliged to pass that in which was seated the old man.

Halting in the centre of the corridor down which they had made their way, the companions paused.

From the interstices of a door on their left stole a thin ray of light.

A jingling, clicking noise sounded from within the chamber.

The ringing as of gold.

Turpin, placing his eye to the key-hole for a few seconds, was intently engaged peering into the chamber.

Then starting back, he drew the arm of Eustace in his, and stole onwards along the corridor, reaching the end of which he stayed his steps.

"Eustace, we are now close to the room in which Sybil is imprisoned. Do you away at once. I will watch here to give an alarm."

Requiring no second bidding from his friend, Eustace, who, with throbbing brain and with feverish impatience, had followed his companion along the corridor, darted away, and in a moment was lost in the darkness.

"So, then, he is gone. Now, Dick, to your part of the business. Whilst your friend secures the daughter, do you ease the old man of some of his superfluous cash. It was no use," muttered Turpin (whilst proceeding slowly down the corridor), "to make Eustace acquainted with the fact, that I saw old Fairley counting out heaps of goldfinches (guineas) when I peeped through the door, or that I determined to make that money mine. He would but have persuaded me to forego my purpose; but as we've cracked the crib, why, damme, I'll carry away something in the shape of payment for my trouble." With a chuckle and a low laugh Turpin made his way to the chamber in which he had discerned the miser counting his gold; but hardly had he arrived at the door before he heard the sound of footsteps within. Darting back, Dick, with a curse, stole softly but quickly down the stairs, as the door of the room in which the miser had been seated was thrown open.

There was a stream of light through the corridor.

Ralph Fairley for a few moments stood, lamp in hand, gazing into the darkness before him; then, muttering to himself, locked the door of the chamber he had quitted, and disappeared along the passage.

A few minutes afterwards Dick stole back, and very speedily picked the lock of the door secured by the miser, and stole into the chamber.

A low chuckling laugh escaped his lips as he entered.

"Now for the gold! Ha! ha! ha! Robbed of his daughter and his hoards, the old man will go mad and cut his throat out of spite.

Exclamations of joy and chinking of gold now sounded in the chamber so shortly before tenanted by the miser.

Dick Turpin secured a rich prize that night at the Hemlock Manor House.

When, leaving his friend Eustace, proceeding down a dark, narrow passage, he arrived at a door at the further end opening into a chamber used as a lumber-room.

Passing through this, he again emerged into a passage, at the end of which was another door.

This bar to his further progress was locked, but this did not long stay our hero in proceeding onwards.

Failing to pick the lock, and trembling with excitement at the thought of a meeting with her he loved, without hesitation, and forgetting that he might cause an alarm, he dashed himself against the door, which, with a loud crash, burst open the lock from the force against it, torn from its fastenings.

The sound of a slight scream rang upon the air, as if close to the chamber.

Eustace was now in a large, deserted room, in which there was scarce any furniture.

By the dim light that stole from a casement, he perceived the wall was hung with oil paintings, some of which were dropping to pieces with decay.

A thin, pale ray of moonlight now darted in the room, the luminary of the night at length breaking forth from the heavy clouds.

The sickly rays of the pale moon made the room look ghastly and sombre.

With hurried steps Eustace passed on, reaching another door, which was standing open.

Beyond this was a narrow corridor, at the end of which were four or five steps.

Descending these, our hero found himself facing a strong oaken door that he discovered refused all his efforts to open.

About to dash with all his force against the solid wood that barred his progress, he was stayed by the sound of voices within.

Voices that caused him to start, and bend eagerly forwards.

How his heart throbbed as he caught the tones of the sweet Sybil's voice, which anon were drowned in the fierce, angry exclamations of her parent.

Another way of entrance had been used by Ralph Fairley to visit his daughter's chamber.

The terrified, anxious manner in which Sybil entreated her father to leave her to her rest, was well understood by Eustace.

She each moment expected the arrival of her lover.

Should they meet, the unfortunate girl shuddered for the result.

"Hark you, Sybil; by the mother who bore you, and whose bones now lie mouldering in the grave, I swear to follow up this man to whom you have given your heart till I see him swinging on the gibbet. You shall leave this chamber only on the day that beholds the accursed highwayman perish on the scaffold. I will crush or kill you."

"Father—father, mercy! Speak not thus! You have no cause for this hate you bear him who saved your life."

"'Tis false; 'twas all a plot arranged among the burglars—a trick to gain my friendship."

"No, father. On my soul, you wrong him. Both you and I would have perished that night months back, had it not been for Maltravers and his friend."

"I care not. I hate, hate this man with an intensity of passion that will not be appeased but by his death. For yourself, girl, as I have said, I will crush or kill you; by the bones of your dead mother I swear it. I have registered an oath in heaven to give up my pursuit of this man, Eustace Maltravers, only with my life. He has robbed me of you; he has robbed me of my gold, and I will see him swing—swing upon the gallows."

There was a loud shriek and a heavy fall.

The key now turning in the lock, the door was thrown open.

For a moment the miser stood, lamp in hand, gazing spell-bound upon a dark figure before him.

A howl of demoniac fury then burst from his lips as he started back, still glaring with wild and frenzied stare upon the form that stood firm and erect before him.

"Eustace Maltravers! Curses light upon him, he is here!"

With feverish haste, the old man thrust his right hand into his bosom.

With a shriek of terror, aroused from the faintness that had seized upon her a few moments before, Sybil now started forwards, and threw herself at her father's feet.

"Father, father! touch him not. 'Twas I that brought him hither. He has hastened here at my bidding. Vent on me, then, your anger; but spare, oh! spare him."

Wildly the poor girl clung to her parent's knees, whilst, with eyes literally blazing with fury, the miser glared upon the figure of Eustace, who, with folded arms, stood calmly looking upon the enraged miser.

"So, then, you have escaped your prison-house, felon and midnight marauder, but better had you remained in Newgate cells; better had you entered the den of the savage panther than ventured hither."

There was a loud, savage laugh, and a shriek of wild terror, followed by a thundering report; then all was still.

The lamp, falling from the hand of the miser, lay extinguished upon the ground.

The pale, blue, and sickly rays of the moon alone lighted up the strange and terrible scene in that lone chamber of the Hemlock Manor House.

With the senseless form of Sybil in his arms, Eustace stood glaring in horror and affright upon a hideous object at his feet.

The moonbeams threw a ghostly light into that lone chamber, darting full upon the figure of the miser, Ralph Fairley.

Ghastly, horrible, and hideous the old man looked as he lay, weltering in a dark, crimson pool, upon the floor.

His white hairs, soaked in blood, partly hid from view a frightful wound in the forehead, from which the crimson tide of life welled out in streams.

The face, one mass of torn flesh and broken bones, looked grotesquely horrible in the moon's rays.

Suddenly and terribly had the miser perished.

The pistol he had levelled and fired at Eustace had burst to atoms, the butt and pieces of the barrel crashing into his own skull.

Uninjured, Eustace stood gazing, speechless and spell-bound, upon the strange and hideous sight before him.

The few servants of the Manor House and Dick Turpin, entering the chamber, started in horror at the terrible sight of the dead miser.

Sybil Fairley, now mistress and heiress of the miser's wealth, upon recovering from the deadly swoon into which she had fallen, pale, livid with horror, bade the servants leave the chamber.

The door then locked, alone in his hideous pool of blood, the miser was left in the deserted room.

With her brain near turned to madness, Sybil Fairley sought not her couch that night, the two friends, Eustace, her lover, and Richard Turpin, remaining with the distracted heiress in the Hemlock Manor House.

CHAPTER XXX.

THE VISITORS AT THE "BOLD HORSEMAN."—GEOFFERY NEWTON, BOW-STREET RUNNER, AND LORD WALSINGHAM.—THE CONVERSATION.—THE PANEL IN THE WALL.—A SECRET REVEALED.—DEPARTURE OF EUSTACE, AND MEETING AT THE HAUNTED MILL.—THE NOBLE HIGHWAYMAN AND THE VILLAIN LORD.

THE morning following the death of Ralph Fairley, Turpin and Eustace made their way to the "Bold Horseman," Sybil first going to London to acquaint the few relations of her family with her father's sudden decease.

The light of the early morning's summer sun and the cheering condolements of her lover somewhat raised the drooping spirits of Sybil, who, of course, horror-stricken at her parent's horrible death, felt not the pangs and distress she would have done had the author of her being played a father's part.

From her infancy Ralph Fairley had exercised an undue authority over his child. Loving nought on earth but his gold, he would have sacrificed his daughter for mammon. A being of fierce and terrible passions, stern, cruel, and relentless in his hate, there was nought about the wretched man to win love from his kindred or respect from mankind.

The moment that saw Sybil on the road to town beheld Eustace and his friend wending their way to the inn kept by George Watson.

For fear of their enemies, the runners, the highwaymen took the secret passage from the old mill.

'Twas as well, as it afterwards appeared, that they did so.

Arriving at the door opening into the stable known as No. 2, Turpin, kneeling down, pressed a little knob, and the secret panel flew open.

Closing to the entrance, Turpin now pulled a ring let into the wall over the rack that contained the fodder for the horses.

A tinkling sound was the result.

A few moments afterwards, the jolly, rubicund face of George Watson appeared at the door of the stable, which had been locked from the passage without.

"All right, George?"

"At present, yes, my flower; though five minutes back I sighted a couple of strange horsemen down the road."

"Say you so? Well, for the present, we will make ourselves comfortable in the closet."

"Right you are, Dick. Follow me."

The two friends, walking along with the landlord of the

"Bold Horseman," left the stable and made their way up a flight of wooden stairs and then along a mildewed, dusty, dark passage that ran behind the walls of the old house. At the end of the passage, a small door admitted them into an apartment so small that it was not inaptly termed the closet.

Every convenience for comfort, however, was in this chamber.

A couch, two chairs, a table, a little stove, and other trifling articles were crammed in it, but the closet was evidently built but for one or two persons who might be at peril of their lives for a hiding-place.

It was stated by George Watson that the inn had once belonged to an old Jacobite, who had built the closet as a hiding-place for the Royalists who might be flying from the crop-ears.

Be this as it may, the closet was admirably suited to answer the purpose of Eustace and Turpin. Watson was much startled upon hearing the tragic incident of the night before at the Hemlock Manor-house, and with a muttered anathema upon all misers, and the deceased Ralph Fairley in particular, the jolly landlord withdrew to fetch refreshments for his friends.

"Well, my dear pal, what do you intend to do? Now Providence has removed the old man, nought stands between yourself and the lovely Sybil. Of course, you will not stop in London, or follow up your profession as a knight of the road?"

"Alas! Dick, I know not what I shall do!" murmured Eustace, gazing pensively into the countenance of his companion.

"Not know what you'll do? Why, of course, you'll splice the pretty Sybil, the rich heiress of the Hemlock Manor, trip it over to France, and enjoy yourself for the rest of your days, you lucky dog!" In vain Turpin, finding a cloud still hung upon the brow of his friend, endeavoured to rally him and cheer his spirits. Only deep sighs and exclamations of despair escaped him. At length, pressed by Turpin to explain the meaning of his distress, Eustace exclaimed—

"Dick! the events of last night have entirely altered matters with respect to myself and Sybil. If her parent was still alive she would fly with me to evade that parent's tyranny; but now he is dead, and Sybil Fairley is the rich heiress of the Hemlock Manor and all the old man's wealth."

"Well, of course she is, Eustace, and you, her future husband, will share those riches."

"Never, Dick, never!"

"How? You are mad! Will you not marry her?"

"No."

"For why?"

"Am I not, Dick Turpin, a thief—a common highwayman—a knight of the road?"

"Granted!" exclaimed Turpin, coolly eyeing his excited companion.

"And you would have me wed with the heiress of Ralph Fairley?"

"Yes; that's just what I would have you do. And I'll come down on a visit to your villa or castle in La belle France."

"Dick, I can never be the husband of Sybil Fairley."

"Nonsense, man! You'll think differently by-and-by. Your nerves are unstrung by the scene of the past night. Here comes George. We'll see if some of his old wines won't put better life into you."

George Watson now made his appearance, laden with refreshments, but bearing an uneasy, disturbed look upon his jolly features, that caused Dick to lay aside the bottle he had seized upon the entrance of his friend.

"How now, George? What's up?"

"The hounds are on the track!"

"Say you so? Then we must stick to the closet till night."

Speaking in a whisper, Watson, whilst pointing to the wall of the closet on his left, exclaimed—

"Look you, Dick! I've put them in the Blue room. They halt here for an hour."

"I understand. We may learn their movements by being in the closet here. Who are they?"

"Geoffery Newton."

"Curses on the hound! I owe him one, and I'll soon pay the debt. How many runners with him, George?"

"Six."

"The devil! He means it."

"There is another in his company who is desperately bitter against Eustace, and offers any money for his capture."

"Who the deuce is he?"

"No other than Lord Walsingham."

Eustace, who had till now been absorbed in a reverie, started up, exclaiming—

"Why or wherefore, I know not; but ever since the night I met with the young nobleman, when attacking with you, Dick, the York mail, have I been pursued with the same relentless hate as that evinced towards me by the late miser, Ralph Fairley. A cruel fate seems to bring upon me the revenge and hate of those to whom I inflicted but little harm. Let them, however, look to it. I will not be hunted thus. Like the deadly serpent, I'll turn upon and sting them! Ralph Fairley has fallen—fallen by his own hand, whilst, in a fit of fury, endeavouring to slay me. Perchance this Lord Walsingham may bring upon his own head a terrible punishment whilst pursuing me thus with his causeless malice. But, hark! the sound of voices proceeds from the Blue chamber. Away, Watson! they may require your presence. The runner, Newton, may have his suspicions aroused if you are away."

Eustace and Turpin now placed their ears against the wall that separated them from the other room, called the Blue chamber, and from which distinctly could be heard the voices of the thief-taker and Bow-street-runner, Geoffery Newton, and the noble Lord Walsingham.

"You tell me, Geoffery Newton, that you can ensure success in your pursuit of this man?"

"Yes, my lord. I'll run him down, though the devil himself aided him to escape!"

"Do so. Lodge him once again in jail, let me hear that he has perished on the scaffold, and name your own reward!"

"Hem! You want him hanged?"

"Yes," replied the nobleman, with a muttered execration.

"Well, you see, my lord, he ain't an old offender; he might, perhaps, get off with a trip to Botany."

"I would sooner know that he was dead! Surely, you can manage that! You are pursuing him now; he is an escaped felon! Can you not contrive at your next meeting to lodge a leaden bullet in his skull? Bring me news of his death, and I will hand you the sum of five hundred guineas!"

"It is a goodly sum you offer."

"Do you agree to earn it?"

"Ay, though 'tis a ticklish business, and one that before I go further in I must have cash down for."

"Swear to follow up this felon to the death, and I will this moment hand you over one hundred guineas! The rest shall be yours when you bring me the news that this highwayman, Eustace Maltravers, is dead."

"There needs no oath from my lips, my lord, to assure you of my purpose. When Geoffery Newton says a thing he means it. I have said I will do your bidding, and I will. I hate this man! He has defied me, thrice escaped me, and I've sworn to capture him or perish in the attempt! You wish him dead. Be it so. He shall die! I have a shrewd suspicion that he has gone to, or will go to, the Hemlock Manor House near here. Either this inn, or the residence of his mistress, will be the first place he will fly to. I shall proceed to the manor within the hour. Do you, my lord, stay at the inn with a couple of my trusty runners."

"Be it so. Here, Newton, are notes for one hundred pounds. Execute your purpose, let me hear that Eustace Maltravers is numbered with the dead, and the remainder of the sum I have promised shall be yours!"

"Thanks, my lord. Do not fear; I will earn the money, and the highwayman shall perish!"

Newton, rising, then left the room; the two friends, Eustace and Turpin, gaining an insight into the chamber, in which Lord Walsingham and the thief-taker were, through a sliding-panel, cleverly contrived in the wall of the closet.

The hand of Eustace shook as it rested on the shoulder of Turpin, while his whole frame trembled with suppressed passion, as he listened to the cold-blooded plot arranged by his enemies for the securing of his death.

"Dick," exclaimed Eustace, in a hoarse whisper, whilst

his fingers nervously clutched the pistols in his belt, "these two men must die! 'Tis their lives or mine! They hunt me thus with a hate that will alone be satisfied by my death! I will turn upon them. They have changed my forgiving nature to one of passion and revenge. There is some potent reason in this hate and malice of the villain who offers the wretch, Newton, payment for my death! And, by the heavens above me! I will fathom it."

In his passion and excitement, Eustace drew back the sliding-panel.

About to dash into the chamber in which Lord Walsingham was seated, our hero remained motionless with astonishment, as he noted the horror upon the countenance of his foe at his sudden appearance.

Eustace, with pallid features, his dark eyes fixed intently on his enemy, moved not from the panel. Lord Walsingham for a few seconds remained transfixed to his chair. Then, with a cry of terror, started up, and, like a demented being, darted from the chamber.

Shutting-to the opening, Eustace exclaimed—

"Come, Dick, let us leave the inn by the passage to the old mill. I must and will unravel this mystery in connexion with the villain who was so strangely struck with terror as I appeared before him. But now, come, we will depart at once. Making our way to the Hemlock Manor, we will boldly face the villain Newton, and then let him look to it. I am now bent upon revenge; and, by the devils whom my enemies serve! I will pause not in the execution of my just vengeance upon those who hunt me thus to the death. Come, Dick, come!"

Despite the entreaties of his friend, Eustace persisted in leaving the inn, and a few minutes after the scene at the panel with Lord Walsingham, the companions were threading the secret passage to the old ruined mill.

Finding his attempts to turn his friend from his purpose fruitless, Turpin followed in his steps, determined to aid him in his revenge upon his foes.

Making their way from the bottom of the old pit or shaft, the companions pursued their path till at length they emerged from the narrow opening, covered up with brushwood, that came out upon the dried-up bed of the stream that had originally fed the mill.

From thence they made their way into the old ruin by an entrance at the back, and were about to emerge from the mill in the direction of the high road, when Eustace, with an exclamation of rage, drew back.

Turpin, about to ask him the cause of his return to the shelter of the ruin, now gave utterance to a deep-breathed curse.

Standing just without was the form of Lord Walsingham, with three runners by his side. He was apparently awaiting the arrival of Geoffery Newton, who the friends perceived hurrying forwards from the direction of the Hemlock Manor House.

His search futile at the residence of the late miser, the thief-taker was returning to the inn.

"We must go back, Eustace. The closet in the 'Bold Horseman' must be our hiding-place till our foes have gone."

"I will not return. I have vowed to have revenge upon these men; and I will effect my object, Dick, though I swing for it."

"But the odds are too many for us this time, Eustace. Seven runners, with his lordship, are more than we can hope to conquer. We must await a more favourable opportunity. Doubt not Geoffery Newton and Lord Walsingham will fall into our power; and, when the moment comes, we will send them to their master, the Devil. Come, let us return to the inn."

"Do you return, Dick; I will come anon."

"I go not without you, old pal. Damme, if you are beat on the matter, why, we'll have it out, and luck be with us. I'll see to my barking irons, and then have with you for a tussle with our friends the runners."

"Hush, Dick! Newton returns, curses on him! He is furious at not lighting upon us at the Manor."

Even as Eustace ceased to whisper these words to his companion, the runner, Newton, uttering fierce oaths and cries of rage and disappointment, arrived at the mill, without the door of which stood the nobleman and his companions.

"Well, my lord, the fox has doubled on us; but, by ——," muttered the officer, with a terrible oath, "I'll run him down before another sunrise. There has been queer work at the Manor. Old Fairly is dead—blown his own brains out, so they tell me, in a conflict with some burglars. Maltravers has been at the house with that daring and much-wanted Dick Turpin, or Richard Palmer, as he calls himself. However, I'll trap them both, or my name ain't Geoffery Newton. And now, before we return to the inn, lads, let us search this old mill; our men might be inside, who knows? Owen and you, Hartley, follow me."

"All right, Newton."

The officers, following their leader, prepared to enter the mill, when Newton stopping them, and drawing back, with a chuckle called to Lord Walsingham, who had remained gazing moodily at the decayed ruin that reared its height before him.

"My lord, I shall require four hundred guineas of you to-night."

"What mean you?"

"I am going to put an ounce of lead into the brains of the man you hate," ejaculated Newton, with a devilish chuckle of glee.

"I do not understand."

"I've trapped the fox."

"How?"

"The highwaymen are even now in the mill."

"Ah! say you so? Curses, then, upon them!" A dark, fierce look of rage and gleam of Satan-like triumph wreathed the features of Lord Walsingham.

"Softly. We must be wary. Our men are armed and desperate. Even as I was about to enter the mill I heard the click of fire-arms put on cock. We must fight for it. Owen, get the darbies ready."

"All right, Newton."

"Hartley, see to your barking-irons. We must rush in; but keep your head down, without you want an ounce bullet in it. I presume you will wait here without?"

"No; I will enter the mill with you."

"You had best stay behind. A chance bullet might end your lordship's career."

"I care not."

"As you will. Proud to have the honour of your company. Now then, lads, come on."

"Hold!"

With a cry of momentary alarm Newton and his officers started back.

"Hold!"

Again that startling cry rung upon the air, proceeding from within the mill.

"Look here; it arn't no use, my lads; you're as good as booked for the stone-jug. Will you, before we proceed further, submit to become our prisoners? No nonsense."

"Ha! ha! ha!"

A shout of such derisive laughter greeted this speech of Newton, that with a volley of oaths the thief-taker, followed by his men, at once rushed into the mill.

There was the loud report of pistols and screams of rage and pain, followed by a shout of yelling laughter.

Then, for a moment, all was still, the silence being broke by Geoffery Newton.

With horrible imprecations he, with his men, searched in vain through the mill for the highwaymen. They had gone.

The old mill was tenantless.

But well Newton knew his men had been there, as he picked up from the floor a knife, upon the handle of which was engraven the name of Richard Turpin.

Like some angry and disappointed beast of prey, for a few minutes the runner stood glaring round the dark interior of the old mill.

At length his eye alighted upon the broken and decayed woodwork at the back, through which streamed a thin ray of light, for all within the old ruin was dark and drear.

With a howl of fury, Newton rushed to the opening, and, followed by the determined Lord Walsingham, found himself presently afterwards in the bed of the old stream.

But in vain a close search was instituted for the missing ones, they were not to be discovered.

Followed by the officer, Newton, Lord Walsingham, with a smile of secret triumph, with his eyes fixed upon the ground, now kept in the track of some footprints in the soft earth, that ceased upon gaining a mass of brushwood.

"By the fiends, my lord, we are on the scent ; and we shall have them at last."

Discovering the opening behind the tangled brier, without the least hesitation Lord Walsingham, followed by the runner, tore his way through.

In another moment both were in complete darkness.

Thick and black as a funeral pall.

The voices of the runners without, who had only just missed the presence of their officer, sounded strange and hollow in the dark, underground passage.

"Hold, my lord ; before we proceed further here, I'll call some of my men."

A low laugh now fell upon the ears of the officer and his companion.

A second of time elapsed, then the sounds of a fierce struggle woke up the echoes in the secret passage.

One cry for help only escaped the lips of Newton.

Overpowered, bound, gagged, and helpless, he was then drawn swiftly along that darksome, secret way.

Dragged along with no gentle force by a strong, powerful hand.

The sound of footsteps, and the smothered, gurgling noise behind, told the helpless officer that his companion was also secured.

Not a word was uttered by their captors during their journey along that underground passage.

At length the man who dragged Newton along in his powerful grasp, paused as they reached a wall that forebade their progress.

A moment afterwards a small opening appeared to the eyes of the enraged and astounded officer, and through this his captor, followed by another bearing Lord Walsingham along, made their entrance into a small chamber, that, dark as pitch, resembled a funereal vault.

There was a low murmuring converse for a few moments, then the sound of flint and steel, and a broad ray of light diffused itself through the chamber.

Though a bold, daring ruffian, a cold shudder darted through the body of Geoffery Newton, as in the captors of himself and Lord Walsingham he recognised the persons of Dick Turpin and Eustace Maltravers.

From the frowns and dark looks upon the features of both of their captors, the runner had but little hope of escaping with life.

Lord Walsingham, apparently undismayed by his critical and perilous position, coolly and calmly gazed upon the two men, one of whom he had pursued with such causeless malice and bitter enmity.

"Well, Eustace, the tables are turned ; my device wasn't a bad one to secure our foes. And now we have have them safe in number one, what is your purpose ?"

"A terrible, but necessary act."

"You mean to silence them both for ever."

"Yes. They now know the secret of the 'Bold Horseman ;' we dare not let them free ; besides, they have pursued us to the death. They have thrown the dice, and must stand the hazard of the die. The game is ours ; not I and you, but they must perish."

"Just so. How shall we do the trick ?" ejaculated Turpin, coolly pulling out his pistols and proceeding to load them.

A livid pallor now spread over the faces of Lord Walsingham and the runner as they heard their captors proposing their death.

"You would not murder us ?" gasped Newton.

"You jest ; you but play with our fears. You would not, could not, crimson your hands in our blood !"

"And why not, Lord Walsingham ?" exclaimed Eustace, who with folded arms gazed immoved upon the writhing form of his foe, bound and helpless at his feet.

"Because it would be a cowardly assassination."

"And what was your orders to that wretch an hour back ?" ejaculated Eustace, pointing to the runner. "Why, to hunt me to the death. I was not to be dragged back to joil ; the laws might not condemn me to the scaffold ; therefore, to gratify your accursed malice, I was to be shot like a dog by that villain, whose livid features betoken him the coward assassin that he is. But you are both outwitted. You have played your game with the cards and lost. We hold the winning ones. You are in our power, and, by the heavens above us, you shall mete out to us the stakes, and those stakes, as well you guess, are death ! Turpin, are you ready ?"

"Yes, captain, I have put a nice little leaden pill into these barking-irons of mine. Only say the word, and, curse me, if I don't soon end the career of clever Geoffery Newton and blot out a name in the peerage."

Cocking the pistol he held in his hand, Turpin took his stand by the wretched prisoners, waiting but the orders of Eustace to fire.

Cries for mercy, mingled with oaths and threats, issued from the mouth of the thief-taker, who rolled upon the floor of the darksome chamber, wild with fury and terror of a near approach to death.

"Shut up yer dominoes-box, or, damme, I'll finish you before orders," said Turpin, giving the howling officer a kick that sent him from one corner of the apartment to the other.

"Dick ! Dick ! are there no means but death ?" exclaimed Eustace, seizing Turpin by the arm, and drawing him to the further end of the underground chamber.

"None. 'Tis their lives or ours. Let them go, and before to-morrow's sun rises they will be again upon our track. As well spare the savage tiger—as well fondle the deadly snake, as spare these men. Pity them not. Curses on them ! were they not prepared to bury their bullets in our skulls ?"

Turpin glared savagely upon the helpless forms of the enemies in his power. Of a sterner, harder nature than his companion, no ray of pity, no feeling of compassion entered his breast at the thought of mercilessly slaying the foes they had secured and held in their power. Without remorse the highwayman was prepared to pistol the runner and his employer where they lay.

"There is no resource but their death ?"

"None."

"And you will do it, Dick ?"

"Ay, captain, with as little hesitation as I'd end the life of a mad dog."

"Were it not best to tell Watson ?"

"No. Why should he know it ? I can soon hide their bodies in No. 1 here. Leave all to me."

"It is a terrible measure, Dick."

"Ay, granted ; but a necessary one."

"Might we not bind them by a fearful oath ?"

"Think you such as they would value an oath ? Let them free, and a few hours hence the 'Bold Horseman' would be beset by Bow-street runners."

"There is nothing to be done, then, but to slay them ?" ejaculated Eustace, who, although he saw all that Turpin pointed out to him, shuddered at the idea of taking the lives of his foes.

"If I could think of any other measure, I would avail ourselves of it ; but there are none."

"You think not ?"

"I am sure of it. Let them go, you give yourself and your pal up to the hangman's hand. I am not particularly in want of a dance at Tyburn ; and, to save our own lives, why, damme, I'll take theirs."

The converse between Eustace and his friend, carried on in an under tone, had been unheard by the two captives, who, with shuddering horror, glared upon every action of the highwaymen, into whose hands they had fallen ; but, as Turpin advanced towards them, with his pistols raised, and Eustace with folded arms stood at the further end of chamber, apparently indifferent to their fate, cries and shrieks for mercy burst from the mouths of the prisoners.

"Help ! help ! help !"

"Mercy ! mercy !"

"What mercy would you have shown to us, you jail bird ?" ejaculated Turpin, with the butt of his pistol smashing in the front teeth of the struggling and frantic officer, who, his mouth and face streaming with blood, shouted loudly for help. "I couldn't let yer go without a mark of my regard. There, you are free of your bonds ; and thank Eustace Maltravers there for your life, not me." Turpin, unfastening the rope that had confined the limbs of the runner, now drew back. Staggering to his feet, Newton, spluttering and speaking strange and thick from the loss of his teeth and bruised jaw, exclaimed—

"Dick Turpin, I'll have a fearful revenge for this night's work. My lad, you shall swing at Tyburn yet."

"Pshaw ! don't be a fool. Keep your tongue quiet, or, damme, I'll bullet yer, despite the commands of the captain there." A glitter in the eyes of the highwayman, and a hectic flush on either cheek, told the officer that the enraged knight of the road was quite capable of fulfilling his threat. Clearing his mouth from the blood that

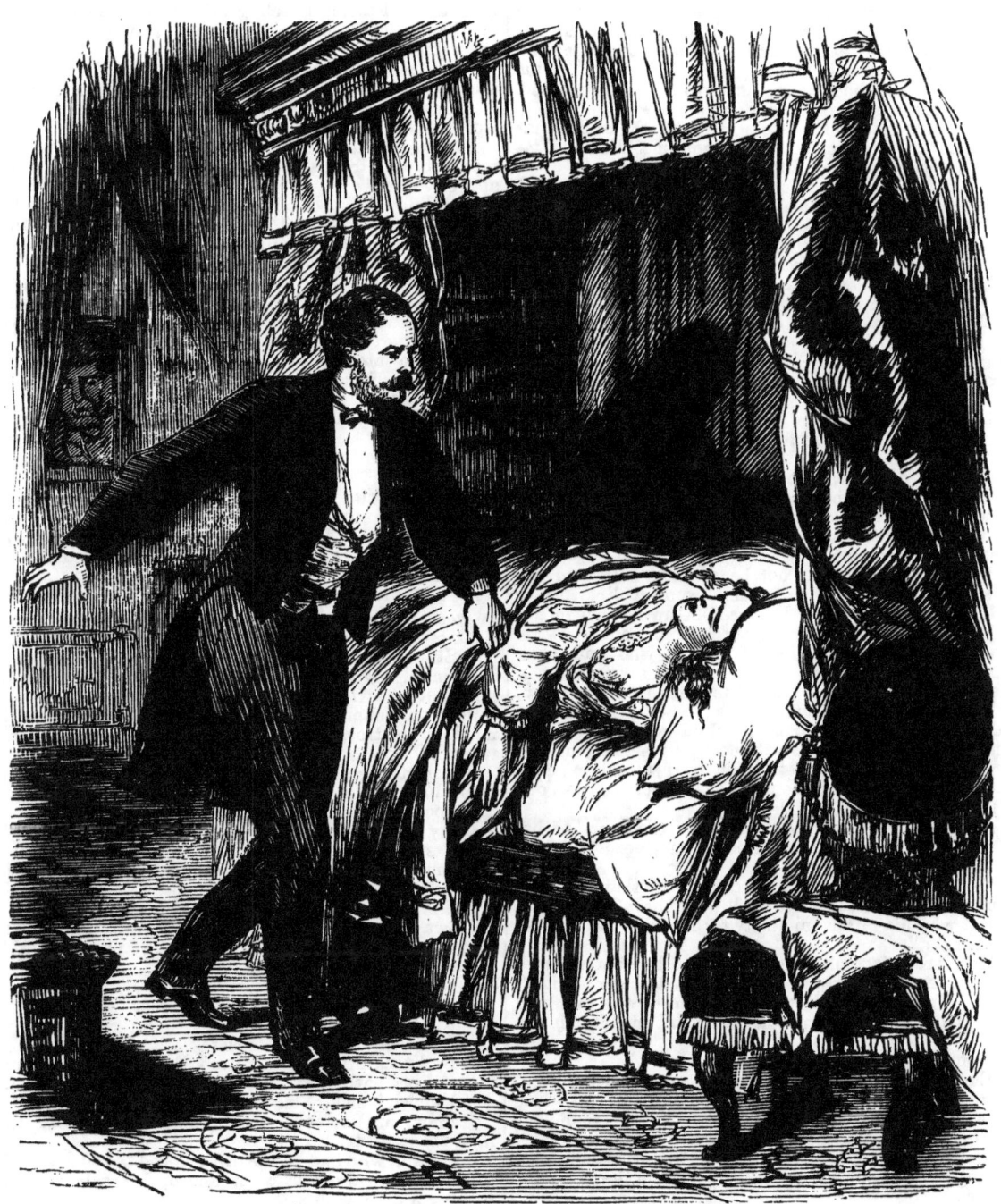

LORD ARLINGTON AND THE BEAUTIFUL VICTIM.

almost choked him, the runner gazed uneasily upon Eustace, as he gasped out the question of whether he was free to go.

"Upon swearing by all that's holy that you will keep secret what has taken place here to-night, blotting out for ever the remembrance of it from your memory. Geoffery Newton," exclaimed Eustace, "you may go. I want not your blood upon my soul, though you would have murderously taken mine at the instigation of that man." Eustace here pointed to the form of Lord Walsingham, who lay cowering and trembling where he had been thrown by Eustace on entering the apartment.

"I am free to go, then?"

"You are."

"'Tis well. Nor shall you find Geoffery Newton forgetful of the fact that you have saved him from death. Turpin, you have marked me for life; but no matter; better a few teeth out than an ounce of lead in my skull. From to-night it will be always my endeavour to avoid you both. Whilst in the service of the law, I must do its behests. We must remain foes, but I swear never to reveal aught of this place, or to forget that you spared the man who was hunting you to the death."

"See you keep to this, Newton. Farewell. Nay, no more thanks. Adieu, and remember that you owe your life to Eustace Maltravers and Dick Turpin."

"I shall never forget it. I am but a Bow-street runner; a man without heart or feeling; nor till to-night did I know I had enough grace or good in me to estimate a favour. You are a noble highwayman, Maltravers, and 'tis a cruel fate that has thrust you in the path of crime. Farewell. From to-night count Geoffery Newton, the Bow-street runner, your friend."

"As you will, Newton. Farewell."

"Show him the way out, Dick. I would be alone with his lordship here."

Turpin, taking the hand of their late foe, conducted him through a secret panel out into a darksome passage, leading to the entrance by the mill.

A look of alarm spread itself over the face of Lord Walsingham as Turpin and the runner disappeared, but on again glancing at the features of Eustace, he seemed reassured, and rising to his feet, having been freed of his bonds by Turpin, he staggered over to the man whom he had so relentlessly pursued, and exclaimed—

" And what is to be the fate of the man who bribed that one whom you have spared, to slay you in cold blood ? "

" What should be your fate, Lord Walsingham ? "

" Death ! I know it—I feel it ! Eustace Maltravers, I have been under the influence of a fiend. You know not what terrible matter it was urged me on to pursue you as I have done ; but your nobleness of heart shown to me this night makes me resolved to tell you all. Listen ! "

Glaring wildly round, the nobleman, clutching Eustace by the arm, exclaimed—

" Twenty years ago my eldest brother died — died at sea, leaving in England a widow and infant child to mourn his loss. That child, Eustace Maltravers, stood between me and rank and power. A twelvemonth after my brother's death my sister-in-law followed her husband to the other world. The child still lived, lived to thrust me from all the fond desires of my ambitious soul."

" My lord, distress not yourself with recollections of the past. Let me lead you hence."

Eustace, with bewildered air, gazed upon the convulsed features of his companion, who seizing his arm, stayed his steps, exclaiming—

" No, no, no. Take me not hence till I have told you all, lest I repent, and call back from my lips that I would now make known. Eustace Maltravers, when my brother's child was but one year old, I had him removed — given to the wife of a man who had been banned by the law, and whom I had saved from a felon's death. The child passed for this man's nephew, but he himself knew not it was the offspring of my brother. I then gave out the child was dead. The object of my ambition was attained. I married ; had an only son ; that son now lives. You have seen him ; first met him when, with your companion, you robbed the York mail."

" And was the fact of that robbery the cause of his and your own relentless persecution of me, Lord Walsingham ? "

" Yes. Had you not robbed him of that jewelled miniature, had he not met you, all would have been well."

" But why his bitter animosity to one who did him so little harm ? "

" He feared, trembled, lest a secret I had entrusted to him was, after the lapse of years, about to come to light. In you, Eustace Maltravers, he recognised the one who could push him from his proud estate and level him in the dust."

" I, my lord ? How ? What mean you ? "

" Eustace Maltravers, you are my son's cousin. You, you are the child whom I, twenty years ago, gave into the hands of the wife of Guy Essington. Heap your curses on the head of your father's guilty, guilty brother."

Sobs of heartrending agony shook the breast of Lord Walsingham, who fell, moaning piteously, at the feet of his nephew.

The chamber for a few moments appeared to Eustace, to be whirling round and round with him.

His brain was dazed, confused by what he had heard.

At one moment he fancied the miserable man at his feet was mad.

Then with a cold shudder, and thrill of joy and pain, strangely mingled, he remembered how wonderfully the portrait in the jewelled locket resembled his own.

A thick, husky, burning feeling was in his throat.

He felt as if he could shriek wildly with joy.

Now could he claim the hand of his Sybil, and lead her proudly to the altar.

The sound as of bells rung in his ears.

The before darksome chamber seemed to the eyes of Eustace filled with a thousand lights.

In the midst of the yellow glare he beheld a face dancing before him.

'Twas the face of the young Lord Walsingham.

The wildly-shrieked words, " You will spare my son ! you will spare my son ! " sounded like thunder in his ears. The lights then seemed to vanish, and with a cold, nervous thrill, Eustace awakened from his dreamy trance to be-

hold the aristocrat kneeling at his feet, and holding up his hands beseechingly to him, shrieking with terrible earnestness—

" Eustace Maltravers, I have told you all ! but you will spare—you will spare my son ! " Then with a shriek, as of dying agony, Lord Walsingham sank senseless at the feet of his injured nephew.

Raising the form of Lord Walsingham in his arms, he made his way from the underground chamber to the inn above.

Standing by the couch, upon which reclined the form of his uncle, Eustace, with a happy smile upon his features, patiently awaited his return to consciousness.

Ere that moment came, however, Turpin—his face flushed with passion—burst into the room, exclaiming—

" Haste away, Eustace, lad ! A dozen of the accursed runners, headed by the whelp of a son of my Lord Walsingham there, are in the house ! Away with you ! Ah ! we are too late for the secret passage ! We must retreat by the back of the house ! "

Bang ! bang ! bang !

Shouts, cries, and pistol-shots sounded in the inn.

CHAPTER XXXI.

A SCENE AT THE OFFICE IN THE POULTRY.—THE RIVAL CLERKS.—EXULTATION OF NAT STEVENS, AND FURY OF EPHRAIM RASSELTON.—IGNOMINIOUS EJECTMENT OF THE HEAD CLERK OF THE LATE RALPH FAIRLEY.—THE RENCONTRE WITH RESURRECTION BILL.—THE PLOT.—A PROJECTED BURGLARY.—ROBBERY AND REVENGE.

IT was the day following the death of the miser, as the clock of Bow Church gave out the hour of twelve, that Nat Stevens was startled from a reverie in which he had been indulging (much to the annoyance of Ephraim Rasselton), by hearing a loud summons at the hall door, and to the astonishment of both the clerks, the pretty waiting-maid of mistress Sybil Fairley gave admittance to her mistress.

" Something's up, Rasselton ! " exclaimed Nat. " Miss Sybil here in town, who was yesterday a close prisoner at Hemlock Manor-house at Harrow, proves that either old Fairley has done the decent thing, and let his daughter have her own way, or else, being a girl of spirit, she has a second time given the old buffer leg-bail, and cut and run from her cruel parent."

" The latter is the most likely thing ; and, eh ! eh ! eh ! I'll away at once to Harrow, and let Mr. Fairley know that his disobedient child is here. Eh ! eh ! eh ! I'll go at once."

" No you won't."

" Who will prevent me ? "

" I will."

" You ! eh ! eh ! eh ! How ? "

" By knocking you down, and then locking you up in the scullery with dirty Sal Gooding, the cinder woman."

" Eh ! eh ! eh ! You had better not try it."

" Why, my flower ? " ejaculated Nat, assuming a belligerent attitude.

Ephraim, who had before experienced the effects of Nat's fistic powers, drew back in alarm, his sallow features turning a dirty white.

" Stand back, or I'll have you locked up ! Eh ! eh ! eh ! Old Fairley has taken my advice. Eh ! eh ! You'll be kicked out at the end of the quarter ! "

" Indeed ! Take care, humpy, that you aint kicked out before."

" He told me to give you your dismissal ; but I've kept the good news. Eh ! eh ! eh ! I didn't mean you to know anything about it till the last minute." A low chuckle escaped the lips of Ephraim.

" Oh ! that's it, is it ? So I'm to be turned out, am I ? and that, too, at the instigation of a measly, dirty, grovelling, lickspitting, tale-telling, half-made specimen of an ourang-outang like you ! Well, it don't surprise me. Old Fairley is a cussed bad parent, a miserly old hound, and Ephraim Rasselton is just suited to his dirty work."

" Eh ! eh ! eh ! He is too clever to keep a pauper any longer at his office, to whistle popular melodies and cut up the pens ! Eh ! eh ! eh ! "

Coolly turning up his coat-sleeves, Nat, taking his station between his fellow-clerk and the door, exclaimed—

" So, so ! Cheek is your little game, is it ? Now just take a good stare at the sunlight, old dot-and-go-one, for

I'm going to bung up your eyes, so that you won't see daylight for a week. I'll give yer a keepsake before I go."

"Stand off!"

"I'm to be kicked out, am I?"

"I'll have you locked up! eh! eh! eh! Lay finger on me and you shall be sent to jail! eh! eh! eh!"

"I will chance that, my ugly-mug. A pauper, am I? Well, if I don't make your hide pay for that, damme, cut me for the simples, and shove me in the stocks!"

"Keep back! Help! murder!" Rushing aside to avoid a blow from the enraged Nat, Ephraim Rasselton fell over the stool by his fellow-clerk's desk, and, yelling with rage and alarm, lay kicking out his feet, at the same time that he fingered nervously a knife he drew from his bosom unnoted by Nat. The latter, about to drag the howling cur and villain from the ground, was stayed in his purpose by Nancy Watson who, bursting into the room, with a strange look of joy and terror mingled, exclaimed—

"Oh! Nat, such news! Poor Mr. Fairley has been and shot himself! Miss Sybil is here, and desired me to tell you to shut up the office directly."

"Old Fairley dead? oh! here's a lark!" ejaculated Nat, losing all sympathy for the miser in the exulting thought that Ephraim would now be defeated; for well he knew that Sybil hated the sight of her late father's head clerk. "Now shall I be kicked out? Get up, humpy. There's the door, and I dismiss you on my own hook. Cut and run. Make yourself scarce while you have a chance." Giving the astounded and cowering Rasselton a kick, Nat threw open the office door, ordering Nancy to see the enraged clerk out of the place.

"Nat Stevens, you shall suffer for this!" shrieked Ephraim, as, livid with passion, he limped towards his determined fellow-clerk.

"What, still on the cheeky game? then blowed if I don't give you a keepsake, old fellow. One on your smeller won't spoil your beauty, because you never had any."

There was a loud shriek from Nancy, as on Nat striking out at Ephraim, the latter, with eyes glittering like fiery sparks with terror and rage, with deadly intent rushed upon his aggressor, knife in hand.

Fortunately the ready eye of Nat had discerned the dangerous weapon in the other's grasp.

With an oath, Nat seized the wrist of the infuriated Ephraim, and nearly twisting it from its socket, caused the wretch to drop the knife with a shriek of fury and pain,

"You murdering, snivelling, backbiting, revengeful ape, take that one on your smeller as a remembrancer from Nat Stevens! Take that! and that! and that! to help yer on your road to your master, the devil!"

With fierce energy Nat, first dashing his clenched fist between the evil eyes of the helpless Ephraim, deluging his hideous features with a dark, muddy, ensanguined stream; then, at each fresh ejaculation, gave such a vigorous kick upon an unmentionable part of the other's person, that caused a horrible howl to issue from his lips.

Reaching the door leading into the street, Nat threw it open, and, with a last, malicious, hearty kick, sent the wretched Ephraim howling into the road.

"There, if you sit down easy for a month, I'll eat my head," exclaimed Nat, as, with a shout of laughter at the speechless and enraged Ephraim Rasselton, he closed the door.

Staggering to his feet, and glaring savagely upon some boys and passers-by who were laughing at the strange and ignominious ejectment of Ephraim from the money-lender's office, he dashed to the door, muttering—

"I will have his life! I will have revenge! eh! eh! eh! I'll have his heart's blood for this!"

"Hallo! mate. Who's flurried your milk? Put by your sticker, you fool, without yer want the grabs on yer; and come along with me, and tell me all about it. Has old Fairley kicked yer out? Cuss yer, don't stare so viciously at me, or by ——, I'll twist yer neck as soon as I would a blind puppy's."

Resurrection Bill, for he it was who had been startled by the sudden appearance of Ephraim from the miser's office, now dragged the enraged dwarf from the spot, presently turning down Wood-street, and thence into a narrow court.

The resurrection man, who remembered the person of the deformed clerk, thought that possibly the latter might aid him in a nefarious project he had entertained in respect to the miser.

"Now, look here, my rum cull. What's up? What lay has been smoked? Has yer been piped making free with the wedge (plate) or goldfinches (money) of old Fairley?"

"Eh! eh! eh! what's that to you? Who are you?"

"One that may be of service to aid you in your revenge upon old Fairley."

"Eh! eh! eh! I think you'd find that rather difficult."

"Why so?"

"Because—eh! eh! eh!—the old man's dead."

"Dead? Ten thousand devils! Then the cursed Eustace Maltravers will drop into all the miser's rowdy. Curses on him! but this shall not be. I'll yet revenge the fate of poor Viper. Are yer sure of this news?"

"Yes. Eh! eh! eh! it's quite correct."

"How did the old man die?"

"By his own hand, so they tell me."

"Indeed! Well, it matters not. If the old man is ready for a parson's lodging (grave), it's pretty sartin he won't require any more of his goldfinches; so it don't signify our helping ourselves to summat. Now look here. Suppose we both take a trip down to Harrow, and see if we can't do a big thing at the residence of the old boy what is now made cold meat on. What do you say? Will yer like to join me in a crack on the crib, and so revenge yourself on the lot on 'em?"

"Eh! eh! eh! I knows the whole ins and outs of the Hemlock Manor House."

"In course you does; that's why I asked yer to join in the crack."

"Eh! eh! eh! we share, of course?"

"Oh! yes. You'll always find Resurrection Bill act on the square. And now, hark ye. My bitterest foe, Eustace Maltravers, will, in course, be down at the Manor with Miss Sybil Fairley. Now I mean, come what will, to cut his throat from ear to ear."

"Eh! eh! eh! cut his throat?"

"Yes, just so," ejaculated the ruffian, with a horrible oath.

"Eh! eh! eh! Would you mind, if I join you in this business, assisting me to cut another?"

"Aid me in my revenge upon Eustace Maltravers, and I'll cut fifty throats if you wish."

"Eh! eh! eh! then we will together go to the Hemlock Manor. He whose life I've sworn to have will journey, doubtless, to the house to-night with the miser's daughter. We will surprise them in their sleep, and, eh! eh! eh! we will have their blood. And then, ho! ho! we will give them a bonny funereal pyre. We will fire the Manor, and so in the ruins hide the secret of our crime."

"Devilish good idea! Curses on it! you are one of the right sort. It shall be so. We will talk more of this. Come with me, and we will arrange our proceedings within doors."

"As you will. Ha! ha! we will have brave sport to-night. Nat Stevens shall welter in his blood, and I'll shriek in his dying ears 'twas my hand gave the fatal blow."

"All right, mate. For myself," muttered the resurrection man, "I will have this night the blood of Eustace Maltravers to throw at the feet of the Night-Hawks, or become myself food for worms. But my time ain't come yet. The leader of the Red Band ain't yet booked for a leap in the dark, or the grasp of Stiffening Dick. But howsomever, come on, my pal, and we'll arrange this little business of profit and revenge."

Following the herculean form of the housebreaker, the stunted dwarf figure of Ephraim hobbled on, the enraged clerk giving ever and anon vent to his devilish chuckle of satisfaction, as he thought of attaining his revenge.

"Eh! eh! eh! They shall all perish in the flames that shall destroy the Hemlock Manor," he muttered, rubbing his hands with elfin glee.

CHAPTER XXXII.

THE WILLOW GRANGE.—CAPTAIN LESLIE AND HIS VICTIMS.—THE FURY OF LIZZY HEYWARD.—THE THREAT.—THE STRUGGLE.—THE KNIFE.—THE OPEN CASEMENT.—RETRIBUTION.—TERRIBLE FATE OF THE SEDUCER.

THE morning following the abduction of the unfortunate Bessie Templeton from the Cedars at Kensington the sun rose bright and joyous upon the old gothic turreted-roofed building, known as the Willow Grange.

At the window of a large chamber in an upper story of the Grange was the figure of a young woman gazing down from the casement, which was open. The unhappy girl, so pale, rigid, and ghost-like, seemed as though meditating a frantic leap into the grounds many feet below.

The rising sun cast its golden saffron rays full upon her features.

They were fixed in an expression of passion and despair.

The hands clenched, were raised as if in supplication to the One above.

Whilst the eyes of the unhappy girl glared wildly round, and then were cast with a frenzied stare at the horrid depths below.

One leap—one dash from that height, and all would be at an end.

But Lizzy Heyward, for she it was who had been brought with the unfortunate Bessie Templeton by the villain Leslie to the old Grange, paused at the thought of suicide.

"Might she not yet secure revenge upon her seducer? Might not a terrible retribution yet overtake her destroyer?" she asked herself, as she stood by the open casement.

The young girl was suddenly startled from her reverie by hearing a low laugh behind her.

Turning from the casement, a half-shriek escaped her lips, whilst the livid pallor on her cheeks changed to a hectic hue.

In the apartment she discerned the figure of a man.

The bright rays of the sun shone full upon his form.

Upon the features of the intruder there rested a grim, satanic smile. With a curl upon the haughty lip, he exclaimed—

"So, then, fair Lizzie, cousin of mine, you meditate destruction? A leap from that casement would soon, indeed, end your troubles; but methinks you shudder at rushing into death? But, by the fiends, girl, you shall suffer a thousand deaths ere I satiate my revenge. You have defied me, Lizzie Heyward; attempted to thwart me in the execution of my project with regard to the girl Bessie; and, by the heavens above me, you shall rue the hour you entered the lists against me. Know, now, that by a forgery I secured wealth by right appertaining to your father."

"Villain! accursed wretch! to tell me this, if it be so. Then 'twas your hand sent my parents in sorrow and misery to the grave? You—you, Captain Leslie, are as much the murderer of my father and mother as though you had buried a knife in their bosoms! There are other means of murder than that of sword, or bullet, or the deadly poison. This is the worst of all assassinations, the murder of starvation. This murder, Captain Leslie, rests on the heads of many in the good city of London, who by fraud deprive the honest man of his own, and thrust him into a pauper's grave. But the day of reckoning comes for all. Mark me, Leslie, your crimes will yet be punished. A divine power will let fall upon your head a terrible retribution in the very hour of your triumph."

"Ha! ha! ha! You are mad, girl; but if this divine power you prate of is to punish me in my triumph, it had best be speedy. Bessie, the sweet Bessie Templeton, is below, and at my mercy. You, too, are in my hands. Nought can tear ye from me, and to-night, ay, within the hour, you shall receive such mercy from me as will give you a foretaste of that which is to come. You shall sleep to-night, girl, in a cold and dark cell, your companions the crawling toad and hideous rat. I much doubt if, after sleeping in the underground chamber to which I shall have you conveyed, if you will talk so glibly of the powers above, or retribution upon the head of one who, had you behaved differently, would have never seen you know suffering or want."

The wild glare in the young girl's eyes now changed to a fixed and deadly stare; the hectic flush that had dyed her cheeks upon the appearance of her villain cousin, again turned the deadly, livid pallor of a corpse.

With a shriek of rage, of maddening fury, she dashed from the casement at the form of her destroyer.

He turned to the door. But with a shrill scream of laughter and shout of exultation, his companion slammed it violently to, locking it, and then hurling the key through the casement.

Captain Leslie was now a prisoner with the enraged girl.

A cold, nervous shudder darted through his frame, as he gazed upon her wild appearance and listened to her hideous shrieks.

He feared the slim, young girl locked with him in that chamber.

He shuddered, and his teeth chattered with terror as his victim, with another of her terrible shrill screams or yells, pulled a knife from her bosom, glaring with a fixed, deadly stare upon him.

Foam in white flecks burst from her lips, that had within the last few minutes turned from their rosy hue to a dark purple.

Two angry spots of red tinged each cheek.

The rest of the features were a livid pallor.

The dark, livid pallor of the grave.

Such horrible, piercing yells now issued from her lips, that Captain Leslie, as the young girl approached him, drew back in terror and shuddering horror.

A terrible truth now burst upon him.

The thought of which caused the cold beads of perspiration to trickle down his brow.

His wretched cousin, Lizzie Heyward, was the victim of a fearful fate.

A terrible disease had fastened upon her.

She was mad!

Her wild shrieks deepening in their shrillness, the frantic gesticulations of the wretched girl, all told the fatal truth.

She was mad!

With yells of maniac laughter, knife in hand, she darted upon her terrified relative.

A curse, and a cry for help escaped his lips.

But no answering cry came back. The few servants of the Grange were wont to hear such sounds of alarm, and paid no heed; besides that, the chamber was a topmost one in the old Grange, and sounds below could not be plainly heard.

A strange, wild scene now took place.

The cowering, villain roue in vain endeavouring to avoid the maddened girl, closed with her, attempting to wrest the knife she held from her grasp.

But endued with a fictitious strength, the maddened victim wrestled bravely with her destroyer.

Shriek followed shriek in rapid succession.

The chamber in the old Grange echoed with the wild yells of the maniac victim of the seducer.

Fiercely, frantically, the young girl and Captain Leslie struggled.

Peals of hideous laughter burst from the mouth of the maddened girl.

At length, with fierce energy, she dragged the roue to the casement.

The morning sun poured its rays full upon the face of Lizzie Heyward.

With a shudder, Leslie noted the demented look on his wretched cousin's face.

Insanity could be traced in the livid features and in the wild eyes.

Strange, horrid jabbering issued from her lips.

"Mercy, Lizzie! Hold your hand!" ejaculated Leslie, paralyzed with fear, as his maniac cousin thrust him half over the frail balustrade without the casement.

Half strangled by the fierce grip the mad girl had retained of his neckerchief, and confused by the suddenness of her attack and horror of the scene, Captain Leslie had lost possession of his powers, and was like a child in the hands of the maddened girl.

The sun pouring its rays in his eyes, he scarce discerned the descending knife.

A moment elapsed, when a wild shriek from the maniac was echoed by a frenzied cry of terror and pain from Captain Leslie.

A dark mass then whirled through the air, falling from the balcony down into the grounds below.

Screams of laughter issued from the lips of the maddened victim of man's base passions.

Leaning far over the frail support, the maniac girl, with shouts of glee, gazed at a dark mass that lay upon the gravel walk many feet below.

The sun shone full upon the huddled-up, coiled-up form.

It moved not; but in a confused heap lay upon the earth.

A mangled and bleeding mass.

A divine Power had indeed destroyed the scoffer in the hour of his triumph.

Captain Leslie, the *roue* and seducer, falling from the balcony above, had been dashed a shapeless mass upon the earth beneath.

He had sown the storm and reaped the whirlwind.

His victim in her insanity had destroyed him.

CHAPTER XXXIII.

THE RUNNERS AND THE HIGHWAYMEN.—A FIGHT FOR LIFE.—THE DEATH STRUGGLE BETWEEN THE COUSINS.—FATE AND ITS VICTIMS.—DEATH OF THE YOUNG LORD WALSINGHAM.—FLIGHT OF EUSTACE AND TURPIN.—THE RUNNERS AT THE OLD MILL.—THE ESCAPE PREVENTED.—APPEARANCE OF AN UNEXPECTED ALLY.—THE FLIGHT OF EUSTACE TO THE HEMLOCK MANOR.

THE noise and shouts of the runners partly aroused Lord Walsingham, who, as Turpin burst into the room occupied by himself and Eustace, started up and looked in an alarmed and crazed manner at the two friends.

"How is this, Dick? The officers in the house!"

"Ay, and headed by the young Lord Walsingham, who vows to shoot you down like a dog. But we shall see."

Turpin, pulling out his pistols, coolly cocked them.

Bang! bang! bang!

"Open the door, in the king's name! It's no use trying to evade us; we must have you!"

"Really you don't mean it, gentlemen," ejaculated Turpin, in a bantering tone.

"Open the door, or we burst it open!"

"Are you in a hurry?"

"Will you open the door?"

"Of course. Who do yer want?"

"Dick Turpin."

"That's me."

"And Eustace Maltravers."

"When will you have us? Now, or when you catch us?"

"Parley no longer with them, Jones, but burst the door."

"I think Jones had better leave it alone."

"Bang! bang!"

"Friend Jones, don't. You'll hurt yourself."

Bang! bang! crash!

The door burst from its hinges, revealing to the eyes of Dick Turpin and his friend a crowd of Bow-street runners, headed by the young Lord Walsingham, who, with a face livid with passion, exclaimed, whilst pointing to Eustace—

"See the escaped felon! Fire upon—secure him!"

"Take my advice, gentlemen, don't attempt anything of the kind. Eustace, out with your barking-irons; we must rush for it."

"Yield yourselves our prisoners."

"Parley not with them, but upon them," exclaimed the vindictive young aristocrat, dashing into the chamber and firing upon the highwaymen.

There was a deep curse from Turpin, who, levelling his pistols at the head of the young lord, fired. The distracted father, seeing the act of the highwayman, darting forwards, interposed his person to shield that of his son, receiving the shot in his chest. With a wild cry of pain, the unfortunate man staggered back, falling to the ground.

A moment afterwards the din of fierce conflict resounded through the room.

Oaths, curses, and firing of pistols making up a scene of horror.

"Down with them."

"Slip on the darbies."

"They can't escape. Hold on to him, Jones."

"I think Jones had better leave it alone."

Turpin, who was held in the powerful grasp of the runner, now stooped down, and seizing the wretched man by the waist, lifted him off his feet, and hurled him, head first among his comrades. His skull, crashing against the oaken table in the centre of the room, was beaten in by the force of the blow.

"There's one rubbed out. Let them have it, Eustace."

Firing a brace of pistols amid the group of officers, Turpin caused a momentary diversion in favour of himself and his friend.

With a dash, Eustace, now accompanied by his companion, bounded from the room.

The enraged runners, like a leash of hounds, yelling and following in their wake.

With lightning speed, Eustace darted down the stairs of the old inn, meeting George Watson, the landlord, in the passage below.

"It's no use trying the front, there are more of the grabs outside; you must take to the passage," ejaculated Watson.

"All right, George. Follow me, Dick," exclaimed our hero, dashing down the passage, followed by his friend.

There was a feeling of terror at the idea of capture, in the bosom of Eustace, never experienced by him before. His brief interview with Lord Walsingham had shown him that he might yet secure the means of an honourable career.

Could he escape the officers now on his track, all might yet be well.

The thought of capture now, of incarceration in a felon's prison, was madness.

Wildly dashing on, Eustace gained the stairs leading to the door opening upon the stables that led to the secret passage.

Dick, close upon his friend, was followed by the young Lord Walsingham and two runners.

The door at the bottom of the stairs was opened by Eustace.

In another moment the friends were in the stable known as Number 2.

Unable, however, to close the door upon their pursuers, they were brought to bay.

There was no escape.

With curses of rage and fury, the two friends dashed upon their foes.

There was a short and desperate struggle.

Engaged with one of the officers, Turpin, with a shudder, beheld the young lord standing in the doorway, with pistol levelled at the head of his friend, who was fiercely resisting the attempt of his antagonist to thrust upon his wrists a pair of handcuffs.

There was a deadly, savage glitter in the eyes of the young lord, that bespoke the malice of his purpose was fixed and determined.

As at length, with an exertion of strength, Turpin hurled the runner with whom he was engaged to the other end of the stable.

There was the loud report of a pistol, and Eustace, with the officer upon him, fell to the ground.

With an oath of fury, Turpin, snatching a pistol from the belt of the man at his feet, fired at the retreating form of the assassin, who, upon the delivery of his dastard shot, darted from the stable.

There was one single short cry of pain, accompanied by a gasping sob, and throwing up his arms with a wild leap into the air, the miserable young man fell a corpse just without the door.

The bullet from the pistol of the enraged Turpin had pierced his heart.

"Curses on the hound! At all events, I've revenged your death, my dear pal!"

Turning round, Turpin now started back with a cry of joy and surprise.

Erect and in life, before him was the figure of his friend.

In a moment Turpin understood it all.

The inert mass from beneath which his friend had struggled, told the tale.

The bullet from the pistol of the young Lord Walsingham had entered the skull of the unfortunate runner, who, ghastly and horrible, lie a blood-stained corpse upon the ground.

The struggle that we have here related occupied but a few minutes of time.

Eustace and his friend, aware that not a moment must be lost, opened the secret way and disappeared from No. 2 as the runners dashed in.

The hounds of the law were once more off the scent.

"Where do you propose to seek a refuge, Eustace?" exclaimed Turpin, as with his friend he hurried along the passage, the shouts of their enemies dying away in the distance.

"At the Hemlock Manor, Dick; and, by this time tomorrow, I will be far away from hence for a period. France shall be my abode; but I have that to tell which will cause you both surprise and joy, for well I know your kind feelings towards me. But, come, let us to the Manor. I am eager that my sweet Sybil should know the change in her lover's career, for from this hour, Dick, I no longer league with the Night-Hawks of London, or remain a knight of the road. A strange and sudden change has taken place in my before wayward fate. Anon you shall know all; but, see, we are at the end of the passage that opens on the dried-up stream of the old mill."

About to dash out from the secret passage, Eustace drew back with an exclamation of alarm and rage.

Turpin, peering through the thicket that hid the mouth of the subterraneous way, gave utterance to a fierce oath.

Standing about the old mill, and loitering in the vicinity of the hiding-place of the highwaymen, were some half-a-dozen Bow-street runners.

"What's to be done, Eustace? We're caught like a fox in a hole."

"There is nothing for it, Dick, but to dash boldly out."

"No, that won't do. There are six to two. We are fatigued—they are fresh. We should be overpowered in a moment. I've only one shot in one of my barking-irons, and no more powder."

"Nor I."

"We are fixed."

"Like rats in a trap."

"Well, we are perfectly safe here."

"I suppose so, Dick."

"Suppose so? Why, of course we are."

"I don't know. Remember the secret of the passage is now known."

"To Geoffery Newton, yes; but he is not among our foes without. Besides, he will not reveal the secret; he will keep his oath."

"You think so."

"Yes. I'd almost stake my life he'll remain true to his promise."

"Well, I don't."

"How?"

"I that was for sparing him, am now the first to mistrust him. And, by heavens, I am right in my suspicions!"

"What mean you?"

"Hark!"

"I hear nothing."

"Listen again."

Turpin, bending his ear to the ground, started up with a deep-breathed curse.

"Well, Dick; what do you hear?"

"The sound of approaching footsteps along the passage. Curses! we are lost! But, by the fiends, the bullet I have left shall crash into the skull of Geoffery Newton."

"There is one hope yet, Dick. It may only be George Watson."

"Oh! no; it ain't George. He is too busy with the officers at the inn to get here."

"Well, if our suspicions are correct, Dick, we will fight our way to freedom or death. I will not live to be dragged back to a felon's cell."

Eustace was aware that other charges beside Lord Walsingham's could be brought against him, and shuddered with horror at the idea of incarceration in Newgate's fearful cells.

Tap! tap! tap!

The sound of footsteps came nearer and nearer.

Turpin, biting his lip, drew forth his pistol, putting it on at full cock.

Tap! tap! tap!

A dark, shadowy form could now be discerned through the thick gloom of the passage.

"Stand aside, Eustace. I want to give it him full between the eyes."

The form of a tall, herculean man could now be plainly perceived, groping cautiously along the subterranean way.

"There is only one, Dick. Be cautious ere you fire."

"That one arn't George Watson, I'll swear! I'll take my oath 'tis Geoffery Newton who approaches. And, by all the devils in ——! I'll plant my bullet in his skull, if I swing for it!"

Raising his pistol, Turpin took aim at the advancing form.

The figure of the man was now within fifteen yards of the spot on which they stood.

About to fire, Turpin let his finger remain upon the trigger, muttering a curse, as he observed the figure before him pause, as it reached a little nook or bend in the passage.

This projection screened the stranger from the fire of Turpin's pistol.

With an oath, Dick was about to dash forwards, when a low voice fell upon his ears.

"Hist! hist! Turpin, is that you?"

"Geoffery Newton, by heavens!" ejaculated Eustace.

"By the holy! 'tis he, indeed. And, damme, he is true to his word!" exclaimed Turpin, as dashing forwards, he seized the outstretched hand of the runner in his. "Well, after this, I'll put faith in the oath of an enemy, be he a beak himself. But how is this Newton, my boy? What brings your here?"

"To give you warning not to attempt an escape from without; the mill is filled by my men."

"What would you advise, Newton?" exclaimed Eustace. "Aid us to escape, and you shall receive a reward for your faithfulness you dream not of."

"Never mind the reward. I owe you a life; and, curse me, if I ever forget the favour. I've heard strange things from the dying Lord Walsingham at the inn; and, though I peril my life, I will aid you to escape with yours. It won't do for you to fall into the hands of the grabs after what I've heard, though for the matter of that, certain parties could soon settle the matter, I'll swear. Your honour knows to what I alludes," added the officer, with a rough respect in his manner towards Eustace, that mystified and surprised Turpin. "Now, look here, I'll go back, make my way to the mill, and draw off the runners. But to give them summat to do, you, Dick Turpin, can go with me. You can have my mare that is saddled at the inn, and make show as we aproach. We shall then give yer a race. I'll prevent anyone catching up with yer, and when we are a few miles on the road, leave the mare, and make off. I'll keep the men back."

"Newton, you're a smart one, and a damned good fellow. The plan you have proposed is a good one, and if I had my own bonny Black Bess instead of your mare, damme, I'd give you all a race in earnest! But come, we will be off. Eustace, I'll see you at the 'Three Tuns,' the residence of Galloping Dick Ferguson, to-morrow at noon, as, of course, you will make your way to London first thing."

"Ay, Dick; but my stay in town will be but short. Newton, be you at the inn. I should like to see you ere I leave England."

"Leave England!" exclaimed the officer.

"Yes; Newton, for a time I will abide at France. In a few years hence I may return, when the brief career of Eustace Maltravers, as a knight of the road and member of the Night-Hawks of London, will be forgotten. But get you gone. Dick, I will be with you to-morrow, when you shall know all. For the present, farewell!"

Shaking hands warmly with the runner, and his friend Turpin, Eustace, with folded arms, watched their retreating forms as they disappeared down the passage.

In a few minutes he was alone.

Alone with his wild, whirling thoughts, that crowded in his brain, making him feel as though in a dream.

The incidents of the past few hours darted before him as he stood alone in that secret path.

Over and over again he asked himself if he was not the victim of some wild dream.

At length he was roused from his meditations by the sound of voices without.

The runners had been joined by the officer Newton.

Calling them together, the group remained for a few moments in earnest conversation with their officer, and presently all left the spot.

Geoffery Newton had kept his promise.

Ten minutes after his appearance all the runners had disappeared.

He had drawn them away from the mill, leaving the means of escape open to Eustace.

With a sigh of relief, our hero made his way out into the dried-up bed of the old mill-stream, and half an hour afterwards was seated, with his loved Sybil, in the drawing-room of the Hemlock Manor.

————

CHAPTER XXXIV.

A DARK NIGHT, AND A NIGHT OF HORROR.—THE RESURREC-
TION MAN AND THE DWARF.—THE BURGLARY.—THE
SURPRISE.—THE STRUGGLE.—TRIUMPH OF RESURREC-
TION BILL. — SUDDEN APPEARANCE OF SYBIL. — THE
PISTOL-SHOT.—DEATH OF THE BURGLAR.—THE DWARF'S
REVENGE.—EXULTATION OF EPHRAIM RASSELTON.—
THE ATTEMPTED ESCAPE.—HORRIBLE FATE OF THE
DWARF.

THE night following the incident related in the former chapter was a dark and dreary one.

In the height of the tempest, two dark figures, emerging from the lane that fronted the Manor House, passed through its gates into the grounds.

The intruders who burglariously made their way into the Hemlock Manor House during that wild storm, was the ruffian Resurrection Bill and the wretch Ephraim Rasselton.

"I'll enter every room in the crib, but what I'll drop on my man," muttered the resurrection man, with a fierce oath.

"Eh! eh! eh! It is a dark night. We shall not be able to find our way out. Eh! eh! I'll make a blaze that shall light us on our road, and—eh! eh! eh!—tho bones of our enemies shall be calcined in the flames; for I'll burn, burn the house, and all that are in it," murmured Ephraim Rasselton, chuckling and rubbing his huge hands with fiendish glee.

"Well, cuss me, it arn't a bad idea o' your'n, but let me get well away with the swag afore yer lights up. Once I'm off with the wedge, yer can blaze away to yer heart's content. With my usual cunning, I've taken care there shan't be many to share the swag, only you and I, and your'n I'll take care of," ejaculated the villain to himself, as Ephraim left him to try one of the other doors.

A few minutes afterwards, the two villains were standing in a large apartment overlooking the grounds at the back of the manor.

A smothered cry of exultation escaped the lips of Resurrection Bill.

He had forced open a bureau in the corner of the apartment, and from its recesses draw forth bag after bag of guineas.

"Here's a haul! By the ——, those may collar the wedge (plate) as likes; I'll be satisfied with the gold-finches (guineas)."

The amount of treasure found in the bureau far exceeded anything that the resurrection man had ever seen.

In his eyes the bags of guineas he had secured were worth a prince's ransom—an inestimable mine of wealth.

For some three minutes, in mute exultation, the burglar remained kneeling on the floor beside the bureau gazing at the treasure.

All was still as death in the old house.

Nought could be heard but the warring elements without.

Save the howling of the tempest and the plashing of the rain, all is silence within the manor.

"Hist—hist! my flower. Kious! does yer want to rouse the crib?"

With a fearful oath, Resurrection Bill turned to Ephraim, whom he fancied had left the room, as he heard a heavy foot without.

To his surprise, he beheld the dwarf busily engaged at a further corner of the chamber, heaping all kinds of inflammable materials together, such as papers, curtains, and every available thing at hand likely to burn.

With a chuckle, he lighted a taper, and stood glaring around with savage joy.

"Eh! eh! eh! they shall all burn—burn! and the morning's sun shall glisten on their calcined bones."

"Kious (silence), hold yer noise, yer devil's whelp! or by ——, I'll slit your weazand in about a minute! Sleek the trap (shut the door), or, take yer davy. I will chive yer like beans, unless yer wants me to make a stiff-'un on yer. Come here."

Ephraim, with a growl of discontent, joined his enraged companion.

"Eh! eh! eh! what do you require?"

"Your silence; or by the fiends, I'll make cold meat of yer. Look here; I have got a good haul; the lay has turned up a trump card. Revenge is sweet, but it will eat very well cold; it's like game, all the better for keeping. I came here to pay off a debt I owes Eustace Maltravers,

not calculating upon dropping on this swag all in ready Stephen (money); no dinging (changing); all ready to a bloke's hand. Now, in course, I takes my hook with the rowdy, and leaves for another time my business of providing my friend Eustace with a parson's lodging (grave)."

"Then you are going to leave the house?"

"Jest so; neither more nor less. Don't yer like it? cos if so, I'm sorry. But here, don't stand there staring at nothing. Collar these bags, and we'll be off."

A fierce oath escaped the lips of the resurrection man, as Ephraim, without replying, threw his taper among the articles he had heaped together in the corner of the room and gave utterance to a shrill yell of demoniac triumph.

A glare of light shot through the apartment, a broad, yellow glare.

Starting to his feet, Resurrection Bill was about to dash at the dwarf, but, with rage and fury in every feature, stepped back towards the casement, as he discerned, fully revealed in the glare, the form of his hated foe, Eustace Maltravers. He who had already thrice escaped his murderous intentions.

Scarce had the yelling shout died upon the lips of Ephraim Rasselton, after the perpetration of his fiendly act, ere the two enemies, Eustace and Resurrection Bill, were engaged in a terrible struggle.

A fierce, desperate struggle.

A struggle for life or death.

Oaths and blasphemous curses escaped the lips of the ruffian resurrectionist.

His antagonist, holding his breath, reserved all his strength for the struggle with his foe.

Well Eustace knew the wretch with whom he had to do.

There was a devilish look of murderous malice in the villain's face.

A look of crime and blood.

Like two huge serpents they writhed and twisted in each other's arms.

For an instant Eustace was uppermost; then, thrown down by the herculean ruffian, he was for a moment powerless in the other's grasp.

Vindictive fury lent additional strength to the frame of the ruffian housebreaker.

Over and over they rolled in a close grip of deadly hate and savage fury.

Now in danger of being enwrapped by the fiery tongues of flame that darted through the apartment, and anon struggling and panting in the direction of the casement at the further end of the chamber.

"Ha! ha! ha! Curses! You escaped me at the old house in Battersea-fields! You laughed me to scorn at the old ken in the Mint! You escaped poor Jem Vaughan, the viper, now blinded by your accursed band; but, by ——, you don't now free yourself from my grip! I as yer hard and fast, and will slit your weazand, and carry your head to your friends!"

Wild chuckles of savage glee escaped the ruffian, as, having firmly grasped Eustace by the throat, he knelt upon his chest and drew forth a large clasp-knife, the blade of which he opened with his teeth.

The blade was a long and glittering one.

A fearful, terrible weapon in the hands of an assassin.

With exulting triumph, Resurrection Bill flourished it in the eyes of his victim.

"I shall chive yer with this till I makes cold meat of yer!" hissed the villain between his clenched teeth. "Nothing can save yer now. Not the fiend himself should drag yer from me. Double-edged Dick shall drink yer heart's blood."

Vainly Eustace endeavoured to throw the villain off his labouring chest.

He was choking, gasping for breath.

The room began to swim round and round with him.

The yellow tongues of fire seemed to dance around him and assume fantastic forms.

The roar of the flames was like the bellowing of wild animals in his ears.

The fire had seized upon everything in the room. To the eyes of the struggling Eustace it appeared like a volume of flame.

A dinging, humming noise rang in his ears.

He was about to lose all consciousness.

The pressure of the ruffian resurrection man's fingers on his throat had produced partial strangulation.

Just about to relapse into total insensibility, he was startled into life by beholding the gleam of his adversary's knife, as the formidable weapon was raised aloft to strike.

The exulting shout of triumph from the murderer's lips was then drowned in a loud report of a pistol.

With a yell of agony, Resurrection Bill started to his feet, and, throwing up his arms, staggered wildly about the room.

Released from the death-grip of his savage foe, Eustace, rising to his feet, made for the door, gazing at the scene before him with a wild, dazed expression.

Just within the entrance of the chamber, pale and wan, like a spectre from the grave, stood Sybil Fairley. With her figure firm and erect, she held in her hand the pistol, the barrel of which was yet smoking from the recent discharge.

Awakened and alarmed by the noise in the house, the brave girl had left her chamber, arriving at the scene of horror in time to save her lover's life.

Ghastly, terrible looked the ruffian resurrectionist, as he staggered about, his hideous face streaming with blood.

The bullet from the pistol of the brave girl had entered his jaw, tearing away the greater portion, with the teeth and roof of his mouth.

Inarticulate sounds escaped the mouth of the wounded ruffian.

Glaring with bloodshot eyes upon Sybil and her lover, the ruffian, mouthing horrible oaths, and scarce articulate vows of vengeance, like one blind, groped his way from the room.

Permitting the disfigured and fainting burglar to pass unmolested, Eustace, with Sybil, hurried to the lower part of the house.

Endeavours were made by the few servants in the Manor to stay the progress of the devouring element, but in vain.

The flames had secured firm hold of the dry, rotten woodwork of the building.

The Hemlock Manor House was doomed.

Ephraim Rasselton's malicious purpose was half achieved.

The house would be destroyed, though the victims of his hate escaped.

A strange, terrible, and wild scene finished the horrors of the night.

Some labourers and servants from the "Bold Horseman," who had arrived at the Manor, having rescued from the burning building some of the most valuable of the property, with its mistress and Eustace, stood in the grounds gazing at the flaming mass.

A grand but terrible sight.

The storm of the early part of the night had passed away.

The huge, black clouds had disappeared, the moon shedding a rich silvery light upon hill and dale.

The burning Manor House sent up huge tongues of flame and showers of sparks in the sky.

Reddening the whole horizon with a hue of blood.

Suddenly there was a cry of horror from the group that were gazing at the burning, flaming mass.

At a topmost casement of the old building appeared a human form.

Wild shrieks of horrible agony peeled upon the air, sounding in the ears of all above the roar of the furnace.

All knew that there was no hope for the doomed being.

A terrible fate condemned him to a fearful end.

There was no means of escape for the wretched creature. Nothing but a horrible death awaited him.

None knew how he came in his terrible position.

Only once during an unusual glare did the shuddering Sybil, in the agonized, shrieking, howling being, discover her late parent's confidential clerk, Ephraim Rasselton.

Eustace, on learning who it was that was thus wildly shrieking for aid that could not be given, guessed by what means Rasselton had entered the Manor.

Sybil and her lover could only imagine that, wandering about the old manor, the wretched creature had got secured in one of the disused and secret apartments, and was unable to escape in time to avoid the ravages of the fire.

It was a fearful sight to behold that human being clinging wildly to the burning casement.

For a few moments the doomed one could be discerned amid the flame and smoke that now poured from the windows.

Then a huge bright tongue of flame dashed out of the casement, enveloping the shrieking form in its fiery folds.

A second of time elapsed, and the figure was gone—buried in the fiery gulf his own hand had kindled.

CHAPTER XXXV.

AND LAST.—LORD WALSINGHAM AND HIS BRIDE.—THE HAPPY HOME.—A LAPSE OF YEARS.—CRIME AND ITS VICTIMS.

FIVE years have passed away.

The scene now changes to a sweet romantic rural vale in Devon.

It is the bright spring time, the hedges with their delicate green foliage, and the pale flowers of the early summer glisten and throw out delicious perfumes in the air.

In the centre of the vale is a large villa, in front of which meanders one of those sylvan streams so common in Devon.

A fanciful and pretty little bridge, built over the stream that runs in front of the villa, leads the wayfarer to the gates of the retreat, in which reside a family known, loved, and respected by all around.

Often, on a bright, sunny morn, a stranger, passing the villa, might observe three merry, bright-eyed, rosy-cheeked children, whose infantile laughter rings joyously in the air.

Accompanying the light-hearted little creatures may sometimes be seen a tall, handsome man, with a lovely woman on his arm.

They are the parents of the children, and owners of the villa.

Friends to the poor—affable to their neighbours—kind and generous to a fault, Lord Walsingham and his wife are loved and esteemed by all.

Seldom do the happy pair, whose whole pleasure and joy seem centered in each other, leave the rural retreat of Honeysuckle Villa.

None would imagine what struggles, trials, and temptations had been gone through, in their early life, by the happy pair, or recognise, in the handsome Lord Walsingham, the once dashing knight of the road, Eustace Maltravers, or in the blooming lady, Sybil Fairley, the miser's daughter, who had never, for an instant, regretted linking her fate with the noble highwayman.

*　　　*　　　*　　　*

Turn we from the bright, happy scene in the country to the sombre, darksome, busy town.

Many of the characters in this romance of real life are gone the journey of death; others still remain.

A large hotel, one of the busiest and handsomest at the West End, is tenanted by a jolly, affable landlord, who has the honour of an acquaintance with the noble Lord Walsingham.

Few of his former acquaintance of years gone by, would recognise Nat Stevens, the landlord of the Star Hotel.

Lizzie Heyward, the victim of the roue, Captain Leslie, Bessie Templeton and others, passed through varied scenes, that may not here be detailed.

Terrible scenes of crime, deeds of black and evil passions, were enacted by a horde of villains, styling themselves the Red Band; or, the Night Birds of London, the history of which may perhaps be given at a future time.

The last scene in the career of the noble highwayman has been disclosed; but, for years after the hero of our life romance had withdrawn himself from the web of crime that had enwrapped him, fearful deeds were executed by the Night-Hawks of London, who, besides warring with society, were implacable foes to the captain and members of THE RED BAND.

NOTICE! NOTICE! NOTICE!

To the Readers of the "Night-Hawks of London."

All those who have read the above work, should see the companion,

"THE ROGUES OF LONDON."

Purchase "The British Traveller," and read the most novel work of the day, "THE ROGUES OF LONDON."

www.ingramcontent.com/pod-product-compliance
Lightning Source LLC
Chambersburg PA
CBHW081211170626
46811CB00010B/3250